THE GHOST THAT CLOSED DOWN THE TOWN

THE GHOST THAT CLOSED DOWN THE TOWN

The Story of the Haunting of South Africa

Arthur Goldstuck

PENGUIN BOOKS

PENGUIN BOOKS

Published By the Penguin Group
Penguin Books (South Africa) (Pty) Ltd, 24 Sturdee Avenue, Rosebank, Johannesburg 2196, South Africa
Penguin Books Ltd, 80 Strand, London WC2R 0RL, England
Penguin Group (USA) Inc, 375 Hudson Street, New York, New York 10014, USA
Penguin Group (Canada), 90 Eglinton Avenue East, Suite 700, Toronto, Ontario, M4P 2Y3, Canada (a division of Pearson Penguin Canada Inc.)
Penguin Ireland, 25 St Stephen's Green, Dublin 2, Ireland (a division of Penguin Books Ltd)
Penguin Group (Australia), 250 Camberwell Road, Camberwell, Victoria 3124, Australia (a division of Pearson Australia Group Pty Ltd)
Penguin Books India Pvt Ltd, 11 Community Centre, Panchsheel Park, New Delhi – 110 017, India
Penguin Group (NZ), 67 Apollo Drive, Mairangi Bay, Auckland 1310, New Zealand (a division of Pearson New Zealand Ltd)

Penguin Books (South Africa) (Pty) Ltd, Registered Offices:
24 Sturdee Avenue, Rosebank, Johannesburg 2196, South Africa

www.penguinbooks.co.za

First published by Penguin Books (South Africa) (Pty) Ltd 2006

ISBN-13: 978-0-143-02505-4
ISBN-10: 0-143-02505-8

Typeset by CJH Design in 10.5/13.5 pt Schneidler
Cover design: Flame Design, Cape Town
Printed and bound by Interpak Books, Pietermaritzburg

For Zianda

Contents

Preface

This is the story of the South African ghost. It is a tale not only of the supernatural, of fear, fright and terror of the unknown, but also of cultural clashes and commingling. It is as much an exploration of mystery and darkness as it is a practical attempt to unravel the evolution of the South African psyche.

This work was inspired, firstly, by the discovery that powerful urban legends have shaped the supernatural beliefs of all the peoples of South Africa. And, secondly, by the realisation that the belief systems of the different peoples have had a powerful influence on one another. The ghost stories of each culture have had a profound impact on the supernatural beliefs of every other cultural group in this country over the past four centuries.

Today, the South African ghost is a complex character that reflects a turbulent history and a harsh existence. It is a unique character that sheds fascinating light on the nature of supernatural experience throughout the world. And, just maybe, it will bring us closer to an understanding of ghostly manifestations. Or, at the very least, an understanding of the beliefs that shape all people's experience of the supernatural.

Acknowledgements

If I said this book would not have been possible without the assistance of numerous people, I would be falling far short of the truth. The reality is that this book should not have been possible at all. I first agreed to write it in 1995, with a 1996 deadline, and extended the deadline every year after that, setting up the ultimate test of patience for Alison Lowry, first my editor, then publisher and now chief executive officer at Penguin Books SA. I was ready to drop the project on numerous occasions while life and a career took priority, but the support and consistent interest of the team at Penguin kept the project alive. So thank you first to Alison for keeping the faith, Pam Thornley for her encouragement from the start and fine editing at the end, Jeremy Boraine for urging me the last few laps towards delivery of the manuscript, and Claire Heckrath for the last push.

At the start of 2005, a decade into the project, I never imagined I would find the time to complete the book, and it wouldn't have been possible without the encouragement and sacrifices of my family: my wife Sheryl and daughters Jayna and Zianda, who cheered me on page by page, chapter by chapter. What a great team you make!

The journalists and broadcasters who kept my attention focused on the book by insisting on interviewing me about the research over the years make up the next category of contributors to whom I am deeply indebted. They include Jenny Crwys-Williams, Kate Turkington, Barry Ronge, Mike Mills, Gwen Gill and all those who called me up from time to time to check on the credentials of 'new' ghosts their listeners and readers had encountered or imagined.

Sadly, I cannot share this book with an even more important category of contributor, namely those who gave me their insights, ideas and stories, but passed away during the time the research was being conducted. First and foremost among these was my first editor, Arthur Markowitz, who taught me the nuts and bolts of my profession when I started out in journalism, and then years later shared with me both his insights and his amazing work on San folklore. Then there were those almost mythical individuals who granted interviews in their last years, namely the Rain Queen of the baLobedu people, Queen Mokope Modjadji V, Regopstaan Kruiper, head of the Xomini clan of the KhoiSan, Margaret Williamson, veteran journalist, author and mentor of writers, Achmat Davids, legendary scholar of Cape Muslim history, and the somewhat less illustrious ghost hunter, Martiens Joubert. If any of their spirits are wandering, I hope they approve.

Expert and inside knowledge and insight was shared by ghost-lore custodian of the Karoo Rose Willis, that wonderful actor and raconteur Patrick Mynhardt, unofficial keeper of the social history of Belfast Julie Beukes, curator of the Bo-Kaap Museum Saleigh van der Schyff, curator of the William Fehr Collection housed in the Rust-en-Vreugd art gallery Johan van Wyk, film producer Bonnie Rodini, one-time tour guide at The Castle in Cape Town Helene Wessels, journalist and publicist David Barritt, and Victor Mathekga, councillor to the Rain Queen.

Many e-mail correspondents also enriched my understanding of and access to urban legends of the supernatural, in particular: David and Barbara Mikkelson, the fascinating California couple who run the snopes.com website that is an essential tool in understanding and debunking urban legends; Brian Chapman from Victoria, Canada, who shared a vast treasure trove of legends; the denizens of the OFF, an e-mail forum that emerged from the pioneering days of electronic bulletin boards that preceded the Internet as a form of electronic communication for the public; the regulars at alt.folklore.urban, the Internet newsgroup that is to urban legend claims what a hot knife is to butter; and a.f.u.'s spin-off online community, the Old Hats.

Thank you to my immediate family, my mother Jessie, brothers Oscar and Charles, sister Daphne Miller, aunts and cousins Gladys and Harold Goldstuck, Alida Taylor and Natalie Ginsburg for their contributions to the tales that piled up over the years. I also received excellent guidance from my late parents-in-law, Leonard and Jean Lack, and brother and sister-in-law, Hilton and Lizette Lack.

Numerous people have made a contribution over the years in the form of stories, tip-offs, suggestions and enquiries that sparked my investigative interests. I have probably not recorded all their names, so if you are left out, please don't come back to haunt me, but feel free to remind me. The list includes John Auton, Fraser Butterworth, Terry Carroll, Terry Chan, Steven Cherry, Paul Clingman, Mike Conroy, Desiré Craig, David DeLaney, Charles Dimmick, Mias du Plessis, Laurie Durand, Harry Dugmore, Sonia Duvenage, Ian Fell, Kenny Ford, Phillip Ghee, Martin Gray, Phil Gustafson, Steve Hayes, Jason Heimbaugh, Alan Holm, Jessie and Greg Jamieson, Angus Johnston, Bob Kernohan, Jackie Klevansky, Hlalele Koddisane, Drew Lawson, Irving Lissoos, Joe Mansfield, Kirsten Martin, Don Mattera, Lawrence Miller, Bill Nelson, Loraine Paul, Colin Plen, Mark Ramsden, Peter Ramsey, William Ramwell, Kyle Rayner, Iain Robertson, Vicki Robinson, Lydia Rolando, Lee Rudolph, Kim Scheinberg, JoAnne Schmitz, Gus Silber, Steve Slaughter, Simon Slavin, Hylton Smith, Simon Spencer, Beccy Stones, Wayne Talbot, Derek Tearne, Harry

Teasley, Richard Thompson, Russell Tiedt, Bruce Tindall, Paul Tomblin, Peter van der Linden, Koos and Milenna van Niekerk, Jaap van Oudtshoorn, Denise Venter, Lindsay Walker, Dave Walsh, Andrew Walton, Ron Weissenberg, Will Wheeler, Sean Willard, Glenys Williams, and Ian York.

Grateful acknowledgements is made to the following for permission to reproduce copyright material: Eric Bolsmann, for permission to quote material from his book *Ghosts of Pretoria* (Be My Guest Publishers, 1997); Jonathan Ball Publishers for permission to quote material from *Haunted Corners: South Africa's Own Ghost Stories* by Margaret Williamson (1993); from *Indaba, My Children* by Credo Mutwa, first published in Great Britain by Canongate Books Ltd, 14 High Street, Edinburgh, EH1 1TE. First published in South Africa in 1964 by Blue Crane Books; Stephen Watson for permission to quote material from *Return of the Moon: Versions from the /xam* (The Carrefour Press, 1991).

Every effort has been made to trace copyright holders or their assigns. The author and publisher apologise if there has been any inadvertent infringement of copyright and, if this is drawn to their attention, will be pleased to make the necessary correction in any subsequent edition.

Why People Die

When the moon dies, he does not altogether die. He keeps his backbone. He waxes. He grows round. He comes back alive.

The people were formerly like the moon. They did not, when they died, become altogether dead. They came back to life.

It is because of the hare that people, dying, now altogether die. It is because the hare contradicted the moon.

The hare was formerly a people's child. He was a male child. He cried because his mother had gone away, while he thought that she had died. Therefore, he cried greatly for his mother.

The moon spoke to the child. The moon said that the child should leave off crying, for his mother was not altogether dead. His mother would again living return. The child, answering, said that his mother would not again return alive, for she was altogether dead.

Therefore the moon became angry. He hit with his fist, cleaving the child's mouth. And the moon cursed the child. He said: 'This person shall become a hare, for he shall always bear a scar on his mouth. Vermin shall be those who will bite him at the place where he is lying. Vermin shall hang abundantly in his head. He shall have no peace. He shall fear not a little. He shall spring away.

The dogs shall chase him and, when they have caught him, they shall tear him to pieces. He shall altogether die.

'And they who are men, when they are dying, they shall also die altogether, for it was one of them who contradicted me.'

It was because of the hare's doings that the moon cursed us in this manner, while he had formerly intended that we should resemble him, that we should not altogether die.

It was because the hare was disobedient that the moon grew angry. Therefore he cursed us with uplifted tongue. Therefore he said:

'Ye, who are people, ye shall not return to life. Ye shall altogether vanish when you die.'

From *With Uplifted Tongue: Stories, Myths and Fables of the South African Bushmen told in their manner*, by Arthur Markowitz, 1956

The Day We Die

The day we die
The wind comes down
To take away
Our footprints.

The wind makes dust
To cover up
The marks we left
While walking.

For otherwise
The thing would seem
As if we were
Still living.

Therefore the wind
Is he who comes
To blow away
Our footprints.

From *With Uplifted Tongue: Stories, Myths and Fables of the South African Bushmen told in their manner*, by Arthur Markowitz, 1956

1

The Ghost that Closed Down the Town

This is the story of the South African ghost. It is not a tale told by madmen, eyes wide with imagined fright. Nor is it the creation of the campfire raconteur, terrifying his listeners with dark inventions and dire warnings.

Rather, it is a journey into the soul of South Africa, an attempt to unravel the vast, contradictory and intertwined beliefs in the supernatural shared by most of the people of this nation.

Ghost stories? Yes, of course. We will share ghost stories aplenty. But I will take you beyond the mere stories, into the foundations of the experiences and beliefs that inspired the stories. I will show you not only the surface images of superstition, revelation and terror, but also an astonishing network of roots that have fused together to anchor a truly multicultural system of beliefs.

The ghost stories of South Africa were documented

several times during the twentieth century, from C J Langenhoven's adapted tales of terror in *Geeste op Aarde* and *Stille Waters*, through Eric Rosenthal's light-hearted excursions in *They Walk By Night* to Margaret Williamson's collected explorations in *Haunted Corners: South Africa's Own Ghost Stories*.

But never has the pattern lurking behind the tales been laid bare. Never before have the ghosts of this land revealed the more earthly, physical basis of the manner in which they manifest themselves, a basis not hidden in the depths of mysterious darkness, but found in the clear light of rational analysis.

I do not claim to have revealed the true nature of ghosts. However, what I have learned about the South African ghost and am about to share with you must surely shed some light on a subject so often figuratively and physically shrouded in darkness.

Today, the South African ghost is a complex character that reflects a turbulent history and a harsh existence. It is also a unique character that sheds fascinating light on the nature of supernatural experience throughout the world.

And, just maybe, it will bring us closer to an understanding of ghostly manifestations. Or, at the very least, an understanding of the beliefs that shape all peoples' experience of the supernatural.

The South African ghost comes in many guises and disguises. It obeys no single set of cultural norms or beliefs. It borrows from Africa, from Europe and from the East Indies. And it may appear in precisely the same form to those who follow religions rooted in Africa, in the West or in the East.

If you believe in the existence of ghosts, you may well

argue that this is only natural. After all, if ghosts exist, would they not exist in the same way for all? In this question lies the fundamental dilemma of the very existence of ghosts.

When we examine the nature of supernatural experiences around the world, in different cultures and belief systems, we discover that ghostly experiences were heavily shaped by religious beliefs and cultural environment.

In this observation both the believer and the sceptic can take comfort. The sceptic might say that the supernatural experience is so firmly grounded in specific beliefs that it is those beliefs, rather than the existence of true supernatural entities, that not only shape, but also cause supernatural experiences.

The believer can use the same evidence to argue that the very fact that ghosts are explained in such diverse and divergent cultures without one 'learning' its experience from another, there must be a basic reality underlying the experience. Otherwise, why would such experiences, or belief in such experiences, arise spontaneously in so many cultures?

Therein lies a vast anthropological discussion for another day.

The path on which I am about to lead you may well answer the same questions, although it is intended to offer an understanding not of the world's separate ghost cultures, but rather of one country's remarkable evolution towards a common culture of supernatural belief.

The ghost that closed down the town

Somewhere in the far reaches of the eastern extremes of Mpumalanga province, near the Swaziland border in a region where traffic lights and rush hour are foreign concepts, lies a small town called Amsterdam. By day, it is a bustling little village, with farmers, businessmen and civil servants going about their unchanging routines year after year; by night, the town comes to a near standstill, with only the occasional passing car or pedestrian, and maybe lights in the windows of the small houses, betraying signs of life.

But one night a week even these vestiges of humanity disappear.

At six o'clock on a Saturday night, as dusk falls, the streets empty entirely. The cars are parked in their garages, the heavy curtains are drawn, and darkness descends along with a deathly hush.

And then, without a sound, a horse and his grimly silent rider come down the main road. Not even the sound of hooves can be heard. As the soundless horse passes the houses and the shops and the municipal offices, the rider looks neither to the left nor to the right, but stares ahead as if transfixed by a destination that cannot be evaded.

If anyone were watching, they would realise that the horseman is a soldier, and that he is wearing a uniform that has not been seen in battle for more than a century. It is the uniform of the Boer army that went into battle against the English at a time when this town could not be called a town.

And then the horse moves off the main road, and it would seem that the onlooker's eyes are playing tricks on him because it passes through a bush without trampling it, and through a tree without bending it. That's when it becomes obvious that the horse and rider are not of this world. The brave – or foolish – onlooker might follow the apparition until it turns towards the old graveyard, the one behind the modern showgrounds, where soldiers of forgotten wars are buried. And then horse and rider disappear, the horse to whatever ghostly pastures long dead animals are led, and the rider back into the grave from which he emerges once a week.

It will be Sunday morning before the people of the town dare venture out once more, with the sun in the sky and the church beckoning them to more holy and wholesome pursuits. And none of them will so much as whisper an admission that they had shut themselves in their homes the previous night; and they will all scoff at the notion that a ghost had closed down their town.

Many people tell this tale in the province that used to be part of the Eastern Transvaal, and even more people believe the story.

But none of these people live in Amsterdam. There, many have never even heard of it, let alone believed it, or seen the ghost. Or any other ghost. Oom Jaap van Oudtshoorn, who has lived in the town since 1937, tells of an old German immigrant who used to ride up and down the main road on a horse, decades after cars had chased all other horses off the road. But he was very much alive, wore no uniform, and had simply moved somewhere else twenty or thirty years ago.

Oom Mias du Plessis, who has lived in Amsterdam for thirty-one years and is said by anyone you ask in Amsterdam to be the man who knows anything there is to know about the town, is quite adamant that there is no ghost: 'People tell a lot of stories, but those who tell ghost stories about Amsterdam have heard the story somewhere else, or they made it up. There was never a ghost in Amsterdam. I once heard a ghost story about an old soldier in the graveyard on the other side the showgrounds, but that was just a story.'

The truth is, there never was a ghost that closed down Amsterdam. And the story is never told in Amsterdam itself, but rather by people who may have visited the area, heard a ghost story somewhere else, associated the two in their minds, and finally also in their recounting of the tale.

Julia Beukes, a down-to-earth personnel officer who could easily qualify as Mpumalanga's unofficial historian, has been collecting stories like this for years from her geographical vantage point of Belfast, a town on the road to Amsterdam. In an interview with the author, she commented:

> That story is an old story. It is like an urban legend. There's a similar story in Dullstroom, where everyone is supposed to close up by a certain time and it would happen at a specific time every evening. Just as soon as the shops have closed, between five and six, if you're still outside and you come to this corner, you see this woman walking around. She looks terrible, as if she's tormented, like a mad person.
>
> Eventually electricity would go off and the lights would go off and everybody had problems with their television sets and things like that. She had that sort of influence.

In Julie's version of the Ghost of Amsterdam, the rider is either headless or seriously injured and is making his way to the graveyard to die. He also has an effect on electricity, with lights going out and the like. 'He's either in soldier's uniform or in the typical clothing of a Boer soldier. It varies. At first I thought he had been murdered, but in the most recent story I heard that some people said he was definitely wounded, as he had been shot in the war. Some said he was headless.'

The more we hear told about it, the more obvious it

becomes that the ghost that closed down a town is a classic example of the ghostly folklore that has evolved over the centuries in South Africa and that attaches itself to likely sounding locations, people and events.

The Anglo-Boer War and the small towns of the Free State and the old Transvaal are perfect settings for much of this folklore.

Probably the best known of all such legends is the tale of the ghost of a British soldier looking for an Afrikaans nurse who ... but wait. Perhaps we should go back in time just a little.

Love and war

It was the year 1900, and the British army was struggling to gain a foothold in President Paul Kruger's Zuid-Afrikaansche Republiek. The guerrilla warfare tactics of the Boers and their intimate knowledge of the terrain meant that an army totalling no more than sixty thousand was playing havoc with the near half-million British troops dispatched to the gold fields of southern Africa.

So it was that the Inniskillen Dragoon Guards, accustomed to token resistance as they wielded their swords and rifles across the world, suffered grievously at the hands of a ragtag Boer army. Many were killed or injured, and prisoners littered the makeshift hospitals of the Republiek.

One of these unwilling patients was Lieutenant John Lawlor, who found himself fighting for his life in a field hospital at Waterval-Onder. In constant attendance, it seemed to him, was an angel of mercy whom he knew only as Maria, the Afrikaner nurse. Clinging to his life, the dragoon fell in love. But then tragedy arrived in that time-honoured way of all wars: a British shell landed on the hospital and Maria was killed instantly.

Lawlor was inconsolable. The combination of a broken heart and a mortal wound was finally too much and he, too, departed from this world. On his gravestone, behind the Wayside Inn at Waterval-Onder, you may still read the inscription: *The only son of his Mother and she was a Widow*.

The grave is set in a grove of trees, well away from the hotel buildings, where we find the last resting place of a few dozen soldiers who died while being nursed there. And there the story may have ended, except that passers-by began reporting the sight of a ghostly soldier keeping a tryst with a nurse under an old pepper tree. And so the legend began.

Every year, on the anniversary of Maria's death, it is said, the couple meet once more in the shade of a tall pepper tree behind the building that served as Paul Kruger's Eastern Transvaal headquarters. The tree eventually burned down, leaving behind only a stump – and it is at this stump that Lawlor and his Maria now meet every year before they take a stroll through the gardens, still pursuing a romance that began generations ago.

Another version has it that, before Lawlor died, and despite his injuries, he and Maria began meeting under the pepper tree. But, sadly, he never recovered fully, and when he died he was buried in the nearby cemetery. Not long afterwards, Maria was killed when a shell fell on the hospital. Now, every October, they meet again at the site where the old pepper tree once stood.

This tale of love requited in the hereafter has a small historic postscript: during the 1980s, the then-owner of the Wayside Inn discovered a plaque affixed to an old tree stump behind the Kruger house in the hotel grounds. It read: *The ghost tree – in memory of William Greig, the seeker of ghosts – died 30th September 1953*. We can only imagine that Greig finally found the answer to his quest in a world beyond ours.

Meanwhile, the tale of Lawlor and his nurse is immortalised in the urban legends that are told to and by visitors to the Wayside Inn. One room (number 12, if you must know), it is whispered, should be avoided, unless you want to hear ghostly voices from the bathroom. In 1990 the *Transvaler* reported that a guest was kept awake all night by the sound of a flushing toilet. Was that perhaps the action of Lawlor's restless ghost, or simply evidence of faulty plumbing?

The same report claimed that Lawlor's girlfriend had committed suicide by jumping over the waterfall that gives the town its name – and that the Kruger Millions are buried under the falls, echoing one of the great rural legends of the old Transvaal.

The same year the *Middelburg Observer* sent a photographer to stake out the pepper tree stump, and subsequently published a photo of, it was claimed, the ghostly couple. The flippant tone of the report told a different story. Tongue firmly in cheek, the report stated that the couple did not want to talk to the newspaper, but merely held hands and gazed into each other's eyes.

Another legend describes ghostly parties in the garden. Yet another declares that a body is buried under every cross-spar of the railway line running behind the hotel on its way to the sea.

And one more tells of Lawlor's ghost chasing treasure hunters away with a horsewhip.

And there are yet more tales of a British soldier and his Afrikaner lady love, doomed never to know happiness in this world.

One of the most famous is that of a couple whose destiny has them repeatedly coming back to a spot just up the main road from Waterval-Onder. A short distance off the

N4 highway between Machadodorp and Belfast stands the Boer War monument to members of the Zuid-Afrikaansche Republiek Polisie who fell at the Battle of Berg-en-Dal in 1900.

It is also, apparently, a monument to doomed love. For it stands on the spot where …

A certain British soldier was stationed at Waterval-Boven during the guerrilla war stage of the South African War (1899-1902), when General Louis Botha was desperately trying to hold off the British advance from Pretoria into the Eastern Transvaal.

One day, while patrolling one of the farms in the area, this dapper British soldier encountered the feisty Afrikaner daughter of the absent farmer. The young beauty of Berg-en-Dal was a flirtatious lass who had no qualms about making eyes at the enemy. The soldier, much encouraged, courted her secretly. They began meeting late at night in a storeroom on the farm of Berg-en-Dal, about 12 miles from the soldier's camp. Simple romance soon blossomed into passionate, though illicit, lovemaking.

But the girl's indiscretions could remain hidden from her compatriots for only so long. Boer soldiers discovered her scandalous affair with one of their mortal enemies. One night they lay in wait for him and ambushed him as he arrived for his rendezvous with his lover. He was summarily executed. His lover came running when she heard the shots ring out in the night and found him lying dead on the floor where they had so recently been lying in each other's arms.

Distraught, she ran to his horse, which was still tethered outside the storeroom. Her heart burning with grief and vengeance, she rode to the British camp and warned the soldiers that the Boers were about to attack them.

The British saddled up, and after a long ride encountered the Boer soldiers in the area to which the girl had directed them, and wiped them out. After the war the woman was ostracised by her community as a *verraaier* (traitor), and she lived out her life alone on Berg-en-Dal. Some say she went mad before she died, but all agree on one thing: the soldier who was buried on the farm returns every year on the anniversary of his death to look for her. He does so to this day.

One could say this story has a happy ending. According to those who speak of such things when a glass of wine has loosened their tongues sufficiently, the girl too, after her death, came back to find her soldier. Finally, they were reunited in death, and now she meets him at the same time every year at a rendezvous at Waterval-Onder, just a few kilometres down the highway heading east.

Says Julia Beukes:

> There's a family cemetery there. Then there's a big cemetery where the Boer soldiers were buried. But just behind this cemetery is what was the old part of a house. You can still see it; it looks like a storage facility. The floor is still there and two of the walls.
>
> I was told by the late Oom Piet Ahlers that he actually saw this woman and man one night while he was driving from Machadodorp to Belfast, in the days before the road was tarred. He said you had to drive very slowly because it was a steep hill and the road made a very sharp turn. He saw them one night, with the horse and all.

As is the tradition in every small community where a ghost is said to be abroad, young men from the surrounding farms and from Belfast itself go ghost hunting at a certain time every year, around October, and always in the middle of the night. But the timing of the ghost hunt does not correspond with the more formal version of this story, which sets it as the first skirmish in the vicious six-day battle of Berg-en-Dal in June 1900. The battle is described today as 'the last set battle of the war' and coincided with Field Marshal Lord Roberts' proclamation of what became the 'scorched earth' policy. Homes and farms suspected of providing shelter or support to the Boers were razed to the ground and, in September of that year, the first concentration camps for civilians were established. It is unlikely that the British soldier would have been able to find his free-spirited boeremeisie living free on a farm in a war zone by October. But when ghost stories evolve into folklore, historical accuracy is the least of their believers' concerns. In any case, for the young folk of Belfast today, ghost hunting on balmy October evenings makes more sense than venturing out in the freezing nights of June.

Of greater concern to historians is the recurring theme of romance between invaders and family members of those resisting them.

The ill-fated romance at Berg-en-Dal seems unlikely even today, considering it blossomed in the months leading up to and following the final great battle of the South African War. The sieges of Kimberley, Ladysmith and Mafeking (today's Mafikeng) had been relieved, and Lord Roberts had taken Pretoria. The Boers took to the countryside, and in June 1900 Paul Kruger arrived at Machadodorp by train, along with his government and even his mint. Machadodorp was declared the last capital of the Boer republic and, in early August 1900, the Boers regrouped at Dalmanutha, near Belfast, for a last stand against the British.

The skirmishes began on 21 August. Six days later, 1500 infantrymen overran Berg-en-Dal koppie, where a mere 74 members of the Zuid-Afrikaansche Republiek Polisie (known as the ZARPS) had held the high ground throughout the battle. The capture of the koppie was almost as significant as Lord Roberts taking Pretoria: it ended the last set battle of the war, and it ushered in the birth of guerrilla warfare. For the next 21 months, until the signing of the Peace of Vereeniging on 31 May 1902, Boer commandos would change the rules of warfare. And 28 000 Boer women and children would die in disease-ridden concentration camps, while the British carried out their scorched earth policy to ensure that they had no sanctuary among their own families.

Who can believe British soldiers and Boer girls socialising, let alone falling in love? For some, this is unlikely enough for them to dismiss tales of ghostly lovers from opposite sides of the South African War. But the truth is that interaction between British soldiers and Boer civilians was an active, integral aspect of the occupation. In a first-hand account of the war, a member of the Royal Canadian Artillery, E W B Morrison, describes the relationship:

> Thanks, largely, to Lord Roberts' policy, the best of relations exist between the troops and the people. The individual British soldier bears no ill-will against the people he is fighting. When the fighting is over and the village or town captured he turns in and helps nurse the baby of the people near where he is camped, and is anxious to be friendly and sociable. If he is stationed there a few weeks he knows everybody in the place, and has made a little circle of friends just as if he was quartered in a town at home.[1]

Stationed in Belfast during and after the battle of Berg-en-Dal, Morrison provided a fascinating account of some of

---

[1] Morrison, p224.

these interactions. For example: 'A couple of rather nice looking Boer girls live near our camp and lately they have been in the habit of coming over in the evenings for a talk.'

It turns out that the girls are hungry for news about when the war will end. On another occasion some of the girls encounter Morrison on his way back from a skirmish and enquire whether any prisoners have been taken. A Boer woman, seeing Morrison sketching nearby graves, asks him to sketch her six-month-old baby. Since it was born while the father was out on commando, he had never seen it, and she wanted a picture to send him.

'The fact of their being able to send these sketches out is additional evidence of the amount of communication that goes on through our outpost lines between the inhabitants and the Boer commandos,' wrote Morrison in *With The Guns*.[2]

In fact, what Morrison reveals is how porous the entire human fabric could be in a time of war. The Boer girls moved freely among their British occupiers and their fighting men in the field. They were even roped in by the British to pass on to their husbands and boyfriends pamphlets calling for their surrender.

Not only would an affair between Brit and Boer have been perfectly possible, it would probably have been inevitable. It may even have been a common occurrence. Certainly, the ghosts of Berg-en-Dal are not the lone spirit lovers in this area.

And there were other wars in southern Africa, other times, and other places that inspired similar tales.

The most famous of all of this country's stories of ghostly love centres on the building known as Kronendal, a

[2] Morrison, p238.

stately restaurant in what is today Hout Bay, once a sleepy seaside village that has been transformed by developers into a noisy tourist town.

The date: some time in the early nineteenth century. The setting: the farm of the Cloete family. The situation: the Second British Occupation of the Cape, which had begun in 1806, a resumption of their brief First Occupation that had lasted from 1795 to 1802 and was ended by a treaty with the Dutch. Now they were settled in for the duration, and established a powerful military presence to ensure that there was no trouble from the Dutch burghers. One of their many military forts was erected at Hout Bay, then nothing but farmland and a beautiful view of the bay.

And from this fort sallied forth a young soldier who, in the manner of all such tales, chanced upon the beautiful Elsa, daughter of Daniel Cloete, owner of what was then the magnificent Cape Dutch homestead of Kronendal. Cloete's parents quickly cottoned on to what was happening and forbade not only the relationship, but even barred the soldier from setting foot within their home.

The closest he could get to Elsa was the avenue that ran past the front of the house. He would stroll nonchalantly past the window, from which she would invariably be looking, but they were never able to get closer than that. Finally, as must happen, the agony of being kept at a distance broke his heart, and he hanged himself from one of the oak trees that still form an avenue running down the hill, and from which the front of the house can be clearly seen.

Elsa, horrified and distraught, killed herself inside the house. Doomed never to emerge from its shadows, she now appears at the front window, eternally waiting to catch a glimpse of her soldier.

When Kronendal was renovated in 1966 by Malcolm Tate and Alasdair Wyllie, they were told that the house was occasionally visited by a ghostly woman, but they could find out nothing more. Malcolm told Margaret Williamson, author of the book *Haunted Corners*, that they had even held a seance, and were contacted by a woman who claimed to be Elsa Cloete: 'Her story was that she was confined to the house while the man she loved was outside and they couldn't make contact. There was this desperate feeling of longing.'

Williamson spoke to numerous people who claimed they had seen or heard something supernatural at Kronendal, or knew someone who did. Her conclusion: there were simply too many variations, and the story had begun spinning off into urban legend almost the moment it was first told.

> In the original story, she did away with herself. That was the story as it was then and it was a very credible story. But then the whole thing dissolves into thin air. When I was investigating the story, I spoke to several people who said they had seen her around Kronendal, and they showed me where they had seen her. She was looking through this window, or through that window, or in this bedroom, or walking through where a door used to be.
>
> I couldn't get the soldier's background at all. I didn't get his name and I didn't get any sort of location except that he was stationed 'over there, you know, by a British fort'. There certainly are the remains of a British fort at Hout Bay, so that was the assumption, but I couldn't authenticate who he actually had been.
>
> I spoke to several people who said, 'Yes, well now, the man was a British soldier and he was stationed at Wynberg military camp', and I would say, 'Wasn't he stationed at Hout Bay?' 'No, no, no, he was stationed in Wynberg military camp.' Now that's over on the other side of the mountain. They couldn't find a name or add:

'Oh, and he hanged himself. He hanged himself on that tree out there.' And this had not appeared in the original story at all. The suicide was another addition.[3]

If you drive past the Kronendal restaurant on the main road from Constantia Nek to Hout Bay, you will be startled more by hearing that it could be haunted than by the hauntings themselves. It's not a very eerie or forlorn sight, this old Cape Dutch home with its freshly painted white walls and green window placements and shutters and white window frames. Perhaps the sign outside, 'Kronendal Garden Restaurant Open' with a very large Amstel Lager logo underneath it, betrays too heavy an element of commercialism to allow for fear, terror, or haunting. Perhaps the '24-hour armed response' sign on the outside is the real scare tactic. More than anything, it's the fact that the building hugs the main road. But then you enter the parking lot and stop under the shade of the large milkwood trees. An atmosphere of melancholy settles upon you, deepening as you enter the restaurant: not necessarily because of any supernatural presence, but rather because the old structure reimposes itself after the violation of the main road in front of the main entrance.

The present management, however, have no intention of cashing in on Elsa Cloete's history. They simply have not experienced anything untoward. Ron Wyatt, one of the present owners who again renovated and relaunched Kronendal as a restaurant on 2 July 1996, says:

... people from previous restaurants say they saw things move or saw this or saw that, but there really is nothing here to prove it or prove otherwise. Everything that

[3] Interview with the author, 13 January 1997.

happened here so far, you can always account for. The noises are all explainable. I don't think anyone's ever walked into the room where she's supposed to be sitting and seen her there. No one's ever seen that, never seen a person, never seen a soldier hanging from a tree. They used to say in previous restaurants if you moved a chair in front of the window it would be moved back in the morning. I've had chairs over there about a hundred times with nothing happening.

In a stiflingly hot loft upstairs a small window faces the sea. But all a ghost would see from there would be the traffic passing by and ... a grove of trees. But even the trees do not give any promise of supernatural possibilities. Very clearly through the thinning branches can be seen the rapidly growing town of Hout Bay, an urban scene which dispels any notion of hauntings and hangings.

If British soldiers and Boer girls are still meeting each other, and their compatriots or adversaries closing down towns at nightfall generations later, it is not in this world.

Yet it is not in the modern-day absence of these ghosts or the contradictions about their sightings that we must look for a message. It is in the very fact that the stories are so similar. The ghosts that come out at a certain time of day and frighten the citizenry away, the doomed lovers from two sides of the political divide meeting in a ghostly hereafter, are archetypes: symbolic apparitions that speak to people's inner fears and hopes.

And, more than that, they are classic examples of tales that have crossed the cultural divide between Brit and Boer, English and Afrikaner, who believe and retell these stories with equal fervour.

Ultimately, they must be accepted as folklore rather than real, verifiable experiences. But, at the same time, they help us reach closer to an understanding of the nature of the South African ghost.

Having said that, it is impossible to understand the South African ghost fully without a history lesson that charts the emergence of supernatural beliefs on the southern tip of Africa …

2

From San to Islam

The evolution of the South African ghost can be fully understood only by exploring the supernatural roots of the people who eventually came to make up the South African population. For that reason, this chapter must be a history lesson. But it is also an adventure, as we pick apart the beliefs that fed into the great melting pot from which so many of our hauntings have emerged over the centuries.

The San and their beliefs

The place: Africa. The time: an age that the nations of Europe call the sixteenth century. The continent is dotted with villages and kraals and kingdoms, populated by thousands of nations, tribes and clans, and by as many gods and beliefs.

But far to the south, in a harsh country where deserts and mountains grapple with the shores and their wild seas, the land is sparse and the small-boned people who move from waterhole to waterhole form family groups no more than a few dozen strong. The men hunt and fish, the women gather fruits and berries, and all things belong to all who need them. These are the San people. Many will one day refer to them as the Bushmen.

Closer to the seashore, the distant relatives of the San have introduced sheep and cattle into this unspoilt world. For these herders, who will one day be known as the Khoikhoi, the animals represent wealth, and with wealth comes the quest for land. As a result, the San and the Khoikhoi compete for survival. The herds of the Khoikhoi denude the grazing land, resulting in the disappearance of the game on which the San depend. Consequently, the San see nothing wrong with robbing the herds of the Khoikhoi. The result: generations of skirmishes and even wars.

But some San families have made their peace, and have joined groups of Khoikhoi. The two groups will one day be thought of as one: the Khoisan. In this very marriage lies one of the seeds of the destruction of San culture, although it will play a far smaller role than will their inability to compete with the black warriors from the north and, later, the white invaders from the south.

Eventually, the San will be like sideshow attractions, their rock art barely surviving, their language all but dead, and their culture entirely forgotten. And not even their ghosts will haunt those who were responsible for their passing. For the San do not have ghosts.

They communicate with the spirit world, but their spirits bear little relation to the ghosts from other lands or cultures. They are the spirits of animals, of trees, of the sun and the moon. The medicine men with their songs and their magic herbs dance themselves into a trance in which they become animals with the legs of men, or men with the bodies of animals. And they communicate with other beings which themselves are animal or insect or something in between.

These people do not believe in ghosts. They believe that, when a human being dies, it 'altogether dies'. No one and nothing comes back from the dead.

The San and their ghosts

Looking back on those times, it is easy to identify the historical forces that destroyed the San. But hidden beneath the centuries lies a second destruction that has gone unnoticed: their spiritual death. This was not merely the death of those who shared a common belief, but the death of the belief itself. And the one belief that could have lived on after they had gone, a belief in their own spirit lives, did not exist in the first place.

While other peoples might gain scant comfort from the notion that their passing could be avenged by their spirits, the San did not even believe that they could one day reach back from the spirit world and influence the things of man.

Today no one can explore the spiritual beliefs of the San in their natural setting. Urbanisation, laws and exploitation have utterly changed the way of life, and thus the culture, of the San.

The last of the great scholars of San culture, Dr W H I Bleek, translated much of their oral culture during the nineteenth century, but based only on interviews with prisoners at the Cape of Good Hope. These were mostly members of the /Xam clan of southern Cape Bushmen, although his sister-in-law and research collaborator, L C Lloyd, later worked with children brought down from the Namib desert. Bleek died in 1875, and thirty years later his work was published thanks to Lloyd's efforts. Their translations never reached a mass audience, however, since they took an academic, linguistic approach which rendered even the English translations of the carefully transcribed texts almost meaningless.

At about the same time that Bleek was active, a German missionary recalled only as Schwarz lived and worked with the San in the Kalahari and made his own efforts to collect and translate their poems and stories. He eventually retired to Germany, but found himself unable to adapt to Europe after a lifetime in the desert. In 1928 he once more set sail for Durban on the steamship *Toledo*. On the ship he met a young German-Jewish emigrant by the name of Arthur Markowitz. The seventy-something missionary and the eighteen-year-old youth found a common interest in chess and established an immediate rapport. The old man soon had Markowitz spellbound with tales of the San. Schwarz died a few years later, but not before leaving all his written records to Markowitz, along with the vivid descriptions of the social life of the San with which he had regaled Markowitz.

Markowitz would later spend some time with the Bushmen in the desert, but he was unable to find the world that Bleek and Schwarz had researched, and it was on the works of these men, and the stories Schwarz had told him, that he finally relied when, in 1956, he produced a collection called *With Uplifted Tongue: Stories, Myths and Fables of the South African Bushmen told in their manner*. The style was almost unrecognisable from the only previous attempt at this kind of work: Bleek's 1905 anthology.

The reason for this was Markowitz's own poetic touch as well as the manner in which he wove in Schwarz's colourful descriptions of the way the San saw the world. 'Bleek was a pure scientist and Schwarz was a human being,' Markowitz explained in 1997, a few months before he passed away at the age of eighty-seven.

Bleek had written in a report sent to the British government in 1871: 'The Bushmen are a hunting race, strictly monogamous, without chiefs, worshipping moon, sun and stars, speaking a most harsh clicking and guttural monosyllabic language, with an extensive mythological traditionary literature.'

But it was only with Markowitz's collection that the beauty of that mythology, not to mention the range of beliefs of the San, could be appreciated for the first time.

I was not even born when Markowitz wrote his book, but three decades later he eagerly shared his tales of these people who were now extinct.

And then, in 1988, I met the patriarch of the Xomini clan, Regopstaan Kruiper, who was believed to be ninety-five years old. He was the unlikely star in a war movie being produced as a propaganda exercise. The understanding was that in return for his participation in the movie his family would be given a game farm where they could resume their old way of life.

For the wizened old man with watery eyes sunk in a deeply wrinkled face, it was a final quest for dignity for his people. Sadly, the production company behind the film failed amid claims of mismanagement, and the Xomini were reduced to poverty once more.

Kruiper himself was unimpressed by the supposed glamour of acting in a film, his philosophy embracing what intellectuals would call an existential approach to life. But his words, spoken in a rapid-fire Afrikaans loaded with metaphors, were prophetic: 'For me one day is like the next, and one place is like the next. I have suffered terribly ever since people came to take away the land where the animals were. I cannot find a place to stand firm. Wherever I step, I slide. I slide. I am still in the wind.'

Kruiper has since passed away, the last living link with the San that Bleek had found still attempting to hold on to the ancient way of life as late as the end of the nineteenth century. Kruiper's words echoed a poem that was first recorded in print by Bleek, and later adapted by Markowitz from a combination of Bleek and Schwarz's writings:

The day we die
The wind comes down
To take away
Our footprints.

The wind makes dust
To cover up
The marks we left
While walking.[4]

Regopstaan Kruiper knew this poem, and he realised that, even while he was alive, the wind was already blowing away his footprints. He had no vision of coming back to haunt those who tormented his people, for he knew that once he died he would be 'altogether dead'.

[4] The South African poet Stephen Watson was yet another explorer of San culture who came across the poem, in the form recorded by Bleek, and adapted it to his own poetic style in his anthology, *Return of the Moon: Versions from the /Xam:*

When a person dies
A rain starts falling,
filling, erasing his living footsteps,
filling the hollows
of a dead man's footsteps

Cape of Slaves

In 1488 Bartholomew Diaz landed at present-day Mossel Bay and encountered the Khoisan for the first time. On that journey he named the Cape of Good Hope (Cabo da Boa Esperança), but he died in a storm off the same coast two years later. That was to be the beginning of the Cape's reputation as the Cape of Storms, a reputation that would inspire one of the world's great ghost stories.

Meanwhile, in the year 1510, the Viceroy of Portuguese India, Francisco d'Almeida, decided to attack a Khoikhoi kraal at Table Bay. But the local inhabitants were well versed in defensive measures and used their oxen to create a barrier, counter-attacking with spears and stones. No fewer than fifty-eight of the heavily armoured Portuguese were killed, and later buried near the mouth of the Salt River.

The ghosts of the Europeans were mounting, but it was not until 1647 that the first temporary settlement was established to challenge the Khoikhoi. A Dutch ship, the *Haerlem*, was driven ashore by a gale at Table Bay and assistant merchant Leendert Jansz was ordered, with fifty-eight men, to guard the rescued cargo until the next fleet arrived a year later. He was subsequently required to prepare a report on the suitability of Table Bay as a site for an outpost of the Dutch East India Company. The result was the arrival, on 6 April 1652, of Jan van Riebeeck aboard the ship *Drommedaris*. Within days, he ordered the construction of the Fort of Good Hope, the forerunner to the Castle which looms large in the history of South African ghosts.

Van Riebeeck was desperate for slave labour to help with the building of the fort, but was under orders to keep the peace. In 1658, however, the ships *Amersfoort* and *Hasselt* arrived in Table Bay with cargoes of West African slaves from the Portuguese colonies. Some had been seized off slave ships bound for South America, others had been purchased from the Portuguese. The slaves were intended for the use of the Dutch East India Company, but free burghers – farmers who had been released from service and granted land outside the settlement – were allowed to buy a small number.

This source of labour soon dried up when the East India Company's main commercial rival, the West India Company, acquired the sole right to trade slaves along the West coast of Africa. The solution was obvious: import slaves from the Dutch East Indies. The Malays, as they were inaccurately known, were more educated than the slaves from Africa, and quickly made their mark on Cape society. The records show that as early as 1656, East India Company employee Jan Woutersz freed a slave by the name of Catharina Anthonis from Bengal because he wanted to marry her. The marriage was frowned upon and, according to the Reader's Digest *Illustrated History of South Africa*, Woutersz was promoted to the position of supervisor on Robben Island as 'a way of putting the couple out of sight'. His successor in these matters, one Jan Stael, had better luck when he married Maria van Bengalen (her surname imposed by the Dutch to denote her origin), one of Jan van Riebeeck's personal slaves. She had already learned Dutch and something of Christianity, and was considered an acceptable wife.

The scene, clearly, was set for a cultural commingling that would echo down the centuries ...

Men of power

The place: De Kaap de Goede Hoop. The date: 13 May 1667. The Dutch ship *Pollsbroek* weighs anchor in Table Bay. On board are three prisoners in chains. But these are no ordinary prisoners. They are the Orang Cayen – Men of Power and Influence – of Indonesia.

Their homeland is under the colonial yoke of the Dutch East India Company, a hold threatened only by the Orang Cayen. To break their power, the authorities have arrested their leaders, and sent them as slaves to the colony at the Cape.

The implications are enormous, although hidden in even the revised histories of the new democratic South Africa. The three prisoners were Sheikh Abdurahman Matebe Shah, the last Sultan of Malacca, and his two religious advisers, one of whom was Sayed Mahmud, who would later be buried on Islam Hill, Constantia. They were captured after the fall of the fortress of Soeroesang and, rather than make martyrs of them by executing them, they were sent into political exile at the Cape.

They were followed, a few years later, by Sheikh Yusuf of Makassar, also known as Sheikh Yusuf al-taj al-Khalwatial-Maqasari. His father had been a near-mythical figure who was believed to have been immortal, and Sheikh Yusuf himself was said to have been engulfed in a mystical light from heaven when he was born.

According to Yusuf da Costa and Achmat Davids, Sheikh Yusuf was born in 1626 in Goa on the island of Celebes (today known as Sulawesi), the son of Makassarese nobility, and the nephew of King Bissu of Gowa. He spent several years studying Arabic and traditional religious sciences in Mecca, and eventually returned to Banten, West Java, where he taught the Islamic doctrine of Khalwatiyyah.[5]

The Dutch were still struggling to gain control of other Sultanates in the East Indies, and Sheikh Yusuf sided with Sultan Ageng in his fight against the Dutch. Sheikh Yusuf

---

[5] Da Costa & Davids, pp129-135.

was captured in 1683, exiled to Ceylon and then sent to the Cape of Good Hope, arriving on board the ship *de Voetboeg* with forty-nine followers in 1694.

Already regarded as a saint in the East Indies, he received a royal welcome from Cape Governor Simon van der Stel, but his connection to the Orang Cayen of Indonesia made him an instant threat. He and his followers were sent to the farm Zandvliet, in what is now the Macassar area. The Zandvliet farm quickly became a sanctuary for runaway slaves and a kind of headquarters for the propagation of Islam in South Africa. As a result, it is regarded as the birthplace of the first true Muslim community in South Africa. Sheikh Yusuf died on 23 May 1699, and was buried at Faure on a hill overlooking Macassar.

His remains are said to have been taken to the original Makassar (now Ujung Pandang) in 1705 and placed in a tomb in Katangka Village. His tomb at Faure, however, is still a place of pilgrimage today, and even the Indonesian authorities cannot state with certainty that Sheikh Yusuf's body lies in Makassar. Moreover, two other sites are also said to mark the last resting place of Sheikh Yusuf.

In a September 2004 interview on the normally propagandistic radio station Voice of the Cape, Professor Dr Abu Hamid of the Hasanudien University in Makassar, Indonesia, gave a remarkably rational perspective. He said that extensive research had shown that the other three graves where the Indonesian national hero's personal belongings (like scarves) are to be found, were largely ceremonial.

Abu Hamid said it was possible that a dispute arose among the children of the cleric about where he was to be buried once his family had been given permission to return home after his death. It was believed that one of his daughters, who remained in the Cape after marrying the Rajah of Tambora, had refused to let her father's remains be exhumed and returned to his homeland. According to Abu Hamid, 'This could have meant that the returning children had taken sand from his grave and carried it, along with some of his personal belongings, to three other destinations where ceremonial gravesites had subsequently been set up.'

The Indonesian ambassador, Abdul Nasir, summed up the issue perfectly in the same broadcast: 'Since Sheikh Yusuf had been a well-loved saint, it is accepted that mysteries cling to such people, which do not confine them to time or geography.'

On that note, Saleigh van der Schyff, then curator of the Bo-Kaap Museum in Cape Town's Malay district, takes up the story of the Sheikh's voyage to the Cape in an interview conducted for this book on 14 January 1997:

> One of the legends relating to Sheikh Yusuf is that, while they were coming over by ship, the people on board were short of drinking water. He went over to the side of the boat and stuck his toe in the water. They put down a bucket of water, they lifted it up and the water was fresh water and people drank it. This is just one of the legends told about some of the things he did.
>
> As far as legend goes, these people are what we call Auliyah, Friends of God. Through their strong religious belief they have this power that the ordinary person doesn't have, they would do miraculous things like this. It doesn't come from within themselves, it's a power granted them, like any person with a special talent.
>
> Sometimes you hear of a person with a kind of illness that doctors can't cure ... and then often they are referred to someone who has a special strength; to find a cure by spiritual means.
>
> You have a natural tendency to draw a comparison when you see these things, like sangomas and people

> who have been granted a special power. Sangomas use their powers quite openly, whereas someone who was granted a special power within the Muslim community wouldn't be someone using their powers openly; it might be an ordinary person and he would maybe be gifted. Perhaps people will know of it and they will ask him for advice, and he would do it in that way.

As closed as such secrets were, they quickly became known to and understood by the early Dutch community that would later evolve into the Afrikaner community. And the culture that emerged in that community was in no small way thanks to the Malay influence. It is an influence that has been played down by the ruling establishment for centuries since. As in other countries and other centuries, the distance between master and servant has been part of the fabric of the ruling ideology.

But that fabric has finally worn away, and research that has uncovered the reality is now far more readily discussed and debated.

In the Cape Muslim community, however, that relationship has always been understood. The late Achmat Davids, renowned historian and broadcaster, researched the impact of the supposed slave culture on the rulers of the time and came up with controversial conclusions. On 14 January 1997, a few years before he passed away, I was fortunate enough to spend time with him while he was working on his own book about his findings. Sitting in the lounge of his small home in the Malay Quarter of Cape Town, he was eager to explain:

> I would not be surprised if, in the legends of the Afrikaner, they should have drawn heavily on the legendary traditions of the South East Asian slaves, by

virtue of the fact that social conditions were much more intimate than we might like to believe.

The Cape style *huisie* was a single sort of dwelling, a single room dwelling, which slave and slave master shared. A lot of acculturation took place. I've argued the case with Afrikaans academics that this kind of acculturation led to linguistic change and led from Dutch to Afrikaans and that the real speakers of this language were not the Dutch but the slaves.

Afrikaans as a language does not in fact conform in grammar to the Dutch of Holland but rather to the Malaya-Polynesian languages. So it's not merely a transposition of lexical items, but rather in the construction of the language. And if Afrikaans was a creole, then it must conform to the grammatical constructs not of its native speakers but of the learners of a foreign language with a tendency to simplify a vocabulary and impose a grammatical construction. I think this is what happened.

In other words, Afrikaans is the product of acculturation, a product of the different cultures coming together and people having to learn it. Boeremusiek has its origin in the krontian of Java. Cape Malay music makes use of the Dutch lyrical musical style which is very much part of the pandoor of Indonesian society. So we have that kind of cultural mixing.

Afrikaans became a language here. It was the fact that Indonesian slaves they brought with them spoke so many languages and dialects that they had to learn Afrikaans because they could not communicate with each other, nor with their masters. For survival some form of communication was necessary. So it combines all those languages with Dutch. They found evidence for this. They found for instance that Afrikaans cannot exist without the word *baie* from the Malay *banja*.

This brings us to the most controversial aspect of Davids' research: that the ruling but uneducated Dutch settlers were deeply influenced in their culture, beliefs and language by the highly educated slave population who ran their kitchens and, often, their homes.

> Whereas the slave owner couldn't even read his own Bible, his slaves could write in at least four languages. Although the minor culture might have been dominant in the sense of being the owner, he lacked in cultural artefacts.
>
> When two communities share in such a way, with the one being dominant in the sense of having a culture, a written means of transmission of ideas, and a literary tradition, we see it influencing another group of people who ought to have been dominant but lacked literature and lacked culture.
>
> So the one with the cultural knowledge, of course his ghost stories and *toor* stories and witchcraft are in fact the cultural dominant things that become imposed on the less cultured group.

The more accepted version of the story, naturally, is that Malay culture gradually faded away under the influence of the Dutch. In his 1945 anthology entitled *Tales from the Malay Quarter*, the renowned Afrikaans writer and academic I D du Plessis paid tribute to this culture, but reinforced the standard view:

> The Cape Malays have made a fascinating contribution to South African folklore, a contribution which is a curious mixture of East and West. They are a conservative community; but it was inevitable that contact with the Europeans of the Cape for close on three hundred years, with almost complete isolation from their homeland,

> should lead to the loss of much which they had brought with them and the adoption of much that was new. Language and dress were modified under European influence until both were all but lost by the middle of the nineteenth century. Their own songs were replaced by those of Holland, not without some concessions to the East. Stories from the *Thousand-and-one Nights*, entangled with the fairy tales and fables of Europe and Africa, took on a new quality and became the legends of the Cape.[6]

While this view supports the contention that South Africa's spiritual legends are deeply ingrained with cross-cultural influences, it sees largely the manner in which Malay culture absorbed Dutch influences. The more powerful process, it seems, was the manner in which Dutch culture was subsumed by Malay culture without the Dutch even knowing it.

'Exactly,' Davids confirmed. 'So the Afrikaner will consult the Malay doctor, believing in his superiority as a bearer of knowledge, and therefore also believing in the reality of what might not be there, like when a spell is allegedly cast on him. There are many methods for doing these things, some extremely technical. There are spells to win a girl's love, there are spells to cast evil, there are spells for virtually everything, and some of these things are recorded.'

Spell-casting is indeed at the heart of the beliefs that many Afrikaners held in 'Islamic magic', better known as *goëlery*. Ironically, but not surprisingly, it became a powerful element of Afrikaner supernatural belief.

This concept, and the premise of this book that supernatural experience is often a cultural experience, is closely aligned with a concept of history that Davids was exploring before his death: 'We are looking here at myths and legends

---

[6] Du Plessis, 1945, p9.

in the making. Myths and legends, in a historical sense, give a spirituality to history.'

This spirituality does not belong only in the past, either. One of the core legends of the Cape Muslim community has it that the Western Cape is protected by a circle of more than twenty holy tombs, known as kramats, which are said to shield the Cape from earthquakes, fire, pestilence, war and the like. According to the legend, as long as the community obeys the commands of Allah, these tombs will protect it.

They include the tombs of Sheikh Yusuf of Makassar and Tuan Guru, and are located in both accessible and hard-to-reach spots, including the best-known and most visited of all, that of Sheikh Muhammed Hassan Ghabi Shah al Qadri on Signal Hill, along with kramats at Constantia, Robben Island, Faure (Sheikh Yusuf's tomb), Caledon and Bain's Kloof. [7]

---

[7] The following list of Cape Town kramats is supplied in *Guide to the Kramats of the Western Cape:*
Robben Island: Tuan Matarah (Sayed Abdurahman Motura)
Simon's Town: Sayyid Musa (Sheikh Suleiman / Abdul Samad)
Muizenberg: Sayed Abdul Aziz
Klein Constantia: Sheikh Abdurahman Matebe Shah
Constantia (Summit Rd): Sayed Mahmud
Constantia Forest: Sheikh Abdul Mutalib
Oudekraal: Sheikh Noorul Mubeen
Bakoven: Sayed Jaffer
Camps Bay: Sheikh Ali (Sayed Bassier)
Signal Hill (Ridge): Sheikh Mohamed Hassen Ghaibie Shah
Signal Hill (Army Camp): Tuan Kaape-ti-low
Bo-Kaap (Tana Baru): Tuan Guru
Bo-Kaap (Tana Baru): Tuan Sayeed Alawie
Bo-Kaap (Tana Baru): Tuan Nuruman
Vredehoek: Sayed Abdul Malik
Deer Park: Sayed Abdul Haq
Mowbray (Cemetery): Sayed Moegsien Alawie & Sheikh Abdurahman ibn Muhammad al Iraqi
De Waal Drive: Sheikh Abdul Kader (Biesmillah Shah Bawa)

Davids traced the legend back to 1807, the year that Tuan Guru died and his tomb was erected. Supposedly the holy man himself had made the prophecy before his death.

Because these tombs have an existence in reality, and are identifiable, they make for potent symbols. In our interview on 14 January 1997, Davids told me:

> I'm trying to look at the Indonesian Malaysian way of recording history, in which history is not merely a sequence of events, but the appropriation of symbols. I asked myself why, in the writing of the history of the Cape, these things were not included. Then I started looking at the circle of tombs around the Cape, and I found that the legends which are there are created in another way. There is an interplay here between the old question of Islamic symbolism and the understanding of these symbols in a way that also explains history.
>
> I relate, for instance, the story in Islamic Tradition that after one of the big battles the Prophet is engaged in the battle of the mountain. Hamzah, the son of the Prophet's uncle Abi Talib, gets killed in the battle and, on his burial, the legend goes, the earth shook, because it refused to accept his body. I think that even if the event did not occur in history, the legend was necessary to give to Hamzah that elevated status of a great warrior – even the earth refused to take his body after he disobeyed the command of his leader.
>
> I see that type of legend-as-history and history-as-legend manifesting in the Cape as well. Symbolism and history become interwoven. I find it in Indonesian history and the whole emergence of Islam in Indonesia. It contains a very interesting mix of symbolism to give spiritual meaning to history. I've found it in the life of a more modern person, Imam Abdullah Haroon, the Imam

who died in political detention (on 28 September 1969). When he died there was an earthquake, and he has been transformed into a cult hero. It was related to the circle of holy tombs, which protects the Cape from earthquakes.

With the death of Imam Haroon, the first major earthquake occurs in the Cape (the devastating earthquake that struck Tulbagh and Ceres occurred on 29 September 1969), on the night of his burial, but also on the third and the seventh night. And again on the fortieth night. It's of spiritual significance: these are the nights the soul is supposed to depart this earth in stages and they are normally nights spent in spiritual restoration. It's an old Cape tradition, as it is in Indonesia and also in other parts of the Eastern world, but it's much more strictly adhered to here than anywhere else.

There are related stories: it was a windless day but, all of a sudden, as the body was carried into the graveyard, things blew off a roof ... We have all the elements for the making of legends, even in this modern day and age.

Davids was fascinated by the legends, but not seduced by them. He cast the cold light of academic rationality on every legend claimed as truth. Even the 300-year-old story of Sheikh Yusuf's foot in the water came under this lens: 'This is one of the miracles that I relate from that journey. But I suspect that it was his knowledge of the ocean and where the estuaries of the rivers were that gave him that sort of insight.'

His stories are a catalogue of the powers of the Orang Caten:

- Tuan Guru (Imam Abdullah Kadi Abdus Salaam, the first Imam of the Cape's oldest mosque, the Auwal Mosque built in Dorp Street in 1798), for instance,

turned potatoes into stones on Greenmarket Square in the 1770s, before he was imprisoned on Robben Island at the age of 79 and incarcerated there until he died at 92. A version of the story was told in the *Sunday Times* by Heather Robertson in 2000: 'Apparently a Boer selling potatoes at the market refused to tell Tuan Guru what he was selling because he didn't talk to freed slaves. Tuan Guru touched the bags and walked away leaving the Boer horrified to find his potatoes turned to stones.'[8]
- Tuan Sayed Alawie of Yemen (who spent 11 years in prison for converting slaves, before becoming the first Imam of the Cape Muslims) entered the guarded slave quarters undetected, carrying the Koran, to convert the slaves. And whenever he went to a farm, he always found food for the slaves.

Even the legend of the circle of holy tombs, says Davids, is not an original Cape creation: 'It is in all probability modelled on the belief of the Orang Ulu – indigenous peoples of Sarawak – that there are 44 kramat in Jahore, acting as guardians for the benefit of the local people and those who require assistance from outside. This is why the Jahore area is free from earthquake and even tremor, as well as Malaysia as a whole.'

Other clearly apocryphal stories of the holy men of the Cape were collected by three students of Pinelands High School in Cape Town, under the coaching of the University of Cape Town's Tasneem Fakie:[9]

- Sayed Abdul Malik was brought to the Cape from Batavia near the end of the eighteenth century as a slave, and

[8] Robertson, *Sunday Times*, 24 June 2000.
[9] http://library.thinkquest.org/C0120708/main/Welcome.htm

became a 'Malay Doctor and Priest'. He was a colleague and confidant of Tuan Guru, who appointed him the executor of his estate and guardian of his two sons. Legends of his miraculous appearances abound, including many reports of the friendly 'old Malay man' who indulges in conversation with students in the playground of St Cyprian's School – near Malik's shrine in Upper Buitekant Street: 'It is claimed that he disappears as quickly as he appears.'

- Tuan Nuruman, who arrived in Cape Town in 1779, was housed in the slave lodge that is today the Cultural History Museum at the top of Adderley Street. Fellow slaves described him as their priest, their doctor, and their 'wonder-worker'. Tradition has it that when he prayed he was engulfed in a strange light which radiated from his body.
- Sayed Abdul Kader's kramat at Caledon, according to legend, is mysteriously protected. 'During severe floods in this area, it was always this site which was never under water.'
- Sheikh Ali, also known as Sayed Bassier, is a mystery figure buried along the Signal Hill Ridge on the Camps Bay Drive side. Legend has it that 'a stone mason, in search of special rocks along the mountainside, stumbled across a fascinating rock which resembled the form of a man lying on the ground. On touching this rock, it became alive. The living rock then instructed the humble stone mason to advise the authorities to discontinue building a school on this site. Apparently the authorities agreed, and the stone mason became the custodian of this grave.'
- Sheikh Abdul Mutalib's grave was found in 1972 in Constantia Forest by woodcutters: 'Strange things happened to their donkeys and their carts, especially at

about one o'clock on Friday afternoons. There was this special spot over which their animals refused to go. Some spiritualists were consulted and they confirmed that a kramat lies buried at that spot.'

- An unmarked grave on Devil's Peak, just above De Waal Drive, fenced with an oblong iron frame decorated with stars and crescents, is thought by some possibly to be the tomb of Sheikh Abdul Kader. 'A legend about him circulates in the community. This legend relates that a certain Junaid Mazier reported that he was curious about a man who, on Fridays after the midday prayer, would walk towards the slopes. Wanting to know where the man was going, he decided to follow him. On reaching the mountainside, he saw the man walking towards his grave, enter the grave and disappear.'
- Near Oudekraal lies the tomb of Sheikh Noorul Mubeen. He was imprisoned on Robben Island in 1716 but, according to legend, he escaped and made contact with slaves in the area, teaching them Islam. In one version of the legend he swims from Robben Island and is discovered by slave fishermen on the shore. They hide him and nurse him back to health and, when they discover that he is a holy man, they start taking lessons from him. Another version, however, contends that he walked across the Atlantic Ocean from Robben Island. It doesn't end with his death, though: 'A present-day legend tells of a spirit on horseback from Robben Island who still comes to take lessons from his teacher. He is seen, so they say, at about midday on a white horse coming across the ocean from Robben Island.'
- Tuan Matarah, also known as Sayed Abdurahman Motura, who was also imprisoned on Robben Island, has inspired a similar legend: it is said that he walked across the water to visit associates in Cape Town.

- Tuan Masud is a mysterious figure believed to be buried at Worcester, along the road leading from Rawsonville: 'Legend has it that an artisan, working and sleeping in a tent at a building site at Worcester, was one night awoken by a voice, calling the name "Masud" and beckoning him to come outside. He obliged and saw a man on a white horse who requested the artisan to follow him. He did so for a time until they reached a certain spot. The man and the horse disappeared. He returned to his tent and went back to sleep. Next morning, when he went to investigate, he found the grave on the spot where the man and the horse had disappeared.'

Many of these tales are clearly not only apocryphal, but also archetypal, meaning that they followed certain forms that have a long history in folklore, such as men on white horses, figures disappearing into their graves, and places where animals refuse to go.

Davids understood both the political significance and the mythical status of these tales: 'I think these are mere creative legends for a community that had been subjugated into slavery and wanted to develop an elevated status. But fascinating stuff.'

In this context, the tales told by Eric Rosenthal of 'Malay Tricks'[10] appear somewhat quaint. Most are silly stories of poltergeists, bewitched children and adults, and people being struck in the face with bizarre objects like dried fish and tobacco rolls.

But one story strikes a powerful chord: the life's work of a distinguished Cape Muslim personality Hadji Sullaiman Shamahomed to restore the tomb of Sheikh Yusuf (or Sheik Joseph, as Rosenthal had the name) in the early twentieth

---

10 Rosenthal, p36.

century.

As a preliminary, Sullaiman Shamahomed bought the portion of the farm Zandvliet on which the structure stood, and then called on a leading Cape Town architect and took him to the kramat, about which Europeans were mostly ignorant in those days. It was a dilapidated structure, arranged inside 'after the manner of a four-poster bedstead, hung about with ostrich eggs and ornaments of the Christmas tree kind, very gaudy and garish'.

'How much are you prepared to spend?' the architect asked the Hadji.

'Spend?' enquired Sullaiman Shamahomed. 'I have no money, nor will the descendants of the Holy Man give any themselves. Yet it is my one ambition to carry out the scheme, and I believe it will be done in God's good time.'

Attracted by the old man's personality, his red tarboosh and morning coat, the architect drew a set of plans of which he made him a present. For seventeen years nothing more was heard of him. Then one day in 1926 Shamahomed reappeared with the good news that he could now build 'with the help of Allah'.

A contractor had been found and sufficient money raised to make a start. Some distance from the old tumbledown structure arose the new tomb, to which the body was shortly to be removed. The Sheik's descendants objected even more strenuously than before, declaring that only evil would follow the desecration of the original tomb.

Calamity stalked their words. The builder went insolvent on the job and took poison. His replacement was beset with new worries. His domestic animals died; mysterious black figures threatened him; his drinking water was poisoned. Yet somehow the work was completed and the day arrived in 1929 when the Saint's remains were to be removed to their worthier resting place. In an elaborate effort to keep the matter secret, the transfer was to be carried out at new moon and at midnight. A lorry was standing by to carry the coffin and, beside the tomb, the concrete lay dry-mixed, when once again appeared the black figure. The contractor found his tools were missing when he left home and strange marks were scrawled in tar upon his gatepost.

Twenty-four hours later Hadji Sullaiman Shamahomed went to his room to close off his accounts and offer thanks for the completion of his self-imposed task. He was found the next morning, stiff and cold, still sitting at his desk.[11]

There is of course one crucial flaw in this story: no one knows for certain where Sheikh Yusuf's body lies. There is a good chance that it was removed from the Cape more than two hundred years before. But then, what do a few centuries matter in the world of myth and legend?

[11] Rosenthal, pp39-40.

3

Castles and Curses

Sitting at the sidewalk tables at The Castle of Good Hope's restaurant, De Goewerneur, where the hamburgers will haunt you long after the atmosphere is forgotten, you look out at De Kat, a defensive wall which houses the one-time Governor's residence, fronted by an ornate entrance portal set above a short staircase.

The parade ground between you and De Kat was the heart, for two centuries, of the city's civic life. Here, the changing of the guards would take place before the governor, standing at his portal, or he would read out announcements of importance to the citizenry.

It is easy to sit there now and conjure up in your mind the scene of old-time soldiers marching about, or citizens in their seventeenth and eighteenth-century finery strolling across the grass and paving stones. The yellow walls, the green and white wooden window frames, the mountain in the background looming over it all: it simply reeks of history.

If you take the traditional tour of the Castle, you will hear fresh-faced students talk animatedly about historic personalities and modern renovations. In between, they tell you matter of factly about implements of torture, reigns of terror and the dungeon known as the Donker Gat, or Black Hole.

'... research has revealed that these two rooms were most probably used for torturing purposes,' Stellenbosch University student Helene Wessels is telling her audience. She continues:

> You will note that it consists of two rooms. There's also a good reason for that. According to Dutch law, nobody could be executed unless he or she confessed to their crimes. Of course, they had several ways to make you confess. You will note these two iron beams sticking from the wall. The person was handcuffed here and then whipped. There's also a hook hanging from the ceiling. The person was blindfolded, hung there upside down and then, when the soldier on duty let go of the rope, the person went through the floor head first.
>
> While one person was being tortured, another was kept in the room. He or she heard the first one screaming and decided to confess. You will also note an upside down horseshoe on that first green door. People were very superstitious in those days and they believed that that horseshoe indicated bad luck for those two rooms.

Bad luck indeed for those invited inside for interviews.

Despite describing these gruesome incidents in the casual way you would offer someone a koeksister recipe, the guides have little room in their scripts for ghost stories. However, if you're lucky enough to find one of the more helpful or knowledgeable members of the team, the stories begin spilling out. After her shift, Helene agrees to help and tracks down a sheaf of clippings and typed reports that no one else seems to know about. The reports about supernatural experiences from individuals based at the Castle over the past century present a rough and unordered history. Tales of great and fearsome personalities mingle with the eyewitness accounts of ordinary soldiers and clerks. Combined with the research of some of South Africa's leading ghost hunters, one conclusion becomes obvious, at least on the surface: the Castle is haunted by entire generations of ghosts.

Built between 1666 and 1679 as the successor to Van Riebeeck's original Fort, and the oldest inhabited building in southern Africa today, its very construction inspired the first resident ghost of the Cape of Good Hope.

The ageing Reverend Johan van Arckel departed from Holland in 1665, eager to bring a greater formality to God's work at the Cape of Good Hope. Soon he was an integral part of the civic life of the community. As fortune would have it, he arrived in the year in which it had been decided that the Fort would be replaced by a new castle. He gave his blessing to the building operation and, in January 1666, intoned the prayer of thanks at the laying of the foundation stone. It was to be one of his last duties, however, for he died a few weeks later. It is said that he was buried near the foundation stone, not merely in the grounds of the Castle, but in the very walls of the bastion that would be named Leerdam.

To this day, the Reverend prowls the battlements between the Leerdam and Buren bastions, sometimes moving over towards the Oranje bastion, surveying the unfinished pastoral work he left behind.

And, should you stand on the forlorn patch of grass on the Leerdam bastion, you cannot but shiver at the sense of loneliness and desolation that slowly creeps over you, even in the middle of a hot summer's day. Is it the Reverend seeking your company?

When veteran journalist and ghost hunter Margaret Williamson was hunting down the ghosts of the Cape for *The Argus* around 1970, a natural stop on her trail was the Castle. As fate would have it, the officer commanding Western Province Command, and hence commander of the Castle, was one General Magnus Malan, later to become chief of the South African Defence Force and then Minister of Defence. But he showed as little imagination at the Castle as he did later during an ignominious stint in government, which saw him demoted to the Ministry of Water Affairs before his retirement.

In her book *Haunted Corners* Williamson tells a delightful story of the General, the General's aide, a supercilious captain who scoffed at her quest, and a dim tour guide. While she was in their office, they were issuing orders to a hapless conscript, their 'gofer', who was eventually instructed to show her around, just to get her out of the officers' hair. The conscript turned out to be the most informed person among the military gathering.

'After the Captain and Malan and everybody laughed at us with scorn, we said thanks very much and were leaving,' she recalls now. 'The Captain told this recruit, Martin van Breda, who had to fetch the tea and things like that, to take us anywhere we wanted to go. We went outside and he said, "Come along, and I will show you where you hear the footsteps."'

Whose footsteps?

Perhaps those of the apparition witnessed one cold night in 1947? The story is related in typed notes in Afrikaans and kept at the Castle, but they appear to have been translated from Eric Rosenthal's 1949 collection, *They Walk By Night*. Rosenthal put together his account shortly after the event:

On an evening in July 1947, Corporal M J Boonzaaier, of the Union Defence Force, received a strange report.

He was stationed at the Castle in Cape Town when the guard filed in, saying they had just encountered a ghost. Two of the men, walking round the battlements of South Africa's oldest building, had come upon a misty something, unmistakably like a man, but nearly eight feet high.

'We tried to surround it in a pincer movement,' said one of them, with a touch of modernity, 'when we were staggered to see it step out over one of the ramparts and vanish into space. We looked down about fifty feet into what used to be the moat, but there was nothing there.'

A buzz of conversation arose in the guard-room. Two of the Red Caps, or Military Police, admitted that they too had recently seen the spook and now the Corporal felt it was his duty to make some enquiries of his own.

Accompanied by Lance Corporal H S Botha, Private H C Barnard and Private P D Holder, he went upstairs and peered into the Cape Town winter night. The men were standing between the well-known Oranje and Leerdam bastions when they again saw something white hovering along the battlements. It passed from one side to the other, being sufficiently luminous to show up against the background of Table Mountain.

The soldiers held a conclave and decided to try out a rational check. One of them said: 'Maybe it is someone trying to fool us by dressing up in a sheet.'

'We can make sure of that,' said the Corporal. Back in the guard-room, he told Private Sneygans to find a sheet and do his best to provide a ghostly apparition.

When he returned in his white cloth, the soldiers greeted him with a horse laugh. 'It's no good,' they said. 'You don't even know the beginnings of how to haunt. You aren't even transparent.'

Becoming serious, they agreed there was no resemblance between the spook who had faded over the battlements and Private Sneygans in his sheet.

This, however, was not the end. On a Saturday evening one of the troops rushed down into the guard-room with the news: 'It's here again!'

There was a stampede upstairs and they had just reached the place in question when a bell rang vigorously below.

'That's from the guard-room,' exclaimed one man, 'but there is nobody there!'

By this time Corporal Boonzaaier decided to make a report. The officer on duty scratched his head and passed it on to the Commander of the Castle who, finding no instructions in the Military Code about how to deal with ghosts, went on with his work.

Three times, at intervals of three days, the spooky happenings were repeated. At three o'clock in the morning, one of the men on guard duty came from the Leerdam bastion: 'I went as cold as ice and then began to sweat like anything. It was most uncanny. I won't go over that part again at night.'

The report notes that the Military Police were given instructions to be on the lookout for practical jokers, but none were found.

The events reminded veterans of an incident back in 1915. In broad daylight, a sentry had seen a man dressed in eighteenth-century costume leaning over the parapet between Leerdam and Oranje, staring down at Darling Street. Suddenly the man disappeared. The soldier ran away and refused to return to his post, despite the threat of a court martial.[12]

---

[12] Rosenthal, pp1-3.

If the 1915 report is to be given any weight, then we should perhaps look for another name behind the Ghost of Leerdam, for the Pastor van Arckel would probably not have been dressed as an eighteenth-century gentleman back in the rough and ready days of 1666. Of course, few among us could tell the difference between an eighteenth and seventeenth-century costume, but let's give that veteran the benefit of the doubt for a moment.

Let us sit down at De Goewerneur and let our gaze rest once more on the balcony of De Kat.

The year was 1729. Governor Pieter Gysbert van Noordt, an irreligious man who demanded rigid discipline of his men and was given to fits of fury at the slightest hint of disobedience, stood at the balcony. In his hands he held a fateful document – nothing less than the passing of the death sentence on four soldiers from the Castle garrison.

The soldiers had planned to desert but were apprehended, and gave themselves up without a fight. The Council of Justice (Raad van Justisie) decided to banish them to the colony of Batavia, and also approved their fellow-soldiers' own version of rough justice: the accused had to run ten times through a gauntlet of soldiers who beat them as they ran. The four were then thrown into the Donker Gat, to await deportation.

Van Noordt, however, would have none of this 'light punishment'. He summarily ordered that the four men be hanged. The Council protested vehemently, pointing out that the soldiers had not carried out their desertion.

The governor's response was typically arrogant and to the point: 'Ik neem het op mij' ('I take it upon myself'). The Council was unable to oppose what was in effect a governmental decree.

It was a Friday morning, between eight and nine o'clock,

when the men were told they would be hanged, and that the sentence would be carried out the very next morning. The doors to the Donker Gat were opened, but the guard at the door was doubled.

As was customary, that night the condemned men were served a dinner prepared in the governor's own kitchen. But they were too busy praying and singing to concern themselves with a final earthly pleasure.

At eight o'clock the next morning Van Noordt stood at the balcony. The entire garrison was at attention on the parade ground. At nine o'clock it marched to the front of the governor's residence, and the condemned men were led out of the Donker Gat to the front of the balcony. They stood there, glowering at Van Noordt.

Unperturbed, he read out the details of their crime, and then pronounced their sentence. As the men were led away to the gallows erected outside the Castle grounds, Van Noordt retired to the great hall of his residence where he was in the habit of resting in an old plush chair and contemplating his little empire.

Meanwhile, the condemned men kneeled in front of the gallows, saying final, heartbreaking prayers for each other. Even the members of the Council of Justice were moved to mourning and soon the sound of wailing arose from the entire throng as the garrison surrounded the gallows. The first three men were led to the ropes, and executed. The last one stepped forward but, before they could put the rope around his neck, he said, 'Wait! I have something to say.' He turned in the direction of the Governor's residence and shouted out:

'To you, Governor van Noordt! I call on you at this very moment, before the Judgement-seat of God, the Almighty Father, that you must give reckoning for my soul, and the souls of my condemned companions!'

The man was then hanged, and the Council returned to the Governor's residence to inform him that the executions had been carried out.

They found him in his easy chair in the great hall. Motionless. He was dead. With an expression of utter terror frozen on his face.

That is not where the story ends. Even before it was due to move into the realms of the supernatural, several more acts had to be played out. The first occurred immediately after the discovery of the body. A prisoner in the Castle suddenly began screaming: 'Noordt is dood! Nu is er geen nood!' ('Noordt is dead; now there is no longer any need for fear'). Folklore remembers the prisoner as one Winkelman, and tells us that he was later released and promoted to the rank of sergeant.

If that tale is almost biblical, than Noordt's last act played out in the world of man was Shakespearian. It is said that the Council of Justice ordered that two coffins be made for Van Noordt, the first a rough box, and the second an elaborate casket. The first coffin was sent to the governor's residence, and Van Noordt's body was placed inside. A team of slaves was then ordered to remove the coffin from the Castle at midnight, and bury it at Paarden Island. The slaves were threatened with death should they reveal what had been done. Mindful of summary executions at that moment, the secret remained with them.

At the official funeral, a fine coffin of Indian wood was buried with no body inside.

To this day, Van Noordt is still trying to regain his power at the Castle. But, it is whispered by some, he may be looking for the beautiful coffin that was intended for him, and he may yet be dangerously angry at the insult of his final, anonymous burial place.

The wonderful thing about the Castle's ghost stories is that so many of them can be traced to real personalities who once lived and died there. But in this very traceability lurks the evidence that many of these connections are no more than legend.

Take the ghost of Lady Anne Barnard.

Andrew Barnard, appointed Colonial Secretary of the Cape after its conquest by the British, arrived at the Castle in May 1797. His wife, born Lady Anne Lindsay, brought her aristocratic upbringing to Cape society and dazzled all who encountered her. After she died, Margaret Williamson says, 'an elaborately gowned, smiling figure is supposed to float around the ballroom when evening parties have reached their zenith'.

As Williamson herself records in her collection *Haunted Corners*, however, Lady Anne 'stayed only five years, and died in England'.

Even the tale of Van Noordt appears to evaporate, ever so slightly, when placed under the interrogation lights of serious scholars. So, for instance, G E Pearse writes in *The Cape of Good Hope* that Van Noordt did in reality die in his chair, but not at the Castle: he was seated in the gardens at Government House on 23 April 1729. But Pearse acknowledges that the governor had been in good health only a few hours before, and had that day signed several documents, which still exist.

I have heard many tales of incidental hauntings at the Castle: footsteps that supposedly cannot be explained by science; transparent figures walking through the walls, off the parapets and down the halls; a sad-eyed lady in grey and a large black dog with fire in its eyes; strange voices in strange places.

Can it be that the atmosphere of the Castle, so steeped in

history and, at times, in horror, inspires belief in supernatural experiences, even when they did not really take place?

If this were indeed the case, I believe that there would be even more stories to tell. Even if the Castle is the most haunted building in all of Africa, most of its ghosts can be pinpointed to a time and place of events that have imprinted themselves on the minds of those who experienced them.

But, more significantly, most of the ghosts appear to be rooted in the history rather than the atmosphere of the Castle.

Take the Lady in Grey. No one knows who she was, but sightings were reported by historically identifiable people. One of these was Emily Daniel, daughter of the Brigade Major of the British garrison in 1860, who awoke one night to see a shadowy woman with her face in her hands. A few days later her sister, one Mrs R G Scott, also witnessed a 'lady in a grey jacket'. In the 1880s, Governor Bartle Frere's wife, Lady Frere, encountered the apparition in her bedroom where she was examining a ball gown she was about to wear, with a terribly sad expression on her face. On another occasion, Lady Frere is said to have described the woman as 'our ghost'.

She was spotted again during the Van Riebeeck tricentenary celebrations in 1952, when the organiser of an exhibition of antiques at the Castle spotted her – except that this time she was dressed in a red gown.

Eric Rosenthal reported in a later edition of *They Walk By Night*: 'Only a few years ago the skeleton of a woman was dug up near the old sally-port of the Castle opening on to Table Bay. Since then the Grey Lady has not been seen.' No one seems to be able to trace the source of this report, but all who take an interest in these matters agree with Rosenthal's prognosis for the non-return of the ghost.

Which leaves us with one clearly identifiable ghost at the

Castle, once we have sifted through all the sightings and experiences: Governor van Noordt.

Both the Grey Lady and Van Noordt are associated with a legend about underground tunnels that linked the Castle to city landmarks. Tuynhuis, formerly the State President's residence and before that Government House, and Rust-en-Vreugd, a national monument that has been turned into an art gallery, are both said to have been linked to the Castle by underground tunnels. Consequently, most sightings of the Grey Lady were reported at Government House. None other than Princess Margaret, who stayed there with her family during the Royal Visit to South Africa in 1947, is said to have spotted her.

Rust-en-Vreugd, on the other hand, is associated with Governor Noordt. And it has been described as The Most Haunted House in South Africa, although there is no significant body of supernatural folklore associated with it.

The entrance to the building at number 78 Buitenkant Street is rather unimposing. You walk first through a garden that appears almost wild in an organised manner, before coming to a house that is obviously very old but, more than that, bizarre in its construction. It seems to have been chopped off at the ends as if to make room for the roads running by. The stairs leading up to the front door are also not immediately obvious, giving the impression that even the staircase has been chopped off, leaving the frame of the house standing in splendid isolation. In the broad daylight of early afternoon, lights burn in some of the windows, as if a different time is followed inside the house.

And indeed, people are living there, namely – at the time of visiting – Johan van Wyk, curator of the superb William Fehr Collection of Cape art, maps and other Africana housed in the gallery.

Before he says another word, Johan van Wyk insists: 'I

don't believe in ghosts at all.'

When he moved into Rust-en-Vreugd with his wife and child in October 1994, no one had mentioned ghosts to him. He had been instructed in great detail, however, on how to operate the alarm system that would protect the gallery at night.

'I did not know about the stories, so I wasn't influenced at all. Then, one morning we heard footsteps, heavy footsteps for about twelve strides, upstairs. It was 2 o'clock in the morning, and we were asleep downstairs. Both my wife and I woke up simultaneously and thought, "What the heck is that?" But we have an alarm system that picks up anything and it didn't go off.'

In an interview on 13 January 1997 Van Wyk maintained it could not have been the floorboards contracting as the house grew cold in the early morning:

> That has a particular sound. You know, wood creaking, irregular. This was regular, like footsteps. I don't believe in this sort of thing and nor does my wife, but it has happened three or four times already. At times you can have it in succession and then not hear it for months. We haven't heard it for months.
>
> There's a second occurrence which happens in the flat. The kitchen of the flat was built at the same time as the house, but the main house originally stopped at the kitchen.
>
> We heard a noise coming from the kitchen. It sounded like footsteps of a child who has a club foot. There is a greater emphasis and greater weight applied to one foot as opposed to the other. It probably goes for about sixteen, eighteen steps, so that you can clearly hear it actually approaching you. Now I sleep upstairs in the main bedroom and you can hear this thing sort of approaching

the children's bedroom and then it just stops.

On one particular occasion, it happened around 5 o'clock in the morning and we just left it. The second time it happened I thought, well, it's now or never, so I dashed downstairs and the dog was fast asleep and the children were both in bed. I had thought it was one of the children.

We've often heard, during the day, noises upstairs in the gallery as if there's someone up there. We've never seen anything, only ever heard noises. It's very interesting that in that book *Haunted Corners* they mentioned the footsteps and it's exactly the same as we've been experiencing. And I did not know anything about that publication at all when we began experiencing it.

The first time when we heard the twelve footsteps, that was quite frightening. But it wasn't a supernatural feeling. I've been in supposedly haunted buildings before and you continually have this feeling of an eye or something just watching you all the time. You don't get that feeling at all here.

Plumbing problems – the usual source of strange noises in old houses – have been ruled out. What has not been ruled out is yet another legend of Governor van Noordt: that his body was not buried at Paarden Island, but in fact did come to rest at his out-of-town retreat, just above the present Roeland Street.

'According to tradition,' writes Margaret Williamson, 'Rust-en-Vreugd stands on the site.'

What we have, then, is a personality and a series of noises. There have been tales of figures seen in the upstairs windows, of forlorn ladies with their babies awaiting the return of their men from the seas, but none of these have any consistency. Williamson tells of a young woman who experienced several strange sightings and feelings in the building's days as a nursing college in the 1940s, but these have not been repeated. Moreover, no one who has been resident at Rust-en-Vreugd has ever reported an actual sighting; only the noises.

Should we believe these to be the product of ghostly happenings? If even Johan van Wyk who has experienced more of these phenomena than any previous occupant of the building still does not believe in ghosts, should we be any more convinced by mere reports of the noises?

For now, let us say only that Rust-en-Vreugd certainly does not compete with the Castle for the title of South Africa's most haunted building. There, at least, ghosts still get some respect.

4

Riders in the Storm

Is there anything lonelier than a deserted country road on a moonless night? Anything more silent than an unmarked path that turns off into the darkness? Imagine you are driving along just such a country road, approaching that very turn-off. The skies are loud with thunder, and flashes of lightning send shadows streaking among the trees and across the road. And then you see the turn-off to nowhere.

Can there be a sight more forlorn? Can there be a scene more likely to set your imagination racing? It is easy to picture an old, deserted house at the end of that turn-off. Or to imagine scenes of unspeakable sadness playing themselves out somewhere in the darkness. Or some phantom being roaming through the night.

All these thoughts flash through your mind in a moment, as briefly as the flash of lightning that suddenly illuminates the turn-off as you drive past, searing your eyes and, for a heartbeat, blinding you.

And then you become the victim of a conspiracy. The light,

the night, your eyes and your imagination conspire with your memory, and convince you that you saw something move ...

Most of us have had this kind of experience. Some have rationalised it to the point of accepting it as a trick of the light and the imagination. Some have built it up in their minds into a conviction of a dramatic encounter with the supernatural. Memory adds details, like style and colour of dress. Imagination adds the expected, like face and expression.

Am I being cynical? Over-rational? Perhaps. But is this scene any different from momentary sensations we all have of, for instance, thinking we saw someone move in the shadows, next to a driveway or in a garden at night? In the modernised urban environment, we imagine we have successfully banished wild creatures, insects and ghosts. Yet we imagine intruders. In less built-up areas, we imagine ghosts. In both situations, our imaginations turn visual patterns into seemingly logical conclusions, based on our expectations of the setting, atmosphere and type of stresses or tensions that exist in the specific environment.

The reality is that we have a basic need to make sense of whatever we see. In other words, when our eyes are presented with a jumble of visual jigsaw pieces, such as a night-time scene of light and shadows, our minds are obliged to turn that jumble into a pattern that can be recognised and interpreted.

What then, of those tales that are told again and again by travellers on the same lonely country roads, or stormy seas, or even angry skies? What if the same ghosts are seen in the same place by many different people? What if these ghosts even have names, histories and destinies?

South Africa has played host to many of these, both famous and infamous, along with the unknown and anonymous who have haunted our paths and passages. In modern times, the most famous ghost this country has produced is without a doubt the White Lady of Uniondale. We explore her sad role later in this book. But long before we encounter her on a twentieth-century roadside, we must explore older routes, and ghosts of more ancient times.

The Flying Dutchman

'At four a.m. the Flying Dutchman crossed our bows.'

That brief, matter of fact statement is possibly the most famous line in the history of the supernatural.

It was recorded on 11 July 1881, by Prince George, a sea cadet who later became King George V. In 1880, he set off on a round-the-world sea voyage in a squadron under Prince Louis of Battenberg. He and his brother, Prince Albert Victor, were required to keep a diary of their experiences, and this journal was later published as *The Cruise of H.M.S. Bacchante*.

The bland declaration of the appearance of the ship called the Flying Dutchman in effect gave the royal seal of authenticity to what until then had been more of a legend than a firm belief. At least, among non-seagoers, it had been a great story. Seafarers took it very seriously indeed.

For the origins of the Flying Dutchman, we must go back another 250 years.

In 1641, history tells us, a sea captain by the name of Hendrik van der Decken who was in the employ of the Dutch East India Company embarked on a journey he had made many times before: to round the Cape of Good Hope en route from Batavia in the East Indies to Amsterdam.

But as he approached Table Bay, legend has it, he encountered strong winds that prevented him, time and again, from entering the bay. He then cursed the heavens, it is said, and vowed that he would round the Cape even if he had to sail until Doomsday (which, indeed, he has). Profanity cannot go unpunished in the world of myth and legend.

Some versions of the legend maintain that Van der Decken set sail on Good Friday, and that setting out on a long journey on such an auspicious date meant that the captain was doomed from the start. Whatever his sin, however, the one item we know from history is that the ship never made it into Table Bay, and was never seen again – well, not in solid form, at any rate.

There followed two centuries of tales told by sailors and travellers, and an ever-increasing fascination around the world with the Flying Dutchman.

The heart of the story was always Van der Decken's attempts to hail other ships, in the hope of sending a boat with a batch of letters from himself and his crew – a desperate effort to get word to the homes they would never see again. Sadly, the tale went, no one would ever accept the letters – for to do so would condemn the recipient to the same fate as the Flying Dutchman.

One of the best descriptions, reported by Eric Rosenthal as recorded by Victorian marine authority W Clark Russel, who in turn was told the story by an old Capetonian seafarer, does not miss a detail:

> The Flying Dutchman is described as having a very curious low-built bow, with a mass of timbers curving at the head to the immensely thick cutwater. Her bowsprit is sheered to an angle of forty-five degrees; at the end of it is a round top, and standing perpendicularly up out of

this top is a small mast with another top at the head of it, big enough to admit of its occupation by two or three men. A heavy, very square yard hangs by lifts under the bowsprit, and on the little perpendicular mast she carries what may be called a spritsail yard, the foot of whose sail spreads on the yard beneath. She has topsail and topgallant yards, with large round tops at the head of her lower masts, and smaller tops, but of a like character, at her topmast's heads, instead of cross-trees. She has a very lofty stern, with a kind of castle at the after end of the poop, where the taffrail should be; and it is here where Van der Decken takes his stand, trumpet in hand, when a vessel heaves in sight and he desire to speak to her. Her mizzen-mast rakes aft, and carries a triangular sail set on a gaff, with another jib-headed sail that sets flying outside. The break of the poop comes to before the main-mast, so that that spar pierces the poop-deck, while the athwartship-rail sets up, so to speak, on either hand the main-mast. The high bulwarks end abruptly just abaft the forerigging. She is pierced for eight guns, but it is not certainly known whether she still carries the quaint old pieces that grinned in her heyday through her ports. The ancient Dutchman affirmed that his great-grandfather used to say she was painted a pale yellow. Time, probably, has left to the struggling fabric but little of her old garnishings.

There can be no doubt, however, that the above description is that of Van der Decken's ship that sailed from Batavia for Holland in or about the year 1641 on a voyage which, through the wickedness of her profane master, will never come to an end as long as old ocean continues to roll.[13]

[13] Rosenthal, pp7-8.

If the story had not captured the imagination of Europe before Russel's account, it certainly did in the second half of the nineteenth century. In the 1840s, the German composer Richard Wagner chose it as the theme of a new opera: *Der Fliegende Holländer*.

When the opera was staged at Covent Garden in London a few decades later, it made a huge impact, stirring the imaginations of Princes George and Albert Victor no less than anyone else's.

Their journal entry itself was surprisingly non-committal:

> A strange red light, as of a phantom ship all aglow, in the midst of which light the masts, spars and sails of a brig two hundred yards distant stood out in strong relief as she came up on the port bow. The lookout man in the forecastle reported her as close on the port bow, where also the officer of the watch from the bridge clearly saw her ... Thirteen persons altogether saw her. Whether it was the Van Diemen, or the Flying Dutchman, or who else must remain unknown ...

The princes interrupted this tale with a series of exuberant verses from Wagner's opera, including:

> Saw ye the ship on ocean main,
> Blood red her sails and black her mast?
> On highest board, with features pale, her Captain stands in storm and blast![14]

Most 'official' versions of the tale suffer from a similar inconclusiveness. The closest we come to the legend in formal documentation is a log entry for the Royal Navy

[14] Rosenthal, p12.

ship HM *Leven*, commanded by Captain W F W Owen, who was conducting a survey around the Cape coast along with the HM *Barracouta*. On 6 April 1823, he thought he saw the *Barracouta* about two miles away.

> This was considered extraordinary, as it was known on board the *Leven* that the other vessel's sailing orders must have dispatched her leagues away from the place in which she was now seen. Captain Owen bore down to speak, but the other put her helm up, though she was observed some time afterward to lower a boat. Next day the *Leven* anchored in Simon's Bay. The *Barracouta* arrived a week later. On inspecting her log it was seen that she was three hundred miles from the spot where it was believed she had been described. Twice the *Leven* sighted the phantom ship. On the second occasion the Dutchman lowered a boat, but Captain Owen, perfectly aware of the penalty that would attend his undertaking the delivery of a letter for Van der Decken, packed on canvas and took to his heels as fast as his ship would carry him.[15]

Other versions included a description by R Montgomery Martin, compiler of a book on South African Statistics. His experience, which occurred in 1835, was preceded by what we would today call a dead giveaway. 'We had been in "dirty weather", as the sailors say, for several days, and to beguile the afternoon I commenced after-dinner narratives to the French officer and passengers (who were strangers to the Eastern seas) current about the "Flying Dutchman" '.

The punchline came, inevitably:

> Suddenly the second officer, a fine Marseilles sailor, who

[15] Rosenthal, p9.

> had been among the foremost in the cabin in laughing at and ridiculing the story of the Flying Dutchman, ascended the weather-rigging, exclaiming, 'Voilà le Volant Hollandais'. The captain sent for his night-glass, and soon observed: 'It is very strange, but there is a ship bearing down upon us with all sail set, while we dare scarcely show a pocket-handkerchief to the breeze.'[16]

The ship disappeared as suddenly as it had appeared, with nary a glimpse of a fierce captain. The Royal version, too, omitted Van der Decken. Not only that, but according to Eric Rosenthal's account, '... the Royal narrative does not tally with the traditional version of the Flying Dutchman yarn. The *Bacchante* met the mystery vessel beyond the Cape, not on the Atlantic side, from where the legend says the ship is ever trying to round the famous foreland.'

Three other sightings were recorded by Rosenthal, one off Muizenberg in 1939, one from a passenger on the mail ship *Cape Town Castle* in 1955, and a final sighting by the master of a Dutch freighter in 1959. All are vague, or tend to take it for granted that any sighting of a ghostly windjammer must be the Flying Dutchman.

There are three astonishing aspects to this tale:

- Firstly, the time-honoured and age-old heart of the plot, namely the captain of the doomed ship hailing other ships with a request for messages to be carried home, has never appeared in the documented sightings. Only Owen's log tells of a boat being lowered, but even he assumes its intention from knowledge of the legend, rather than because of a ghostly plea.
- Secondly, despite the testimony of the most apparently

[16] Rosenthal, pp9-10.

reliable kinds of character you could have hoped for in Victorian times, namely royalty, naval officers and statisticians, there is far more evidence for the impact of a famous legend than for the existence of the Flying Dutchman.

- And, finally, there is a startling similarity to the legend of the White Lady of Uniondale. She, too, is linked to a real person who died while travelling in a storm. She, too, has been trying to find her way home ever since. Her tale also has Easter as an ingredient in its plot. And, of course, a number of eyewitnesses tell of seeing her, and even the authorities have confirmed aspects of the eyewitness accounts. Yet the accounts themselves are contradictory and questionable.

Could the Flying Dutchman have been just another vanishing hitch-hiker legend who was lucky enough to get more than his fifteen minutes of fame?

On the road

Let us return to those deserted country roads, the unmarked paths. And let us follow the treads of wagon wheels as they roll into ... the Spokeveld. The veld of ghosts.

> 'On the southern edge of the Great Karoo between Patatus River and the Soutkloof, is situated the bleak and desolate tract commonly known as the Spooky or Haunted Country, which is popularly believed to be the peculiar residence of ghosts and demons,' wrote Major A B Ellis of the West India Regiment, while stationed at the Cape during the nineteenth century. The supernatural creatures come in a variety of forms, he said, but 'the

> most frequently seen is a spectral wagon which, with phantom drivers, rushes furiously across the veldt in the still hours of the morning just preceding daybreak.'[17]

In a detailed narrative in Ellis' 1887 book, *South African Sketches* (quoted verbatim in Eric Rosenthal's 1949 work, *They Walk by Night*), he tells the story as told to him by one Lotterodt, a traveller who had been going by post-cart from Ceres to Beaufort West. Lotterodt was accompanied by the driver, Anthony de Beer, a Cape Town man, and another passenger.

During the trip one of the wheels was damaged and they stopped at Patatus River at nightfall to repair it, starting out again at 3am.

'It was a bright starlight night, and bitterly cold,' Ellis recounted. 'We were all nodding in our seats, dreaming no doubt of comfortable beds, when the cart suddenly stopped short, nearly throwing us out.'

De Beer cursed the horses, then got down to see if there was a problem with the harness. Still, the horses refused to move. Finally, he whipped them until they started off reluctantly. But they stopped again after a short distance.

> Anthony began cursing, when I thought I heard the sound of wheels, and stopped him to listen. True enough, over to our right we heard the cracking of a whip, the cries of a driver, and the rumble of wheels coming fast towards us. It was coming along at a furious rate on a dark night, over stones, rocks and bushes, where a man could hardly drive forty yards in the daytime ... in a few seconds we could see the mules, ten, twelve, fourteen of them, with heads down, tearing along at full gallop, and

[17] Rosenthal, p66.

> a mass of foam and steam.
>
> De Beer shouted: 'Where the hell are you going to?' Someone or something yelled: 'To hell!', followed by a burst of devilish laughter that made my blood run cold.

De Beer whipped the horses to move them out of the way, but they stood frozen, snorting and trembling, their manes bristling. The men leaped from the wagon and ran. The oncoming span of horses, 'with wagon leaping after them', missed their horses and wagon by inches.

> As they went by, there came the coldest blast of air that I have ever felt. It made us feel as if our blood had been turned into ice; and, just as the wagon was passing us, the driver turned his head round to us and pushed back his hat. Good heavens! What a face was that we saw ... it was the face of a white man, ghostly pale, like that of a corpse, and the jaws were tied up with a white cloth. The eyes seemed to look us through and through.
>
> ... All in a second the crash, rattle and rumble ceased and not a sound was to be heard. At the same moment the wagon disappeared.

There was a sequel, however. Legend had it, in those days, that the Phantom Wagon charged down on any vehicle it came across and smashed into it, dooming all those on board – unless someone was brave enough to challenge it. But ... the challenger would then die within a week. And sure enough, on the journey back, De Beer had an accident in Hottentot's Kloof. He, his cart and his horses were found smashed at the bottom of a ravine.[18]

[18] Rosenthal, p147.

Now we move forward in time, all the way to the 1980s. Ernest Meyer and his wife are travelling along the national road between Albertinia and Mossel Bay in the southern Cape. Near Cooper's Siding, they see a car with lights blazing rushing towards them from the Mossel Bay direction. Meyer dips his lights ... and the other car disappears. As they pass the spot where the car should be, they feel an icy coldness – but see nothing. It is a straight road, and there are no turn-offs.

This story was told as a first-person account to Margaret Williamson, who recounted it in her collection, *Haunted Corners*.[19] As if that were not enough of an echo of the Phantom Wagon of the Spokeveld, she also recalls the Phantom Lorry of Riversdale. As one-time women's editor of *The Argus*, she regularly published letters from one of her readers, Peggy Morris. In 1989 Peggy wrote to Margaret about a strange event on the road to Gouritsmond.

'We were returning home from a dance at Riversdale very late one night,' wrote Peggy, 'when we saw quite clearly an old-fashioned lorry, the type with a high square cabin, the headlamps shining a deep yellow, parked at a dangerous bend in the road.

'My husband slowed down for safety, which gave me a chance to see a man bending over the radiator part of the lorry. I noticed his hat – a trilby like you see in old films. We passed by carefully and glanced back to see that all was clear ... It was! The phantom lorry from another era had gone. The whole spectre had disappeared. I went cold with fright.

'The locals told me "The lorry often rides". He crashed in that area a long time ago.'[20]

Such phenomena cannot be explained in what we like to

[19] Williamson, pp16-17.
[20] Williamson, p17.

call rational terms. Neither the supernatural nor the human imagination have an accepted scientific basis. Yet, there are many theories that do offer explanations or, at least, understanding of such events.

One such theory is a starting point for understanding why so many stories are told of ghosts on the road, and why so few of them are consistent. Why, for example, is every encounter with the Uniondale Ghost, supposedly the spirit of Maria Charlotte Roux, killed on that dark stretch of road in 1968, entirely different? Why is she wearing a long white dress on one occasion and slacks and duffel coat on another? Why is she silent for some, but delivers hysterical screams for others?

In Chapter 5 we will look at the way that legends emerge from the archetype of the vanishing hitch-hiker. This does not, however, explain the random encounters with 'roadside' ghosts along all manner of desolate routes.

The Encyclopedia of Ghosts and Spirits finds a clue in an encounter in Lincolnshire in 1967.

On the night of 28th January, John Watson was driving a car in a rally, with his mother and a navigator as passengers. As the car rounded a bend, Watson saw a dark figure on horseback, dressed in traditional highwayman garb. He slammed on brakes to avoid a collision, and the figure vanished. His passengers saw nothing.

A year later, while organising another rally in the same area, Watson was approached by Pete Shenton, who told him he had seen the same figure, and pointed out the same spot. And, as with Watson, the passengers in the car had seen nothing.

Why do only the drivers see the figure? Ah, therein lies a world of meaning, if we can accept the suggestion of John and Anne Spencer, the *Encyclopedia*'s authors, 'that it is the degree of concentration on the road which creates a minor "altered state of consciousness" in the driver, whilst the other passengers remain marginally more relaxed'.[21]

The Lincolnshire highwayman, however, creates a dilemma: 'To explain away one such apparition as "highway hypnosis" is in fact popular with sceptics whereas this case of two different reports of a very similar figure at the same location would seem to suggest more than that.'

Indeed, rather than explain away the supernatural, the concept of 'highway hypnosis' may reinforce it: 'perhaps highway hypnosis itself creates a state where a genuine external event can be perceived as a result of the altered state of consciousness'.

There is a central problem with this argument, as with any claim for supernatural events being accessible only to people with special abilities or attitudes. It traps us in a logical loop of the 'you can only see if you believe and you will only believe if you see' variety.

And once you allow yourself to be caught in one logical loop, you may well be caught in them all. Chris Brazier, introducing a startling November 1992 special edition of *New Internationalist* on the paranormal, summed up the problem: 'Gullibility is like a minefield surrounding the paranormal. Being a fully fledged New Ager is in some ways akin to embracing Catholicism – having taken a leap of faith you accept the whole territory.'

We will return to that special edition, but for now I will acknowledge that Brazier does only use this perspective as an argument against the supernatural. Being 'unprepared to accept any paranormal occurrence whatever the evidence', he says, 'also smacks to me of religious commitment: faith in Western rationalism as holding the answer to everything.'[22]

[21] Spencer, J & A, p194.
[22] Brazier, p1.

When it comes to roadside ghosts and phantom hitch-hikers, however, Western rationalism holds an answer that is very satisfactory indeed to some.

John and Anne Spencer, in particular, believe that

> there are certain aspects of this particular type of report which suggest that it is also – more than any other type of ghost report – the product of folklore and mythology … The circumstances of the reports are often too 'pat' compared to other ghost reports; the hitch-hiker can frequently be identified, and the way that the hitch-hiker will have left the car often seems to leave no room for ambiguity, which is uncharacteristic of the general range of ghost reports.[23]

In other words, if the story is too good to be true, it often isn't.

[23] Spencer, J & A, p194.

5

The Lady Vanishes

Legends, tales of terror and ghost stories have always shared a close relationship. What town or city does not have at least one supposedly haunted house and a variety of stories, or legends, to explain the haunting? Usually, such stories circulate among the local inhabitants, particularly adolescents, for whom haunted places have always had a curious fascination.

Among these are often stories that people grow up believing to be indigenous to their neighbourhood only to discover, as they move away or come into contact with people from other towns or cities, that the same stories are claimed for numerous other locations.

When this happens you are probably no longer dealing with a ghost story, but rather with an urban legend.

Popular adolescent urban legends include the horror tales of lovers' lanes, escaped lunatics and cars that won't start in terrifying circumstances.

The clear non-psychological purpose of such stories is to

scare the hell out of friends and fellow students, or at least to give them shivers up the spine during those late-night storytelling sessions adolescents and students delight in. There is also the theme of the underlying cautionary tale – playing pranks can have tragic consequences. And, of course, there is the element of confirming the irresponsible behaviour of 'the youth of today'.

However, such warnings, meanings and variations seem trivial in the light of the 'genuine' ghost stories which have had such a powerful impact on the public mind that they have become part of modern folklore.

The Uniondale ghost

The best-known South African ghost story is undoubtedly the Lady in White or the Uniondale Ghost. The tale is repeated in major South African magazines every few years, usually just before Easter.

This ghost even has a name: Maria Charlotte Roux, who was killed in a road accident near Uniondale in the Eastern Cape on Easter morning, 12 April 1968 at 4.30am.

According to the police report of the accident, the driver of the car was her fiancé, one G M Pretorius, 21 years old. He was driving at about 100 kilometres per hour when he moved his right hand from the steering wheel and lost control of the car. Maria, who was asleep in the passenger seat, was flung from the car and killed.

The story is now taken up by David Barritt, a journalist who has written extensively about the case. Writing in the *Sunday Times* Magazine on 29 March 1987, he comments that it was a tragedy that would eventually have been forgotten, except that people began seeing Maria's ghost:

Mr and Mrs Leonard Fraser from Cradock … on Easter Friday 1973, were the first to see her. 'We were on our way to Oudtshoorn,' said Mr Fraser. 'At around midnight I stopped the car on the Willowmore-Uniondale road and got out to stretch my legs. The road was deserted when I got out but suddenly a figure dressed in a long white dress appeared beside me. I got such a fright that I dived straight back into the car and drove off. As I tore off down the road I could still see the figure standing there.'

… The most convincing account is that of Mr Anthony le Grange, then aged 41, who saw the ghost on 1 May 1976.

At about 7.15 that night, Mr le Grange was driving along the Uniondale-Willowmore road when he saw a dark-haired girl, dressed in duffel coat and slacks, standing at the roadside. 'She wasn't hitch-hiking but because it was cold and raining I stopped the car,' he said. 'She opened the door and got in. I noticed that her face was very pale. I asked her where she wanted to go and she said "Porter Straat twee, de Lange". These are the only words she spoke to me.'

Mr le Grange started his car and drove on. 'I didn't know where Porter Street was so I turned to ask her and she was gone.' He was nonplussed. 'I just didn't know what to do so I drove to Uniondale police station and reported what had happened.

'Of course the policeman didn't take my story seriously. He told me to forget it and continue my journey. I was mystified and confused but what could I do except do as he said. I got back in my car and carried on toward Oudtshoorn.

'Just outside Uniondale I heard the most chilling sound I have ever heard in my life. It was a hysterical scream of fear and shock and it came from inside my car. To me everything stopped, my flesh went cold and prickly and I felt as if I had no blood in my veins. I was completely terrified.

'At that time I had never heard of the girl ghost but now when I think about that scream I think I was hearing the sound the girl made at the time of the crash.

'I turned the car round and went straight back to the police station. I told the policeman what had happened and said, "Look, the woman is still in my car." I made him examine the car with me. We found nothing but there was no way I was going to drive off alone so I insisted the policeman follow me in his van.

'I drove off at a steady 70 kilometres an hour, after having first made sure all the doors were securely locked. The policeman followed closely behind me.

'Just outside Uniondale the right rear door of my car slowly opened and closed, exactly as if someone got out and then shut the door behind them. I stopped the car and the policeman came up to me and asked if I had seen it. All he could say over and over again was: "How about that?" '

The policeman who witnessed what happened that night is Cornelius Potgieter, now a sergeant based in Vryheid, Natal. He confirmed Mr le Grange's story in every detail.

Barritt reports that Andries Vermeulen, who was then Uniondale's magistrate, launched an investigation. He collected sightings, and was given positive identification after showing a picture of Maria to the witnesses.

Barritt also spoke to a Uniondale resident, Charles van Rensburg, who claimed to have helped a University of Pretoria scientist investigate the sightings. Van Rensburg said the scientist eventually contacted the ghost, and told her she was dead and that her spirit was now free. 'Since then no one has seen the ghost,' said Van Rensburg.

Penny Miller's comprehensive collection of traditional folk stories, *Myths and Legends of Southern Africa*, published in 1979, includes the tale as 'The Spectral Hitchhiker'. She briefly tells the Le Grange version, and then goes into further detail about another incident which had also been recorded by Barritt:

> Mr Dawie van Jaarsveld from Johannesburg was going to visit his girlfriend at Oudtshoorn. He decided to take the road through De Rust, but it was growing dark and beginning to rain dismally. He had actually lost his way when he arrived at the first turn-off to Barendas. He was surprised when the headlights of his motorbike shone on the figure of a girl wearing dark slacks and a blouse. She was soaking wet as she stood watching him. Touched by her plight, he offered her a lift into town and helped her don his spare crash helmet; he even gave her an earphone so that she could listen to music as they rode. They set off briskly for Uniondale and travelled the next 17 kilometres to the second turn-off to Barendas. Just at that point he felt the back wheel skid slightly and thinking he might have a puncture he stopped to investigate. The girl had gone. With a growing sense of horror, he saw that the spare crash helmet was still firmly fastened to his motorbike and the earphone he had given her he found firmly plugged in his own ear! By the time he reached the Petros Café in Uniondale he was in sore need of the cup of strong coffee that was given to him.

Barritt's version of the story places it on 31 March 1978. It has Van Jaarsveld feeling 'something about her that made my flesh go cold' before she climbed on the bike. As he was driving along, he started feeling unnaturally cold, and speeded up to 120 kilometres an hour. When the wheel skidded slightly, he looked in his rear-view mirror to make sure the girl was all right. She was gone. He thought she had fallen off and went back to look for her, until he realised his spare helmet was bouncing against his back. It was still clipped to the luggage rack. Barritt does not mention the earphone.

Yet another version, reported by Cynthia Hind in *Fate* magazine in July 1979, has Van Jaarsveld suspecting a flat tyre, looking round, and seeing, or rather *not* seeing, the inevitable.

Hind went to the Petros Café, where the proprietress confirmed that the man had arrived at the café looking 'like he'd seen a ghost' and that he had claimed to have met the phantom hitch-hiker.

Hind also went to the ultimate destination mentioned in versions she had heard: the Louterwater farm, where Van Jaarsveld had been going to meet his girlfriend. Residents at the farm confirmed that he had arrived in a nervous state and that he had repeated his experience to them.

Cynthia Hind went to look up Constable Potgieter to check on Le Grange's story. Potgieter confirmed the story, except that he said he had accompanied Le Grange after the desperate man's first – not second – visit to the police station. When the car door had opened, the constable said, he had heard a maniacal laugh.

Meanwhile, a Lieutenant Giel Pretorius of the South African Air Force contacted the press, claiming he had been the driver of the car in the original incident. He said his fiancée had been flung from the car when a powerful wind threw it from the road and flung it over an embankment. He produced a photograph of his fiancée, which Mr le Grange said could have been the girl but he was not certain.

Hind also did the obvious: she went looking for 2 Porter Street. The only one on record in the Cape was in Worcester, and that was the address of a boys' hostel. She was unable to contact Lieutenant Pretorius, or Maria Roux's mother, who had apparently moved elsewhere.

As mentioned earlier, this is South Africa's best-known 'true' ghost story and, despite all the seemingly factual evidence, it is also one of South Africa's best-known urban legends.

The case has fascinated folklorists, as it happens to be the best documented version in the world of one of the most enduring and widespread international urban legends.

Jan Harold Brunvand, the Utah academic who popularised the term 'urban legend' through his various books on the subject, even named his first book after this brand of urban legend: *The Vanishing Hitchhiker*. The book does not even mention the Uniondale ghost; there are so many others to choose from. The traditional version of the legend goes like this:

A man is driving on a lonely road one dark and stormy night. Peering ahead through his windscreen wipers, he suddenly sees a hitch-hiker at the side of the road. It is a young woman, wet and bedraggled from the rain.

He picks her up, and she gives him her address in the next town. After a while, he turns to speak to her – and she's gone. All that remains is a puddle of water where she had been sitting. Terrified, he speeds into the next town, and goes to the address she had given. A man opens the door, takes one look at the traveller's face, and says sadly, 'You gave my daughter a ride, didn't you?'

Astonished, the traveller asks how he knew. The father

says this is not the first time. His daughter had died in a motor accident ten years ago on the same spot where she'd been hitch-hiking on this night, and she had been trying to get back ever since. He thanks the traveller for having tried to bring her home.

The Uniondale ghost fits the legend perfectly, except that the travellers never get to meet the parents. Ironically, however, the 'true' story has passed into the general pool of South African urban legends in exactly the version involving the parents.

It is told as having happened to travellers in various parts of the country, and usually includes the parents meeting the traveller at the door. In one version, which I recall hearing on radio but have been unable to track down, the traveller knocks on the door, tells the parents he had given their daughter a lift and she had disappeared.

That's impossible, they say. She had died exactly a year ago, in a motor accident. Suddenly he sees, over their shoulders, a portrait on the wall of a young woman: the hitch-hiker to whom he had given a ride.

The wake-up call

A different approach to the legend has a young man driving across the country, usually from Cape Town to Johannesburg or from Johannesburg to Durban:

The traveller is exhausted, and finds he can hardly stay awake, but he has to get to his destination by the next morning, and cannot stop to rest. He sees a hitch-hiker on the side of the road, and thinks that perhaps having company will help keep him awake.

He gives a ride to the hiker, a young man. The man is rather tense, and every five minutes he asks the driver the time. The driver gets quite irritated, but eventually finds himself waiting in anticipation for the next query.

By the time he sees the lights of Johannesburg (or Durban) he is wide awake. He turns to the hiker to make some comment ... and the man is gone.

The next day, at a meeting, he recounts this strange experience.

Another man at the meeting, suddenly wide-eyed, says, 'That was my son!'

It turns out that his son had died on that same road some years before after falling asleep behind the wheel. Every now and then, his father would come across someone who had picked up a hitch-hiker, who in turn had kept the driver awake throughout a long trip by constantly asking for the time, or striking up conversations relating to getting home safely.

Penny Miller, in *Myths and Legends of South Africa*, tells of another female ghost hiker, supposedly haunting the verges of Du Toitskloof in the Western Cape. But this one is rather more difficult to authenticate because 'whoever takes her in their car is always involved in a fatal accident'.

Jan Brunvand classifies these legends under 'Roadside Ghosts'. The Vanishing Hitch-hiker, he says, is a prime example of the adaptability of urban legends. It is also the classic automobile legend. 'This returning-ghost tale was known by the turn of the century both in the United States and abroad,' he says. 'It acquired the newer automobile motif by the period of the Great Depression, and thereafter spawned a number of subtypes ... some of which themselves stemmed from earlier folk tales.'

All the accounts traced by Brunvand were told as 'true'

stories, which supposedly happened to friends of the narrators. No less than fifteen distinct plots are recorded, with numerous variants on each plot. One of them, involving the portrait-identification element, has been traced back to St Petersburg, Russia, in 1890. It was actually reported in a Russian newspaper called *The Citizen*, published on 16 December 1890. It does not involve cars, but instead a priest who is asked by a woman in the street to give sacraments to a sick man at a certain address. The priest goes to the house, but the healthy looking man who lets him in doesn't know what he's talking about. The priest then sees a portrait on the wall. He points to it. That was the person who had made the request, he says. It is a portrait of the man's long-dead mother. In terror, the young man takes communion from the priest. That night, he dies.

'The quest for the ultimate origin of the Vanishing Hitch-hiker and its variations pretty well comes to a halt at this point,' says Brunvand, 'at least until further nineteenth-century and foreign prototypes are discovered. But updated and localized treatments of the legend continue to flourish in modern folklore, suggesting that the old ghost tale must have some important appeal to contemporary folk.'

Brunvand draws attention to a prototype, which he insists is not related to the modern hitch-hiker, in the New Testament, Acts 8:26-39. An Ethiopian in a chariot gives a ride to the Apostle Philip, who baptises him, then disappears.

The Sandringham Dip

South Africa alone boasts numerous versions of the vanishing hitch-hiker.

Johannesburg residents who hear the story of the Uniondale Ghost for the first time agree that it is true, but that it actually happened in the Sandringham Dip, part of what was once a dark, deserted stretch of road called Club Street that links the Johannesburg suburbs of Sandringham and Senderwood.

According to this version of the legend, there is a tombstone beside the road at the bottom of the dip. Because of the trees and weeds in what appears to be untended and undeveloped municipal land, people don't usually notice the grave.

But if you drive down the dip at exactly midnight, you will see a woman in white standing on the side of the road next to the grave. Some people have given her a ride, but when they turn to talk to her she vanishes, leaving only a small pool of water, or a breath of chill wind.[24]

At the time I first heard the story in the early 1990s, I examined the spot. There was no tombstone there. I never did drive down the dip at exactly midnight. My excuse is that there was always somewhere else to go, and I'm sticking to it.

But there was a chilling epilogue to the story. The ground next to the road, on the side where the tombstone supposedly stood, belonged to the Rietfontein Hospital, the management of which eventually decided to clean it up for development in the late 1990s. In the process, they discovered a graveyard in the area alongside the road, and consulted their records. It turned out to be the graves of patients who had died of cholera decades before and who, to avoid contamination, had been buried in an isolated part of the grounds.

The hitch-hiker may have been a figment of many imaginations, but give or take a few metres, the grave itself was very real!

---

[24] Goldstuck, *The Leopard in the Luggage*, p302.

That would have been enough to give the ghost new life, so to speak, but progress has no respect for the imagination. Shortly after the discovery of the graveyard, the road was widened into a well-lit, double-lane avenue, and the atmosphere of gloom and foreboding is history. And so is the ghost.

Vera, the hitch-hiking ghost of Meadowlands

In the Soweto suburb of Meadowlands, it is said, a ghost by the name of Vera terrorises taxi passengers.

According to one version of the legend Vera was murdered by her lover in 1957. Another maintains that she was a gangster's girlfriend and was killed in crossfire during gang warfare in the early 1960s.

Whichever way she met her fate, she spent the next forty years trying to get home by boarding a taxi in Meadowlands. If a taxi began to pull away from a stop in that suburb with an empty seat, Vera would quickly take the seat – and the taxi would never reach its destination. The more benign versions of the legend merely have her disappear en route.

As a result of these stories, it was said, taxi drivers refused to pull away from stops in Meadowlands until every seat was filled. This alone tells us that the story is mere legend, because taxi drivers are always in too much of a hurry to hang around Meadowlands in the hope of filling that last seat.

Another version claimed that as a result of Vera's haunting people avoided Meadowlands after sunset. Which, of course, raises the problem of what the thousands of residents of Meadowlands do with themselves after sunset!

These clear signals of the story being an urban legend did not stop a self-proclaimed 'ghostologist' by the name of Dr

Ismail Ballim from claiming in *The Star* of 5 October 1992 that he had brought Vera's reign of terror to an end (page 282).

As a bizarre footnote to the township life of the Vanishing Hitch-hiker, a similar story is told in Tembisa on the East Rand. Here, it seems, a ghost dressed as Michael Jackson – yes, the infamous pop star – stands on the side of the road, trying to catch a ride home. No one has ever claimed to have given him a ride, but he is assumed to be the ghost of an impersonator killed on the side of the road while trying to get a ride home from a lookalike contest.

Authenticating the legend

If you're still not convinced that the Uniondale ghost is an urban legend, perhaps you need a close encounter with a book called *The Evidence for Phantom Hitch-hikers*, by Michael Goss. It is published by the Aquarian Press in conjunction with the Association for the Scientific Study of Anomalous Phenomena, and investigates the numerous hitch-hiker stories told around the world, from New Zealand to New York.

Goss comments that 'the 100-plus (stories) upon which this present book draws is far from an exhaustive sample. Taken as a group, the individual variations within these hitch-hiker narratives do not disguise the obvious fact that we are dealing basically with the same story.'

The real contrasts in the stories lie in the way they conclude. Most end up explaining exactly who the ghost was, while others defy us to find a better explanation.

Goss has one warning which should be a red flag to Uniondale believers:

> ... folklore warns us that in hitchhiker stories police involvement is flourished as another pseudo-corroborative narrative element, one that enhances the credibility of an inherently incredible tale; by that the police took the thing seriously we are led to believe that the preceding part of the narrative was 'serious' (authentic) as well.

Goss discovers that 'there have been cases featuring named witnesses, some of them subsequently interviewed by investigators who found no blatant evidence of fabrication'.

The Uniondale ghost is given extensive coverage by Goss. He discusses an earlier version by David Barritt, from the 18 July 1980 edition of *Scope*, as well as Cynthia Hind's investigation for *Fate* magazine.

He comments:

> Looking with some difficulty past the assorted discrepancies in these accounts – applauding also that someone went to the trouble of trying to check the story by interviewing available witnesses ... it depends as usual on the credibility of unsupported eyewitnesses, but there are two of them, two reporters and two separate incidents pointing in the direction of a ghost that obeys the folklore tenets concerning the tragic origins and regularized (anniversary) appearances.

Goss's final conclusion about the legend is that 'there is sound evidence pointing to the Phantom Hitchhiker being a classic fabrication – a supernatural tale told as a matter of truth because that is part of the narrative convention ... Outside that convention, the story is obviously not true: (it is an) urban legend.'

And if you are still not convinced, perhaps the time has

come to contact the person who has spent more time than any other researching the Uniondale ghost, David Barritt.

When I went to see him in the late 1980s, he kindly dug out his records on one of the most popular stories he had ever written. He answered several of the questions foremost in my mind – not to mention the minds of many folklorists who examined the reports, but never bothered to question the reporter.

First of all, why did none of the stories ever quote the parents, except in one brief mention that has the mother moving to another town? Why was the fiancé only brought in second hand, and never actually quoted? Why was there no awareness of the international nature of this story?

Barritt confirmed that he did contact the parents, but the moment they heard what he was calling about, they refused to speak to him. 'I do definitely remember contacting her former fiancé, Pretorius,' Barritt said. 'He didn't want to discuss the matter either, saying she was dead and should be left in peace.'

Barritt has seen his story published many times. The original target of his article was the American sensationalist tabloid *National Enquirer*, which immediately puts a question mark to how seriously the story can be taken. Barritt himself did not deny this, but pointed out that the *Enquirer* went through a stage 'where they wanted every claim checked up as thoroughly as possible – and they paid for it. I had the luxury of going down to Uniondale in 1978 and spending some time in the Eastern Cape following up the various leads.'

Barritt's most reliable witness was Le Grange, not only because his story was backed up by both Potgieter and a second policeman on duty that night, but also because of what happened to Le Grange next.

'This is the part I really like about the story,' he said.

'Le Grange's wife told me that before that night he was a hard-drinking rabble-rouser. Overnight, there was a complete metamorphosis. He gave up drinking, and became a churchgoer, which he never had been.'

Barritt further revealed, however, that the story told by the other witness, Van Jaarsveld, had not stood the test of time quite as well: 'I think he was not the most reliable of witnesses. He contacted me some time later to say he'd seen other ghosts. I wouldn't put a high credibility rating on his story.'

Having spoken to the people involved and the people who witnessed the reactions of those people, did Barritt believe this was the one authentic version of the vanishing hitch-hiker?

After making it clear that he does not believe in ghosts, he continues:

> ... that story made more of an impression on me than any other I've written – largely because of the testimony of Le Grange and the policemen I spoke to, as well as the Frasers, who were the first to report seeing the girl.
>
> The stories weren't second hand. They were the first-hand testimony of three highly credible people who didn't have any reason to make up a story. There were no friends of friends involved. People like Le Grange have never heard of urban legends. He was a simple fellow. But something happened that night that changed his life profoundly.

Michael Goss cuts to the heart of the matter when he says that even if a witness does report the experience to the police, and the police respond, and it goes on record, 'we can still dismiss the thing: police involvement or not, there is still absolutely no guarantee that the witness was speaking the truth. And even if he was, the truth as he perceived it may not correspond with the truth of what actually happened.'

No matter which way you turn, as far as the sceptical enquirer is concerned, you still lose.

On the other hand, perhaps the phantom hitch-hiker is very real, and she's still out there, standing by the Barendas turn-off, waiting forlornly in the rain for the next unwitting traveller – perhaps you? – to give her a ride.

6

The Rain Queen

The world is flat as you head out of Pretoria on the N1 highway, but as you leave the metropolitan sprawl further and further behind, the landscape undulates, hills roll into view and valleys drop away before you. From the tree-swept hillsides in the foreground to the misty blue mountains in the distance and the vast sky hanging its clouds of grey and white, this region begins to earn its nickname, 'The Great North'.

Passing from historic towns like Modimolle (formerly Nylstroom) and Mokopane (formerly Potgietersrus) through the bold commercialism of Polokwane (formerly Pietersburg), you finally find yourself on the narrow tar road to Duiwelskloof. Here large trucks ply the treacherously cratered road, and a railway line in the distance carries steam locomotives into the rural heartland. The lights of Turfloop University far off to the right make for an unlikely carousel in the night.

The road winds, twists, turns and dips, down mountain

passes, down, down, as if you're descending into hell itself. And indeed, the road finally leads you into the isolated town of Duiwelskloof[25] – the 'devil's valley'.

It takes its name not from the world of darkness, but from weary nineteenth-century travellers whose ox wagons became stuck in thick mud.

Death appears to be very much part of the economic life of Duiwelskloof, for no fewer than three funeral parlours greet you before you reach the curiously named Imp Inn. It seems an appropriate name for an overnight stop in a quest for South Africa's most famous supernatural being. The owners of the Inn, however, dismiss any notion that the name might be related to this land's infamous imp, the tokoloshe.

In this part of the world, superstition about the power of the tokoloshe pales before the rumours and myths of a far greater power, one that can change the very weather and turn war into peace. For here we are on the edge of the realm of the Rain Queen.

✪

It is early in the sixteenth century. White settlements have yet to appear on the southern tip of the African continent. In Bokhalaka, the land of the Kranga people in Zimbabwe, the Monomotapa Kingdom still flourishes. But all is not well in the royal household. The daughter of King Mambo has fallen in love with her own brother. Their relationship remains a secret, until the day Princess Dzugundini falls pregnant.

---

[25] Following years of debate, during which the African National Congress wanted Duiwelskloof renamed after one of its deceased leaders, it was renamed Modjadjiskloof on 11 June 2004.

Great is her shame, but even greater is her fear. She knows her father will kill the prince when he finds out who is responsible. She beseeches her mother, the queen, to help her escape, and late one night flees with a group of loyal servants. Before she goes, however, Dzugundini violates her father's trust one more time: she steals his magical tools, the medicine he uses to make rain. Her mother has taught her the art of rainmaking, and she will use this force to build her power in a new land.

After many years, she arrives with her followers in the dark forests of the Molototsi River valley, and begins to build her own kingdom.

By the year 1800, Dzugundini's people have grown into a powerful tribe, but it is racked by its own internal conflicts. Finally, the chief, Mugodo, calls upon the spirits for counselling. He is told that his own sons are plotting against him, and that he must marry his daughter, whose female children will lead the tribe from now on.

Mugodo obeys the spirits' instructions to the letter: he puts his sons to death, takes his daughter for a wife, and builds a secret village for her on a mountain deep in the forests. She first gives birth to a son, who is strangled before he has taken a dozen breaths. And then, finally, a daughter is born to her.

She is named Modjadji – 'ruler of the day' – and she is kept away from all but the most necessary human contact. When Mugodo dies, Modjadji becomes queen. But still she shuns contact with the outside world, instead preparing to use the magic spells which have come down through her ancestors for a thousand years.

Her skills as a rainmaker spread throughout the land that is coming to be known as South Africa, and soon ambassadors from all the tribes come to make offerings to the Rain Queen, begging her to send rain. And soon her land becomes known as lo Bedu: 'the land of offerings'. Her people come to be known as the baLobedu, and they live in peace through an era when the assegais of Shaka and Moselekatsi wreak devastation upon the rest of the land.

Some believe she has three breasts. Some believe she will live for ever. All believe that she alone has the power to bring rain to their thirsty lands.

Queen Modjadji died in about 1860 and was succeeded by her daughter, Modjadji II. But it was no ordinary succession. According to legend, both the first and second queens took their own lives, committing ritual suicide by drinking poison made from the brain of a crocodile. Modjadji III, it is said, was persuaded by missionaries not to follow the same course, and ruled from 1895 to 1959. Modjajdi IV also died of natural causes in 1980, passing the throne on to her daughter, Mokope Modjadji V who died in 2001.

It was the second Rain Queen who inspired H Rider Haggard's mythical tale *She*, the immortal – and white – beauty who reigned over a magnificent kingdom somewhere in the heart of Africa for 2000 years. As a result of Haggard's story, many came to believe that the first Rain Queen had been a white woman.

Even the great Afrikaans writer Eugène Marais insisted that the first Rain Queen had been a white woman. Writing in *Sketse uit die Lewe van Mens en Dier* published in 1928, he quoted as his source both a Boer commander and a local tribesman.

The soldier, one Commandant Henning Pretorius, had the job of bringing tribes under the heel of the Zuid-Afrikaansche Republiek in 1890. At Modjadji, he provided a show of strength by firing his weapons over the village, and then demanded an audience with the Rain Queen.

She was carried to meet him in a curtained litter covered in zebra skins, and the crown princess briefly pulled aside one of the curtains to reveal – according to Pretorius – an ancient woman with blue eyes and greying brown hair. Later, however, Pretorius claimed to have met the queen at her invitation, and noted that she was light in colour, but not white. And he made a startling claim: that she was the daughter of a white man and a woman from St Helena. In a letter to *Die Volkstem*, published on 14 September 1892, he wrote: 'She grew up to be intelligent and beautiful and learned the art of making rain. The elders spread the story that she had no beginning and no end ...'

Marais also recounted the story of a tribesman who had accidentally seen the Queen during her youth, and had fled for his life. He described her as a white woman with plaited brown hair. However, his story was also filled with the stuff of legend: of a peace-loving princess who became a vicious sadist once she was crowned, and tempted men to see her so that she could have them killed. And, for someone who saw her only once, he had uncommon knowledge of her origins: that she was a Boer child taken captive by a war party, and brought up by the king's barren wife.

When these legends were recounted by veteran journalist Jack Blades in *Sunday* magazine in 1991, he quoted Professor Eileen Kruger, who had lived with the Lobedu and written the best-known book about them, *In the Realm of the Rain Queen*, as telling him that she had never heard the tribesman's story.

Even if we were to believe such mundane origins, however, much of the mystique surrounding the Rain Queen has been firmly entrenched for at least a century. For instance, the Rain Queen may never get married to a man. According to tradition, she is neither man nor woman. But, as if she were a male tribal chief, she presides over an entourage of women who are regarded as her own wives. She does have children though, and is seen as both mother and father to them. No man may claim her children. Almost as great as the secret of her rainmaking power has been the secret of their parentage.

The last Rain Queen, as well as all her predecessors, required all to remove their shoes before entering the royal kraal. And the queen before her even demanded that her counsellor, through whom all questions had to be put to her, lie flat on his stomach when he addressed her.

Of course, none of this speaks of the supernatural, except insofar as it underlines her independence from the traditional world of men, and her need to concentrate all her spiritual energies on her traditional role as the Rain Queen.

To strengthen both her own spirituality and others' belief in it, she spends one month a year, at the time when the rainy season is meant to begin, in total isolation. Cut off from all contact with the outside world, she prays and fasts in her 'palace' – a large white-walled house with a red-polished stoep built by missionaries in 1927.

Making rain, however, was said to require more than just her magical spells and medicines. A Lutheran missionary stationed at Ga-Modjadji village, Reverend Phillip Masekwameng, explained the 'transaction' to *Frontline* magazine writers Laura Yeatman and Patrick Bulger in 1985: 'They collect water in a horn which they sprinkle when they go home. The queen used to be given gifts like cattle and goats but money is used now ... The rainmaking ceremony is held once a year. It's a big festival with dancing, singing and plenty of maghewu.'

Until recently, it was firmly believed that Modjadji and Modjadji alone in all of southern Africa had the power to bring rains from the heaven. So great has been her power, that no war has threatened the baLobedu in the four centuries of their existence.

How real is that power? How supernatural a being is the Rain Queen?

✪

The year is 1998. Queen Mokope Modjadji V will reign for a few more years, before her passing[26] results in her title being assumed by a young, modern successor.[27] After lengthy negotiations with one of her counsellors, I am finally advised that the Rain Queen has agreed to grant me an audience on a Sunday in February.

✪

It's still summer, yet the mist drenches the mountains in the early morning as I travel out of Duiwelskloof. The road to the village of Modjadji passes through a rural sprawl of houses, homesteads, settlements, and stores, teeming with people trudging to work or school. Modern cars speed along, overtaking horse carts and hooting at pedestrians.

At a small settlement where the only landmark is the Maduneleng filling station, a sign points the traveller up a rough dirt road to Ga-Modjadji. Women carry huge bundles of firewood on their heads and small boys lug sacks over their backs as the road winds through lush bush.

Tight curves cut into the mountain, rocks forced loose by rain and traffic, and people suddenly appearing out

---

[26] On Thursday 28 June 2001, the Rain Queen died at a clinic in Polokwane from renal and congestive cardiac failure.

[27] On Friday, 11 April 2003, 25-year-old Princess Makobo Modjadji was crowned Modjadji VI, queen of the baLobedu people, at Ga-Modjadji. She was the first Rain Queen to have received a high school education.

of the bush, force a slow, bouncing progress as you carry on upward, ever upward, out of the valley. From time to time a group of children rushes out of the forest, hands outstretched. It may be the realm of the Rain Queen, but it is still a poor land.

At last the road levels out and a small village appears, with the obligatory administration offices commanding the entrance, and a church alongside.

A young man leads me down a narrow alley of reeds that form a rough, high fence. At a very narrow entrance in the fence he asks me to remove my shoes. I am taken into a large, though ordinary-looking kraal. I am asked to wait in a hut where a lounge suite fills the main room, along with an old Sanyo boom box blaring out hymns on Radio Sotho. Presently Victor Mathekga, a royal councillor who has a part-time role as interpreter for Queen Modjadji, arrives and asks me to wait a while longer before I can state the purpose of my visit to the queen. She has been told of my visit, which had been arranged with one of her nephews, but wants clarity.

Victor finally returns and tells me the queen is ready. He leads me through a maze of huts, past the hundred-year-old Mohlapu tree – a gnarled outgrowth that is linked to the Rain Queen legend – to a large white house with the year 1927 carved next to a steep staircase leading up to a veranda.

And there, sitting on a piece of linoleum, is a woman I can only guess must be the Rain Queen.

She has an imposing face which seems almost to have been carved out of ebony. It is a strong face, with large brown eyes and an absolutely inscrutable expression. She wears no regalia. Quite the contrary, she is wearing a golf shirt bearing a Matheke Retailers logo, almost as if it was the first thing she came across as she was getting dressed.

On her head is a colourful *doek*, but there is nothing unusual about it. And her dress is one that anyone in the community might wear.

Suddenly I realise that my expectation of royal finery is highly presumptuous: why should she dress like a queen for a meeting with a stranger?

I take my lead from Victor and sit down on the floor facing her, and he tells me that Queen Modjadji will now hear me. After much negotiation, however, it is made clear that she will answer no questions about the history of the Rain Queen or even her own early life. These must be put to her council of elders, in a meeting for which another appointment must be made. However, she is willing to talk about her present views and circumstances.

I have to put my questions to Victor, who will translate for the queen, and then translate her answers for me. She speaks only her own Lobedu language, and neither reads nor writes. She accepts, among the gifts I have brought for her, a book, which Victor assures me her daughter, the teenage crown princess who intends studying at university, will read to her.

My first question is about her lifestyle and her confinement to the royal kraal. I had heard in Duiwelskloof that she goes shopping in the town of Tzaneen like any normal consumer, except that she is escorted by her bodyguards. Have the rules changed so dramatically? She rejects such gossip.

> I don't just go out and enjoy just like everyone else, going anywhere. In our tradition, I am not allowed to go out with anybody. I remain here. Everybody must come here. I don't go to town, here and there. No, no, no, no. It's only through the bodyguard. I can tell them, 'I'm worried about this and this and this – go and take this and this and this.' It's not for me to go outside and do just like you.

She never leaves the head kraal, Victor insists.[28] 'She remains here. Anybody who wants to see her must come here.'

This respect for tradition extends to her followers who are spread out over a wide region, which she describes as covering the area between the Groot Letaba River in the south and the Klein Letaba in the north, and out to the edge of Giyane near the border of the Kruger National Park.

While the vast area does not all fall under her formal control, she has about a hundred indunas who report to her from across the region. A more compact area around Modjadji earned her the right of representation in the parliament of the former homeland of Lebowa, but now her power is more of the nature of a traditional chieftainship.

Victor points to a complex of kraals in the distance.

> You can see the kraal here? Can you see those kraals, just like this one? It is not the people from here who built it, it is the community. She says, 'Come and build my kraal, then bring this and this and this and this', and they definitely help. She has more than a hundred headmen under her. Then she just sends a message to each induna and the induna must tell the people that Her Majesty needs such and such a thing.

The Rain Queen not only understands the possibilities of modernisation, but actively embraces them. For one thing, she dispatched a member of the royal family, Prince Madlakadlaka, to appear before the new South African government's constitutional hearings in 1995. His mission? To make representations on behalf of the baLobedu commu-

---

[28] She broke her own rule under special circumstances on 31 October 2000: she paid a courtesy visit to former President Nelson Mandela at his residence in Johannesburg to thank him for supplying her with a four-wheel drive vehicle and for funding the construction of a school and a clinic at her village.

nity, objecting to the non-recognition of khiLobedu as an official language of South Africa.

'I needed that very much,' she says, shaking her head sadly. 'I am very unhappy because my language is not being recognised. Most of the authors write English books and Afrikaans and Northern Sotho. What I need is the Lobedu books to be written.'

Equally, she would like to see far greater development in the area. Not only the power lines erected by Eskom that hang so incongruously over the village, or the phone lines that reach into a few dozen houses on the mountain. She would like to see nothing less than a tar road leading right up to the entrance of the royal kraal.

Is she not afraid of the modern world?

'No, no, we want to build things. A tar road is the first thing we want. I am very happy to see people, even from overseas, but the only problem is the road, some people don't want to come because of that.'

I ask about her ordinary, almost humble appearance, and the fact that it appears that she does not want to act as if she is important.

Her answer speaks of a hidden nobility. 'As long as my people know me, they know that I am Her Majesty, that I am ruler. Besides that, I feel just like anybody. I don't want to make a show of it now, to make like I'm important, because my people know me.'

What about religion? It is said that Modjadji III was converted to Christianity in 1896, but the local Lutheran minister says the present Rain Queen has never been baptised. Is she a Christian?

Victor talks to her, and then answers on her behalf.

> You see what she is now saying, because of what people feel – take myself, I am a Lutheran and the other one

Zionist – she doesn't belong to any church. As long as any church can come and pray for her, here, she allows them. The Zionists, the Lutherans, the Romans, Dutch Reform, they can come and pray for her. But she does not take any religion.

She is in fact born Christian. Traditionally we are Christian, but she doesn't say this church is better than that church. She believes in God, in the same thing as all of them.

Which brings me to the central question in the entire mythology of the Rain Queen. Does she truly have magic potions and herbs to bring rain?

Victor laughs. 'It's just a story.' Then he translates for Queen Modjadji.

She echoes his laughter, and replies emphatically: 'No. No medicine, because we are not doctors. No muti. It's like praying. The people are telling us there's some muti here for the rain. No, there's no such thing, just only to pray and to believe in God.'

In other words, the Rain Queen's power to make rain is not unlike the stance of religious leaders who call on their followers to pray for rain during times of drought. The difference, of course, is that Modjadji is so much more powerful a focus for such prayers.

I had feared that this question would bring a stony silence from the Rain Queen. Instead, for the first time, she smiles and laughs, like an adult who has come across a teenage child who still believes in fairy tales.

When I present her with the gifts I had been advised to bring, she begins talking freely for the first time. One of the gifts is a wood carving showing a ritual tribal scene around a campfire.

'Now I can be a sangoma,' she laughs as she holds it in

her hands. 'People used to say because I'm using muti, I'm a sangoma. A sangoma is a special person, you see. Those people are going to the sangoma and everything and then they are saying I will be a sangoma now. All because of the story.'

The matter of fact manner in which she sweeps aside her entire mystique is astounding. Later Victor will tell me that she repeats most of these statements to visitors who come to write about Queen Modjadji, but that the visitors later tell the story the way they would prefer it to be heard.

Leading me back through the huts, he points out the family shrine, a fig tree embedded in what appear to be carved circles of clay. There is little centrality to it, little indication that this is the focus of the royal family's attentions when they meet to pray for rain. Indeed, the entire emphasis at the royal kraal is on functionality. No frills, no pomp and ceremony, no attempt to create a sense of awe or occasion on one's arrival. The one factor that has been dispelled utterly and completely is the belief in the Rain Queen as a supernatural figure.

An entirely unexpected consequence of meeting her is the realisation of the exaggerated extent to which myth and legend flows around the reality of the Rain Queen.

Perhaps times have changed; perhaps generations ago it was important for her to be imbued with a supernatural aura. Now, in a time of increasing commercial encroachment, the entire area is a rural sprawl and it will take very little to turn it into urban slum. The Rain Queen must enter the modern world to have any hope of retaining power in her own realm.

There was a time, it seems, when the supernatural myths surrounding her were created by her own ancestors to strengthen and protect their tribe. Later it was annexed both by the British, in the form of H Rider Haggard's enduring legend of an immortal white African queen, and by the Boers, who believed that the Rain Queen was one of their own lost children.

The Rain Queen is thus one of the great cross-cultural legends of the supernatural. But in its very mobility between cultures has always been the evidence of the legendary rather than factual nature of her powers. That her tale could be hijacked by any culture, and yet remain rooted in the tribal heartland from which it first emerged, attests to a need in all cultures in South Africa to claim a role in the supernatural mythology of the land.

But the story does not end there.

On 11 October 2004, the area around Ga-Modjadji reverberates with the noise of hooting cars and cheering people. It is the Monday after the first rainmaking ceremony by the new Rain Queen, Makobo Modjadji VI. The weather forecast for Limpopo Province has been bleak, with grey skies that would bring no rain. But today, the skies open, and tears of joy are seen everywhere in her small kingdom. Nor are her followers the only beneficiaries.

'From Monday last week, rains fell in many different parts of the country and even on Monday this week, rain was falling in the Letaba district,' Alex Japho Motala reports in a Tzaneen newspaper.[29] He explains the significance in great detail:

> Five different families in the Royal dynasty each hold rainmaking rituals on successive weekends; with the first being held by the Moalwe on October 9, followed

[29] *Mopani News*, 22 October 2004.

by the Mathekga this past weekend, the Molokwane in Phakong village this coming weekend 23 October, and the Mampeule and Matshwi due to hold their rituals on 30 October.

The Modjadji Royal Family, who are world-renowned for their rainmaking powers, delighted many when rains fell on Monday, 9 October, two days after the first rainmaking rituals held by the family of Maolwe gave the Bolobedu something to smile about.

There was also much satisfaction and pride that they had contradicted a forecast by the South African Weather Bureau that there would be no rain in Limpopo this month.

Meanwhile, hundreds of people from all corners of Limpopo have converged on Bolobedu for the period 9 to 30 October to see Rain Queen Modjadji VI calling on her ancestors to bring rain to Limpopo.

The Royal Family strongly believe that more rain is still going to fall during the weeks ahead.

During the ceremonies, while speaking to her ancestors, the Queen poured a traditional mageu, called Mphapo, onto a sacred piece of ground called Thokoleng at the foot of a tree said to be more than 100 years old.

The Mphapo mixture was then fed to a black cow called Mokgadi, which is also known as 'Kgomo ya Thokola'. Finally, the Mphapo was given to members of the Royal Family to drink.

The ceremonies concluded with traditional dances by elderly people connected to the Royal Family.

Speaking to *Mopani News*, the spokesperson for the Modjadji Royal Council, Mr Victor 'No Mistake' Mathekga, said the Mphapo drink was given to members of the family to heal their illnesses and also to pass the Royal powers on to them. 'It also brings luck to the

> family,' he added.
>
> Asked about what makes the rain fall, Mathekga said the Royal Family received their rainmaking powers from a horn which had been given to their forefathers while they were still living in what is now Zimbabwe back in the 16th century.
>
> 'Because of the wars which were taking place in Zimbabwe in those years, our forefathers moved down South and settled in Bolobedu. We then started to speak to our ancestors who responded with rains that sent rivers flowing to their banks and dams filling up. Since then we have performed our rainmaking rituals annually in October and we have never failed,' he explained. Mathekga further said that because the Royal Family's 'supernatural rainmaking powers' enabled Bolobedu to receive a high annual rainfall it could be called 'The Evergreen Paradise'.
>
> However five of ten people spoken to by *Mopani News* said they believed that rain came from God, and not from any human being. They said anyone who claimed to have powers to control nature deserved to be severely punished by God.[30]

If it appears that the new Rain Queen is happy for the myth of her supernatural abilities to be rejuvenated, consider the most unlikely aspect of the 2004 event: for the first time in history, the Rain Queen allows her rain-making ritual to be photographed. Full-colour photos of the ceremony, including one of the Rain Queen pouring mageu at the foot of the hundred-year-old Mohlapu tree, cover the front and second pages of the *Mopani News*. At one and the same moment, they offer a glimpse into the mystique of the Rain

[30] *Mopani News*, p2.

Queen, and demystify the entire concept of rain-making. Faith in the supernatural becomes the equivalent of praying for rain.

In the last week of February 2005, the next chapter in the legend of the Rain Queen opens: Queen Makobo Modjadji VI gives birth to a baby girl. The Rain Queen has a successor.

The chairman of the Modjadji Royal Council (MRC), Kelly Modjadji, tells the *Mopani News*: 'We decided to name the girl Masalanabo after the former Queen Masalanabo Modjadji who reigned between 1854-1895 to honour our ancestors for this precious gift.'

Once again, Alex Japho Motala takes up the story:

> Asked about the father of the child, Kelly said he was not in a position to reveal his identity and had still to consult with the family.
>
> However, sources in the MRC confirmed that the child's father was former Greater Letaba Municipal Manager, Mr David Mohale.
>
> 'That is why the council kept the arrival of the child secret at first, because the father was a commoner,' they explained. 'According to Lobedu tradition, the Queen is not permitted to marry. Marriage takes place in the sense that the Queen is seen as a man who marries a woman from every headmanship in the kingdom to keep the royal blood going.
>
> 'The Queen's "wives" (Bahlanone) reside in the Royal Village. The children are fathered by men from the nobility (Bakholola). The biological fathers, however, may not claim fatherhood since the Queen is considered as the "father".

'As for the Queen, she was supposed to be married to any man from the royal blood,' they said.

Further investigation revealed that while most in the Royal Council and family celebrated the new baby, a certain minority group was perturbed by its arrival.

It was alleged that some people in the family believed that because the father was not of royal blood, the baby would only bring bad luck to the Royal Family. In times past, a boy child or one born to a commoner was strangled immediately after birth without anyone knowing about it.

'That was done to say sorry to our ancestors and ensure that rain fell afterwards,' *Mopani News* was told.

Meanwhile, other elders in the family saw the arrival of a girl baby as a blessing from the ancestors. A big party was reportedly thrown during February at the Royal Kraal to celebrate the pending arrival of the baby. Various tribal kings and queens and headmen were invited.[31]

And who then is David Mohale (also known as David Mogale)? None other than the boyfriend of Queen Makobo Modjadji VI. The truth is, she was not meant to take on the role of Rain Queen for a long time to come. Queen Mokope Modjadji V's daughter, Makheale Modjadji, had been groomed for the role, but died at the age of 37 on 25 June 2001, just a few days before her mother. Princess Makobo was Queen Modjadji V's granddaughter, who was enjoying a normal working and social life when she was suddenly called to the throne of the baLobedu. She was expected to give up her boyfriend and embrace an austere and highly regulated life of ritual. Ironically, the birth of her most likely heir put her new life into a very different context.

---

[31] *Mopani News*, 18 March 2005, p1, under the headline 'Joy as Modjadji Rain Queen has baby girl'.

In short, the Rain Queen was finally revealed as a mere mortal but, it seemed at the time, few begrudged her the happiness this brings. But the happiness was short-lived. On Sunday, 10 June 2005 she died in Polokwane Medi-Clinic after being admitted on the Friday before. She had been vomiting, and the family decided to seek help. The official cause of death, according to Sapa, was chronic meningitis. Mohale claimed that she had either been bewitched or poisoned by members of the Royal Family who disapproved of their relationship.[32]

Instantly, a major row erupted as an alternative royal council, instigated by Mohale, claimed the right to bury the Rain Queen. To add to the confusion, it was reported that the queen's 25-year-old younger brother, News Mpapatla Modjadji, had gone missing. According to some reports he was pursuing a business opportunity in Uganda. After days of feuding, the Rain Queen was finally buried on 20 June.

But there was one last twist: the night before the burial the hut in which the coffin was kept caught fire. The police and fire brigade were called and the coffin was removed before it could be damaged.

It will take up to a year before a new Rain Queen is crowned. Despite this, and despite the brief and controversial reign of the sixth Rain Queen, it seems that the legend is not about to die.

As if to underline the power of the legend, the government of Limpopo province acknowledged it in its message of condolence:

---

[32] *Sunday Times* online report, 20 June 2005.
http://www.suntimes.co.za/zones/sundaytimesNEW/topstories/topstories1119265271.aspx,

> The people of Limpopo pride themselves with the Modjadji dynasty which has always remained the only Royal House in Africa where a woman reigns supreme as a Queen, with supernatural powers capable of making rain. The sacredness of the Modjadji Kingdom and the humility of Her Majesty stand as distinguishing features of Limpopo on the world tourism map. Her Majesty the Queen was a symbol of hope and unity throughout the Province and our country.[33]

It was probably the first time in the twenty-first century that a government had officially accepted the existence of the supernatural. The early Rain Queens must surely be looking on with approval.

---

[33] South African Government Information, *Message of condolences from the acting Premier of Limpopo, Joyce Mashamba, on the passing on of her Majesty the Queen of Bolobedu, Makobo Modjadji*, 13 June 2005, http://www.info.gov.za/speeches/2005/05061314451001.htm

7

When the Tokoloshe Comes Calling

People from the district of Ohrigstad say they chased a man from their village after finding evidence that he kept a tokoloshe. The man then approached a white farmer and suggested that he fire all the black labourers on the estate as he could do their work all on his own. The farmer promptly followed his advice, but his curiosity was aroused. One night he visited the fields and found a large number of small creatures tilling the land, with his new employee acting as the supervisor.[34]

This story is told by Lazarus Seitsho, a lecturer who collected the tale while researching witchcraft beliefs in Mpumalanga province.

If it is comical in its absurdity, it also represents a lighter side to the darkness of beliefs in the paranormal. It is more

[34] *Weekly Mail & Guardian*, 27 January 1995.

usual for tales of the tokoloshe to be replete with sexual violence and fear-filled nights.

'Social workers receive frequent complaints in this region from people who say they were raped by a tokoloshe,' says Seitsho. 'When a woman wakes at night with wetness between her legs, she will probably believe that she has been sexually accosted by this supernatural being.'

The implication: it is more about belief in the creature than about its actual existence. Indeed, if the creature could be proven to exist, it would probably be far more benign than the hideous beliefs that surround it:

> A tokoloshe is believed to have an uncanny power called 'moshoshopansi': to make it go under. It can extend its penis to any length and send it underground into the genitals of a sleeping or unsuspecting woman ... many of my informers tell me that divorce ... is caused by tokoloshes raping wives of migrant labourers. When a woman loses interest in her husband, it is often interpreted as being the result of rape by the tokoloshe.[35]

In that brief observation lurks a world of meaning. It speaks of scapegoats, refusal to face reality, inability to accept responsibility when it all goes wrong. At the same time, though, it is impossible to ignore the exaggerated sexual symbolism of the tokoloshe.

Isak Niehaus, a senior lecturer in the Department of Anthropology and Archaeology at the University of Pretoria, argues that the tokoloshe 'symbolises the potential animal-like craving for uninhibited sexual expression'.

In his book *Witchcraft, Power and Politics*, he suggests that the creature 'provokes thoughts about the separation of

[35] *Weekly Mail & Guardian*, 27 January 1995.

spouses and the sexual deprivations that accompany labour migration'.

This is hardly a new insight. Niehaus quotes a 1974 paper by W D Hammond-Tooke: 'Women are ... imagined to take daemon lovers to fulfil their sexual needs and to wreak vengeance on men. The most obvious symbol of women's resentment is the compensatory image of the enormous penis of the thikoloshe.'

Niehaus, however, is one of the few observers to connect this sexual imagery to the ape-like appearance of the tokoloshe:[36]

> The meaning of this association derives from the perception of the baboon as sexually promiscuous and as an appropriate human double ... Unlike other animals they share many features with people ... The symbolic appropriateness of the baboon as the instigator of unwanted sexual intercourse also derives from the perception that baboons are dangerous, strong and ugly.

The connection is not spurious. Credo Mutwa, in his seminal work *Indaba, My Children*, argues that the tokoloshe we know today is indeed a baboon.

'All foreigners in Africa have heard of a tokoloshe. But their idea of one, if they have any, is that of a hairy, human-like elf that lives in the water and is sometimes tamed by wizards to terrorise people. This concept is, like so many others, false.'[37]

But it is also no mere superstition, he insists. And he knows precisely how it came into existence.

---

[36] Niehaus, p53.
[37] Mutwa, p490.

The first tokoloshe

Many generations ago, before the Bantu had moved south of the Zambezi, an old wizard avenged himself on a foul tyrant who had killed all his wives and raped his daughters before flinging them to the crocodiles. The name of this wizard was Mulundi, and that of the tyrant, Kambela.

... Kambela became very scared of the old wizard whose powers were widely known and he stayed in his kraal with all gates tightly shut. His evil warriors guarded him day and night. But the old wizard had seen a weakness in the stockade of the chief's kraal and he already knew how to exploit it. What he did was copied by all wizards since – and thus the tokoloshe came to be created.

Growing just outside the stockade was an old leafy tree, an ancient marula that had seen much and whose spreading branches extended well across the stockade. One night Kambela lay in his hut in solitude and sullen anger; he had just drunk a great pot full of strong beer to drown his fear and calm his heart.

... Weary from panic, Kambela slept, but not for long. He opened his eyes and beheld a sight which was to be the last thing he saw on earth. Poised over him was a squat little figure oozing the very essence of evil. It wore a hideous skin mask and a costume made of the skin of baboons. Dangling from a skin round his neck was the partly decomposed head of a woman. It held a bow and poisoned arrow at the ready.

Kambela tried to scream but his voice died in his throat as a hardly audible hoarse croak. The first tokoloshe that ever walked this earth released the taut string of the bow and Kambela felt the arrow sink deeply into his bowels.

He died with a look of terror on his face.

A sound of mad laughter shattered the moonlit night and every warrior in the kraal felt his blood freeze ... The warriors dashed back to Kambela's hut and had to force the door open. They found him dead, but there was no assassin's footprint and no trace of how he managed to enter the hut. Mulundi passed his secret on to other wizards and even today tokoloshes turn the hair of people white and baffle the police who are called out to try and solve many unaccountable murders.[38]

So what is the tokoloshe? Mutwa has the answer to this question, too. But strangely, in the light of the above, he rejects the supernatural:

A tokoloshe is not a ghostly or supernatural phenomenon. He is a physical human being, and he operates along perfectly scientific lines. Mulundi had used a very small pigmy whose weight he had drastically reduced with a severe diet. He had furthermore turned the little creature into a zombie by a simple interference with his brain. A sharp awl can do the trick. He was posted up the marula tree and along a branch that reached across the roof of Kambela's hut. With a long thong he lightly descended upon the roof of the hut and wriggled his skeletal little frame through the grass roof. He escaped the same way.

This weird practice has today been perfected into a fine art. Cases are known to me where wizards are known to have arranged the faked death of a particular person whom they have selected for a prospective zombie. The person is actually buried, but exhumed the same night and revived. He is then turned into a zombie and, many

[38] Mutwa, pp490-491.

days or weeks later, heavily decorated with parts of other people's bodies, also exhumed from graves, the puppet is induced to pay a particular victim an unexpected visit. The victim simply dies of fright. It is as simple as all that. Any chance eyewitness will relate a beautiful tokoloshe story to the police, and the police will dismiss it as so much nonsense.

In later generations the wizards perfected their art of tokoloshe-making and they started breeding tokoloshes from childhood. As recently as 1922 there was a secret tokoloshe farm kept by a gang of wizards in the Drakensberg in Basutoland.[39]

Perhaps they later migrated to the northern reaches of the Drakensberg, from where they could be hired out to the farmers of Ohrigstad?

The return of the zombie

South Africa shares a curious parallel with West Africa and the West Indies in one aspect of the paranormal: the belief that witches or wizards are able to revive the dead (or near-dead) and turn them into slaves to do their bidding. South Africa is unique, however, in offering a parallel between zombies and other supernatural creatures – ie the tokoloshes – in this context.

In both cases, according to academic and expert opinion, the creatures do not start out in their fearful forms, but are conditioned, trained and manipulated into becoming tokoloshes and zombies.

Belief in the existence of zombies is rife in rural South

[39] Mutwa, pp491-492.

Africa as well as among many urban dwellers. Usually, however, they are not associated with tokoloshes. Nevertheless, the purposes both serve on behalf of their owners are so similar that they seem based on the same psychological needs and fears.

The most famous zombie tale of them all is the urban legend about Paul Ndlovu, the star singer of hit pop group Mordillo during the mid-eighties.

On 27 September 1986, Paul was officially buried after dying in a car crash. But even as he was being buried, a chilling rumour came to life: Paul Ndlovu had not died in the car crash; it was someone else's body in the grave; Paul had been kidnapped by an inyanga, who had turned him into a zombie – one of the living dead – and was using him as a slave.

Friends and family of Paul claimed to have seen him at an inyanga's home, and he was then spotted by acquaintances throughout what was then the Transvaal.

In early 1989 journalists even travelled with Paul's mother Kate to Bochum in what was then the Northern Transvaal, where he was allegedly being kept.

They arrived at a heavily guarded kraal, where they were introduced to an inyanga by the name of Mapoulo. They were told to pay R100 each if they wanted to see Paul.

While they were talking, Mapoulo suddenly waved her arm, and there, standing at a spot not far from the group, stood a man who looked like Paul Ndlovu! He was about nine metres away, and the journalists weren't allowed to approach him. After a few moments, he was ushered away.

Ike Motsapi, one of the journalists and an old friend of Paul's, was dazed: 'My thoughts went back to my memories of Paul and I was soon sure that whatever I had thought to be true – that Paul was dead – had been turned upside down.'

However, when he followed up various other leads on the story, Ike realised that all may not have been what it had seemed. He came across numerous rumours of rival showbiz figures being behind Paul's death. All dismissed the tales as rubbish. The police at Bochum called the zombie story 'absolute nonsense'.

Ike then learned that Paul was due to be sent back to his mother on 6 May 1989, when a massive celebration would be held. But the event never took place.

A year later, there was still no more news of Paul. Except, of course, for a record company executive who 'spotted' Paul alive, behind the wheel of a delivery vehicle in the Johannesburg traffic. And a nurse who had known Paul 'saw' him in Nelspruit in Mpumalanga. And, no doubt, numerous other people who have seen Paul Ndlovu in one place or another.

The Paul Ndlovu rumour had become a fully fledged urban legend – the modern version of ancient fairy tales, and a sophisticated version of traditional oral legends.

Bad tokoloshe, good tokoloshe

If, for argument's sake, we accept Credo Mutwa's account of the nature of tokoloshes as true, then it is clear that the tokoloshe is a perversion of nature, both literally and figuratively. Belief in the tokoloshe would also, therefore, reflect an overturning of nature's ways. For example, says Izak Niehaus, sexual intercourse with a tokoloshe has the opposite effect of 'moral sex', which is intended for procreation. Sex with the tokoloshe, by contrast, causes infertility or 'makes women abort or give birth to horrible, deformed creatures'.

If nothing else, the arguments and explanations presented

here tell us that the tokoloshe has occupied a great deal of thinking among researchers and writers. In the world of experience, the tokoloshe weighs equally heavily on the mind – when people take it seriously. Early published records tend to repeat superstition rather than actual experience. Phyllis Bard, writing in *The Friend*, the now defunct Bloemfontein newspaper, gave this description in 1921: 'Mr Tokoloshe is an imp from Hades ... dark water pools.'[40]

Eric Rosenthal gave the account of Mrs Minnie Martin, wife of an official in Basutoland (now Lesotho), who lived there from 1891 until the end of the century:

> There is in Basutoland a little creature of whom all stand in awe. He is not much bigger than a baboon, but is minus the tail, and is perfectly black, with a quantity of black hair on his body. He has hands and feet like an ordinary mortal, but is never heard to speak. He shuns the daylight, and abhors clothing, even in the coldest weather. Evidently he is above such sensations as heat and cold. This wonderful creature is 'Tokolosh', the Poisoner, the Evil One, whose deeds are cruel, revengeful, apparently unlimited. He has power to kill, to afflict in every imaginable way, to send mad, or to visit with unknown sickness; but to do good is beyond his power. There are several of these little people in the country. They generally are employed by the witchdoctors to do their dirty work.
>
> ... Whether there really are creatures in any way answering to the description of these little people or not I cannot say. My own belief is that these doctors keep Bushmen who act the part and impose upon the superstitions of the Basuto, for there is certainly some

[40] Rosenthal, p159.

truth at the bottom of this, as I can prove from personal experience.[41]

Mrs Martin then describes a brief sighting of a small black creature one night when the moon was almost full. It is amazing, in that context, that she is still able to reject belief in the tokoloshe as a supernatural creature.

Unusually for a book written by a white man in the first half of the twentieth century, Rosenthal also quotes a first-hand account from a black woman, Flora Ntshantshe, described as 'a person of the greatest respectability ... a Christian and a leader in her church'. The account was given by Mrs Ntshantshe to Estelle Hamilton-Welsh, wife of a high-ranking English officer and herself a 'lifelong friend of the Xosa people' and well known as a collector of articles used in tribal customs:

> One night in 1916 when I was sixteen years of age (said Flora Ntshantshe), I was walking back to my parents' home in the location at De Aar, where I lived, after spending the evening with a girl friend of mine in the village. It was bright moonlight and suddenly coming towards me was a strange-looking object. At a distance I was not quite sure if it was an animal or a child.
>
> As he got nearer, imagine my terror when I saw it was Tokolosh. He was short and fat with a fur cape or animal skin round his shoulders. His eyes were like lights, yellow, shining brightly and looking evil. He looked hard and very angrily at me, but otherwise took no notice of me, but he was evidently going to something much more important and was in a great hurry.
>
> I shook with terror and watched him hurrying up

[41] Rosenthal, pp159-160.

> the street. I wondered if any evil would befall me or my people, but I think his thoughts were elsewhere and he was too concerned with thinking about something else to worry about me. I dared not speak about it to my parents that night. We never speak of him except during the day. He can hear us at night and we get soundly slapped by him if he overhears us speaking of him.
>
> He loves children who have no fear of him. He plays amongst them many games in the moonlight. I had two brothers – Temba, who is dead, and Tongintaba, who saw a lot of him. They did not speak of him, but one night they seemed to be having such fun and there was so much laughter I asked why. They said: 'We will tell you in the morning,' and then I knew at once Tokolosh had been there. They told us the next day how nice he was to them and they had great fun with a small very round stone he threw to each in turn. When holding this stone they became invisible. He warned them to play no pranks and go away from him while invisible or something terrible would happen to them. They liked this game best of all.[42]

A full eighty years passed between the time of this supposed incident and the broader popularisation of such 'friendly' versions of the tokoloshe. While most accounts, stories and even jokes focus on the evil deeds of the tokoloshe, Greg Doolan decided to take a 'new' approach. He created the cartoon character Prince Thabo, 'a tokoloshe from the new South Africa'. In an animated TV series and in a range of books illustrated by Dean Foster, 'South Africa's own super hero' emerges as a modern interpretation of Flora Ntshantshe's tokoloshe who 'loves children who have no fear of him' and plays with her brothers.

[42] Rosenthal, pp162-163.

In the introductory tale, 'Prince Thabo's Calling', he is shown learning magic powers, wearing a ring that could make him invisible, and being sent to frighten a young girl. He fails in his task, is kicked out of the tokoloshe clan, and then dedicates his life to good deeds.

This is as far from Credo Mutwa's version as it is possible to get, but it also probably represents one of the final chapters in the story of the tokoloshe as the most feared creatures ever to stalk the South African subconscious.

Tokoloshes for the New South Africa

But perhaps the evolution that has occurred is a case of the end of the old and the beginning of the new tokoloshe. With the dawn of the new, democratic South Africa in 1994, tokoloshes discovered politics.

In the months leading up to the 1994 elections, a researcher at the Human Sciences Research Council, Anthony Minnaar, decided to look into the extent to which black superstitions would affect the polls. However, he made little headway because of the secrecy surrounding the issue, he told Reuters in an interview published by the *Sowetan* on 15 April 1994.

'There's definitely a belief that the other side will bewitch the polls,' he said. 'I couldn't quantify it because people didn't want to talk about it. But some inyangas said they had been approached for muti for protection during the election.'

Minnaar referred to two powerful fears he had found among the superstitious:

- Blacks believed spirits could watch where they put their cross, leading to repercussions later, or could take control of their minds and make them vote for a party they did not support.

- The shape of polling booths could also be significant for black voters – tokoloshes lurk in corners but would not be able to hide in round booths.

The latter had already become a widespread urban legend, which incorporated the 'fact' that the blocks on the ballot paper had been changed to circles in the rural areas – because of superstitions about tokoloshes hiding in corners.

Both of these variations, however, seem to be a white interpretation of tokoloshe legend, as the fear of the tokoloshe is usually specific to his invading homes, and to his coming out at night to do his nefarious deeds. Applying the belief to voting stations seems like wishful thinking on the part of those whites who would like to believe that blacks are too superstitious to run a country. If this were not the case, and the belief was real, should we not have expected complaints to the Independent Electoral Commission of tokoloshes interfering in the voting process?

On the other hand, Minnaar's case is backed up by the fact that the major parties contesting Namibia's first free elections in 1990 had agreed to call in neutral inyangas from outside the country to hold 'cleansing' ceremonies of polling stations. 'The inyangas were paid big money. The idea was that they would free the polling stations of any spells put on them and that it would be safe for everyone to vote.'

With election fever mounting, anthropologists reported that witch-burning and muti killings were increasing. Professor Robert Thornton, head of the University of the Witwatersrand's anthropology department, said people whispered about vampire-like blood-suckers turning people into zombies or changing their blood into cash.[43]

[43] Goldstuck, *The Aardvark and the Caravan*, pp105-107.

Such desperate measures, however, seemed to be left behind after the elections in favour of a new strategy that would be more in keeping with the political awakening of all South Africans.

The following report appeared in an Eastern Cape newspaper in 1998, complete with straight-faced comment by the police:[44]

Woman claims tokoloshe invasion

by Mkhululi Titi

QUEENSTOWN – A 42-year-old Queenstown resident's difficulties with 'tokoloshes' in her home drew no sympathy from the local police or President Nelson Mandela's Office and she is still struggling with her strange visitors.

Ms Nothemba Bekebhu, a remedial specialist at the local education support centre, claims that on Wednesday night she saw five tokoloshes sitting on sofas demanding their rights.

'These strange people, with only heads and no facial features, are demanding houses like all other people in the country ... I saw them sitting in my house,' she said.

A terrified Ms Bekebhu, who is also a sangoma, said the tokoloshes demanded to talk to Mr Mandela and she decided to dial 1023 and was apparently given Mr Mandela's office number.

'A man answered the phone and I told him my problem ... he then asked me to give the phone to my visitors, but unfortunately they refused to talk,' she said.

As the problem worsened in the house, she immediately phoned the local police on 10111, but none of the policemen took her seriously, she claimed.

When a *Daily Dispatch* reporter visited her home, Ms Bekebhu appeared panicky and appeared to have been crying.

---

[44] *Daily Dispatch*, 2 October 1998.

She was pushing the handset of the phone under the couch so that police could hear the tokoloshes talking, but no voices were heard.

Ms Bekebhu claimed the tokoloshes could have been brought into the house by a domestic worker whom she fired.

The sitting room was full of thick smoke from her mutis, burnt in an effort to chase away the tokoloshes. Ms Bekebhu was undecided yesterday about whether she should leave her house and seek shelter elsewhere.

Police spokesman Captain Thembisile Patekile confirmed that Ms Bekebhu called him, but said it was difficult for the police to help her as she was not being intimidated by human beings.

While one would have hoped that the tokoloshe of the new South Africa would be more committed to democratic procedures, this version is perhaps even more fitting: the modern tokoloshe, as it appears in this tale, is a firm believer in the most important distinguishing feature of our constitution, namely equality before the law and human rights for all.

Um ... did I say ... human?

8

The Many Haunts of Daisy de Melker

It was not yet dawn when trainee nurse Moira Vimpany prepared for the last hour of her shift. She was stationed at the old Johannesburg General Hospital in Hillbrow and on this night was looking after Ward 4, the children's ward.

At about 6am a little boy, who had been admitted after being kicked by a horse, called her. 'Who's the lady in the long white dress over there by the tent? She came through that door,' he said, pointing to where a little girl was sleeping in a steam tent. She had had a throat operation, and was on the way to recovery.

'I reassured him that everything was fine, but cold chills crept up my spine and my hair stood on end. The door he spoke of led on to a balcony and was firmly locked every night. There was no one near the little girl's bed.'[45]

[45] *Personality*, 1 October 2005, p33.

Telling the story years later, Moira confessed that only her professional training prevented her from fleeing. When she left the ward at 7am, the little girl was doing fine and all was calm. But when she returned an hour later, she heard that the little girl had just died. The doctors were baffled, and the autopsy could not determine the cause of death. But Moira was in little doubt what was to blame or, rather, *who* was to blame.

For this was the very ward in which South Africa's infamous murderer Daisy de Melker had once worked as a nurse. Her first husband was believed to have been a patient in the same hospital. This meant, everyone assumed, that her murder spree had started while she tended to patients in this very ward.

For many years, new nurses were terrified by the old-timers' stories of a woman in a 'long white dress, apron and vest' who walked about Ward 4 at night.

'Many nurses even prayed that they wouldn't see their names on the roster for night duty.'[46]

Amazingly, just one day before this account appeared in *Personality* magazine in 1993, a letter was published in *You* magazine from Mrs J Batzofin of Port Elizabeth, also on the subject of Daisy de Melker. She reported:

> Daisy de Melker was a porteress at Transvaal Memorial Hospital for Children. We nurses were told she was arrested there and her ghost haunts the baby ward.
>
> Of this I had definite proof on more than one occasion. She always warned us when a baby was going to die and in which cubicle, and it always happened.[47]

---

[46] *Personality*, 1 October 2005, p33.
[47] *You*, 30 September 2005, p6.

Clearly, it was a time for people to remember Daisy. A month later, *Personality* published another account from a reader in a regular section called 'It Happened To Me'.

This version was headlined 'I spoke to Daisy's ghost'. The writer, Faye Batlofin, elaborated on the claim made in Mrs Batzofin's letter, and may well have been the same writer, with her name mistyped by one of the magazines:

> The baby ward was divided into cubicles, each holding four cots. We normally kept the cubicle doors shut, and also made every effort to keep unwelcome draughts out of the ward.
>
> But there was one draught we couldn't keep out. You'd be quietly going about your work and suddenly feel a cold breeze brush against your cheek. Immediately a chill would run down your spine – and not just because the breeze was cold. With pounding heart you'd wait for what you knew what was coming next and, sure enough, one of the cubicle doors would open.
>
> That was the signal to immediately phone for the doctor on duty.
>
> 'Doctor, come quick!' you'd say. 'One of the babies is in trouble.'
>
> But even as you said it you knew it wouldn't help. Whenever that cold wind blew and one of the cubicle doors opened, it meant one of the babies in the cubicle was going to die. There was no variation in this pattern.[48]

Strangely, there is no evidence whatsoever that this ghost – if such it was – had any link to Daisy de Melker.

True, Daisy had been particularly ruthless. In three carefully planned murders, she had put arsenic in the food

[48] *Personality*, 5 November 1993, p74.

of two husbands and her son, and then collected the life insurance payouts. True, she had worked in the hospital. True, nurses experienced many inexplicable sounds, screams and movements, not to mention the occasional claim of sighting a lady in white.

It is clear, however, that the infamy of Daisy de Melker fitted so neatly into the legend of 'The Messenger of Death', as Faye Batlofin described the presence, that it became part of the legend.

The fact is, there is hardly an old hospital in South Africa that does not have a claim to a ghost or two. Margaret Williamson explains it simply: 'Most hospitals form the epicentre of a few ghostly legends, and this is not surprising. Hospitals see life, and death, in the raw. The stories arise through the true dramas and tragedies which are constantly being played out in their theatres and wards, and take in a whole range of human emotions.'[49]

She tells of the ghost of a swashbuckling highwayman at the Eaton Convalescent Home at Dieprivier in the Cape, ghosts of devoted nurses at the Victoria Hospital in Alphin Hill at Wynberg, and a 'lady in grey' at the old Somerset Hospital in Greenpoint. The latter is identified with Sister Henrietta Stockdale, known as the Florence Nightingale of South Africa. She was the force behind the first nurses' training centre in South Africa. On tours of inspection, she would sleep over at the Somerset, in a small room up a staircase at the top of the building. And her ghost, it is said, is seen both in this room, on the stairs, and in the wards.

Groote Schuur Hospital in Observatory, where Dr Chris Barnard performed the first heart transplant operation, boasts an entire flock of ghosts. Most have no names, or only first names. Children's wards are particularly susceptible,

[49] Williamson, p128.

just as they appear to be in Johannesburg.

If hospitals attract ghosts thanks to the dramas and tragedies played out in the wards, then courtrooms have an equal claim. But only one courtroom ghost gets to carry a name: none other than Daisy de Melker.

She is said to haunt court number 3 at the Johannesburg Supreme Court. Here, writes Margaret Williamson, 'Doors mysteriously open and shut, and a creepy atmosphere made everybody scared of court 3.'

Court 3, the legal history books tell us, is the courtroom in which Daisy de Melker's trial began on 17 October 1932, and where she heard her sentence of execution pronounced thirty-nine days later. She was hanged on 30 December 1932 and, for the next seventy years she made sure no one forgot her. And if they did, she could remind them at yet another of her, er, haunts: aside from her last home at number 70, on the corner of Turf Club and President Streets in Turffontein, she was also believed to have lived in a house in the Johannesburg suburb of Bertrams.

Today these houses look little different from when she lived in them during the first half of the twentieth century. Legend has it that she still haunts the Bertrams house, but neither the present residents nor their neighbours provide any corroboration. She even has an alleged presence in Kimberley, at 22 Tapscott Street, where she once stayed while visiting her sister.

For decades, her ghost has been said to stalk the cells of the Old Fort in Hillbrow – situated on what was called Hospital Hill until 1994, and since renamed Constitution Hill. It is now the site of South Africa's Constitutional Court – and is still supposedly haunted by Daisy.[50] While awaiting trial, she was kept here in the Women's Gaol, a

[50] 'Mbeki opens Constitutional Court', Sapa, 21 March 2004.

double-storey building in the prison complex.

'One of the inmates recorded that when she was arrested and brought there it was so graceful a hall that she expected to see beautifully gowned ladies being whirled about in waltzes – instead she found naked bodies being strip searched before being committed to the adjoining cells,' wrote Neil Fraser, Executive Director of Partnerships for Urban Regeneration, in his weekly newsletter distributed via the City of Johannesburg website.[51]

Many years later, after the 1976 Soweto uprising, Winnie Madikizela-Mandela was detained there and was said to be so shocked that prisoners were not allowed to wear underwear or stockings that she led a successful protest on their behalf.

'Now it is hung with large format screens of see-through mesh on which are printed the images of some of those who were confined in this place, common criminals side by side with activists,' writes Fraser.

And one of those images just happens to be Daisy de Melker. But even this physical presence does not satisfy the public psyche. Her ghost remains, even as the Women's Gaol is transformed into the Women's Centre, home to the Commission on Gender Equality.

Why this obsession with finding Daisy everywhere she may have set foot?

A psychology master's thesis produced at Rand Afrikaans University by S-A Maritz, entitled 'Women who kill: A psycho-legal literature review', offers part of the answer:

> Daisy brought to life much of the feared evil cruelty of killing for financial gain in absolute cold blood. She represents to many the picture of pure evil and as such

[51] Citichat, 23 August 2002.

> provides a fascination so far removed from our own civilised existence. Eventually good does however prevail, and in the description of her final moments one gets the sense that evil has been banished by the rightful judicial process – all is well again ...[52]

This suggests, by implication, that her ghost represents ongoing reassurance that overturning the natural order, in the way that Daisy did by murdering the very people who trusted her and depended on her, will result not only in swift punishment but also in eternal damnation. Maritz indirectly links Daisy and two other infamous South African women murderers, Marlene Lehnberg and Charmaine Phillips, to that symbol of supernatural female evil, the witch:

> Questions surrounding issues such as good and evil, the inherent nature of man and society's responsibility to victim and perpetrator are conjured by stories like these ...
>
> The evil, cold-blooded witch using poison as a weapon of choice, the spurned lover seeking to fanatically remove the obstacle in her love triangle and the blushing lady who, offended, kills to protect her virtue and motherhood. Three very different women and very different motives yet united by society's horror at their deeds.[53]

From an urban legend perspective, the most fascinating aspect of Daisy de Melker's many hauntings is how little evidence there is for any link between supposedly supernatural events and the name associated with them. Mere association with Daisy de Melker, it seems, confers on a building the status

[52] Maritz, October 2003, p42.
[53] Maritz, October 2003, pp48-49.

of being haunted by her. What an energetic ghost!

It seems that there is something very compelling about the afterlife of famous or infamous people who have been executed. The Tower of London is perhaps the best spot in the world to witness such lingering spirits. First, there was Lady Jane Grey, who was proclaimed Queen of England after the death of Edward VI in 1553, and reigned for just ten days before being arrested and subsequently executed. According to John and Anne Spencer, she has reappeared many times since.[54]

Then there was Sir Walter Raleigh, imprisoned in the Tower on and off for fifteen years before being executed in 1618. The Spencers describe him as a 'persistent ghost' at the Tower – but also report his spectral presence at Sherborne Castle in Dorset, his former home.

Royalty makes up probably the single biggest category of personality ghosts, with almost every late monarch of the United Kingdom having an afterlife in one castle or another. In Paris, Queen Marie-Antoinette still hangs around more than two hundred years after being guillotined. She is part of the tableau of spirits supposedly witnessed at Versailles on 10 August every year, which was first described by two English schoolteachers, Miss Moberley and Miss Jourdain, in 1901. Aside from the ghost story itself, urban legend now has it that the scene reappears annually on 10 August.

In the *Encyclopedia of Ghosts and Spirits* John and Anne Spencer analyse a dozen ghosts of the famous in detail, and draw some telling conclusions:

> Henry VIII's wives in particular must be amongst the most frequently reported famous ghosts, at least in England. Does this indicate that there is some special

[54] Spencer, J & A, p77.

quality which makes these famous people come back when many less famous seem not to? Probably not, although there might even be an argument in support of that suggestion: famous people usually become so because of some single-minded sense of purpose which drives them forward where lesser people would sit back and rest on their laurels. Perhaps that determination lets certain spirits rest less easily.

More probably, however, the high frequency of reports of famous people is attributable to the viewpoint of the witness reporting the sighting. If a ghostly figure in a long flowing dress is seen walking through the corridors of Hampton Court Palace it is far more exciting to believe you have seen the ghost of Jane Seymour than merely one of her ladies-in-waiting or indeed a servant girl or other 'ordinary' person.[55]

A more recent phenomenon is the appearance of showbiz ghosts, like Rudolph Valentino, who died an untimely death in 1926 at the age of thirty-one, of a perforated ulcer. He is claimed to haunt the bedroom of a beachside home where he once lived in secret in Oxford outside Los Angeles. Residents have described 'ghostly echoes of depraved days of parties, sex, drink and drugs' and even sightings of ghostly figures.[56]

Sometimes, according to the descriptions of eyewitnesses, there is no mistaking the identity of such 'famous' ghosts. In most cases, however, the connection is circumstantial. If Daisy de Melker's many hauntings proves anything, it is not that ghosts don't exist. It proves, rather, that even ghosts that may be authentic are subject to the phenomenon of the urban legend.

---

[55] Spencer, J & A, p77.

[56] *People*, 22 March 1993, p8.

9

The Haunted Imagination

Sound of silence gives you that eerie feeling

LONDON – The haunted feeling given off by certain buildings is the result of low frequency 'infrasound' vibrations, according to a team of British scientists who have conducted a series of experiments in a concert hall.

Richard Wiseman told a conference in the northern English city of Manchester on Monday his tests showed extreme bass sounds, like those emitted by some church organs or from the wind on windows and chimneys, could have a profound effect on feelings.

'It makes people feel extremely strange, even though they can't tell whether it's there or not,' Wiseman, a psychologist at the University of Hertfordshire, said.

'It has implications for claims about hauntings, and things people think they feel in religious settings like cathedrals.

'What appears to happen is that people have odd sensations that they cannot explain, and so they attribute them to supernatural causes. It could lead to people having weird experiences in churches and attributing them to God. If you are in an old house, you might attribute the same thing to a ghost,' he added.

Wiseman said he had tested the effects of infrasound on 750 volunteers at a concert hall in London, where a special additional instrument – an 8m pipe – was switched on and off secretly.

This produced inaudible vibrations at 17 hertz, whereas the audible range is from 20hz to 20khz.

The concertgoers heard four pieces of contemporary music, two with the infrasound added. When subsequently asked to describe their feelings, reports of 'strange feelings' rose 22 per cent.

Wiseman said the sensations reported from the South Bridge Vaults in Edinburgh, which he has studied, were an example of the effects of infrasound, generated by traffic moving overhead.[57]

The experiment described here proves only one thing: that in one particular location at one particular time, creepy sensations had a rational, physical explanation.

However, if it were to be replicated at different times at numerous locations, both supposedly haunted and 'ghost-free', with the same results, we have a fairly convincing 'proof' on our hands.

Nevertheless, the Wiseman argument is as solid a theory as most of the arguments in favour of paranormal explanations. And it also matches a powerful argument based on the workings of the human mind rather than of the human soul.

'We certainly cannot deny that people have the experiences, but we can question their interpretation, argued Susan Blackmore, author of *The elusive open mind: Ten years of negative research in parapsychology*, among other, in the early 1990s.[58] 'Perhaps they have misinterpreted as paranormal something which is quite normal.'

[57] Sapa-DPA, 12 September 2003.
[58] *The New Internationalist*, November 1992, p7.

The most famous example that underpins such arguments is a common experience of individuals the world over, which usually begins in their teens. It is one that I have experienced many times over the past thirty years, and originally assumed to be paranormal. I finally discovered it was a phenomenon almost as old as written records, and as mundane.

It is called Old Hag, or Sleep Paralysis. It usually occurs during the REM (rapid eye movement) phase of sleep, which is associated with vivid dreams and a near-paralysis of the muscles. The paralysis, say medical experts, is intended to prevent us from acting out our dreams.[59] However, as the muscles 'freeze', something may awaken the sleeper. And sometimes, for some reason, the mind snaps awake but the muscles don't. The subject tends to experience heightened awareness at the same time as an inability to move even a finger. The experience is accompanied by a range of sensations, from bright lights to a buzzing in the head to a feeling of floating above one's body to a physical presence alongside the bed to a crushing force pushing down on the chest or holding the entire body down.

It is natural to panic when this happens, and it's understandable to experience it as a supernatural event. The crushing sensation, in particular, has been ascribed through the ages to an old witch sitting on the victim's chest – hence Old Hag.

In some cultures an event of this nature is regarded as indisputably supernatural, and causes the phenomenon of Sleep Terrors. In India, in particular, there are documented instances of relatively young people dying of heart attacks as a result of the fear inspired by sleep paralysis.

A research team at the University of Waterloo in Canada

---

[59] http://paranormal.about.com/library/weekly/aa112000b.htm

has made a study of sleep paralysis, and even developed a measurement system for it: the Waterloo Sleep Experiences Scale. It is designed 'to assess the prevalence of sleep paralysis and a variety of associated hypnagogic and hypnopompic hallucinoid experiences: sensed presence, felt pressure, floating sensations, auditory and visual hallucinations, and fear.'

They offer a deeply academic definition, but also one that covers the gamut of Old Hag sensations:

> Sleep paralysis, or more properly, sleep paralysis with hypnagogic and hypnopompic hallucinations, has been singled out as a particularly likely source of beliefs concerning not only alien abductions, but all manner of beliefs in alternative realities and otherworldly creatures. Sleep paralysis is a condition in which someone, most often lying in a supine position, about to drop off to sleep, or just upon waking from sleep realizes that s/he is unable to move, or speak, or cry out. This may last a few seconds or several moments, occasionally longer. People frequently report feeling a 'presence' that is often described as malevolent, threatening, or evil. An intense sense of dread and terror is very common. The presence is likely to be vaguely felt or sensed just out of sight but thought to be watching or monitoring, often with intense interest, sometimes standing by, or sitting on, the bed. On some occasions the presence may attack, strangling and exerting crushing pressure on the chest. People also report auditory, visual, proprioceptive, and tactile hallucinations, as well as floating sensations and out-of-body experiences (Hufford, 1982). These various sensory experiences have been referred to collectively as hypnagogic and hypnopompic experiences (HHEs).
>
> People frequently try, unsuccessfully, to cry out. After

seconds or minutes one feels suddenly released from the paralysis, but may be left with a lingering anxiety. Extreme effort to move may even produce phantom movements in which there is proprioceptive feedback of movement that conflicts with visual disconfirmation of any movement of the limb. People may also report severe pain in the limbs when trying to move them. Several recent surveys including our own suggest that between 25-30% of the population reports that they have experienced at least a mild form of sleep paralysis at least once and about 20-30% of these have had the experience on several occasions. A few people may have very elaborate experiences almost nightly (or many times in a night) for years. Aside from many of the very disturbing features of the experience itself (described in succeeding sections) the phenomenon is quite benign. It was thought in the past that it was a significant part of the so-called 'narcoleptic tetrad', but recent surveys of non-clinical populations, such as ours, suggest that the prevalence may be as high among the general population as among diagnosed narcoleptics.[60]

The University of Waterloo team points out that nocturnal attacks have been connected to myths and monsters across time and cultures, and even dig up an argument, more than a century old, that the 'night-mare' is the origin of all mythology.[61] They dismiss this notion, but agree that 'the pervasiveness of the nocturnal attack in mythology, religion, and legend is quite striking'. Their guest list of night-time intruders includes:

---

[60] University of Waterloo website, http://watarts.uwaterloo.ca/~acheyne/S_P2.html

[61] University of Waterloo website, http://watarts.uwaterloo.ca/~acheyne/night_mare.html

- Ardat lili or Lilitu, an evil Sumerian spirit, 'one of the earliest Hag-demons' who could fly and who 'frequently attacked men in their sleep'. Some see her as the prototype for the Hebrew Lilith and the Roman Lamia;
- the Greek ephialtes (one who leaps upon), mora (the night 'mare' or monster), pnigalion (the choker) and barychnas (the heavy breather);
- the Roman incubus (one who presses or crushes);
- the German mar/mare, nachtmahr, Hexendrücken (witch pressing), and Alpdruck (elf pressure);
- the Czech muera;
- the Polish zmora;
- the Russian Kikimora;
- the French cauchmar (trampling ogre);
- the Old English maere (mab, mair, mare-hag), hagge, (evil spirit or the night-mare);
- the Old Norse mara;
- the Old Irish mar/more;
- the Newfoundland Ag Rog (Old Hag);
- the Spanish pesadilla.

In a series of studies published in 1999, the University's 'sleep team' – J Allan Cheyne, Ian R Newby-Clark, and Steve D Rueffer – produced astonishing findings. Firstly, a paper entitled 'Relations among Hypnagogic and Hypnopompic Experiences Associated with Sleep Paralysis' showed the extent of Old Hag and the range of experiences associated with it:

> Consistent with results of recent surveys, almost 30% of 870 university students reported at least one experience of sleep paralysis. Approximately three-quarters of those also reported at least one hallucinoid experience, and slightly more than 10% experienced three or more. Fear was

positively associated with hallucinoid experiences, most clearly with sensed presence. Regression analyses lend support to the hypothesis that sensed presence and fear are primitive associates of sleep paralysis and contribute to the elaboration of further hallucinoid experiences, especially those involving visual experiences.[62]

They also conducted studies among older groups and came to the conclusion that sleep paralysis most often begins in adolescence.

Several large samples have produced consistent means of 17 years of age, with a sharp increase after 10 and an even sharper decline from 17 to the mid-twenties. The results do suggest, however, that sleep paralysis episodes can begin at virtually any age, although it is rare for this to happen after 30.

The same team then published a paper titled 'Hypnagogic and Hypnopompic Hallucinations during Sleep Paralysis: Neurological and Cultural Construction of the Night-Mare', in which they developed a model for categorising and understanding the experiences associated with sleep paralysis, and which revealed the cross-cultural parallels and similarities in the experience:

Hypnagogic and hypnopompic hallucinations (HHEs) accompanying sleep paralysis (SP) are often cited as sources of accounts of supernatural nocturnal assaults and paranormal experiences. Descriptions of such experiences are remarkably consistent across time and cultures and consistent also with known mechanisms of REM states.

---

[62] *Journal of Sleep Research* (1999), 8, pp313-317.

> A three-factor structural model of HHEs based on their relations both to cultural narratives and REM neurophysiology is developed and tested with several large samples. One factor, labeled Intruder, consisting of sensed presence, fear, and auditory and visual hallucinations, is conjectured to originate in a hypervigilant state initiated in the midbrain. Another factor, Incubus, comprising pressure on the chest, breathing difficulties, and pain, is attributed to effects of hyperpolarization of motor neurons on perceptions of respiration. These two factors have in common an implied alien 'other' consistent with occult narratives identified in numerous contemporary and historical cultures. A third factor, labeled Unusual Bodily Experiences, consisting of floating/flying sensations, out-of-body-experiences, and feelings of bliss, are related to physically impossible experiences generated by conflicts of endogenous and exogenous activation related to body position, orientation, and movement. Implications of this last factor for understanding of orientational primacy in self-consciousness are considered. Central features of the model developed here are consistent with recent work on hallucinations associated with hypnosis and schizophrenia.[63]

Having suffered all three of these 'factors' – Intruder, Incubus and Unusual Body Experiences – I was personally amazed by how my awareness of Old Hag having a physical cause entirely changed my experience of it. I learned to ride out the sensations, wait for them to subside, and then roll over and go back to sleep – perhaps after flexing a few muscles to make sure they were still in working order!

The important point, however, is that a little knowledge

[63] *Consciousness and Cognition* (1999), 8, pp319-337.

changes the individual's experience of what may at first seem a supernatural event.

And then there is such a thing as too much knowledge, which is what would occur if you read a paper written by a member of the 'sleep team', J Allan Cheyne, who decided to drill down into one of the specific experiences associated with Old Hag, namely the Intruder:

> A 'sensed presence' often accompanies hypnagogic and hypnopompic hallucinations associated with sleep paralysis. Qualitative descriptions of the sensed presence during sleep paralysis are consistent with the experience of a monitoring, stalking predator. It is argued that the sensed presence during sleep paralysis arises because of REM-related endogenous activation of a hypervigilant and biased attentive state, the normal function of which is to resolve ambiguities inherent in biologically relevant threat cues. Given the lack of disambiguating environmental cues, however, the feeling of presence persists as a protracted experience that is both numinous and ominous. This experience, in turn, shapes the elaboration and integration of the concurrent hallucinations that often take on supernatural and daemonic qualities. The sense of presence considered here is an 'other' that is radically different from, and hence more than a mere projection of, the self. Such a numinous sense of otherness may constitute a primordial core consciousness of the animate and sentient in the world around us.[64]

Got that? To get you out of the endogenous activation state that has surely just been induced, and to resolve the

[64] *Journal of Consciousness Studies* (2001), 8, pp133-150.

ambiguities inherent in such threat cues, here is a simpler argument, from Susan Blackmore: 'The way to understand the human mind is not to invoke spirits, souls, telepathic powers or psychic vibrations but to understand how our minds naturally lead us to misinterpret the world around us.'[65]

She then proceeds to offer a scientific explanation for illusions in general:

> Let's take the example of a dream that comes true. Suppose you dream that your favourite cousin is being buried in a coffin and the very next morning you get a call to say that she died in the night. What would you think? If you're human at all you'll probably think it must have been precognition (seeing into the future) or telepathy (mind to mind communication). You might try to calculate the odds of it happening just when you dreamed it. Could they be 1,000 to 1? 100,000 to 1? Surely they must be astronomical, mustn't they?
>
> ... One British statistician, Christopher Scott, has calculated how often death dreams should come true by chance. He assumes only that each person has one death dream in their lifetime and works out how often that should coincide with the death of the person dreamed about. Allowing for how many people die each night, even in a small country like England, he concludes that this startling coincidence will happen to someone once every two weeks. Now each of these events is pure chance, but the people involved will certainly think it was psychic – and be wrong.[66]

---

[65] *The New Internationalist*, November 1992, p7.

[66] *The New Internationalist*, November 1992, pp7-8.

After discussing various examples of illusions and their medical or scientific rationales, Blackmore comes up with a controversial conclusion:

> All this implies that psychic events may be just an illusion. The obvious comparison is with visual illusions and the comparison is closer than you might think ... Our natural tendency is to look for pattern and meaning in everything around us. When we see patterns we cannot explain we look for explanations. If none is to be found we conclude it must be psychic – and we draw the wrong conclusion.[67]

Such statistical, psychological and medical explanations for supernatural experiences are not enough. After all, if there were a single physical-world explanation for all these events, they would be experienced in a similar way across all cultures, and in all times. But in the case of Old Hag, there is a consistency that is almost unknown in other forms of supernatural experience. The University of Waterloo, not surprisingly, has scoured the literature and found a cross-cultural menagerie of sleep terrors:

> These experiences ... are by no means limited to western culture. In St. Lucia, West Indies, an attack of kokma comes at a time that the individual is just falling asleep or just waking up. The sensations include pressure on the chest, inability to move, and anxiety. The kokma is the spirit of a dead baby that haunts an area, attacking people in their beds. In a familiar pattern, they jump on the victim's chest and clutch at the throat. The victim attempts to cry out, or in some other way to get

[67] *The New Internationalist*, November 1992, pp8-9.

> another's attention, someone that might scare off the kokma. Informants described the babies clutching at their throats. The notion that the attacks are thought to be initiated by dead, unbaptized babies is also found in Ireland ... In Thailand experiences referred to as phi um (ghost covered) and phi kau (ghost possessed) involve pressure, immobility, and something black covering the body. In Japan kanashibara ('to tie with an iron rope') is a common and widely known experience. In Korea, people are afflicted by ka wi nulita ('scissors pressed'), an experience felt to be brought on by fear. In the Far North one speaks of agumangia (Inupik) or ukomiarik (Yupik) in which 'a soul' tries to take possession of the paralyzed victim. In Laos, da chor is described as follows: 'You want to listen, you can't hear; you want to speak, you are dumb; you want to call out, you cannot; you feel you are dying, dying; you want to run away. You piss with fear in your sleep'.[68]

David J Hufford, in a landmark 1976 paper,[69] found that

> (1) the experience is wide-spread, at least in Western culture; (2) it has been regularly reported for more than two thousand years; (3) it has been attached to a variety of narrative frameworks ... but regardless of the framework, the experiential features have remained basically the same; (4) this consistency of detail, apparently rather independent of tradition, is the most surprising and difficult to account for.

---

[68] University of Waterloo website, http://watarts.uwaterloo.ca

[69] 'A new approach to the "Old Hag": The nightmare tradition reexamined.' In W D Hand (Ed.), *American Folk Medicine: A Symposium* (pp73-85). Berkeley: University of California Press.

This contradicts a central theme of this book, which argues that supernatural experience is dictated by cultural context. The University of Waterloo sleep team makes the same point:

> This is, of course, quite inconsistent with the cultural source hypothesis that such experiences are induced by knowledge of cultural traditions. Subsequent research has made clear that these experiences are by no means limited to Western cultures. Also striking in this connection is the similarity of the descriptions of the SP experiences across all cultures, including industrialized culture which appears to have no commonly accepted popular myths to offer cognitive support to the experiences.

But there is one key difference between Old Hag and most other kinds of supernatural experience: Old Hag has a proven and commonly accepted rational and physical basis, ie the experience itself is not imaginary – it is what the mind makes of the experience that is usually imaginary. Most other supernatural experiences, however, do not result from or in an obvious set of physical responses. The experiences are, in many cases, the result of trying to find an explanation for 'patterns we cannot explain'; and the quest for an explanation tends to occur within a strictly cultural framework.

Each culture has its own understanding of the supernatural, which results in different expectations of supernatural events, which in turn clouds the actual experience of these events. And this does not even take into account how these expectations and consequent experiences evolve over time.

The popular Marshall Cavendish series entitled *The Unexplained*, which was updated every decade or so and reissued in weekly instalments through newsagents over three or four years during the late twentieth century, offers evidence of this evolution both in its publishing history and in its own pages.

An edition published in 1992 carried an article entitled 'Fashions in phenomena' that put it quite succinctly:

> The early history of Spiritualism produced floods of ectoplasm, hosts of full-bodied materialisations, and enough apports to stock a department store. Yet, before and after the period bridging the late 19th and early 20th century, such phenomena of physical mediumship were almost unheard of. Fashions in phenomena have changed, and with them fashions in physical research. Indeed, the investigators of today have all but deserted the séance for laboratory tests of metal-bending, ESP and the like.[70]

Not entirely coincidentally, *The Unexplained* makes the case for a psychological explanation too, although couched in the terminology of the scientific world's one acceptable venture to the borders of the supernatural, the science of the subconscious:

> To most of us, the things we perceive in our everyday lives are solid and real. They are the tangible proof of that state of existence we agree, by consensus, to call reality. It therefore seems preposterous that the furniture of reality could be subject to the whims of something as ephemeral as fashion. But there can be as many definitions of reality as there are people to perceive it. Research into the nature of coincidence has established strong links between the subconscious mind, of both individuals and the collective, and the phenomena of

[70] *The Unexplained*, Marshall Cavendish (1992), p1226.

reality ... a consensus can influence reality by creating its own separate 'bubble' of reality.

The crazes or obsessions that can grip a community, as well as an individual, exemplify this.[71]

The most famous example of all is probably the phenomenon of witch-burnings of the seventeenth century. In the town of Salem, any behaviour or action by a woman that diverged from the norm in the slightest was deemed paranormal or, rather, witchcraft and the perpetrator faced being burned at the stake.

More localised examples are episodes of hysteria at specific schools, related to supposed paranormal events, such as the pinky-pinky ghost/monster that invaded some South African schools in the mid-1990s (see Chapter 15). As discussed later, that, too, is an example of a rumour that came from nowhere, entered the imaginations of impressionable schoolchildren, and suddenly took supposedly solid shape in the shadows of numerous school buildings.

It would be entirely fair to argue that these are all paper tigers, or paper ghosts, easy targets set up in order to knock them down in the name of science.

And indeed, pure physics can be invoked to prove that it is the *non*-belief in ghosts that is unscientific.

'The languages of eastern mystics and western physicists are becoming very similar,' says Gary Zukov, scientist author of *The Dancing Wu-Li Masters*, a groundbreaking work on the New Physics. He argues that the 'non-participating observer' is a scientific impossibility and a person who carries an attitude of objectivity is in fact prejudiced.

Albert Einstein himself started his formulation of the Special Law of Relativity with a conscious decision to

---

[71] *The Unexplained*, Marshall Cavendish (1992), pp1226-7.

disregard common sense.

And then there's the matter of Heisenberg's Uncertainty Principle. Dr H shocked the world of Victorian science by proving that there was no such thing as 'exact science'. At its most mundane, the theory says that there are limits beyond which we cannot measure accurately, at the same time, both the position and the momentum of a moving particle.

'These limits are not imposed by the clumsy nature of our measuring devices,' says Zukov, 'but rather by the very way that nature presents itself to us. In other words, there exists an ambiguity barrier beyond which we never pass without venturing into the realm of uncertainty.'

To round off this conspiracy against all that is normal and rational, British Nobel laureate physicist Brian Josephson, writing in *Physics Today* in 1992, argued that 'psychic phenomena may be both consistent with physics and conceivable in rational terms'.

But, wait – these are all individuals who did not make it their life's work to prove the existence of the supernatural. Susan Blackmore did. And, finally, she stopped:

> I long ago threw out my own previous beliefs in a soul, telepathy and an astral world, but even then I kept on searching for evidence that my new skepticism was misplaced, and for new theories that might explain the paranormal if it existed. I kept doing experiments and investigating claims of psychic powers. Finally I have given up that too.
>
> One of the reasons I have given up is probably a trivial and selfish one – that I have simply had enough of fighting the same old battles, of endlessly being accused of being scared of the truth or even of trying to suppress the truth; of being told that if I don't come

> and investigate x (my near-death experience, my psychic twin, Edgar Cayce, the miracle of Lourdes, D.D. Hume, or the haunted pub round the corner) that proves I have a closed mind. It doesn't. It only proves that after years of searching for paranormal phenomena and not finding them, I am no longer prepared to spend my precious time and limited energy in documenting yet another NDE (near death experience), setting up more carefully designed experiments to test telepathy in twins, going over all the reams of published argument about Cayce, Lourdes or Hume, or sitting up all night waiting for the ghost that (because I am a psi-inhibitory experimenter) will never come.[72]

And finally, let's hear it from those killjoys at the *Skeptical Inquirer*: '... in the entire history of modern science, no claim of any type of supernatural phenomena has ever been replicated under strictly controlled conditions.'[73]

So if, on a dark and stormy night, you look out of the window and see a moving shape or light that cannot be explained, and suddenly feel the hair rise on your head, you might assume that you are experiencing a ghostly vision. Probably, though, you are just scaring yourself witless.

---

[72] 'Why I have given up.' In P Kurtz (Ed.), *Skeptical Odysseys: Personal Accounts by the World's Leading Paranormal Inquirers*. Amherst, New York: Prometheus Books, 2001, 85-94.

[73] The Columbia University 'Miracle' Study: Flawed and Fraud, *Skeptical Inquirer* magazine, September 2004.

10

Haunted by Fear

We move now from the theory of fear to the reality of fear. While an understanding of the Old Hag syndrome may help us to understand many supernatural experiences, it doesn't take us any further in appreciating the sheer terror that can accompany such experiences. The following stories are usually told as true stories, but when they are all read together their true nature emerges.

The big catch

During the Second World War a South African soldier on a French battlefield somewhere was persuaded to stand guard in a mortuary, apparently as a prank by his fellow soldiers. In the mortuary lay the bodies of many deceased soldiers, arranged on benches, awaiting a decent burial.

Naturally, the soldier was nervous, but he was a soldier and he would do his duty. That night, sitting on one of the benches in the swirling darkness, things began playing on his mind. He became increasingly nervous, suspecting every shadow, seeing movement in every flicker of light and darkness.

Suddenly, it all got too much for him and he leapt to his feet, intending to flee. As he did so, however, someone grabbed his jacket from behind and pulled him back. Completely terror-struck, the poor man had a heart attack and died.

The next morning his comrades found him lying dead on the bench. On closer examination they found that his jacket had got caught on a nail sticking up out of the bench.[74]

I first heard the story on radio in the early 1970s. Anyone who listened to Springbok Radio in those years will remember Ten O'clock Tales, a weekly dramatisation of tales of the supernatural. A church bell tolled ten times to introduce the show, and those sounds were enough to bring out the goosebumps even before a word had been said, perfectly setting the scene for half an hour of hair standing up on the back of the neck. This tale was perfect – a combination of fear, shock and surprise.

More than a decade later, in 1987, I heard a completely updated version. A friend told me that it had happened to a friend of his father, while they had been students at the University of the Witwatersrand medical school:

> During orientation, or initiation, as it was then called, my father's friend had to spend the night in a haunted house somewhere in Johannesburg. Part of the dare was to knock a nail into a table in one of the rooms, to prove he'd been there.
>
> They dropped him off at midnight outside a spooky,

[74] Goldstuck, *The Rabbit in the Thorn Tree*, p101.

big old house that was so dark inside that even the shadows threw shadows. He made his way with a small torch through the long, dark passages to the room with the table.

All the time, he could hear strange creaking sounds in the house. He was not to know it was the seniors trying to scare him and he started to get jumpy. Finally he found the room, but by this time he was so nervous he was ready to jump at any unexpected object, even a chair, which appeared in the light of his torch.

As he was knocking the nail into the table, he suddenly saw shadows moving in the room. They were caused by the hammering motion of his arm, but all logic had deserted him. His imagination was working overtime.

Deciding he wasn't going to spend another second in the house, he turned to run. Just then, someone grabbed him by his coat and jerked him back. He promptly died of a heart attack.

The next morning the seniors found him lying there, his coat stuck in the nail he had driven into the table.[75]

The real South African prototype of this story may well be from Cape Town.

A South African version was reported in Jan Harold Brunvand's fourth book of urban legends,[76] along with various other legends grouped under the title 'The Graveyard Wager'. It was sent to Brunvand by Professor G L Maclean of the University of Natal, who had first heard it twenty or thirty years before, when university students were still required to wear academic gowns at their evening meals:

One evening at dinner, three medical students at the

[75] Goldstuck, *The Rabbit in the Thorn Tree*, p101-102.

[76] Brunvand, *Curses! Broiled Again!*, W W Norton, 1990.

University of Cape Town were talking about a body they had seen lying on the mortuary slab at the hospital adjacent to the medical school.

They dared each other to take a knife, sneak into the mortuary in the dark, and plunge the knife into the corpse. One student accepted the dare, and the others waited outside while he went in.

A few minutes after he entered the mortuary, they heard a scream, and fled in terror.

The next morning their colleague was found lying dead on the floor, the knife firmly plunged into the corpse, and also through the long sleeve of his black academic gown. The fright of thinking he had been pulled back by the corpse caused him to die of a heart attack.

Brunvand writes that the legend is so old that folklorists even have a number for it. In the Types of Folktale, a standard index of folk-narrative plots, it is listed as 'Type 1676B, Clothing Caught in Graveyard'. Variations have been recorded since the Middle Ages.

Now, thanks to those wonderful folk from the University of Cape Town, I have a couple of entirely different variations on the theme.

Death by disinformation

When first-year students were being initiated some years ago a group of freshmen were taken down to the shunting yard. There was one totally deserted area where several tracks went round a corner. One of the tracks had fallen into disuse, but the new students weren't aware of this. What happened was that if you were lying on the unused track, you couldn't see that a train coming round the corner on the track next to you wasn't on your track. You would immediately think it *was* on your track.

The first student was tied down on the unused track and thought it was a big joke. He saw a train approaching and started to get a little panicky, but still assumed he would be untied in time. His companions then said they'd decided not to untie him, and they pretended to walk away. The train went past and the guys went back to untie him. The student was dead. When the train had come round the corner, he had died of a heart attack.[77]

The story is still told as a true tale, particularly at schools and universities. Witness the tale of a schoolboy by the name of Bradford, of Florida on the West Rand, another of the callers to a 702 talk show on urban legends:

> Look, I don't know how true this is, but our principal always tells it to us. He says you mustn't play jokes because he heard from another person that some people were feeling very rowdy and got hold of his friend.
>
> He had a phobia about trains. They went down to a train line. There was an empty line next to it and they tied him down there, blindfolded him and went away.
>
> A train came past and they thought it was a big joke but when they got back there he was dead. I don't know how true it is.

That wasn't the only alarming initiation stunt those whacky Cape Town students dreamed up:

> They blindfolded one of the guys and they put him in a coffin. They told him they were going to bury him. So they carried him down stairs, up stairs, down passages,

[77] Goldstuck, *The Aardvark and the Caravan*, p28.

round buildings, until he could have no possible idea where he was. Then they took him to a ground floor window, and made loud statements about the grave being ready, being deep enough and so on.

Then they slowly lowered the coffin out through window, until it reached the ground outside. And they threw rice over it. From inside the coffin, each fistful sounded like a spade of sand landing on the coffin. The kid screamed and screamed and screamed, but they ignored him.

After about fifteen minutes, they opened the coffin, ready to burst out laughing at his terror-stricken face. Except that he was stone cold dead. He'd died of a heart attack.[78]

It is clear that these stories are all variations on the Clothing Caught in Graveyard type, but the last two move away from the stuck clothing, taking the falsely induced heart attack with them. This emphasises rather than reduces the urban legend nature of the stories, as it shows just how mobile the themes within urban legend themes can be.

The haunting that never was

Ask anyone in Tshwane, the metropolitan region that incorporates Pretoria, which is the most haunted location in their area, and few will hesitate in pointing to what they call either the 'Erasmus Castle' or the 'old Armscor building' or simply the 'spookhuis' (ghost house). The building, built in Bavarian style in 1903, belongs to Armscor, whose headquarters is next door, but has been declared a national monument.

---

[78] Goldstuck, *The Aardvark and the Caravan*, p28-29.

Standing high up on the ridge from which the suburb of Erasmus Kloof takes its name, it looks out on to a broad valley stretching southward. Nearby is a cave believed to have been a Stone Age dwelling, surrounded as it is by extensive evidence of ancient artefacts and activities.

It is a foreboding old building, with ungainly turrets and odd-shaped extensions jutting out in all directions. This gives it the creepy, unwelcoming appearance of the classic horror houses of movies that are designed to inspire fear. Inside, it is gloomy and oppressive. Of course, it simply has to be haunted.

An informant who worked there for Armscor in the 1990s told me: 'On the second floor there are no pipes, yet one day water came gushing through the ceiling on to the ground floor. There is a whole family haunting the house. At the beginning of the century some of the Erasmus children had leprosy and they were locked up in the house. Their ghosts are still there today.'

The castle is an obligatory stop on the Mystery Ghost Bus Tour, the 'moving theatre' created by Mark Rose-Christie, in which patrons are taken on a bus tour of haunted spots by a professional tour guide.

And then there is the reality behind the hauntings: the ghosts were a figment of a movie-maker's imagination.

A few years ago Thersia Rossouw of the University of Pretoria had a rather unusual paper accepted as her thesis for an MA degree in cultural history. Its topic? The history of Erasmus Castle.[79]

She tracked down the descendants of the original Erasmus family who had owned the building, and the true story unfolded. 'Many of the myths could be explained, while others

[79] 'Die Erasmuskasteel (1903) in Pretoria – 'n Kultuurhistoriese Studie', University of Pretoria, 2003.

could be regarded as tall tales,' she writes in her foreword. 'The legends that exist about leprosy and that the children were all born with leprosy could also be put to rest.'

One chapter of the thesis is devoted to the origins of the building's reputation for being haunted. The most telling lines are these: 'The researcher attempted to establish the origin of the "Spookhuis" label. According to the Erasmus family it was the result of a film that was shot on the site ... Later it emerged that it appeared in two films ... Mr J R Erasmus (Emus) was the owner of the house at the time both films were made.'

One of the films was believed to have been made in 1946, providing us with a date – to within a decade, at any rate – of the origin of the legend. Sixty years later, it has taken a firm grip on the imaginations of Pretoria residents, and it refuses to go away. Offer the average Pretorian a chance to spend a night in the 'castle', and the likely response is, 'no chance'. Their response is based entirely on the fear of what might be there, rather than on what is there in reality.

The myth of the haunted castle of Erasmus Kloof confirms that belief in ghosts and fear of ghosts does not depend on the actual existence of ghosts, but can be inspired by something as mundane as a movie.

To borrow from Franklin D Roosevelt's famous words,[80] we probably have nothing to fear of ghosts but fear itself.

[80] In his first inaugural address on 4 March 1933, talking about the Great Depression, he said: 'So, first of all, let me assert my firm belief that the only thing we have to fear is fear itself – nameless, unreasoning, unjustified terror which paralyzes needed efforts to convert retreat into advance.'

11

Ghosts go to the Movies

'Every good theatre has a ghost,' is one of the mantras of ghost hunters the world over. Troy Taylor, founder of the American Ghost Society, makes the term his own both literally[81] and figuratively as he explores the progress of American theatre ghosts from musty theatres to moviedom. His explorations seem to suggest that, if you dig hard enough round an old theatre, it will be a shock if you *don't* come up with a 'true' ghost story.

Theatres seem a natural home for ghosts, what with the psychological weight of all their many superstitions and traditions. And since the average ghost likes its haunts old, dark and gloomy, old theatres make a perfect setting for their performances. Taylor has his own firm set of theories:

> What is it about a theater that seems to attract a ghost? Could it be that the entire range of the human emotion is often expressed inside of a theater, from happiness to

[81] *The Ghost Hunter's Guidebook*, Whitechapel Press, 1997.

sorrow to fear? Perhaps these expressions of emotion attract spirits who need such energy to exist. In some cases, tumultuous events that occur in the buildings also leave an impression behind. Such impressions are often regarded as hauntings.

Theaters also demand a great love and devotion from the staff members who work there and in many cases, these same staff members return to their favorite theaters after death. Many of them remember the theater as the place where they found their greatest happiness, while others return because of some unfinished event that was never completed in life.

We deal with theatre ghosts elsewhere in this volume (see Chapter 13). However, there is a family of ghosts that enjoys the limelight, the glitz and glamour of the movie and TV worlds, and even the harsh glare of modern technology. So much are they attracted to this most visible form of show business, that the movie-making Mecca of Hollywood boasts enough ghosts to fill several books and documentaries. During 2004, the History Channel aired a documentary in South Africa entitled 'Haunted History: Hollywood'. The marketing for the show summed up the allure:

> From the ninth floor of Hollywood's Roosevelt Hotel, the ghost of an actor endlessly paces the hall still practicing his lines ... In a haunted movie studio, lights swing and turn themselves on long after the living workers have gone home ... Historians and eyewitnesses alike recount the strange events going on here ... They explain that the ghosts of Hollywood are not like ghosts anywhere else. Some were famous ... Others died in obscurity. Now they inhabit a shadowy world called Haunted Hollywood.[82]

[82] DSTV channel 68, Monday 23 August 2004, 23:10.

Before returning to South Africa, let us set the scene with a few tales that reveal just how common these stories really are. Books on the phenomenon include *Hollywood and The Supernatural* by Brad and Sherry Steiger, *Hollywood Haunted* by Laurie Jacobson and Marc Wannamaker, and *Ghost Stories of Hollywood* by Barbara Smith.

Troy Taylor has scoured all these sources and compiled the best Hollywood ghost stories in the Haunted Hollywood section of his Prairie Ghosts website.[83] Both the movie studios where films are made and the theatres where they are screened provide the backdrop.

The most famous movie theatre of them all, Mann's Chinese Theater, built in 1927 by Sid Graumann and originally named Graumann's Chinese Theater, boasts a haunted interior and exterior. This is where the tradition began of stars leaving their hand and footprints in the concrete of the sidewalk, and it is that very sidewalk that is said to be haunted. Taylor takes up the story:

> In 1982, while enjoying a drink at a local bar, actor Victor Kilian struck up a conversation with a stranger. The authorities believe that the two of them must have left the bar and went to Kilian's apartment. It was here that the actor's badly beaten body was discovered the following day. His apartment, located just a block away from Mann's Chinese Theater, had been burglarized. His killer was never caught but apparently Kilian has never given up his pursuit of the man who killed him. Local lore has it that his ghost still walks the route from the Chinese Theater to his apartment, perhaps hoping that his murderer will return to the scene.
>
> It is also believed that the interior of the theater is

[83] http://www.prairieghosts.com/hollywood.html

haunted as well. The stories have it that a ghostly little girl named Annabell roams the backstage area of the theater, tugging on curtains and appearing to startle staff members.

Numerous other cinemas are also said to be haunted, most notably the old Warner Pacific Theater on Hollywood Boulevard. It was built by the four Warner brothers, Harry, Albert, Sam and Jack, with the intention of using it to host the premiere of their new project, a risky 'talking movie' called the Jazz Singer. Sam Warner was in charge of the building project and, 'when he realised that the theatre was not going to be ready for the opening, he stood in the lobby and cursed the place'[84].

Just twenty-four hours before 'The Jazz Singer' opened in New York on 6 October 1927 Sam suffered a cerebral haemorrhage and died in Los Angeles. The Warner Pacific Theatre opened six months later and, it is said, Sam Warner's spirit has been in attendance ever since:

> Since that night in April 1928, random sightings of Sam Warner have taken place at the theater and in the administration offices above. People who live nearby report seeing him in the lobby, walking back and forth and looking frustrated and tired. Late one night in the 1970s, two men on the late night cleaning crew saw Sam walk across the lobby and enter the elevator. He stepped into it and pushed the button, then the door closed and the elevator went up. When a security guard made his rounds through the lobby, the startled men told him what they had seen and then quit on the spot! The guard however was not bothered by the story. He only

[84] http://www.prairieghosts.com/hollywood12.html

wondered why a ghost would use an elevator.

While Sam has not been seen in recent years, the security company that watches over the theater when it is closed are quite familiar with his comings and goings. When things are quiet, they often hear him in the offices upstairs, moving chairs around, scratching on doors or tapping on things to get attention.

A new twist has emerged in recent years. Paul Miller, director of the USC Entertainment Technology Center Digital Cinema Lab, which used the old theatre, wrote to Troy: 'While the elevator is no longer operational things still do move around suspiciously. It seems Sam may have a propensity for high technology items. Cell phones, PDAs, and digital cameras frequently turn up missing in the theatre, never to be seen again.'

Finally, there is the Pantages Theater, which was acquired by the reclusive tycoon Howard Hughes in 1949. He set up two offices on the second floor, and hung out there until the mid-1950s, after which it fell into disuse. The theatre was restored in 1967, and the legend began: staff working on the second floor reported feeling a presence, especially in the conference room, which had once been Howard Hughes' office.

Karla Rubin, an executive assistant at the theater, notes that 'there's something about the temperature of this room – a coldness ... I often feel a wind go past me where there's no air-conditioning on.' She and other employees have frequently heard bumping and banging sounds for which they could find no explanation, as well as the clicking of brass handles like those on desk drawers. Every once in a while, a cold wind will blow through the executive suite as well and when it does, it brings with it the faint aroma of cigars.

Karla Rubin also states that she has twice caught sight of an apparition, a tall man that she believes to be Howard Hughes. Dressed in modest business clothes, he has been seen rounding a corner in the remodelled suite where his original office door was once located.

Perhaps inevitably, a female ghost hangs out in Hughes' old, er, haunt. However, there is no romantic connection. She dates back to 1932. That year, a female patron died in the cinema during a screening. Ever since then, says Troy, when the auditorium is dark and quiet, the voice of a woman can sometimes be heard singing in the silence: 'The voice sometimes comes during the daytime and sometimes at night and recently, her voice was even picked up on a microphone during the stage setting for a live performance.'

Theatres, as suggested above, almost demand ghosts. But movie studios? Where barely a movement goes unnoticed or unrecorded? You bet. One of the most famous film sets of the twentieth century, Universal Studio's Stage 28, created especially for the 1925 version of 'The Phantom of the Opera', is said to be haunted by none other than the man who played the phantom in the movie, Lon Chaney.

Employees and visitors to Stage 28 have long maintained that it is haunted. For years there have been sightings by electricians, designers, carpenters, art directors and security guards of a man in a black cape who seems to come and go without warning. Those who have got more than just a glimpse of him say that the cloaked man is Lon Chaney himself.

In addition to studio employees, many visitors who do not know the history of Stage 28 have reported seeing the man in the black cape, often running on the overhead catwalks. Even security guards who have laughed off the idea of a resident ghost admit to being 'spooked' by lights that turn on and off by themselves and by doors that open and close on the empty stage at night.[85]

This is an archetypal movie ghost legend: a charismatic man who plays a charismatic phantom in a legendary movie comes back to haunt the set on which the movie was made. If you buy that one from the home of fantasy, you will buy any other illusion Hollywood tries to sell you.

The South African movie industry has neither the illustrious past nor the alluring characters which Hollywood boasts. But, just lately, as this country's movies start breaking into the international mainstream, it is digging up the ghosts to match.

Story of an African ghost

Destined to become a South African evergreen legend, the story was first reported by Jeanne van der Merwe in February 2004:

> A ghostly presence joined the cast and crew filming 'The Story of an African Farm' on location near Matjiesfontein, witnesses claimed.
>
> The film, starring Swaziland-born actor Richard E Grant and local actress Karin van der Laag, will be released at the Cannes Film Festival in May.
>
> Producer Bonnie Rodini said she first met the ethereal resident of the farm Zoute Kloof when she was location hunting eight years ago.
>
> Rodini recalled how the hair on the back of her neck stood up one day when she was photographing the derelict farmhouse. 'I called somebody outside to come with me, walked on and took a picture.'

[85] http://www.prairieghosts.com/hollywood5.html

When Rodini had the film developed, she saw something on the wall that she had photographed. 'I turned the print upside down and saw it was a woman in a flowing white dress.'

Later, after the farmhouse was restored for the movie, Rodini was reluctant to tell fellow crew members about the farm's ghostly resident.

'Some of the crew felt a presence in the house while we were filming, especially people from the art department who spent a lot of time in the house,' she said.

By the end of the six-week shoot, security guards had also seen the woman. 'One night the security guards heard a noise and saw a woman in white storming down the passage of the farmhouse,' said Rodini. 'A few nights later, she opened the front door and you could see her from the yard.'

But it was not only at Zoute Kloof that the cast had strange experiences. Video operator Marco Rinaldi had to move out of his room in the Lord Milner Hotel in Matjiesfontein after repeatedly waking up with a strange feeling in the middle of the night. 'It felt like someone was continuously looking over my shoulder,' he said.

Local historian Rose Willis is convinced the 'ghost' that haunted the set is that of Louisa Margaret Green, the wife of a civil commissioner.

'She was travelling with her husband Henry, who was on his way to become the civil commissioner of Colesberg in the 1860s, but then she fell ill with dysentery and died at Zoute Kloof,' said Willis. 'Her ghost has been seen often ... She wears a *kappie* (bonnet), has a small waist and wears flowing white clothes that look like they come from the 1860s.'

John Siems, manager of the Lord Milner Hotel, was not surprised at Rinaldi's experience.

'There have been many visitors here who told me they saw ghosts late at night. I've been here for seven years and I used to feel scared when I had to close up the lounges late at night. At times I have felt the hairs on my neck stand up late at night.'[86]

A *kappie*? The symbol of Afrikaner *Voortrekker* culture? On the wife of a colonial official? Rose Willis informed me that she had not referred to a kappie at all, but rather to a Victorian bonnet.[87] And then the story was taken up by various other newspapers over the following days. And the details began to change, very much in the nature of urban legends, where the 'facts' evolve to improve the dramatic effect of a story. The *Cape Times* reported:

> Producer Bonnie Rodini started scouting for locations in the area eight years ago on the farm Zoute Kloof.
>
> At the time, she said yesterday, she saw the female ghost for the first time and took a picture of her.
>
> 'I remember I saw this woman with a flowing white dress and I took a picture of it. I still have the picture.'[88]

Edna Isaacs told a slightly enhanced version in *Die Burger*:

> According to Bonnie Rodini, the movie's producer, she saw the ghost for the first time on a photograph.
>
> She said that eight years ago she was doing research for the movie and had been photographing a farmhouse in Zoutekloof when she had a 'strange feeling'.
>
> 'When I had the photos developed, I saw the outline of a woman in a flowing white dress. In the photo, the

[86] *Sunday Times*, 29 February 2004, 'Things go bump in the night on film set'.
[87] e-mail correspondence, Rose Willis, 23 June 2005.
[88] *Cape Times*, 2 March 2004, 'Producer has picture of ghost on movie set'.

> woman is rising towards the ceiling,' she said.
>
> ... (Rose) Willis said she did research on (Louisa) Green after stumbling across her grave on the farm. According to her, Green's ghost is often seen sitting on the stoep and walking in the hills.[89]

When I queried the variations with Bonnie Rodini herself, she said that the *Sunday Times* version was the most accurate. Unfortunately, she could not locate the original photo.[90]

Let us leave Louisa Green on her Karoo stoep, and follow the signals of that symbol of modern existence, the television, to the bright lights of the big city.

Undercover angels

At the Randburg headquarters of M-Net and Multichoice, which respectively brought pay TV and satellite TV to South Africa, a purpose-built studio plays host, periodically, to the local version of the international reality TV show 'Big Brother'. In this show, for those who claim higher minds and refuse to take it in, a dozen or so 'housemates' enter the studio under the 24-hour scrutiny of TV cameras, and each week one is voted out of the house. The last person remaining wins a million rand.

When the first series aired here in 2001, the 'housemates' all became instant celebrities. The press analysed every comment, and every relationship. Emotions and attitudes were picked apart, and no rumour was left unturned. One of the housemates who made an enormous impact, given

89 *Die Burger*, 2 March 2004, 'Film set "featured" a ghost'.

90 e-mail correspondence, Bonnie Rodini, 20 June 2005.

that she was the second to be evicted, was Lara Plumstead, who distinguished herself with both a constant sniff and the first romantic tryst in the house. In the days following her nomination for eviction by the voting public, she was emotionally devastated. After her eviction was confirmed and she left the house, the following report appeared in *Die Burger*:

PORT ELIZABETH – Rumours that angel-like beings 'surrounded' Lara during her most vulnerable moment have been confirmed to Lara's father by the producers of the Big Brother series.

According to Michael Plumstead, a viewer sent an e-mail message to Big Brother producers saying that she had seen two 'beings' on Lara in her room on Sunday between 9.30pm and 9.45pm.

'According to this woman, the two beings were a middle-aged man and a woman with shoulder-length hair, who were around Lara's head.

'The producers examined the videotapes and confirmed the incident. My first impression was that it must have been a reflection on the glass in front of the camera, but according to the producers the images were recorded by an infrared camera in the room,' he said.

Although Plumstead has not yet seen the video images himself, he believes it could have been guardian angels, possibly even his own father who died a while ago.

'The woman said that the man had a side parting in his hair that was on the opposite side to where my dad always had his hair, but it is difficult to say without having seen the videotape myself.'

He said that his family grew up with ideas of guardian angels and fairies.

'I believe that angels always surround us, and they make their physical presence clearer when someone undergoes emotional strain. The stress Lara experienced on Sunday after her nomination was the worst stress she has yet been under in her life.'

He believes the guardian angels were definitely there to comfort her at a difficult time.

'The people who saw the images said the presence of the beings was friendly and comforting, and it looked as if they were part of her,' he said.[91]

The most notable aspect of this story was that it appeared on the front page of the newspaper! The report was not quite typical of Big Brother coverage, but certainly epitomised the extent to which the slightest happening was built up into a major story.

From the perspective of delving into the supernatural, the astonishing aspect of this story lies in the conclusion to which the single protagonist leaps: based on hearsay, he decides one angel is possibly his late father – even though the hairstyle is supposedly different. The story encapsulates the manner in which individuals will place an interpretation that strengthens their world view – or netherworld view, for that matter – on events that appear supernatural.

Of even greater interest, however, is the idea that angels or ghosts are not unhappy with an ultramodern setting in which the ever-present eye of a TV camera subjects them to public exposure.

As with the ghosts of Hollywood, this reflects the adaptation of the supernatural to the ultra-physical. In the South African context, it suggests that the supernatural, be it ghosts or angels, has come out of the closet and into the limelight. It will take many decades and many more haunted TV and movie sets, however, before we can begin to expect such legends to become ordinary tales of everyday spectres, rather than the stuff of newspaper headlines.

---

[91] *Die Burger*, 22 September 2001, p1, 'Engele het Lara kom beskerm – pa'.

12

Of Hosts and Ghosts

For as long as people have travelled, they have found rest along the way at inns, lodging places and, in recent centuries, hotels. Along with such establishments came the inevitable places of relaxation and entertainment, from bars to brothels to gambling joints. By their very nature, such establishments are haunted by the hopes, aspirations and intentions of itinerant human beings, usually accompanied by tall tales and wild imaginings.

The longer the establishments exist, and the older their structures and facades, the more likely they are to take on that essential accessory of any self-respecting old building: a resident ghost.

In some countries, hotels are even ranked according to the quality of their ghosts. While these are not exactly the kinds of grading that convince discerning travellers, they add a mystique and allure that shiny new towers can't match.

In the USA, for example, you can find several listings for

the 'Top 10 Haunted Hotels in the United States'. One of the best is by Charlyn Keating Chisholm, who compiles listings of hotels for the About.com online information guide.

She adds a few helpful hints: 'Even if you are brave enough to stay overnight in a haunted hotel, there are no guarantees you'll see a ghost. Staying up all night, being in the right place at the right time, and quietly observing changes in temperature, smells, and sounds in the room can all help your odds of a close encounter with a restless spirit.'[92]

In other words, ghost hunting is a gamble in itself. And hotel phantoms, unlike the ghosts of Hollywood, tend to be a mundane lot. In several of Chisholm's top ten, for example, their only manifestation is 'abnormal readings' by paranormal investigators. Others are far too obvious, like Myrtles Plantation, built on an ancient Indian burial ground. Shades of the Poltergeist movie? As Chisholm says, when ten murders have been committed in the hotel, who needs poltergeists?

The archetypal hotel haunting story is Stephen King's *The Shining*, which had ghosts infesting the entire establishment. The fact behind the fiction is Stephen King's stay in the supposedly haunted Stanley Hotel, where he slept in room 217. However, it is room 418 that is said to offer real ghostly activity. Note: one haunted room at The Stanley, versus dozens in *The Shining*. Since when was fact stranger than fiction?

There are many parallels between American and South African haunted hotels. Both countries were first settled by Europeans in the seventeenth century. Both saw land-grabbing explorations into the interior, a frontier culture

[92] http://hotels.about.com/od/hauntedhotels/tp/mosthaunted.htm, December 2004.

that shaped the nation, and an influx of slaves as cheap labour was used to tame the land. This means that the very idea of a haunted house dates back to the same period in both countries. Of course, both also boast a run-down or creaking old hotel in almost every town, with ghostly guests to match. The bustling, modern cities also throw in their odd haunted establishment, of course, but it is the old and the isolated that seem most welcoming to the discerning ghost.

The big difference between the two countries is that haunted America is exhaustively documented, whereas South Africa's hauntings enjoy only sparse anthologies. References above to the American experience are intended for illuminating the South African experience, rather than filling in its gaps. If you will forgive this intrusion, you are ready to come travelling.

Charlotte's web of tales

Our journey starts at the oldest hotel in KwaZulu-Natal. Opened in 1854, the infamous Nottingham Road Hotel is known to the regulars in its pub simply as Notties. It hosts one of the most famous ghosts in South Africa, Charlotte, who has become a media personality in her own right. The KwaZulu-Natal Tourism Authority's website sums up all the tales in a rather light-hearted style, which captures the spirit in which the locals also talk of the ghost:

> No one even tries to dismiss 'Charlotte' as a prank ... her antics would demand the skills of Harry Houdini to imitate! Victim of an unsolved murder 'back in the day', as locals put it, 'Charlotte' has remained in residence at the Nottingham Road Hotel, charming generations

> of its owners, staff and guests with her alluring ways. She rearranges the flowers according to her own taste, and should someone thoughtlessly include a bloom not to her liking, 'Charlotte' will simply remove it from the vase. Locals believe that 'Charlotte' once plied the oldest profession, a reputation based both on her vanity – mirrors are moved around – and her fondness for making men, in particular, aware of her presence. A word of advice to any single man intent on downing a number of Tiddley Toads in the 'Notties' pub – if you fling your clothes on the floor before falling into bed, be prepared for 'Charlotte' folding them neatly on the dressing-table chair – she's an old-fashioned kind of girl! In addition to gliding through hotel hallways at night, 'Charlotte' can be heard holding lengthy conversations with who-knows-whom, and although Number 10 is her favourite boudoir, she loves to ring the bell calling room service to Number 22, perhaps because there's no such room! Obviously a bit of a tease, 'Charlotte' is regarded as part of the hotel family, and her friendly demeanour ensures that no one ever considers calling in the ghostbusters![93]

During the mid-1990s, Charlotte became the focus of intensive media attention as one journalist after another tested the supernatural and their own nerves in room 10. In 1993 Terry van der Walt was disappointed to spend an undisturbed night there. But there were some juicy titbits to add to the legend, supplied by the regulars at the bar:

> Off-duty barman Graham Riley (38) told us about the copper kettle that used to sway about on a hook in the rafters above the cash register, taps that were switched

[93] http://nottingham.kzn.org.za/nottingham/about/7.xml, June 2005.

> on in the haunted room and a fussy customer who was 'punished' by the ghost.
>
> It was three years ago, when the hotel was under different management and the weekend had been made particularly long by an elderly woman who complained incessantly.
>
> 'On the Sunday she came down to reception and her mouth was still going and eventually the owner said, "You can have it on the house, but I never want to see you again." When she got to her car, all four tyres were flat. She had to get them pumped up at the garage.
>
> 'It was then we realised the ghost was on our side and she had punished the woman for being against the hotel,' he said.
>
> ... I was shocked, but sceptical, when a local told me he knew a man who went to bed in room 10, saw the lusty lady at the door in her long white gown – and passed out. When he woke in the morning he was sprawled on the floor in a spent state and he swore he had 'done it' with her.[94]

Van der Walt was also advised that the ghost made an annual parade around the grounds on August 3 and 4 every year. A year later, Colin Mitchell, former editor of *Personality* magazine, did his duty for the magazine by spending a night in number 10.

However, everything pointed to the legend of a ghost rather than the presence of one. First, there was the receptionist:

> ... when I telephoned to book Room 10, Andrea Henshaw, the receptionist at Notties, casually mentioned that I

[94] *Sunday Star*, 18 July 1993, p5, 'The happy spooker'.

was pretty brave.

'*Is* it haunted?' I queried.

'I don't know,' said Andrea. 'You just won't catch me going into it. Any of the other rooms, sure ... but not Number 10.'[95]

Then came the owner:

Dinner is behind me. I've chatted to some of the locals in the pub and Eddie Albrice, the patriarch of the family syndicate which runs Notties, has told me a bit about the spirit ... that when she's around she's decked out in a diaphanous gown.

... This, Eddie said, is what he's been told. Nope, he hasn't personally bumped into her. Neither has Eddie's wife Maria. Nor their son Fred. Nor daughter Christine. Son-in-law Peter Brown hasn't clapped his cockney eyes on her either. They have, however, heard a lot about her in the time they've been at Notties.[96]

But not everyone claimed only hearsay encounters:

In the five years Sally and Mike Hoy ran the hotel, Sally says, there were several reports by people who'd had encounters with the ghost of Notties. One of them was an Eskom employee who stayed at the hotel while working in the area.

'He was booked into Room 10,' Sally explains, 'but refused to stay in it after he'd gone up to it several times and found everything topsy-turvy. The bedding had been stripped, the mattress had been thrown from the bed and

[95] *Personality*, 5 August 1994, p89, 'The Ghosts' Inn'.

[96] *Personality*, 5 August 1994, p89, 'The Ghosts' Inn'.

his clothes had been strewn around the room. He was a pretty level-headed sort but he flatly refused to stay in Number 10 ever again.'[97]

And Mitchell? He had a solid, undisturbed night's sleep, despite leaving the door unlocked and the window wide open.

I paid my own visit to Notties Hotel during mid-2005. Hotel manager Simon Spencer kindly gave me a tour of the premises and showed me to number 10, where I was left alone to absorb the atmosphere.

The room is nondescript, with two distinctive features.

Firstly, and most strikingly, it is an exceptionally cold room. Shivers up the spine or a sudden cold sensation should come as little surprise to guests.

Secondly, the first floor room has a window that opens directly on to a tin roof that runs round the hotel above the ground floor. If the window were left open, it would be no problem for someone to sneak out of a nearby room on to the roof and hop into number 10. It would take only the mildly mischief-minded to come up with a prank or two to give Charlotte renewed life.

Back downstairs in the pub, the manager will not commit himself to any ghostly belief. He has heard some of the stories, he says, but has no evidence to offer for their truth.

In short, the ghost of Notties Hotel is really the urban legend of Notties Hotel.

To find a ghost, the rule sometimes seems to be: just find the oldest pub or hotel in a particular city. That certainly holds true in Pietermaritzburg, capital city of KwaZulu-Natal.

---

[97] *Personality*, 5 August 1994, p89, 'The Ghosts' Inn'.

Several buildings, mostly former government establishments, enjoy a ghostly reputation. But the best documented of all is the ghost of the Polo Tavern. Ryan Creswell caught up with the story for the *Sunday Times* in 1990:

> A ghost who likes beer is haunting a city's oldest pub – and the landlord has a phantom photo to prove it!
>
> The ghost spirits his way into the carefully locked bar of the 95-year-old Polo Tavern in Maritzburg about once every two months, leaving a half-finished glass of beer on the counter.
>
> Staff at the old tavern used to sleep on the second floor, but they moved out because they were scared by heavy sighs and bumps in the night.
>
> Landlord Philip Botha said the twilight zone story began in 1919 when a policeman died in the doorway of the popular pub.
>
> 'A Sergeant Bosch of the police crashed his Harley Davidson motorbike and sidecar into a pole in front of the pub,' Mr Botha said.
>
> 'His passenger, Anne Smith, later recovered, but the policeman staggered up the tavern stairs and dropped dead in front of the door.
>
> 'His body was taken away and then the police took a photograph of the scene of the accident. When the photograph was developed they saw a faint image of the sergeant climbing the stairs.
>
> 'About two years ago a policeman in the forensic section said they still had the photo because they found the incident so strange.'
>
> A copy of the yellowing photograph, clearly showing the crashed motorbike and the image on the stairs, has pride of place on the wall of the pub.
>
> Some old-timers even claim to have seen the phantom

policeman in the pub, but the landlord admits the ghost stories are usually told after more than a few brews.

Said Mr Botha: 'He's quite a friendly ghost and we hope he stays that way. But strange things have been going on for as long as our old locals can remember.'[98]

Ten years later, in an article in *The Witness* about the ghosts of Pietermaritzburg, Amanda Pasqua-Lotto added two elements that support the theories of the Polo Tavern ghost: Bosch had been a regular at the Polo Tavern, and onlookers at the time the photo had been taken swore that no one had entered the tavern while the photo was being taken. Strangely, however, she attributed the photo to a newspaper photographer rather than the police themselves.[99] A clue to an urban legend at work?

In the same article, Pasqua-Lotto told of another phantom traveller frequenting a place of hospitality. In this case, however, the hostelry in question is now simply an old house – albeit a haunted old house:

> Pietermaritzburg is filled with old houses and it appears that every second one has a 'presence'. There is a special house up Old Howick Road called Ketelfontein. A charming old house with a long history, a murder, a mystery, buried treasure and a ghost.
>
> Ketelfontein was built in 1862 and was a hostelry where the transport riders could change horses or rest overnight before continuing on their journey to Durban from Johannesburg.
>
> One stormy evening a traveller arrived with a horse so exhausted that it was unable to continue to Durban. The stables had no fresh horses left to exchange with him so

[98] *Sunday Times*, 19 August 1990, p9, 'Mine Ghost!'
[99] *The Natal Witness*, 28 July 2000, 'Things that go bump in the night'.

the man had no option but to rest up for the night.

This man was no ordinary traveller. He had driven his horse so hard because he was being pursued by the police as he was in possession of stolen diamonds. During the night the police arrived and a gun-battle ensued with the traveller coming off second best. His body, horse and possessions were searched and no diamonds were found. It is believed that he realised he would be caught and disposed of them by throwing them down a well or burying them somewhere on the property. They have never been found – either by the traveller, who comes back often to look for them, or by anyone else.

If you happen to see spectral figures digging around there at night they just may not all be real ghosts.

The rule about a city's oldest hotel or pub starts and ends in the KwaZulu-Natal midlands. The rivals for the title of oldest hotel in Durban, the Royal Hotel and the Britannia Hotel, have no great reputation for spectral guests. In the oldest city in South Africa, Cape Town, where a ghost is a crucial accessory for any historic building, the oldest hotel, The Tudor Hotel on Greenmarket Square, is equally unencumbered by ghostly reputation. The same applies to the Cathcart Arms Hotel in Grahamstown, believed to be the oldest hotel in all of South Africa – it was first opened as a 'Brewery and House of Accommodation' in 1831.[100] And another claimant for the title, 'South Africa's oldest existing inn,[101] D'Ouwe Werf in Stellenbosch. Not to mention the 'third oldest hotel in South Africa',[102] the Queen's Hotel next to the Ostrich Museum in Oudtshoorn.

---

[100] *Dispatch*, 18 September 1997, p7, 'Historic Grahamstown hotel to be sold'.
[101] http://www.ouwewerf.com, June 2005.
[102] http://southafricantravel.org/stay.htm, June 2005.

Even the likely sounding Bathurst Inn and Pig 'n Whistle Hotel, labelled 'The oldest licensed pub in South Africa',[103] does not lay claim to a single ghost, at least not publicly.

What's a ghost hunter to do? Not believe a word you hear when told an old hotel is *not* haunted? It's a rare hotelier that won't cash in on such notoriety, however. Says Margaret Williamson: 'In Britain, some hotels which started out all spectreless have invented a spooky story or two so that they can join the magic circle, and South African hoteliers seem to appreciate the value of a good ghost.'[104] She adds that old inns are particularly ghost prone, but those that she identifies as most haunted are not necessarily the most ancient. Her only excursion out of the Cape takes us to The Mountain Park Hotel in the foothills of the Drakensberg near Bulwer, built in 1942 and opened in the 1950s.

As a resident of Cape Town, the rest of her haunted hotels are found in the Western, Southern and Eastern Cape. They are:

- The Edward Hotel in Port Elizabeth, opened in 1904
- The Lord Milner Hotel in Matjiesfontein, built in 1899
- Swiss Farm Excelsior in Franschhoek Valley
- Old Mill House Lodge at McGregor near Robertson
- The Royal Hotel in Knysna, originally St George's Tavern, built in 1847

Rose Willis, the acknowledged expert on the ghosts of the Karoo, provides a few more haunted hotels from that arid region:

- Haunted paintings in the Swartberg Hotel in Prince Albert, perhaps not there any more because it has since been sold, but figures were at times seen on the paintings

[103] http://www.pigandwhistle.co.za/tours.html, June 2005.
[104] Williamson, p162.

and at other times not;
- The gambler who still plays poker in one of the back rooms of the Swartberg Hotel – he is said to have come from the old gold fields nearby;
- A certain country inn, 'but the owners of the hotel do not like her mentioned – they truly get the "horries". She is said to be the wife of the last De Villiers and she burned to death in the house when a lamp overturned and her skirts caught alight.' [105]

Only three of Margaret Williamson's hotel ghosts have any, shall we say, substance. Let's start at the Edward, where the ghosts are of even more recent vintage than the hotel itself.

> Reginald Lambson, the proprietor when the King Edward Mansions Hotel opened, died in 1931 and his son Ronnie took over. On New Year's Day in 1972 71-year-old Ronnie and his wife Helen were slashed to death while they were sleeping in their suite. A kitchen hand, Michael Mxolisi Maqina, had apparently brutally attacked the couple and then hidden himself under the sprung wooden dance floor before making his escape from the hotel. He was later arrested, found guilty of the double murder and executed.
>
> That led to the scary stories that the ghosts of the murdered and murderer walked the hotel. Staff refused to go near the place where Maqina had hidden or the hotel suite where the Lambsons had been slain.
>
> And certain staff members are convinced that Ronnie Lambson has never left. He is still seen walking around the hotel at night, checking that all's well with the Edward.[106]

[105] e-mail correspondence, Rose Willis, 23 June 2005.
[106] Williamson, p163.

Yet again, we can detect the signs of an urban legend at work rather than a truly supernatural phenomenon. The sheer horror of the event, rather than actual supernatural experiences, was enough to give rise to the ghost stories. In other cases, it seems natural that there should be a ghost, or that a particularly interesting character should be returning to an old haunt. Such is the case with the ghost of the Royal Hotel.

> The coastal town of Knysna has a fascinating ghost: an ancient mariner who haunts the Royal Hotel. Although he has been dead for more than half a century, he still wanders around the passages in the middle of the night and walks through doors and rearranges the glasses in the dining room and pub. It is, after all, his home ground: he opened an inn on the same spot in 1847. It was called St George's Tavern, and later renamed the Royal.
>
> Captain Thomas Horn was born in England in 1812. He came to Knysna in 1847 after his ship had run aground at Mossel Bay. He settled at Knysna, becoming a well-known figure in the timber trade that flourished there during the nineteenth century, and building his own wooden boat in 1856.
>
> Tom Horn died in December 1885, probably in his tavern, and was buried in the graveyard just across the road. He has never left, though: that is, if the ghost that haunts the Royal is really Captain Horn, which isn't certain.[107]

Several sightings of the ancient mariner have been reported over the years, but Williamson's interview with the then manager of the hotel, Peter Mustoe, once again hinted that

[107] Williamson, p169.

there was an urban legend basis to the stories. She asked whether he had ever met the Captain. He replied: 'I'm afraid not. I have been here only a short while and the gentleman hasn't put in an appearance yet – although I am sleeping in one of the rooms that he's supposed to patronise.'

Finally, there is the hotel that closely rivals Nottingham Road for the title of South Africa's most famous haunted hotel: the Lord Milner in Matjiesfontein. To understand the ghosts of Matjiesfontein, one must know its history. Even the places most steeped in tradition succumb to the power of the World Wide Web, and I am indebted to the official Matjiesfontein website for the following story:

1884, young immigrant Scot, James Logan, purchased land at 'a place called Matjiesfontein', an insignificant railway halt in the depths of the Karoo. The Cape Government Railways had, by then, reached the Kimberley diamond fields, and – following Cecil Rhodes' vision of the 'road to the North', his dream of a Cape to Cairo line – was extending into the Zambezi hinterland. Logan, whose meteoric rise was based on an energetic and meticulous efficiency, had been awarded the government catering contract at Touws River, which lies within the vast spaces of the Karoo.

In those days, dining cars were unheard of, and – aware that travellers needed sustenance on those interminable journeys to the interior – Logan saw the potential of this remote Matjiesfontein halt. He had already found the Karoo air beneficial for his weak chest; and, entranced by the lunar majesty of the landscape, resigned his post and set about creating a village, seemingly in the depths of nowhere, which would make his fortune and become for many what John Buchan (remember *Prester John* and *The 39 Steps*?) would have recognised as a 'Temenos' – a special place of the spirit.

Logan purchased the farm Matjiesfontein and, with his thoroughly commercial instincts, three others which possessed plentiful water. He created what an enthusiast describes as an 'Oasis'; planted trees (inevitably including the ubiquitous pepper) and a garden; built his own still-surviving residence, Tweedside Lodge; and established the famous Hotel Milner which was conveniently completed in 1899, and shortly thereafter served as the Headquarters of the Cape Western Command.

By early 1899, Matjiesfontein had become a fashionable watering place, attracting those who could afford to seek relief for chest complaints in the clear, bright air, entertaining distinguished visitors, some of whom were more parasite than patron. Lord Randolph Churchill is still remembered for 'borrowing' a hunting dog which he never returned.

Olive Schreiner lived in her own cottage here for five years and published the book *The Story of an African Farm* which brought her instant fame and an income to last her a lifetime. Olive later became one of the first voices of feminism in South Africa. Today her small three-roomed cottage is a landmark in the village; Logan, a cricket fanatic, entertained most of the famous early teams visiting the Colony. Rudyard Kipling, on his first call at the Cape, made a special journey inland specifically to visit Schreiner. During the Boer War, Matjiesfontein supported a base hospital, and Logan offered five of his villas as convalescent homes for soldiers.

Virtually all the British Army commanders – Lord Roberts, Douglas Haig, after his post as Commander-in-Chief of the BEF in France, and Edmund Ironside (Chief of the Imperial General Staff, 1940) stayed or were entertained in the Village. Edgar Wallace – ex-trooper, war correspondent, thriller writer – sent his superb 'Unofficial Despatches' from there.

All were celebrated in their time and, even now, some are still remembered.

But why, a century on, does this little village still retain its strange magnetism? It lies in what, to the superficial traveller, must be a wilderness; so remote, apparently so insignificant. And yet, it retains its own unique, very civilised mystique. It is at the very core of this country's history, holding a personality, an integrity and a sense of the past, which even the most transitory visitor may perceive, however dimly.[108]

What more do you need as a seedbed for urban legends, tall tales and, of course, tales of phantom visitors from the past? Another website, that of the Go2Africa travel guide & reservation service, offers a version that punts the hauntings to the hilt:

Matjiesfontein is reputed to be the most haunted town in South Africa. Two stories in particular are fascinating. The Logan family entertained visitors so often that they were always tolerant of the unseen residents. One particular unseen resident caused no trouble except that he/she could not open doors and would rattle the door handles until some obliging member of the family would open it for her. Unfortunately she was slightly sensitive.

One day after Jennifer Buist's wedding she was too engrossed packing her gifts to let the ghost in, the rattling reached an impatient crescendo. Eventually she threw the door open saying 'fine come in if you must, don't make such a damn noise about it'. She felt a puff of cold air rush past her and the ghost rattled her way through the window and was never heard or felt again. Another ghost is supposed

[108] http://www.matjiesfontein.com/About/index.htm, June 2005.

to be a wounded British soldier with his arm in a sling and a bloody bandage around his head who stands at the turn-off to the Memorial Cemetery. Travellers, thinking he is injured, stop to help and he promptly vanishes. The Milner Hotel is also reputed to be haunted by a group of cheerful ghosts. Laughter is heard in empty rooms and the sound of billiards is heard when there is no one there.[109]

Not unexpectedly, Margaret Williamson focused more of her attention on this town than on most others she explored in her decades of ghost hunting. 'The variegated history of Matjiesfontein has led to stories of ghosts that are as colourful and arresting as a Victorian stained-glass door. And even if they're only stories, one wonders ...'

She mentions the bandaged ghost, as well as the famous – or legendary – 'ghost sounds' of a Scottish soldier piping the Lament. Her greatest fascination, however, is with the ghosts of the Lord Milner Hotel itself.

> There are two female ghosts who are live-in guests: one is called Lucy and the other is Kate. Lucy is a vague spectre. Rumours abound of people having seen her floating round the passages and the stairs, wearing a negligee. Someone who died in the building, perhaps? Whoever she is, she's friendly, and too ethereal to be frightening.
>
> Unless, of course, Lucy's is the voice that is heard from time to time emanating from one of the rooms at the dead of night, when a loud quarrel erupts and shatters the Karoo tranquillity even more effectively than a goods train clattering past. It's not only the tranquillity that's shattered: it also sounds as though hundreds of glasses and plates are being smashed to bits.

[109] http://www.go2africa.com/south-africa/karoo/matjiesfontein/, June 2005.

> But when someone goes to investigate, all is quiet and nothing's been broken.
>
> On the Lord Milner Hotel's main staircase, which rises impressively from the hallway, the ghosts of two British soldiers have frequently been seen. '"Guest and staff members have reported seeing these two men, dressed in the army uniform of a century ago," a staff man told me. "They get to the top of the flight and then they disappear. I've never seen them but many people insist they are there."'[110]

The number of times those words come up in the investigation of the supernatural – 'I've never seen the ghost but others say they have' – is one of the reasons that hotel ghosts in particular fit more comfortably into the category of urban legend than the supernatural. But there is one ghost at the Lord Milner that does not go away that easily. This is the ghost of the girl called Kate. Up a steep staircase leading into a turret from the second floor, one will today find a room with a plaque on the door reading 'Kate's Card Room'. The legend goes that she was a young nurse who used to enjoy playing cards with recovering patients in that very room. Williamson takes up the story with a first-hand account:

> Then Kate, who was 19, died mysteriously. And strange things have happened in the turret room and below it. One young hotel guest saw a woman floating round one of the lower passages at about 7.45 one evening ... A few minutes after that the guest and her friend, who knew the hotel well, went up the narrow stairs to the card room. 'I felt that there were people in there,' she told me. And as they walked into the room, which

[110] Williamson, pp165-166.

was empty after all, the locked door leading to the roof started rattling violently and carried on rattling for about a minute.

'We didn't wait to see if anybody was going to appear. We scuttled!' she told me. 'It was terribly frightening.'

Even more frightening was the recent experience of one of the housekeepers, a woman not given to hysteria or over-imaginativeness, who went into the card room at the unwitching hour of 12.30pm. Something brushed past her. She turned round, and saw a woman in a long white dress or a nurse's uniform. Almost immediately the apparition faded away. The housekeeper also scuttled down to the other members of staff, gasping out her story while her hair, she said, 'stood on end'. Kate, looking for her patients or ready for a game of cards?[111]

A game indeed. The ghosts of hotels and pubs share one of two general characteristics: they are either playful and even mischievous, or they are totally unconcerned with events around them. The latter behave in the classic pattern of supernatural 'recordings' of traumatic events which are then replayed over and over again. John and Anne Spencer intimate that such explanations suggest 'that no actual spirit presence is involved and would suggest that at least these particular hauntings were a curious but natural phenomenon'.[112]

In other words, you have nothing to fear of Kate and Lucy, but should be careful of the more physical antics of Charlotte, Sergeant Bosch and Captain Horn. And if you believe that, then you may well be ready to spend a night in Kate's Card Room.

---

111 Williamson, p167.

112 Spencer, J & A, p101.

13

Ghosts of the City

Ghosts have no respect for place. They will haunt a forlorn country farmhouse as readily as a busy urban residence. But the public perception of typical hauntings, if such things can be typical, depends heavily on the cultural and historic background to which that public has been exposed.

'Asked what a "typical" haunted building is like, most people would reply with a description of an ancient rambling mansion or something like the storm-lashed and lightning-illuminated castle in which Dr Frankenstein constructed his Creature in Mary Shelley's tale of "a modern Prometheus",' write John and Anne Spencer. 'No doubt such places have their ghosts, but ... there seem to be no limitations to where you might meet a ghost.'[113]

The preconception they describe is, of course, the European concept of the haunted building. And, while probably the most haunted building in South Africa is indeed a castle,

[113] Spencer, J & A, p21.

the Cape Town Castle is not what comes to mind for the average South African contemplating the whereabouts of ghosts. Mansions also have pride of place in the haunted heartland of Europeans in general and of Britons in particular. In this regard, too, South Africans have thrown off the colonial yoke. Our haunted buildings tend to be more parochial, run-of-the-mill and, well, ordinary.

Statistically, of course, reports of hauntings in South Africa and Europe are equally likely to come from such mundane buildings. But it is in the public mind of South Africans that the ordinariness of our ghosts allows them to flourish.

Every South African city boasts so many ghosts, dispersed so widely geographically and in type, that the twenty-first century has arrived along with a new phenomenon in entertainment: the urban 'mystery ghost bus tour'. Part entertainment, part sightseeing tour, part supernatural lecture, and part pub crawl, it was devised by magician and illusionist Mark Rose-Christie as a novel form of theatre. Professional actors narrate recorded tales played on the public address system inside the bus, and professional tour guides lead the audiences on interactive walkabouts.

Four cities, two large towns and one country area are included, but cities like Johannesburg and Cape Town boast so many spots of horror and haunting that the organisers usually alternate between two different tours of different aspects of those cities' haunted histories. It is likely that any city in the world could host such entertainment, but it is in South Africa that it has become part of the subculture.

For now, let us embark on our own tour of South Africa's haunted cities.

Johannesburg

Elsewhere in this book, the haunts of Daisy de Melker are discussed in detail (page 129). She could make Johannesburg a thoroughly haunted city all on her own, but she has a great deal of help. Aside from the buildings mentioned in Chapter 8, Johannesburg's ghosts inhabit an interesting selection of buildings and are themselves a fascinating array of characters.

One of the most charming is José Dale Lace – the 'first lady' of Northwards Mansion on Parktown Ridge. Both the building and its spectral hostess claim an intriguing history. The mansion was the first large house in Johannesburg designed by renowned architect Sir Herbert Baker, designer of the Union Buildings in Pretoria. Chantelle Benjamin captured the combination of both madam and domain in the *Sunday Times* Metro:

> The house – which cost £21 500 to build in 1904 – shows Baker's eclectic mix of architectural features. It has six types of gables, including the Cape Dutch-inspired one in stone above the entrance, windows in the Tudor, Palladian and Venetian styles; and a majestic hall with a minstrel gallery reminiscent of those in medieval times ... An important influence on the design of the house is believed to have been the first lady of the house, the vivacious José Dale Lace. 'It appears even Baker succumbed to her charms, allowing some unusual and fanciful details to creep into the usual Baker style,' says (curator Neil) Viljoen.[114]

Mrs Dale Lace was born Josephine Cornelia Brink in

---

[114] *Sunday Times* Metro, 13 June 2004, p10, 'The House Where José Lived'.

Richmond in the Karoo. She became an actress, and had affairs with some of the great names of the day, including Edward VII and Cecil John Rhodes. She finally married Colonel John Dale Lace – twice – first in London, a marriage which was never consummated – and then in Cape Town. Their move to Northwards was the beginning of another flamboyant chapter in her life story: 'When she left her Parktown mansion to go shopping, she would have her servants go ahead and blow a bugle to let everyone know that she was coming. She bathed in milk three times a week to keep her complexion, and insisted that the marble tiles receive the same treatment.'[115]

The Dale Laces subsequently went bankrupt, and the house changed hands several times, with successive owners making major – and sometimes disastrous – changes, such as demolishing historic stables to make way for a residence for staff at the Johannesburg College of Education (JCE). A Cape Dutch gateway at the entrance was bulldozed to make way for the M1 highway, no less. During ownership by the South African Broadcasting Corporation (SABC) the front gates were sold to a company employee. Historic gardens simply vanished. But the mansion survived one rather disruptive plan: the SABC television tower now situated in Auckland Park was originally intended to be built on this site. Instead, the Transvaal Provincial Administration took it over for use by the JCE.

Today it is being restored to its original state – as far as possible – by corporate owners Gencor, and tours of the house can be booked though Computicket. And the ghost? Neil Viljoen is adamant that José still lingers, through all the house's trials. Over the years, he told the *Sunday Times*, occupants have regularly seen her near the stairs on the first

[115] *Sunday Times* Metro, 13 June 2004, p10, 'The Cleopatra of Parktown Ridge'.

floor. Lucille Davie, writing for the City of Johannesburg website, reported the following conversation with Viljoen:

> Viljoen tells the story of her ghost lingering in the house. It is said that when a foot touches the second to last step on the staircase, the swish of her skirt can be heard.
>
> 'A year ago a TV crew with a clairvoyant and an infra-red camera came to talk to her. He spoke to her for some time, and asked her a cruel question: "Do you know that you are dead?" To which she replied: "Only now do I know that",' says Viljoen.
>
> But since this conversation, Viljoen says she is more settled and he doesn't have to continually straighten her portrait in the hall.[116]

The City of Johannesburg website offered their list of Johannesburg's oldest buildings in 2003.[117] While no ghosts were mentioned, if you ask around you will hear about hauntings, ghosts and mysterious happenings in almost all these buildings – although in most cases no specific incident can be pinpointed.

Most are old farmhouses, offering a powerful link between South Africa's long tradition of haunted farms and its more famous urban ghosts.

- *Hy Many House*, Frangipani Crescent, Randpark Ridge, built in 1860, and at one stage a second residence of the Dale Laces. Most of it has been demolished by fire and developers with little respect for the past. A small cemetery apparently once stood near the dam that can

---

116 http://www.joburg.org.za/feb_2002/northwards.stm, February 18, 2002, 'Flamboyant José leaves her mark upon the ridge'.

117 http://www.joburg.org.za/2003/feb/feb21_old.stm, 21 February 2003, 'Jo'burg's oldest buildings'.

now be found on the site.

- *Bezuidenhout farmhouse* built in 1863 by Frederick Bezuidenhout on the farm Doornfontein, still standing in the middle of Bezuidenhout Park in Dewetshof, and maintained by Johannesburg City Parks. The ghost of Judith Bezuidenhout (née Viljoen), wife of the original owner, is said to roam the park and small cemetery at midnight. Her father had owned the farm, and the nearby suburb of Judith's Paarl is named after her, so it should come as no surprise that she has a proprietary interest in the area.

- *Emmarentia farmhouse* built on the farm Braamfontein by Louw Geldenhuys in 1887. Named after his wife Emmarentia, as is the suburb in which it still stands today, it has been fully restored. The five palm trees in front of the house were planted by Emmarentia herself – and she may well be tending them to this day. After all, it is just a short walk from the graveyard in Hill Road where she lies buried.

- *Bree Street Police Station,* believed to be Johannesburg's first police station, was built in 1887, complete with Cape Dutch gables. The ground floor is home to a commercial establishment, while the first floor ... ah, therein lies an untold story. According to Lucille Davie, 'The upper floor is vacant and has an unhappy atmosphere with its wooden floors covered by linoleum, its wooden banister painted dark brown, set against its tall 4-metre high ceilings.'

- *Rissik Street Post Office* was built in 1897, after Johannesburg's first post office was demolished. Designed by

President Paul Kruger's architect Sytze Wierda, it acquired its second storey and clock tower in 1905. The building was thoroughly vandalised when the Johannesburg City Council neglected this beautiful relic of the city's origins but, at the time of writing, plans were under way to restore it.

- *The Fort* was built in 1892, with one strange feature: 'Instead of facing outwards to protect the town from invasion, its cannons faced directly into the rapidly expanding town, where Kruger's "enemies", the English-speaking "Uitlanders", lived. A second bastion in the eastern corner protected the road north to Pretoria, Kruger's base – an acknowledgement of Kruger's mistrust of the British.' After the Boer War ended in 1902 it became a jail, holding among other prisoners Mahatma Gandhi, Chief Albert Luthuli, Bram Fischer, Nelson and Winnie Mandela and, of course, Daisy de Melker. Today it is home to the Constitutional Court, but is still claimed to be haunted by ghosts, particularly in the women's section where Daisy de Melker was held.

- *The View* on Ridge Road in Parktown was built in 1896 and owned by Sir Thomas Cullinan, who also happened to own the Premier Mine where the world's largest diamond was found in 1905. Today it is the headquarters of the Transvaal Scottish Regiment and still watched over by Lady Cullinan, who lived in the house until she died in 1963, aged ninety-seven.

- *The Windybrow* in Hillbrow, built in 1896 by Theodore Reunert, is today known as the Windybrow Centre for the Arts. Despite various renovations, it is still a little run-down. With its three theatres, it is a natural magnet for ghosts.

Other buildings that have survived through three centuries, some more renowned than others for their hauntings, include:

- St Mary the Less, Park Street, Jeppestown, built 1889
- The Sunnyside, now part of the hotel, built in 1894
- Markham's Building, Eloff Street, built 1897
- The Three Castles Building, Marshall Street, built 1898
- Kensington Sanatorium, built 1897

Buildings that are also included in the ghost bus tour are the Old Transvaal Children's Memorial Hospital, Eikenlaan/Mike's Kitchen (haunted by 'the ghosts of Mr and Mrs James Goch'), the Roberts Avenue Poltergeist House, Jeppe Boys' High, the Haunted Kensington Castle, Braamfontein Cemetery, and the Langlaagte Station.

As mentioned in Chapter 8, the multiple hauntings of characters like Daisy de Melker and José Dale Lace point to an expectation of supernatural activity rather than its actual presence. And, as has been made clear throughout this book, the first step to *finding* evidence of the supernatural is *expecting* such evidence. Johannesburg, then, can well be said to be haunted by expectations, rather than by the ghosts themselves.

Pretoria/Tshwane

Pretoria, like Cape Town, celebrates its haunted history openly and with relish. No coverage of Smuts House is complete without mention of its ghost, for example. Erasmus Castle, with no real history of haunting, is as celebrated as a 'spookhuis' as any supposedly haunted building in the Cape, and its present owners feel under no compulsion to set the record straight.

We start, however, with one of the most famous and infamous Pretoria structures of all, the Voortrekker Monument. The *Let's Go: South Africa* travel guide perfectly captures the combination of genius and folly behind the building:

> The monument stands as the most potent symbol of the Afrikaners' belief in their destiny as the 'white tribe of Africa', and pays tribute to the 20,000 Voortrekker pioneers who left the Cape Colony in 1834 and 1835. Designed by Gerard Moerdyk and constructed from 1938-49, this massive granite structure is regarded by many conservative Afrikaners as holy ground. Every December 16 at noon light shines through the ceiling onto a symbolic grave to commemorate those fallen in the battle against the Zulus on that date. Gracing the inside wall is a marble frieze (one of the largest in the world) depicting the trekkers' 20-year history (including the killing of 4000 Zulu warriors, the construction of the Church of Vow, and the signing of the Sand River Convention in 1852), and their Great Trek to escape British rule. During the apartheid era, blacks were allowed to visit only at designated times.[118]

White schoolchildren learning the story of the monument also tended to hear – unofficially – tales of Boer trekkers and soldiers choosing the imposing building as their final home, many years after their deaths. There is no consistency or

---

[118] http://www.letsgo.com/SAF/07-Gauteng-296, *Around Pretoria*, St Martin's Press, accessed June 2005.

detail in these stories, however, and they can confidently be said to be mere urban legends.

Not far away from the monument, at the Smuts House Museum on the farm Doornkloof in the outlying suburb of Irene, the haunting cannot be explained away as easily – given that the first source of the claim was Jan Smuts' own wife:

> This humble house of wood and galvanized iron was moved 100km in 1909 to become the home of Jan Christian Smuts (1870-1950), general, international statesman, farmer, lawyer, scientist, author, and botanist. Give the man some credit; he had 26 university degrees. Filled with relics of Smuts' life, the house is an intimate portrait of the historical giant who wrote the preamble to the UN Charter and served twice as South Africa's Prime Minister. Mrs Smuts claimed to have seen the ghost of an old man with whiskers in the Dark Room, and occasional tourist reports corroborate the sighting.[119]

There is one more fascinating detail that is not generally reported: according to Pretoria artist Eric Bolsmann, 'The building was originally an officers' mess which had been transported by the British Army from India to be erected in Middelburg. General Smuts bought the building from the Department of Defence for £300 in 1908 and had it reassembled at Doornkloof at a cost of £2000.'[120]

Bolsmann retells one of the most credible accounts of the Smuts House ghost, by *Cape Times* journalist George Wilson, who stayed with the Smuts family in 1936. In his book *Gone Down the Years*, Wilson recalled his experience,

---

[119] http://www.letsgo.com/SAF/07-Gauteng-296, *Around Pretoria*, St Martin's Press, accessed June 2005.
[120] Bolsmann, p31.

but started out with what was almost certainly an urban legend of the time:

> General Smuts' house was originally an officers' mess for the British troops at Pretoria after the occupation, and it was acquired by General Smuts who had it removed to Irene and built on the site of a pre-existing farm homestead which had been occupied by an elderly Boer farmer of very considerable wealth. On the approach of the British forces, according to the story, he had buried gold to the amount of £30 000 at some place on the farm which has never been discovered.[121]

The scene was set for a very conveniently identifiable ghost:

> The second day I was at Irene I was sleeping in a very comfortable little room next to the dining room, and suddenly woke up at about five o'clock to find that a benign old gentleman, rather like President Kruger in appearance, was standing a few feet from me beside the bed. It was an intensely vivid experience, and I believe I was then wide awake. In any case, I sat up, and put out my hand towards him, whereupon he completely vanished.
>
> At breakfast the next morning Mrs Smuts asked me if I had had a good sleep, and I said: 'Yes, but I had a curious experience about five o'clock', and I began to tell the story of the benign old gentleman. At this point I saw that Sylma who was sitting opposite was making mysterious faces at me, and I realised that in some way I must have put my foot into it rather badly, but I could

[121] Bolsmann, pp32-3.

> not pause sufficiently to collect my thoughts. Then Mrs Smuts said: 'I want particularly to hear about this. Can you describe him?' I described the old gentleman as nearly as I could, and she said to General Smuts: 'There, Oubaas, I always told you the ghost was in the house, and Mr Wilson saw the ghost.' I said that it certainly was a most vivid experience. Mrs Smuts said that no doubt the ghost would appear to me again, and if it appeared I must not do as I had done the previous night; I must not repel it. I must talk to it gently and ask: 'Where did you bury that £30 000?'[122]

Wilson hints at the urban legend nature of the buried treasure, saying 'I found that I had stumbled into a curious little romance, because it was quite a usual thing with those of us who had nothing particular to do to go out on expeditions round the farm with spades and dig diligently in likely spots. But we never found the £30 000. The ghost, Mrs Smuts told me, quite often walked about the house in the very late hours or in the early morning.'[123]

Bolsmann has a well-developed theory of who the ghost is, 'if there is a grain of truth in the tale of the hidden treasure' – a comment that first reveals the suspicions of even this sincere believer in the supernatural. He suggests that 'the elderly gentleman could be Daniel Erasmus's grandson, also named Daniel, who had inherited the third portion of the farm from Michiel Erasmus … Michiel, had died in 1896. It thus could not have been he who hid the gold, for the British forces only advanced in Pretoria in 1900.'[124]

[122] Bolsmann, p33.
[123] Bolsmann, p33.
[124] Bolsmann, p33.

Bolsmann then offers the clincher to this aspect of the ghost story being an urban legend:

> Daniel too is unlikely to have taken such measures. The story of a farmer burying gold worth £30 000 does sound romantic, but he would surely have made certain that the gold would not have been left behind, and Daniel Erasmus had enough time to reclaim his treasure for he only sold his farm to General Smuts in 1908, six years after the British forces had departed.
>
> Nonetheless, it seems that the fable of a hidden treasure had captured the imagination of the people at Smuts House and even President Kruger's treasure was linked to Doornkloof.[125]

Most telling of all is Bolsmann's conclusion about Mrs Smuts' sightings: 'Ouma Smuts may indeed have seen an elderly man walking around the house late at night, and also, as she later claimed, "some little grey men" walking past her through the dining room. Ghosts are supposed to be real – *at least to the people who believe in them*, and Ouma Smuts obviously did.'[126]

Of course, there have been numerous other reports of ghostly sightings at Smuts House over the years. But, if one of the most famous witnesses to the supernatural in South African history had fallen for an urban legend, and the question arises of what else her active imagination may have delivered from the realms of fantasy, then all subsequent sightings are in danger of being interpreted in this context. In other words, such a massive expectation has been created that, as in the hauntings of Johannesburg, supernatural

---

[125] Bolsmann, pp33-34.
[126] Bolsmann, p34.

experiences are inevitable – whether real or not.

Now we move from the outskirts of Tshwane to its busy centre. Our next stop is the Pretoria Magistrate's Court where, conveniently, Liela Magnus spent some time to compile an update of its hauntings for *Beeld*:

> Die een ou spook was vet en die ander ou spook in die Pretoriase landdroshof was maer.
>
> En Lawrence Fisher soek steeds sy skoene nadat hy nege jaar gelede voor 'n streekhof doodgeskiet is.
>
> En 'n beheeraanklaer wat een middag in sy kantoor dood is, loop met sy kierie tot by die middelste hysbak en hou die deur oop voordat hy verdwyn.
>
> Dit is van die spoke wat aanklaers, stenograwe en prokureurs in die streekhof op hul tone hou.
>
> Die derde verdieping is klaarblyklik die plek vir 'spookbedrywighede', terwyl die res van die gebou net nou en dan deur dié 'gaste' besoek word.
>
> 'n Stenograaf het vertel van 'n prokureur wat glo dood is voordat hy sy saak kon afhandel. Hy kom steeds die hof besoek. Soms in 'n wit en soms in 'n blou hemp, en wanneer jy hom nader, verdwyn hy.
>
> Hy is dalk ook verantwoordelik vir die talle lêers wat onlangs in die hof sonder rede omgeval het.
>
> Nog 'n stenograaf vertel van die mense wat in die hof gesels as daar niemand is nie.
>
> Die seldeur word ook soms van binne af geruk – sonder dat daar beskuldigdes in die selle is.
>
> 'n Aanklaer het gesê hy het nie naweke, toe die naweekhowe nog gesit het, deur die selle tussen twee streekhowe geloop nie omdat die hysbak ongevraag op en af ry en die deure oopgaan.
>
> Dït is glo die werk van 'n beskuldigde wat in die gebou

dood is.

Die geklingel van voetboeie kan ook glo naweke in die leë gange gehoor word, saam met die gesprekke van getuies wat glo 'dood is terwyl hulle gewag het om te getuig'.

Sommige tolke en stenograwe wéét van die 'ander' besoekers terwyl ander glo daar is geen spokery in die hof nie. Die ergste wat hulle glo al gesien het, was rotte in die gange.[127]

Rats in the corridors, like rats in the roof of any old house, make for excellent supernatural experiences. And court-houses almost demand ghosts, so narrow is the divide between life curtailed and life redeemed within their walls. Add a few overactive imaginations, and you have one of the most haunted buildings in the city.

Theatres, too, enjoy a heightened reputation for the supernatural, as discussed in Chapter 11. Pretoria boasts several haunted theatres, and there is no let-up in the supernatural entertainment they offer. But sometimes the assumed effect is more sinister than merely amusing. Take this report by Yolanda Barnard from the local newspaper, *Noord-Son*:

Is die spoke in die Breytenbach-teater dalk die oorsaak dat twee dramastudente sowat 'n maand gelede tydens 'n fratsongeluk amper met hul lewe moes boet?

'n Maand gelede het 'n tou waaraan 'n stellasie vas-gemaak was geheimsinnig gebreek en die twee het sowat tien meter ver geval.

Nou loop die storie onder die dramastudente van die Tshwane Universiteit van Tegnologie (TUT), dat een van

[127] *Beeld*, 16 Februarie 2005, p3, 'Spoke hou hofmense op hul tone'.

dié teaterspoke, 'n vet monnik, moontlik 'n aandeel het aan die ongeluk.

Volgens die studente en verskeie dosente wat gereeld aan produksies in die Breytenbach-teater deel het, hou die spook blykbaar nie van al die drama nie en kan partykeer bitter boos raak.

'n Oud-dramastudent, Nadia Valvekens, vertel dat die monnik nie daarvan hou as mense hom uitvloek nie en sal dan met die beligting en klank rondfoeter.

'Hy volg ook die studente na die badkamers en sal toilette sommer vir die lekkerte spoel,' het sy gesê.

Die spook hou glo ook daarvan om saam met die mansstudente te piepie en van die studente het gesê dat hulle hom al saam met hulle in die badkamer gesien en dat die toilette sommer vanself spoel.

Maar dan is daar nóg 'n spook in die teater wat al menige dramastudent, klank- en beligtingsman op hol gehad het. Heather is die bekende verpleegsterspook wat al sedert die begin van die vorige eeu in die teater dwaal.

Volgens Stephen van Dyk, dramadosent, het Heather net soos die teater 'n kleurryke geskiedenis en sy en die teater het al die begin en einde van baie drama beleef.

'Die Breytie, soos wat die teater onder studente bekend staan, was eers 'n Duitse skool en gimnasium, maar is later verander in 'n hospitaal. Heather was glo 'n verpleegster wat nou dwalend na haar kinderpasiëntjies soek.

'Sy weer is 'n vredeliewende spook, wat niemand ooit sal kwaad aandoen nie. Ons het al haar energie gevoel, veral as ons besig is met kinderproduksies. Somtyds sal sy ook in die beligtingskamer sit en voor haar uitstaar,' het Stephen vertel.

Sue du Randt, 'n bekende spookghoeroe van Johannesburg glo dat die monnik dalk nie van al die drama hou nie. 'Baie keer beskou spoke 'n plek as hulle tuiste en hou nie van indringers nie.'[128]

Eric Bolsmann devotes an entire chapter of his book to the historic background and the present hauntings of the Breytenbach Theatre. He believes the hauntings date to the staging of Sophocles' play *The Haunted and the Damned*. Most convincing, however, is his interview with Jan de Brick, then maintenance manager of the Breytenbach:

> 'I have heard her speak on two occasions, once at about 8:30 in the morning and the second time, at the end of 1995, late at night. The question was always the same,' says Jan. 'Waar is my kinders¿' ('Where are my children¿') the pleasant voice asks anxiously. I have heard the voice in the cellar below the stage, where bodies were stored before they were carted away during the influenza epidemic early this century. The voice suggests an educated person who could be in her late twenties or early thirties. On both occasions I asked her who she was, but there was no reply and it felt as though she suddenly vanished.'[129]

Other haunted Pretoria city buildings explored by Bolsmann include:

- The Raadzaal, the Assembly Hall presided over by Paul Kruger during the years of the South African Republic, built in 1888 – ghosts on a staircase (no eyewitness accounts)
- Mea Vota, 62 Rissik Street, Sunnyside, built in 1898

[128] *Noord-Son*, 25 March 2005, p7, 'Spoke Lol in Teater'.
[129] Bolsmann, pp24-25.

– haunted since 1979

- The Old Opera House in Pretorius Street, built in 1903 – haunted by actor-producer Leonard Rayne after his death in 1930
- Die Masker, campus theatre of the University of Pretoria in Tindall Road, Hillcrest, part of a school built in 1922 – haunted by a Christian brother nicknamed Histerie by students (Afrikaans for 'hysteria' – no more need be said!)
- The State Theatre, opened in 1981 on the old Market Square site – footsteps and a 'presence' (all denied by management).

And then there is Zwartkoppies Hall to the east of Pretoria, not exactly an urban haunt but now the well-visited Sammy Marks Museum. Built in 1884, it is said to be haunted by John Murray, a Marks employee and companion who died in 1905. The evidence is largely circumstantial – and the circumstance is called marketing – the museum plays host to a well-publicised 'Ghost Evening With Dinner'. John Murray may well be the ghost that never was, as even the documented cases are not convincing, and attempts to encounter the ghost have all come to naught.

14

Off the Beaten Ghost Path

After Cape Town, Johannesburg and Pretoria, the rest of South Africa's cities tend to take a haunted backseat in comparison. But they do stand out in one very distinct respect: the living residents who share these cities with the ghosts have all but adopted them. They regard their ghosts with an affection that is missing, for example, in the politically charged atmosphere of Cape Town's slave haunts and amid the ghosts of family murderers in Johannesburg. In some cases, like the ghosts that haunt hotels, the affection is even returned!

Some cities, of course, are more haunted than others. In Bloemfontein, for example, aside from schools and theatres, where ghosts are obliged to hang out, the only famous haunting occurs at the Raadzaal, the old government building of the Free State Republic, and even that is only the claim of a haunting.

Pietermaritzburg

We have already met the over-friendly ghost of Nottingham Road Hotel and the drinking companion ghost of the Polo Tavern. We return to these haunts now, but venture beyond the hotels into the less welcoming environs of museums, government buildings and sports grounds.

Once more, I am indebted to Amanda Pasqua-Lotto, who herded together the ghosts of her city in the pages of the *Natal Witness*. Some are mere hints of a presence, but at least three of Pietermaritzburg's ghosts seem to enjoy a rather full afterlife, even if the ends of the first two were somewhat tragic:

> Take poor Miranda for instance. She was the beautiful 19-year-old daughter of a high official at Government House. Unfortunately for her, she fell in love with a groom. They eloped but got only as far as the Star and Garter Inn on the road to Durban before they were caught. The groom was immediately dismissed and Miranda confined to the house where she pined away and died. To this day she roams Government House. Where is Government House? It is the old Natal Training College building at the head of Longmarket Street.
>
> ... One of the most famous ghosts in Maritzburg is the mystery lady in white who inhabits Macrorie House. She was supposedly the wife of the head warder of the jail in Burger Street. She was having an affair with someone high up in Government House.
>
> At this time there was reputed to be a tunnel that ran from Government House to Fort Napier built as an escape route for the governor. It was the ideal place for the lovers to meet.
>
> One night things went horribly wrong for them when

the lady's husband followed her. The enraged husband, using his bunch of keys as the weapon, killed them both directly beneath Macrorie House. Marigold Rei, the present curator of the Macrorie House Museum, has never slept a night there. Not because she is afraid of ghosts, but because the beds are so hard!

... Contrary to common belief, not all ghosts rattle around at night. Some are quite happy to be out and about in daylight like the Alexandra Park cricketers. In summer, if you happen to be in Alex Park late on one of those summer afternoons when the thick fog rolls up from the Duzi and shrouds the cricket pavilion, obliterating the bandstand, stand still and listen.

The voice of the umpire echoes round the field proclaiming 'no ball' or 'end of the over'. Other men's voices join his in the shouting of 'run!' or 'stay!', even a gentlemanly 'well played'. The umpire firmly shouts 'six!' And from the grandstand a refined clapping from a single pair of feminine hands can be heard and a lovely voice cries 'Bravo! Well done!'

The mist lifts and there's no one there. The pavilion is empty and the pitch bare. No one knows who the lone lady in the stand is or who the cricketers are. Or why they play this once-a-year match in the mist.[130]

Since then, the gang has accepted a new member. In 2003, a local family received a series of visits from a ghost with something on her mind:

A Napierville family, following instructions from a ghost, have found a letter in their house written more than 40 years ago by an unhappy former resident.

[130] *Natal Witness*, 26 October 2000, 'Things that go bump in the night'.

The letter, written on December 23, 1961, is addressed to the woman's children, and Martha Coetzee of 65 Langenhoven Road said she would like to give it to them. She appealed to whoever lived in the house at that time to come and collect it.

Coetzee said her 15-year-old daughter Irene was the first to see the apparition. She told her mother that a youngish woman clad in white, with blue eyes and long grey or blonde hair was 'visiting her' at night and telling her to look for a letter.

Later, Coetzee's boyfriend Jacques Steyn also saw the apparition reflected in a mirror, and Irene saw her several more times, her mother said.

She said Irene described the ghost in detail: 'She described to me that the lady's feet didn't touch the ground and that she had a white dress on, her face looked like a bright light and her mouth was moving.'

Irene said the first time she saw the apparition she got a fright, but then she thought the woman was singing.

'She always stood at the lounge window looking at the road,' said Irene.

Last Tuesday Coetzee dreamt exactly where the letter was. She woke her daughter and together they went to the kitchen.

'I told her to look in the fireplace in the kitchen and there it was, in the groove in the oven they used to bake bread in the old days.'

The letter was still in a spotless condition. In it the woman had written that she and her husband had been unhappy for a long time and that they didn't mean to hurt their children.

She wrote that it hurt her as much as it hurt them to see their father with another woman, and that she did not have long to live. She asked her children never to forget her and said she would always love them.

The letter ends: 'Goodbye, my angels, your loving Mother.'

On the outside was: 'You will find this when the time is right.'[131]

It's one of those stories that gets the goosebumps a-rippling. It is just so perfect, with such a neat plot and dramatic sequence of events, followed by a truly sentimental climax, it is almost too good to be true. But there we have full names of the players in the drama, the exact address of the home owner, and the very text of the letter found by supernatural means.

One thing is missing, of course: the identity of the ghost. If the purpose of publicising the events was to track down her children, one might have expected greater efforts to identify her. The deeds office is not exactly foreign to the news media! If anything, this story offers firm evidence that investigative journalism and the supernatural do not often go hand in hand.

One of the most amazing Pietermaritzburg ghost stories of all has, alas, only one witness. Fortunately, however, he recounted his experience in great detail to Professor B J F Laubscher, who published it in his 1963 treatise on the supernatural. In the quaint style of the time, the correspondent is identified only as 'Mr Sp.':

> It was a bright sunny day in May 1938 in Pietermaritzburg. My wife and I who were in this city on holiday were walking along one of the main thoroughfares in a residential area, when we entered a narrow street on our way to friends. This was practically a lane; I noticed

[131] *Natal Witness*, 7 January 2003, 'Ghost directs family to letter'.

that a car was parked on one side facing towards me, and that a little group of people were going down this street. We were walking briskly and soon caught up with this group which consisted of a little old woman, dressed all in black, and a few paces behind were four boys from fourteen to fifteen years of age.

I did not notice anything about the woman's costume to date it, but I was surprised to see that the boys were dressed in a style which had been common during the early years of the century, but which had gone out of fashion since the 1914-1918 war. These boys, although barefooted all wore blue peaked caps, blue polo-necked jerseys and rather long shorts. They had a poverty-stricken appearance and the fact that they were shoeless on a cold day confirmed this. I also wondered why they were not at school. As we passed them I was shocked to hear that they were baiting the old woman, passing such rude remarks as 'Go on, you old witch' and 'You are a witch'.

The poor old woman looked dreadfully harassed and as we passed she entered the front gate of one of the houses. The boys stood in a group in front of the gate and continued to call out to her. Now in the ordinary way I would have choked them off as hooligans but while I wanted to do this something within me prevented me. I seemed to realise somehow that I could do nothing to protect the old woman from her tormentors. As we passed I turned to my wife and asked her whether she did not agree that what we had just witnessed was disgraceful.

She looked at me with amazement all over her face and said that she did not know what I was talking about. I started to explain but her amazement grew, and as I turned round to show her the group of boys the street was deserted. It was impossible for boys to have run away in that short time. I am completely at a loss to account for this event. I am not psychic and this is the only experience of this kind that I have ever had.[132]

For extra measure, his wife added her version of what she had seen – or rather not seen. Unfortunately the exact location of the 'ghosts' was not provided, so we cannot tell today whether it is commonly regarded as haunted. More interesting, however, is the fact that an entire gang of ghosts was sighted. Not only that, but both tormentors and tormented manifested themselves. If we assume that the sighting was authentic, then we must also assume that it did not represent an appearance of ghosts per se. Laubscher has a ready explanation:

This type of experience is called retrocognition, which means knowledge acquired of some past event other than by means of the senses. In reality it is knowledge not inferred from any suggestion or sense impression, but seems to come from beyond the range of a person's memory. The famous 'Petit Trianon' case, which was experienced and described by Miss Moberley who was then principal of St Hugh's College, Oxford, and Miss Jourdain the vice-principal, is a typical example. These two ladies in August 1901, when visiting the Petit Trianon at Versailles, saw a scene in the time of Marie Antoinette, which must have happened more than a century before the time these ladies perceived it.[133]

This is the same story referred to on page 136, and which has now evolved from one of the most famous ghost sightings

[132] Laubscher, pp113-114.
[133] Laubscher, p114.

of all time into one of the best-known urban legends of the supernatural. It is the case that turned retrocognition – literally 'backward knowing' – into a standard term in the ghost hunter's vocabulary. The Time-Life book *Hauntings* offers an excellent overview of the Petit Trianon case, as well as of the historic background of retrocognition:

> Reports of such experiences are not new. W H W Sabine, a scholar of the paranormal, suggests that the description of creation in Genesis was based on retrocognition. Cases continue to arise. In 1963, Mrs Colleen Buterbaugh, a secretary at Nebraska Wesleyan University, said that as she entered a room on campus she was struck by a sudden silence, sensed the presence of an unseen man at a desk, and saw a woman in an old-fashioned dress who then 'just faded away'. When she looked out the window, the secretary related, 'there wasn't one modern thing out there. The street ... was not even there. That was when I realized that these people were not in my time, but that I was back in their time.' As she stepped into the hallway, she said, she re-entered the present.[134]

The Versailles case has been analysed in great detail over the years, including an account by Moberley and Jourdain themselves in a 1911 book entitled *An Adventure*. Fifty years later, biographer Philippe Jullian, researching the life of turn of the century poet Robert de Montesquiou for a book published in 1965, made an interesting discovery. He learned that the poet and his friends had often rehearsed historical plays near the Petit Trianon – and Marie Antoinette was one of their favourite characters. What Moberley and Jourdain may have seen, he argued convincingly, may well have been

[134] *Hauntings*, Time-Life Books, 1989, p39.

these amateur theatrics.

Jullian's theory proved influential. Dame Joan Evans, an art historian and long-time friend to whom Miss Moberley and Miss Jourdain willed the copyright of their book, was convinced that Jullian had hit upon the truth, turning a tantalising tale of retrocognition into nothing but an honest misperception. Acting on her conviction, Dame Joan refused to authorise any further English editions of *An Adventure*. But many who have read the account still fervently believe that the women did, indeed, somehow briefly view a long-dead world.[135]

The claim that the scene manifests itself annually on the same date every year (see page 136), does not add any credence to these beliefs, however. Rather, along with the clues discovered by Philippe Jullian, it adds weight to the belief that the Versailles haunting has indeed become an urban legend.

The relationship between these pieces of history and the encounter reported by Professor Laubscher is that most dramatic examples of retrocognition occur off the beaten path. University towns, castle grounds, isolated airfields and quiet suburbs are far more likely to host such sightings than bustling cities or busy highways.

Durban

Durban may be surrounded by haunted battlefields and creepy country hotels, but the city itself is strangely devoid of ghosts. Perhaps it is the holiday atmosphere that pervades the city, perhaps the crass ways of the visitors from inland, perhaps the ongoing redevelopment that has left only a

---

[135] *Hauntings*, Time-Life Books, 1989, p50.

small number of historic buildings standing.

But if the buildings can't be said to carry even the hint of a presence, one of the highways of Durban more than makes up for it. Not that the highway is truly haunted, but the belief of Durban residents in the ghost of this highway is so powerful that the ghost almost comes to life.

The eThekwini municipality, which includes Durban, is so proud of the supposed ghost, it even includes a profile by Sharen Thumboo in a section of its website devoted to 'Famous Durbanites':

> Highway Sheila has become a household name among Durbanites over the past few decades. Legend has it that she is the ghost of a young woman who was raped and killed in Chatsworth, south of Durban. She apparently roams the Higginson Highway where she's often been seen trying to hitch a lift from passing motorists.
>
> The stories about Highway Sheila date back several decades. One account recalls an incident of an old man who gave a lift to a young woman while driving home on a very cold night. After dropping the woman off at a house, the old man realised that he had forgotten to take back the jacket he'd lent her. The next day the man returned to retrieve his jacket, only to be told by a bemused woman that Sheila had died many years ago. The incredulous man was taken to her gravesite where he found his jacket on her tombstone.
>
> The story, which did the rounds for many years, eventually died down. It resurfaced again recently. Durban newspapers have reported three separate incidents where members of the public have allegedly had close encounters with the restless spirit.
>
> A Chatsworth couple reported spotting Highway Sheila while driving home from a nightclub one night.

On another occasion it was reported that the 'spook' had hitched a lift to the north of Durban, with a helpful motorist. She was also apparently spotted at Redcliffe by a woman who was driving her son home from work, and later by another woman driving her family home, just before midnight.

Although the ghostly one is said to be quite harmless, Hindu priests have conducted a special prayer to ensure that Sheila's spirit can rest in peace.[136]

As you know by now, if you've read Chapter 5, this is a classic rendition of the archetypal vanishing hitch-hiker urban legend. This does not stop residents from insisting that they have seen her, even where more mundane explanations would adequately explain their experiences.

Ironically, this is one ghost story that is indeed known to the media as an urban legend, and is identified as such, but still treated as a valid news story. *The Post* carried the next report on its front page, under the most telling of headlines:

Urban legend Sheila is back on the highway

by Yogas Nair

A Chatsworth couple returning home in the early hours of Saturday morning are still reeling from shock after their hair-raising experience with a 'mysterious Indian woman dressed in black' in Havenside Drive, off Bayview.

According to Nirvana Rupnarain, 30, of Moorton, they were on their way to Havenside to drop off a friend at about 2.30am when

[136] eThekwini Online, http://www.durban.gov.za/eThekwini/Community/history/famous_durbanites/gen/highway_sheila

'sheeee' appeared out of the blue.

Rupnarain said they were passing Protea Secondary when they spotted a tall woman, dressed in black pants and shirt, standing in the middle of the road.

'My first thought was that we were going to be hijacked. She was just standing there and looked frightening with her long black hair hanging on her shoulders and her arms outstretched, almost beckoning for us to stop.'

She said that as the car approached the woman, she stepped out into their path of travel and looked straight at them with her 'wild, glowing, almost spooky eyes'.

'By this time I was hysterical and screaming. My husband Niresh swerved the car to avoid her but she jumped out of the way.'

Rupnarain said they stopped the car and looked back but the woman had disappeared.

'My hair was literally standing on end and I was terrified but still wanted to know what we had seen.'

She said they drove back on the same road but there was no sign of 'Sheila'.

'I don't believe in ghosts but I said a prayer and have vowed never again to go out late at night.'

But her husband Niresh said he was convinced it was either a prostitute or a hijacker.

'I was driving at top speed and this woman just jumped to one side to avoid being hit. I have heard stories about Highway Sheila in the past and unless she changed her dress code from white to black, I'm not convinced she's back.'

Legend has it that Highway Sheila was a ghost who roamed on Higginson Highway and was often seen standing in the middle of the road, pleading for motorists to stop, or hitching a lift.

According to one legend, a Chatsworth grandfather fell prey to Highway Sheila when he stopped to give her a lift.

He apparently lent her his jacket and forgot to take it back from her when he dropped her off at home.

The next day, when he went to collect it from the house where he'd dropped her, the woman who was living there told him that the young woman had died many years before.

It seems he went to her graveside to verify the story and found his jacket lying on her tombstone ... but then this could be just an urban legend.[137]

Which, indeed, it is. But reader interest in the story was so high that the local press kept looking for ways to cover it without themselves coming across as gullible, superstitious and hysterical. Sharlene Packree found a way in *The Independent on Saturday*, tackling it from the perspective of whether there is any truth lurking in a legend, rather than whether there is a legend lurking in claims of a true experience:

Is Highway Sheila for real?

Is she a myth or does she really exist?

Recently, a number of people have claimed to have seen ghostly Highway Sheila in the Chatsworth area, which she is said to haunt.

Legend has it she is a restless spirit who is often seen by motorists in the middle of the road signalling them to stop. One tale has it that a man stopped to give Highway Sheila a lift one chilly night and lent her his leather jacket. When he dropped her off, he forgot his jacket.

The next day, when he returned to her home to pick it up, the woman who answered the door told him Sheila had died many years before. Baffled, the man went to her grave and is said to have found his jacket lying on her tombstone.

The *Independent on Saturday* asked Asherville psychic Faye le Roux, who has heard the legend many times, if Highway Sheila really exists.

---

137 *The Post*, 8 December 2004, p1, 'Urban legend Sheila is back on the highway'.

'Sheila's spirit could be roaming around because, when a person dies traumatically – say by murder or suicide – the soul lingers on earth waiting for the time the person was meant to leave the earth,' she said.

Spirits like Highway Sheila were not dangerous and people who encountered her should not be afraid.

'This poor woman has been portrayed so negatively – she is not evil, but is searching for closure on her death,' Le Roux said.[138]

Hold that thought: it is notable that almost any professional proponent of the supernatural, when presented with a ghost legend, will argue for the reality behind it. But first, Sheila made it on to the front page of *The Post* again courtesy of Yogas Nair, yet another journalist who understood that there was an urban legend at work:

Highway Sheila shifts her haunt

The infamous Highway Sheila has hitched a lift to Verulam under disguise. Myth or fact? I don't know, but according to several locals 'the woman in black' has been seen doing her rounds in the area on the KwaZulu-Natal North Coast over the past few days.

A still terrified Jane Rajpaul, 42, of Buffelsdraai Road, Redcliffe, said she encountered Sheila (hereinafter referred to as Redcliffe Sheila for purposes of identification) on two consecutive nights and has since been having sleepless nights.

Said housewife Rajpaul: 'I was returning home just before midnight last Tuesday after fetching my son from work from Gateway (shopping centre) when I spotted a grey car parked outside a shop at the entrance of Redcliffe. The back doors were open and I saw a woman sitting outside the car, in front of the boot.

[138] *The Independent on Saturday*, 18 December 2004, p3, 'Is Highway Sheila for real¿'

'The woman was dressed in a black top and from her waist down there was just a "white glare".

'Her hair was long and wild and it covered her face. I felt a cold shiver run down my spine and I sped off in fear that she might show her face.'

Rajpaul claimed that the following day she saw 'Sheila' again in exactly the same position at the same time, while returning home after fetching her son. She was again terrified.

'I now use an alternative route because I fear seeing her again.'

She said 'Sheila' was the talk of the town and word was that she had come to Verulam after 'hitching a lift with a man from Chatsworth'.

An adamant Rajpaul said she believed in ghosts and was sure 'Sheila' was a reality and not a figment of her imagination.

She said a friend, who had also encountered 'Redcliffe Sheila' at night, described her as having 'wild eyes and huge teeth'.

Another Redcliffe resident, Nirasha Gurwoo, 23, claimed she had also met the 'spooky' lady.

Said Gurwoo: 'She was untidy, had long hair and appears to be naked from her waist down. I saw her last week at about midnight, at the same spot, next to a grey car, while returning home with my family. She was dressed in black with white from the waist down. I, and others in our car, became terribly scared and drove off. I have been unable to sleep since then,' added Gurwoo, who now carries a knife for protection from evil.

Ever since *Post* reported on the claimed sighting of Highway Sheila in Chatsworth two weeks ago, the newspaper has been inundated with calls from people who claim to have also encountered her.[139]

Despite the hilarious nature of some of these claims, and clearly putting the interests of its readers first, *The Post* joined up with the Umgeni Road Temple and the Divine Life Society to host a prayer meeting at the notorious spot

[139] *The Post*, 22 December 2004, p1, 'Highway Sheila shifts her haunt'.

in Havenside Drive, Chatsworth.

As mentioned above, so strong is the compulsion to accept urban legends as reality, it often leads to attempts at physical intervention, like the attempts by university academics to persuade the Uniondale ghost to find rest. Highway Sheila took this to an extreme, however, with no less than a hundred people pitching up to chase her off. Tasnim Langry delved into the perceptions of the exorcists for *The Post*:

Hit the road, ghosts

In an effort to curb the sightings of other-worldly spirits appearing on Durban's roads, an international organisation hosted a purification prayer yesterday.

More than 100 people from various religious denominations arrived outside the Durban City Hall to pray for the 'purification' of Durban's roads yesterday.

The purification related to prayer by means of cleansing the roads of earthbound spirits lingering after tragic accidents and suicides.

The prayer was arranged by an international religious organisation based in Frere Road, Glenwood, called Sukyo Mahikari, which was founded by Kotama Okada in Japan 46 years ago.

They are working in conjunction with the KwaZulu-Natal Department of Transport. Director for Sukyo Mahikari in South Africa, Glen Nettle, said the organisation existed in more than 100 countries.

... Yesterday's prayer focused on violent deaths and earthbound spirits that seem to linger on Durban's roads. Deputy Manager of Road Safety for the KZN Department of Transport, Bonga Mpofu, said his department decided to work with religious groups to promote road safety ... Mpofu said he believed that these cleansing rituals would help rid Durban roads of lurking spirits ... Sukyo members said they realised there was a problem when reports of 'Highway Sheila' and 'Redcliffe Sheila' appeared in *Post* recently.

Okada, who died in 1971, wrote in his books that those who died in war, in battle, by suicide, in accidents and so on, usually become earthbound spirits and cannot leave their immediate vicinity.

'The spirits will remain within a 100m radius of the scene of his or her death until various rituals are conducted to purify their souls,' Okada had said.

He went on to say that the reason there were such things as cursed railway crossings and intersections was because such spirits attached to people passing by and pulled them in, in order to increase their numbers.

... Father Albert Danker of St Anne's Church in Randles Road, Sydenham, said in his 50 years as a priest he did hear of these incidents being reported which were inexplicable occurrences.

'There is no absolute proof that spirits would want to cause harm to anyone though. Although I don't deny the existence of spirits, I do believe that Durban needs to be rid of those who abuse alcohol, drugs and other intoxicants before driving on our roads.'[140]

Grahamstown

Talking of authorities celebrating the ghosts of their areas, South African Tourism is not averse to sharing a ghost story or two to attract the tourists. In the section of its website devoted to Grahamstown, an article by an anonymous author includes one of the town's great ghost stories:

> One of the first local stories I took to as a journalist student was that of the Ghost of Grocott's. *The Grocott's Mail* in Grahamstown is the oldest family newspaper in the country and was established in May 1870. Two rival typesetters – men by the name of Levey and Shaw

[140] *The Post*, 23 March 2005, p3, 'Hit the road, ghosts'.

– worked side by side but in total silence. They hadn't spoken to each other for 15 years and used to constantly monitor each other's work to make sure there was no slacking.

One Saturday night Shaw had a heart attack and died at his typesetting machine. The next day Levey came on shift and sat down at his machine to work on the Monday edition.

'Suddenly I heard footsteps in the building down below. They started from the direction of the door and came on steadily, through the shop and up the stairs. They tramped across the floor to where I was sitting, and stopped right behind me.

'I knew those footsteps. I'd heard them often enough. It was Shaw, standing there at my back and looking over my shoulders to see how much copy I had set ...'[141]

Grahamstown has many a ghost and it was the first place to host the Mystery Ghost Bus Tour. The list of ghost bus stops offers an insight into the extent of the hauntings: the Stone Crescent Motel, the Haunted Ruin in Poltergeist Forest, the Phantoms of the Passes, Fort Selwyn's ley lines, the Battle of Egazini, the Fort Beaufort UFO, haunted buildings in Artificer's Square, the National English Literature Museum, Woodville Orphanage, St Aidan's Tower Ghost, the murder of little Edith Pinnoch in St Aidan's attic, the poltergeist of Whites Road, the British Soldier at the Rhodes University Administration Building, the unmarked graves at the Botanical Gardens.

Not enough supernatural spots? If you don't like those, we have some more for you. During the 2002 Grahamstown

---

[141] South African Tourism, http://www.southafrica.net/index.cfm?sitepageID =13660, 'City of Saints', accessed June 2005.

Festival of the Arts, the itinerary of the ghost bus also included the Ghosts of Kingswood College, the Grey Spectres of Rhodes University's Hostels, in particular Atherston Hostel, Upside the Ghost Nun at St Peter's, the Blue Lady of Renfrew House, the Olde Gaol that hosted Grahamstown's last public execution, St Aidan's Church, and a Poltergeist House.

Talking of tours, many other large towns host ghost trails. They include the Kimberley Ghost Trail organised by the local tourism office, Rose Trehaven's Haunted Walk in Port Elizabeth, the Stellenbosch Haunted Walk and the Prince Albert Ghost Walk.

Kimberley

Kimberley loves its ghosts, and offers the most well developed of all the ghost trails. The idea of creating the trail was first raised in August 1995 and the official launch of the Kimberley Ghost Trail took place on Wednesday, 3 September 1998.

The official website of the Kimberley Ghost Trail offers an enticing glimpse into the old diamond mining town's best-loved ghosts. These are the haunted highlights:

- Kimberley Club: Established in 1881, the most famous members were Cecil John Rhodes, Leander Starr Jameson (who led the Jameson raid into Transvaal), Barney Barnato, Sir Ernest Oppenheimer and his son, Harry Oppenheimer … The Kimberley Club is reputed to be haunted by a certain Mr van Praag.
- Africana Library: Opened in 1887, it boasts a magnificent wrought-iron gallery, spiral staircase, chandeliers and antique furniture. The tour group enters through the

backyard and gathers at the very spot where a former librarian committed suicide by drinking arsenic. The Africana Library is the site of one of the most active ghosts, believed to be that of its first qualified librarian, Bertrand Dyer.

- Rudd House: Owned by C D Rudd, one of the early diamond magnates, this rambling historical house was known as 'The Bungalow'. It has a number of underfloor hatches and an eerie billiard room displaying stuffed heads and horns of a large number of hunted animals. The house is reputed to be haunted by a phenomenon that creates a terrible sound resembling that of plates, cups, glasses and cutlery falling on the ground.
- Kimberley Regiment Drill Hall: The Kimberley Regiment was founded in 1876 and has famous personalities like Cecil John Rhodes and Harry Oppenheimer as former honorary colonels. The Drill Hall is a turn of the century building that reflects the architectural style characteristic of Kimberley. It is home to a very active ghost believed to be that of Sir David Harris.
- McGregor Museum: Built in 1897 by Cecil John Rhodes as a sanatorium, this magnificent building was used as a luxury hotel (the posh Hotel Belgrave) and later as a convent school before being taken over by the McGregor Museum. It is reported that many ghosts haunt the building, the stairs at the entrance and the staff passages.
- Kimberley Golf Club: The cafeteria of the Kimberley Golf Club is regularly visited by a ghost that appears to be a uniformed British soldier. He walks into the cafeteria and then through the cold drink fridge.

Port Elizabeth

At the time of writing, the most recent addition to the list of cities offering Mystery Ghost Bus tours was Port Elizabeth, which represented a homecoming. Its host is in fact based in Port Elizabeth, as Récah Theodosiou reported in the *Daily Dispatch*:

The man who dares call PE a ghost town

Tiptoeing through a cemetery in the dead of night with only moonlight and a torch to light the way could send chills down the spines of the bravest.

Add ghosts tales and the result is many spooky stops on the new Mystery Ghost Tour to be launched by magician Mark Rose-Christie in Port Elizabeth next weekend.

The story of the ghost at St George's Park Preparatory, told in the school's shadowy garden, is another stop likely to wrack the nerves.

So is standing inside the Port Elizabeth St George's Club in the dead of night while listening to the sad story of an 1820 settler ghost. The tour's luxury bus, filled with eerie music, glides through the dark to landmark cemeteries, schools, hospitals and historic houses throughout the city.

... The stories, drawn from police dossiers, library archives, hospital reports, are highlighted by current residents' stories of first-hand encounters.

Mark recounts the experiences of St George's Preparatory School principal Jan Immelman and his wife, Wendy, who live on the premises.

Wendy said she and her family were convinced there is a ghost at the school. Her daughter often heard footsteps going out of her bedroom, onto the landing and down the stairs. 'We always tried to reassure her she was just hearing the old house creak.'

Wendy said she and her husband believed their daughter for the first time when her mother had a similar experience in the same room years later.

The room where the ghost was heard was, incidentally, the room where the original owner, John Daverin, lived in the house, which was called Knockfierna (Fairies on the Hill) when it was built in 1838 ... Then there is the story of a Provincial Hospital nun ghost, who appears in the older wards and comforts patients at night with a glass of water.[142]

Clearly, the ghosts of smaller cities are gentler ghosts for a gentler South Africa. Perhaps they are a subconscious reflection of a need in our society for a more conciliatory approach towards others. The ghosts of small-town South Africa seem to symbolise the country's new era of hope for peace and prosperity. Times of turmoil, however, may well throw up more ghosts.

142 *Daily Dispatch*.

15

Schooled in the Supernatural

I spent eight years of my school life at boarding school, and this may well have shaped my fascination not only with ghost stories but also with their meanings and origins. It was only in researching this book, however, that I came to realise just what a central role the school ghost plays in shaping individuals' experiences of the supernatural in their adult lives. I have been equally astonished to discover that none of the international guides, histories and anthologies of supernatural encounters and stories has made this connection. It is to a South African collection, Margaret Williamson's *Haunted Corners*, that one must turn for the most cogent summary of the role and impact of the school ghost:

> Schools provide a happy hunting ground for ghosts. Boarders have to endure the traditional night-time trial by spook story. And many schoolgirls, even if they don't actually run around screaming, tend to be credulous and

> often terrified when they hear about the school phantom. Some ghosts that lurk in corridors and classrooms are concocted from the requisite dollop of moonshine, with a dash of imagination and elaboration and garnished at every retelling. In other stories there's that tantalising tang of truth.[143]

In other words, school ghosts are exactly like urban legends.

The ghost of Wilberforce

My first school ghost was called Wilberforce. It is a name that, to many, would recall the famed British statesman William Wilberforce, who fought for the abolition of slavery. Or even Samuel Wilberforce, the orator who raged against the theory of evolution. The former is buried in Westminster Abbey, the latter died in a road accident in Surrey. No famous Wilberforce ever came near Bloemfontein. But there he supposedly roamed, in the suburb of Hilton, where the original premises of Brebner High School stood, along with St Peter's Hostel that housed the boys attending the school from out of town. Although the school did not have a specific religious affiliation, besides being entrenched in the Christian National Education of those days, the hostels were owned by the Anglican Church. The church connection meant that it did not take a great leap to bring the afterlife of a missionary into the night life of the hostel.

The very first story one heard after 'lights out' on one's first night in the hostel was the story of Wilberforce. Not how he came to haunt the place, but how terrible things

[143] Williamson, p116.

had happened in the hostel over the years, all of them the doings of Wilberforce, the ghost of a famous missionary. A long scratch in the institutional green paint along one corridor was the physical evidence of his one-time presence. They were nail-marks he had left along the wall during one especially terrifying manifestation – although no one could recall when exactly this had occurred.

And there was one place where Wilberforce particularly liked to hang out: the sickbay. Woe betide the boy who had to spend a night in that isolated part of the hostel. One dark night, the story goes, a boy with a broken leg was lying in the bed in the sickbay, his leg in a plaster cast. At midnight, he woke up to a chill in the room. And there was Wilberforce, coming through the closed door, floating towards him. In sheer terror, the boy leaped out of bed, jumped through the open window, and ran back to his friends in the main dormitories – broken leg and all.

Rose Willis, the chronicler of ghosts of the Karoo, looked into the story of Wilberforce, and was kind enough to provide the following version of the story:

> The spectre of St Peter's kept the hostel boys at old Brebner School in Bloemfontein in line. According to those who 'grew up' in this now-demolished hostel, this phantom of the passages, William Wilberforce, was much more than a ghost, he was a prankster. 'Often, as you hurried down the passage towards the prep room on a dark moonless night, you'd suddenly feel the hair rising on the back of your neck and you'd just know he was there. When stragglers shot into the prep room white-faced and wild-eyed, we'd know he'd touched them, brushed past them or maybe even ruffled their hair,' said one of the old hostel dwellers. 'The old school passages seemed very long and very dark to a small boy and when

you found yourself suddenly sprinkled with water, or tripping over William Wilberforce's invisible foot, it was terrifying. And, he was just like the fellow in the old nursery rhyme which says: "There is a funny little man, quiet as a mouse, who does the mischief that is done, in everybody's house". William Wilberforce moved things, took things and hid things. And, he did this at the most inopportune times – when you needed your pen to write a test, it was gone, when you knew you'd put a book right there, it had vanished.'

When the old school and hostel were demolished William Wilberforce, it seems, wafted away. Or did he? Is he now the spectre of the streets, the grey, misty shape, some claim have caused would-be car thieves to move along![144]

That climax is a perfect conclusion to the Wilberforce story, as it emphasises the extent to which it is an urban legend, adaptable to the times, the teller of the story, and its audience.

The Grey Lady of Eunice

I have to confess I never did like Wilberforce, either as a supposed presence in my high school days, or as a claimed story from those times. After all, the man he was named after had never come near the city! But worse, the ghost never did anything particularly interesting. Not so my favourite Bloemfontein ghost, the Grey Lady, who was most obliging with regard to her lodgings. Again, I am indebted to Rose Willis for sharing the story:

---

144 Rose Willis, personal correspondence, 30 June 2005.

The old Eunice High School, now part of Bloemfontein's Central University of Technology, had a ghost, The Grey Lady. She terrified the girls and even a charge mistress, who claimed to have seen her floating down an upstairs passage at Eirene House after a power failure one night. The fact that this turned out to be the Matron, Mrs Tennant, in full-length grey dressing gown, walking down the dark passage to reset the circuit breaker, didn't still her palpitations. The Grey Lady was a demanding ghost. At times, such as St Valentine's Eve, chocolates were essential to prevent a serious haunting. These had to be left outside dormitory doors and by morning they'd always vanished. Yet, when Eunice moved to its new school about twenty years ago, The Grey Lady was not simply abandoned. The then headmistress, Joan Posthumus, always fondly called Miss Vos, arranged a taxi. It drove to Eirene House, where it stood for a while with its door open. Then the door closed. The taxi drove to the new school in Jock Meiring Street and stopped at the hostel. The back door opened and quietly closed again. Was it the ghost? Was it a hoax? Who knows? Most believe it was The Grey Lady. She's not been seen much in recent years, but some claim to have 'felt' her.[145]

Emily alias Mary

As with St Peter's Hostel, a sickbay also features in one of the most poignant school ghost stories told by Margaret Williamson, but this one has a slightly firmer basis in fact. It is set in Herschel, an Anglican Church school for girls in

[145] Rose Willis, personal correspondence, 28 June 2005.

Claremont in Cape Town. First, there are tragic losses for both the founders of the school that first stood on the spot. Mrs Rose, who lost her son when he engaged in a heroic sea rescue, and her daughter Caroline Harris started Mrs Harris' Seminary for Young Ladies at Herschel. Caroline's husband, Captain Harris, died soon after he had bought the estate of Herschel as a family home. Almost penniless, Caroline and her mother decided to start the school.

All went well until 1848. Then tragedy struck again. One evening during the school holidays, only two little boarders were still at the school. One was Mary Kelsey, a six-year-old whose widowed father lived in Mauritius. After Mrs Harris had put the children to bed that night the rest of the family were sitting reading when 'fearful screams reached our ears,' writes Mrs Rose, 'a scream I can never forget ... Mrs Harris rushed out of the room, and met one of the little girls, Mary, engulfed in flames.'

Mary had called to a maid walking down the passage to bring the candle, and the maid had put it down on the floor. Mary hopped out of bed and jumped over the candle and her nightdress caught alight; within a second she was ablaze. Everything possible was done to save her but Mary died before sunrise.[146]

The story had a slightly happy ending: when Mary's father came from Mauritius to investigate her death, he fell in love with Caroline, the two were married and went to live in Mauritius. And Mary? Her ghost stayed behind to haunt the dormitories of Herschel. But there was a twist, Williamson found:

> ... some of the matric girls of 1992 ... said she was a girl, a teenager, they thought, whose nightdress had caught

[146] Williamson, p117.

alight and who had died in the sickbay. They knew some girls who swore they had heard ghostly footsteps but they weren't sure whether anybody had actually seen the girl ghost, who was always called Emily ...

The story of Mary has taken a few turns since Mrs Rose's day. Then, Herschel was a single-storey building, so the girl cannot have died in the sickbay upstairs. And the ghost can't be a teenager because the little girl who died was only six. And her name wasn't Emily, it was Mary. But the child who died in flames remains the basic source of Herschel's haunting story.[147]

Nun so blind

Williamson also recounts the story behind several generations of ghosts on the site of Nooitgedacht, an old Cape Dutch house on the slopes of Table Mountain, which burned down in the early twentieth century. That put paid to a supposed haunting by 'a murdered mother and father who were heard forever rushing up and down the passages, desperately seeking their baby'. The voorkamer of the house remained, and became part of the new St Cyprian's school for girls when it was built by the Anglican Church in 1919.

With the new school came a new tradition of ghosts.

The school had been started nearly five decades before it took over Nooitgedacht. It was founded in the city of Cape Town in 1871 by Bishop Robert Gray. After 1877 the school was run by the All Saints Sisters, with Sister Theodora as the first headmistress. The school moved twice before settling at Nooitgedacht. By that time Sister Theodora had died and Sister Hildegarde had succeeded her as head. Sister

---

[147] Williamson, pp117-118.

Hildegarde returned to London soon afterwards, in 1924.

And it's these nuns from St Cyprian's earliest days who are the school's favourite ghosts.

A nun dressed in grey is said to wander through St Margaret's dormitory at night. Generations of St Cyprian's boarders have been terrified by the story, if not by the nun, although hers must surely be a kindly presence. Opinion varies as to whether she is Sister Theodora or Sister Hildegarde. Both seem unlikely. Sister Theodora died in 1910, when the school was situated in Annandale Street at the top of Cape Town, and Sister Hildegarde died in London. There were, however, other nuns who continued at St Cyprian's after a lay headmistress was appointed. Could the grey nun be one of these?

> ... A St Cyprian's 'old girl' told me about a visitor who was walking along the school corridor just outside the voorkamer when she encountered a nun who was wearing a piece of extraordinary headgear, a kind of three-cornered hat.
>
> The visitor went into the library and told the librarian what she had seen. Then, on the wall, she saw a portrait of Sister Hildegarde who had died years before. 'That's the nun!' she said. The visitor had never seen the portrait.[148]

Knowing the ghost could not have been that of Sister Hildegarde, the punchline to the story provides powerful evidence that this is yet another urban legend. And so it goes with school ghost after school ghost. The supernatural, when encountered in a school environment, and especially in a boarding school, can readily be ascribed to the super-imagination at work.

---

[148] Williamson, p122.

The Ghost Run

Before returning to South Africa, let's look at three international examples of imagination running riot at schools, the first with tragic consequences.

Two girls die as ghost sparks stampede

JAKARTA – Two teenage Indonesian girls were crushed to death in a stampede at a Muslim boarding school after hearing what they believed was a ghost, local media reported on Tuesday.

About 100 girls at the school in the East Java town of Greskik were reciting the holy Koran late on Sunday when a woman's ghostly wail ripped through their second-storey classroom, the detik.com news portal reported.

'The loud voice was heard from every direction,' one girl was quoted saying.

Panicked and scared by what they believed was a ghost, the girls fled down the stairs and some were trampled.

Dozens were seriously hurt, said detik.com.

Asked about the ghost, local police chief H Gufron said: 'How can we prove something which we can't see?'

The report did not say if any of the girls actually saw a ghost.[149]

This is, of course, a classic and real example of how belief in a ghost, as opposed to an actual encounter with a ghost, can create as much terror and panic as the supposed real thing. That certainly is the case in the next story, from the same part of the world.

[149] Independent Online, 31 July 2001, Reuters, 'Two girls die as ghost sparks stampede'.

Hungry, headless ghosts hunt Malay kids

KUALA LUMPUR – Headless ghosts that reportedly appeared in broad daylight at a high school south of Kuala Lumpur have prompted students to stay away from classes, said a news report on Thursday.

The timing of the ghost sightings coincides with the Hungry Ghost Month celebrated by Taoists, who believe spirits from hell are free to roam the earth during the four weeks.

Students said they saw the headless figure at the Senawang Secondary School library, canteen and toilet, *The Star Daily* reported.

Government authorities condemned ghost reports. 'I have not heard of anyone being injured from being 'mauled' by ghosts, and it is safe for the children to go to school,' said Zakaria Nordin, chairperson of the Negeri Sembilan education committee.

Parents should not exaggerate the situation or spread rumours that cause anxiety among the children, he added.

According to Taoism, children should not be allowed out at night during the Hungry Ghost Month for fear of running into evil spirits.[150]

More like for fear of running into urban legends. The above examples of mass hysteria are not unusual in the annals of the supernatural. But in most cases there is no evidence whatsoever of any substance behind the panic. In fact, many of these cases can be shown to be urban legends run riot, so to speak. Shortly before the above incidents occurred, Tervil Okoko reported one of the most dramatic examples yet on the continent of Africa for the Pan African News Agency:

Ghosts Invade Kenyan Schools

NAIROBI, Kenya – Two secondary schools in Kenya's Central province have been closed and students sent home following alleged invasion

---

[150] Independent Online, 22 August 2002, SAPA-DPA, 'Hungry, headless ghosts hunt Malay kids'.

by ghosts, the *Daily Nation* has reported.

It indicated that ghosts allegedly invaded Gitogo Mixed Secondary School, about 120 miles north west of Nairobi Thursday night and first targeted boys, who were thoroughly beaten by the ghosts, causing a stampede. The school was closed Friday.

The area police chief, Michael Muthike, said the mixed school had been closed indefinitely. He could not, however, confirm or deny whether there were ghosts in the school.

'As for that (the presence of ghosts) I cannot comment authoritatively because I am not well versed in ghost matters,' he said.

Muthike added the ghosts then invaded the girls' dormitory Friday night, showering the roof with a hail of stones. The girls, too, were sent home Saturday.

The school was completely deserted Tuesday when PANA visited the scene as the teachers were also said to have taken off in fear of being attacked.

In Lari division, less than 30 miles from Nairobi, more than 300 students of Kambaa Girls High School were sent home Sunday after an alleged attack by ghosts.

The students claimed that a senior member of the staff was linked to the evil spirits.

Claims of alleged invasion by ghosts are increasingly becoming a daily story in Kenyan schools, and religious leaders have taken a wide berth on the issue.

Already debilitated by an overloaded curriculum, schools in the country are perpetually living in fear of possible ghost attacks.

The most affected are boarding schools located in the countryside.

However, the authorities seem to have been caught unawares by the phenomenon.[151]

Let's pause here for a moment. It is obvious from the

[151] Tervil Okodo, Pan African News Agency, Nairobi, 19 July 2000.

above that the pupils believed they were being attacked by ghosts, but also that fear was more of a motivation for the children's reaction than the obvious presence of ghosts. An isolated incident of stones being thrown on a roof sounds far more like the work of pranksters than poltergeists. The manner of the spreading of the story is also very much in the nature of scare legends than of real threats – be they physical or phantom. But it gets worse:

On 3 July, students from Wang'uru Girls Secondary School, Kirinyaga district (113 miles north-west of Nairobi), stormed the office of the Central Provincial director of education protesting an alleged invasion of their school by ghosts.

The students said they were terrified by the alleged demons, which they claimed appeared in form of white cats and black snakes.

They further claimed the creatures, which run around their dormitories, had been introduced by their head-teacher.

Earlier in June, the member of parliament for Kandara constituency, Stephen Ndicho, asked the education ministry to resolve a long running dispute at Gathigi Primary school in Maragua District (about 35 miles north of Nairobi) where parents withdrew their children alleging the school had been invaded by ghosts.

Angry parents stormed the school and took away their children for fear that they might be attacked by demons. The parents accused the head-teacher, his deputy, and an assistant teacher of being behind the school's invasion by evil spirits.

On 26 May, two pupils collapsed during a cleansing ceremony to rid the same school of an alleged ghost invasion.

The ceremony, conducted by Rev. Fr Elias Murithi of Gachanjoni Parish, ended in disarray when parents of the collapsed pupils attacked the gathering.

The pupils, however, regained consciousness. On 18 May, the *Daily Nation* carried a report saying a primary school in Kitui district, about 200 miles east of Nairobi, closed and more than 400 pupils were sent home following alleged invasion by ghosts.

A school committee official was accused of having sent the ghosts.

Also in Kitui, pupils of Kathuma Primary School were sent home after demons allegedly invaded the school. The demons were said to have been strangling the helpless youngsters. The parents and school committee consequently raised funds to hire a witchdoctor from the port town of Mombasa to exorcise the demons.

On 4 July 1999, Muthetheni Girls School in Machakos, about 60 miles east of Nairobi, closed after girls claimed attacks by unknown forces.

The girls said demons invaded their St Theresa dormitory and allegedly raped and beat them up.[152]

At this stage, it seems, the hysteria had spiralled out of control. Children had started it – and it can't be ruled out that the motive of some was to get out of schoolwork – but had caught their parents up in the madness of it all. And the claims of supernatural activity were as wild as the accusations hurled in all directions. To their credit, the authorities saw through the whole thing, but their context betrayed an old-fashioned attitude that was not going to help them get through to the kids very easily:

> Education officials and the government are currently grappling with the problem. However, they are undecided on whether to employ the services of a ghostbuster or just dismiss the claims as wild imaginations.
>
> 'An ominous subculture has crept into most secondary schools and this has put our nation's future at stake,' Samuel Kariuki, a senior inspector of schools, said.
>
> He added that the other members of this subculture

[152] Tervil Okodo, Pan African News Agency, Nairobi, 19 July 2000.

are the touts (known for their rough mannerisms) and school dropouts.

He claimed that the subculture is increasingly growing into a cult that would idolise rock musicians and confessed drug abusers.

Kenya's education minister, Kalonzo Musyoka, has dismissed claims of ghost invasion as fertile but dangerous imagination.

He blamed everything on the rise in drug use among school-going children, saying all the claims about ghost invasion are fantasy by drugged children.

Kalonzo also attributed the school closures to delinquency among students, saying if the students were more disciplined, there could be less interruptions in their study.

He called on parents to bring up their children well to make them responsible citizens.

However, the minister feels that there are some elements of witchcraft among the people and he cannot rule out the possibility of some wicked people trying to disrupt the normal running of schools ... But while claims of ghost attacks abound, ghostbusters, fetched from as far as Vanga (120 miles south of Mombasa on the Kenyan-Tanzania border) and Tanga in Tanzania, are making a killing as they are called in daily by desperate clients to defray the effects of the demon attacks.[153]

It is a great pity that the phenomenon was not investigated and researched by sociologists and psychologists, not to mention medical professionals, who could have examined victims and given professional corroboration of the truth or

---

[153] http://www.hartford-hwp.com/archives/36/259.html, PANA, 19 July 2000, 'Ghosts Invade Kenyan Schools'.

myth of the ghostly invasions. At the very least, patterns could have been detected that would have revealed the true nature of, or motivation for, the fears or tensions that led to the panic.

Pinky-Pinky – the all-in-one ghost

In South Africa, we have had an equivalent phenomenon. But here it has been given a name and, in a way, flesh. It was called Pinky-Pinky, and it had the schools of Johannesburg and Pretoria in a frenzy in the early 1990s.

The creature is half-male, half-female, half-human, half-animal (with cat-like features on half of its face). It is short and hairy, wears a dress along one side and trousers along the other, can be seen only by children, hangs around in school toilets, and is partial to girls with pink panties – hence 'Pinky-Pinky'.

First reported at 'white' schools in Johannesburg suburbs around September 1993, it suddenly broke out at 'black' schools in Pretoria townships in September 1994 – this in the years before schools were integrated. Pinky-Pinky's arrival in the townships caused a frenzy among newspapers aimed at black readers, and it was seen as an exclusively 'black' experience.

The best explanation I was given at the time, informally, was that it was a manifestation of examination tension, since it appeared as schools started gearing up for end-of-year examinations. It would begin with the senior kids, for whom year-end exams were a big deal, and then quickly filter through to the rest of the school body.

The implications of Pinky-Pinky are explored further in the Epilogue (p313), but it is clear that he/she/it never went away. And it also turned out that he/she/it was hardly a new phenomenon in 1992. Almost ten years after that outbreak, on 14 September 2002, the renowned South African artist Penny Siopis staged an exhibition at the Goodman Gallery in Johannesburg entitled 'Pinky Pinky and Other Xeni'. The online arts magazine Artthrob explained her motivation:

> In these explorations the story of 'Pinky-Pinky' figures strongly, and gives form to a wide variety of quite different experiences. Pinky-Pinky is a mythical character, a local urban legend. This legend is continually invented and reinvented in the telling. Siopis remembers a 'Pinky-Pinky' experience in her own youth, but it is mostly through the stories of her fourteen-year-old son Alexander and his friends that this work has developed. An urban legend that has been dormant for about two generations, Siopis says: '"Pinky-Pinky" is a hybrid creature; half-animal, half-human, half-man, half-woman, half-everything, half-nothing ... It has one dog's paw and one cat's claw. Its skin is a dirty pink, like the "flesh tint" colour of premixed paints and other commodities (like stockings, gloves, underwear ...). Or sometimes it is white. Some say it is actually black, but "so black" that it appears "white". Still others say he is an albino, because s/he wears a hat for protection from the sun. Many think he is a white "tokoloshe" (actually "pink"). All agree "Pinky-Pinky" is scary – especially for teenagers who are terrorised by it at school. Girls can see "Pinky-Pinky" who threatens to rape them if they wear pink underwear. "Pinky-Pinky" is invisible to boys, but they can feel it by slaps on the face and scratches on the cheek.'[154]

---

[154] http://www.artthrob.co.za/02sept/listings_gauteng.html#goodman2, 2 September 2002, 'Penny Siopis at the Goodman'.

Shades of Kenya? If anything, Siopis' explorations revealed just how versatile school ghosts and demons have to be in order to fit into the pigeonholes created for them, and to meet the fearful expectations heaped on them by impressionable children.

A few years later, Siopis elaborated on her vision of Pinky-Pinky in an interview with Maureen Isaacson:

> Siopis explains that Pinky-Pinky is an urban legend, a kind of pink bogeyman, a pink tokoloshe, half-human, half-creature, who lives between the girls' and boys' toilets at school. For Siopis the legend is an allegory for the anxieties of a society in radical transition.
>
> 'The myth seems to mirror unspeakable psychic states of fear and moral panic in a society at large, but as much as Pinky-Pinky is a perpetrator of violence, he or it could also be a victim of and scapegoat for violent actions: a constructed "something" to blame for social problems.'[155]

That is as eloquent a psychological basis as any you will find for both urban legends and ghost stories of the kind that spark hysteria and panic. Of course, the notion of a ghost as the victim of its own hauntings will sit even less comfortably with some than the idea that most ghost stories are urban legends.

Ironically, once we understand the background and the psychology of school ghosts, it becomes easier to get our heads around concepts like poltergeists and their relatives, such as malicious and destructive ghosts. Yes, many of these phenomena cannot be explained. And yes, science has not covered itself in glory when it comes to explaining the

[155] *Sunday Independent*, 24 April 2005, 'Thirty years in the life of an artist unafraid of the truth'.

supernatural, or specific unexplained events. But when they can readily be explained and understood, as with almost every story of a haunted school, it is pure sentimentalism that holds on to childhood beliefs in ghosts wandering the corridors of learning.

16

Knock, Knock. Who's There?

2001 was a landmark year for poltergeists in South Africa. Not only did a classic example of poltergeist activity make it into the press in fine detail, along with a child's drawing of the guilty entity, but the year also saw the first insurance payout for damage attributed to a poltergeist.

Our first tale, Prega Govender's report of the violent haunting of a family home, easily fits into the time-honoured tradition of poltergeist activity across the world, except for the family's wish to remain anonymous – thereby avoiding the added trauma of sightseeing crowds and the media frenzy that tends to accompany crowd frenzy. This report was accompanied by a drawing that the 10-year-old protagonist made of the creature he claimed he saw:

> Bizarre handwritten messages, lights that switch off mysteriously and rolls of toilet paper that fly through the air have become a regular occurrence at a home in KwaDukuza on the KwaZulu-Natal North Coast.

Even heavy pieces of furniture, including an Imbuia cupboard, move from their original positions to the middle of the room.

The family of five, who have been plagued by these paranormal activities over the past four years, say their lives have become a 'living hell'.

They claim that their 19-year-old-son was forced to flee their home last year and live with relatives in Durban after being terrorised by a poltergeist which has been creating havoc.

The family, who do not want to be identified, said the creature had left their son several notes, written on scraps of paper, warning that his life was in danger if he continued living in the house ...

They said the poltergeist hurled missiles, including eggs, tomatoes and potatoes, at visitors and family members and smeared body lotions and household detergents on walls and mirrors ...

The husband, a 40-year-old fitter, said his youngest son, who is 10 and in Grade 5, had been out of school for more than a month after the poltergeist took control over him. The boy this week described the creature as short, hairy and ape-like with sharp nails.

'It makes a noise and sometimes growls. It speaks Hindi, Afrikaans and Zulu,' he said ...

'We have to constantly watch over my youngest son from morning to night. He often rolls around for hours and hours when the poltergeist takes control over him,' he said.

He said his mother, who is 71, often experienced strange phenomena when she lived with them a few years ago.

'She used to ask me why I was pulling her blanket when I was not even in her room. On many occasions, she found her room lights switched off, although she had them on …

'It's eerie. I was even forced to cut off all outgoing telephone calls after my phone was mysteriously used to ring up numbers at random. When I rang up the people listed on the telephone printout, they could not explain how their numbers were reflected on the printout.'

They had sought the aid of sangomas from KwaDukuza, Pinetown, Umkomaas, Umzinto, Isipingo and Eshowe, but no one had been able to help them.

'We have called in two moulanas as well as two Malawian sangomas. They slept at our house that night and, after they left the next day, the evil spirits were back.

'They gave us things to drink and stuff to burn and sprinkle in the house but it has not helped. People say it's in our minds but that's nonsense. All we want is for someone to help us get rid of this problem,' he added.

His wife said the poltergeist spoke to her mother in Zulu when she visited them a week ago.

'When my mother left here last weekend, she complained of being hit on her arms and body by some strange object. She was sore all over …

'The poltergeist tells us, through our son, that he's king and we are wasting our time.

'It often pinches his private parts. When we move around the house, it throws things at us. It also puts sand in our food and throws rice grains on the floor …

'It says that it doesn't like children and often slaps my other son across his face … It becomes very violent when we scream at it. This thing is driving us mad. All we want is some peace and happiness,' she said.

Lorraine de Wet, a Cape Town expert on paranormal activities who has also experienced poltergeist phenomena, said the spirit affecting the family could be that of a person who has died but whose presence is still in the house.

'It's true that a poltergeist could be working through the boy. The writing on the wall and the smearing of detergents and lotions are typical of the behaviour pattern of a poltergeist. One should certainly not scoff at the claims made by the family,' said De Wet.

She said the family needed to consult a medium, who could hold a seance and help them.

'I doubt whether the boy is faking these experiences,' she said.[156]

The family's choice of anonymity ensured that this case, unlike most other poltergeist reports, did not enjoy ongoing media attention. It is therefore not known whether the situation was ever resolved.

The most revealing aspect of the story is the involvement of a 'channel': an individual identified as the focus of the poltergeist's activity, and through whom most of the destructive energies of the poltergeist are directed. In most documented cases of poltergeist activity in Western countries, the channel is a young girl approaching puberty. While the phenomenon had been recognised for a long time, the theory behind it was first put forward in detail by psychic researcher Hereward Carrington in 1951.

Carrington speculated that the onset of puberty in human beings, combined with other unknown factors, might serve to bring on poltergeist activity. In puberty, Carrington wrote, 'an energy seems to be radiated from the body ... It would almost seem as though these energies, instead of

[156] *Sunday Times* (Durban edition), 15 April 2001, 'Family describe four years of "living hell" in house that is spooked'.

taking their normal course … find this curious method of externalisation.'[157]

The most significant difference between poltergeists and ghosts is that the latter tend to come out at night, while the former tend to work the day shift as eagerly as the night shift. That is almost the only thing the experts agree on.

There is sharp disagreement over what a poltergeist actually is and what forces lie behind its appearances. Even the term poltergeist has sparked a lively debate. William G Roll believes the term is a misnomer, 'since it implies an agency apart from any living organism'. In Roll's view, poltergeists are not noisy ghosts at all, but are instead powerful 'person-centred' phenomena, triggered within the minds or psyches of living, human agents. In other words, what appears to be the handiwork of a restless spirit may actually be traced to uncontrolled psychokinetic energy of living people – specifically, to what Roll and his colleague J Gaither Pratt have termed 'recurrent spontaneous psychokinesis', RSPK for short.[158]

There are many problems with these arguments and others that take for granted the relationship between mental stress or sexual energy and poltergeist activity. Not least is the question of what this energy in fact constitutes. While it is usually hauled out as a 'rational explanation' and therefore not 'supernatural', such energy remains in the realm of the unexplained and unproven by conventional scientific experiment. In other words, the phenomenon that is used to explain away the supernatural is itself a supernatural phenomenon.

The other side of the coin is just how standard the behaviour of poltergeists tends to be. Were this the result

[157] *Hauntings*, Time-Life Books, 1989, pp72-73.
[158] *Hauntings*, Time-Life Books, 1989, p55.

of hauntings and occult creatures, one might expect wide variations in the patterns of their behaviour, and certainly not a neat little set of activities that can be labelled and quickly pigeonholed.

A group of self-proclaimed paranormal investigators in Missouri, USA, calling themselves the Gateway Ghost Hunters Association, have come up with just such a neat categorisation. As quoted by a seemingly adversarial body, the Middle Tennessee Skeptics Organisation – 'Giving Common Sense a Chance' – these categories are:

1. Sense Attacks: The focus hears strange noises in the middle of the night or walks into a room and feels temperature changes.
2. Communications: The sense attacks become demonstrative. Marks and symbols appear on the walls, objects and furniture mysteriously move, doors bang, dishes break, etc.
3. Control: The effects of hysteria begin to become apparent. People around the focus become fearful.
4. Trickster Stage: The moving of objects becomes violent, fires can start at random. Mirrors shatter for no apparent reason. Language on the entity grows foul. Poltergeists have been reported to scream, sob, and moan.
5. Danger Level: Physical attack becomes apparent. Biting, scratching, punching, and sexual assaults may be reported.[159]

Most reports that make it into the media are at level 2, with level 4 the next most common. Those that reach level 5 are less commonly reported but, when they are, they are given far more prominence than the others. The astonishing

[159] http://mtskeptics.homestead.com/Poltergeist.html, June 2005.

aspect of these reports is that there is seldom any variation on these themes.

Let's briefly take a stroll down Buckingham Road in the suburb of Mount Croix in Port Elizabeth:

PORT ELIZABETH – A woman whose home in Mount Croix was said to be plagued by poltergeists has been paid out by an insurance company.

Mutual and Federal Insurance has finally agreed to pay a claim by Irene Dames after the intervention of a public loss adjuster.

Mutual and Federal commissioned Noel Herbiet, an independent fire consultant and electrical engineer, to investigate the causes of 70 mysterious fires which plagued the Buckingham Road house.

In his report, Herbiet ruled out arson and said that the Dames family could not be found responsible for the fires and that Dames had passed a lie-detector test 'with excellent results'. Nevertheless, the insurance company refused to act initially.

According to Herbiet's findings, the fires were suspected to be the work of poltergeists.

'The little known but not uncommon phenomenon of poltergeist activity emerged as a possible candidate to explain these spontaneous fires and related disturbances in the house,' Herbiet said.

After reading a newspaper report in July this year about the fires at the house and the slow response by the insurance company to Herbiet's report, public adjuster George Couvaras offered his assistance.

A public adjuster helps people to make insurance claims.

Yesterday, Dames expressed her gratitude to Couvaras for helping her make a successful claim.

Asked how much she had got, a laughing Dames said: 'I am not sure whether I should tell you that. However, I think it was a good settlement.'

She said she had put the house up for sale and did not intend returning to stay there.

In an interview from Johannesburg, Couvaras said he had had a series of discussions with the insurance company's representatives culminating in an agreement.

'It was clear that Mrs Dames was not involved in setting the fires in any way,' he said. [160]

This 2001 report could well be the first official acknowledgement of poltergeist activity in South Africa, and certainly a first for an insurance company in compensating the victim of such activity.

Such severe damage attributed to poltergeists is the exception rather than the rule. But it is these very exceptions that give the existence of poltergeists their supposed credibility. The most famous of all poltergeists – and possibly the most destructive – is the case study to which all purveyors of the paranormal turn when offering proof of the phenomenon. It is the story of Borley Rectory, and that name is almost never mentioned without being followed by the phrase, 'The most haunted house in England'. Many versions of the tale have been told, and one of the best is the objective approach taken in the Time-Life book *Hauntings*, which describes it as 'one of the most well-documented and controversial hauntings of modern times'. It also makes the point that it owes its fame to Harry Price, the most famous ghost hunter of his day, who got wind of peculiar disturbances at Borley Rectory in 1929. The rectory was built in 1863 as a residence for the pastors of the parish church across the road.

The hauntings can also be divided into two phases: pre-Price and post-Price. First, the pre-Price story:

From the beginning the occupants of the house reportedly had been troubled by ghostly apparitions and strange noises: a headless man and a girl in white, the sounds of a phantom

[160] *Daily Dispatch*, 18 September 2001, 'Claim paid for "haunted" PE home'.

coach outside the house and the sounds of dragging footsteps and loud rapping inside. And there was the spectral figure of a nun, drifting restlessly through the house and garden, her head bent in sorrow.

Local tradition had a romantic explanation for these emanations. It was said that a monastery once stood on the site with a convent close by, and that in the thirteenth century a monk and a beautiful young novice were apprehended while trying to elope. The monk was hanged and the would-be nun bricked up alive in the walls of her convent.[161]

And then came Price.

At about the time Price took an interest in Borley, the rectory began to receive the energetic attentions of a poltergeist. Bells rang, lights flashed and objects flew through the air. Then, in 1930, the Reverend Lionel Foyster and his attractive, much younger wife Marianne moved in, and the supernatural manifestations become more frequent. And a new phenomenon – one that Harry Price considered unique in the annals of the paranormal – manifested itself: mysterious written messages began to appear on the walls and on scraps of paper scattered through the house.

In 1937 – after the rectory had been abandoned as a pastoral residence – Price rented the house for a year and installed a rotating team of observers to document the manifestations. He later wrote two popular books devoted to the case, lectured extensively on it, and discussed it on the radio.

Price's relentless publicising earned Borley both notoriety and the attention of rival researchers, who would squabble for decades over the mysterious events.

Detractors alleged that the entire case was suspect, scoff-

---

[161] *Hauntings*, Time-Life Books, 1989, p65.

ing at Price's investigatory techniques and in particular his crew of amateur observers recruited by newspaper advertisements. Critics even suggested that Price fraudulently orchestrated at least some of the alleged poltergeist phenomena. But in the end the controversial ghost hunter did turn up evidence of a long-ago tragedy that seemed to explain the hauntings – and convinced many that the manifestations were genuine.

The breakthrough came via the planchette, a pencil-equipped device that moves – supposedly guided by spirits – across a board under a sitter's hand, spelling out messages. One alleged spirit, identified as Marie Lairre, related that she had been a nun in seventeenth-century France but had left her order to marry Henry Waldegrave, a member of the wealthy family whose manor house once stood on the site of Borley Rectory. There, her husband later strangled her and hid her remains in the cellar.

In March of 1938, five months after Marie Lairre's introduction, another spirit allegedly promised that the rectory would burn that night and that proof of the nun's murder would be found in the ruins. Borley Rectory did not burn that night. But eleven months later a new owner, Captain W H Gregson, was unpacking books one evening when an oil lamp in the hall somehow overturned and started a fire. The blaze quickly spread, and Borley Rectory was gutted, at last giving Price an opportunity to seek buried physical proof for his explanation of the haunting.

For a variety of reasons, he did not ask Gregson's permission to excavate until 1943. 'Look under the brick floor in the cellar,' one of the spirit messages had implored, and after only a day of digging, Price's crew unearthed a few fragile bones that proved to be the remains of a young woman – evidence, Price concluded, that there was indeed some truth to the story of the murdered nun.

A Christian burial for the bones appeared to provide the ghost of Borley Rectory with the rest that it had long sought. No further haunting activity was reported in the ruined building which was finally demolished in 1944.[162]

Such a rich source of ghostly legends does not quietly go away, however. John and Anne Spencer report numerous subsequent hauntings over the ensuing decades, in the rectory cottage, the grounds of the rectory, and the Borley church across the road.[163] About.com reported in 2001: 'Anomalous images continue to appear on photos taken on the rectory grounds up to the present day. Just last July, 2000, a photo taken behind the church shows a mysterious orb.'[164]

However, these are more common or garden – or church – ghosts, which obey the rules of everyday claims and clichés. Moreover, Harry Price was thoroughly discredited in the years that followed the publication of his sensational books on Borley Rectory. An entry for Borley Rectory in the Wikipedia, the online encyclopedia compiled by volunteers, concludes: After Harry Price's death in 1948, a team of researchers would investigate his claims about Borley and report that the case was 'a house of cards built by Harry Price out of a little more than a pack of lies'. Interestingly, reports of paranormal activity still come out of the area, including the Borley Church.[165]

Paul G Adams, creator of the official Harry Price website, which is 'Dedicated to the life & work of Harry Price' is frank in his summary of the issue:

---

[162] *Hauntings*, Time-Life Books, 1989, pp66-68.

[163] Spencer J & A, pp25-30.

[164] http://paranormal.about.com/library/weekly/aa100900a.htm, accessed June 2005.

[165] http://en.wikipedia.org/wiki/Borley_Rectory, accessed June 2005.

> Harry Price's involvement in the Borley Rectory case was the subject of much debate and examination in the years following his death and this continues unabated to the present time. In the mid 1950s, when the events at Borley were critically examined and reported on by the Society for Psychical Research, Price was accused of being a manipulative liar who falsified evidence in order to use the Borley story to his own advantage, namely for money and fame. Despite attempts at various times over the years to challenge these accusations or provide support for his actions, Price's motives in the cause of psychical research at Borley are still looked at by some modern observers as those of someone fattening up a financial and publicity-laden cash cow rather than those of a sincere seeker of the truth investigating a genuine and long established case of haunting.[166]

Harry Price is just one in a string of psychic researchers whose evidence has subsequently been rejected both by their peers in the world of supernatural research and critics who focus on debunking the supernatural. While a hoax in itself does not damage the cause of the believers, a hoax that is easily exposed but still supported by believers tends to undermine all other claims made by those supporters.

Such was the case in the 1980s when the world's attention focused on a 14-year-old girl, Tina Resch, who was, to say the least, somewhat troubled: 'In 1984, Tina was 14 years old and living in Columbus, Ohio,' records the *Skeptic's Dictionary*. 'Newspaper reports testified to her chaotic household where telephones would fly, lamps would swing and fall, all accompanied by loud noises.'[167]

---

[166] http://www.harryprice.co.uk/Borley/PriceatBorley/priceatborley-intro.htm, accessed June 2005.

[167] http://skepdic.com/poltergeist.html, June 2005.

William Roll, quoted earlier as offering a 'scientific' explanation for poltergeists, was at the centre of the case and of efforts to give it credence. He eventually co-wrote a book entitled *Unleashed: Of Poltergeists and Murder, the Curious Story of Tina Resch*[168] in which he elaborated on the science behind Resch's abilities and poltergeist activity in general.

The case casts a bright spotlight on the irresponsibility often displayed by the media in chasing a story for the sake of sensational headlines rather than exploring the facts. From my own years working as a journalist at both junior and senior level for various reputable publications, I am well aware of the role played by the personal agendas of writers and editors in conveniently 'leaving out' elements that would reveal events in an entirely different light.

So it was with Tina Resch. James Randi, the famous and infamous debunker of psychic claims, succeeded in exposing the hoax behind the 'Columbus Poltergeist', even though he wasn't allowed access to the protagonist. He summed up the story in his electronic newsletter, the James Randi Hotline:

> Tina Boyer (formerly Tina Resch) was the famous 'Columbus Poltergeist' who in 1984 made news all over the world when telephones and other objects began flying all over her home, apparently by spirit forces. I was invited, by the local press and by her parents, to visit there and look into the phenomena. When I arrived I was turned away at the door at the insistence of William Roll, a parapsychologist who specializes in 'poltergeist' claims, who had by then taken up residence at the Resch home and was having a grand time hyperbolizing the events for

[168] Roll, W & Storey, V, Paraview Pocket Books, 2004.

the media.

My investigation thus turned to the photographic evidence, and I managed – by scurrilous means – to obtain copies of ALL the photos in the 36-exposure frame taken by Fred Shannon, the photographer from the *Columbus Dispatch*. In the other frames was the solution to the 'mystery.' The *Dispatch* had chosen to ignore the evidence that was right before them, and were daily running highly positive accounts that supported Tina's wild supernatural claims.

She was discredited, though not to Roll, who continued to study her and to encourage the hoax she had perpetrated.

On October 25th, 1994, Tina pleaded guilty in the beating death of her 3-year-old daughter.

We must ask ourselves whether a proper investigation of the claims that brought this woman to world attention, which might have deprived her of the celebrity status that she attained through support by the 'scientists' and media who encouraged her, might have brought her to a healthier state of mind and adult lifestyle. Such an unhappy child, discovering that she could so easily manipulate the media, becomes an adult who is not in a position to make appropriate choices in life.

Tina had already started her life in an awkward manner, being an adopted child who wanted desperately to find her birth parents, was being blocked in that attempt, and then pulled the 'poltergeist' stunt to attract the media's help. She used them – and the parapsychologists – but to no avail. To be perfectly fair, the media and the parapsychologists used her, too. She went from one disastrous situation to the other, finally to two marriages and two divorces, then to the present sentence of life in prison for torturing and killing her own daughter.

> The blame for this tragedy must be shared by those who promoted the media circus that Tina began.[169]

Randi later added: 'A video camera from a visiting TV crew that was inadvertently left running, recorded Tina cheating by surreptitiously pulling over a lamp while unobserved. The other occurrences were shown to be inventions of the press or highly exaggerated descriptions of quite explainable events.'[170]

Roll insists in his book that she only cheated some of the time, and points to controlled experiments with Resch in his laboratory as proof of his claims. Fortunately for Roll, reviews of his book in the year following its release show just how short the public memory is: they tend to be uniformly glowing in their treatment of his version of the case.

The Eastern Poltergeist

The poltergeist is probably the one supernatural entity that appears to behave in the same way around the world, although the South African experience tends to be subtly different in many cases. While poltergeists have been blamed for similar events from the UK to the USA to the former USSR, the Western poltergeist tends to behave spontaneously – and is more often than not blamed on the psychic energies of young girls or boys entering puberty. The earliest reported poltergeist incidents in South Africa, on the other hand, seem to have stronger links with Eastern traditions, and tend to be blamed on an adult channel or

---

[169] http://www.mindspring.com/~anson/randi-hotline/1994/0032.html, 26 October 1994.
[170] http://skepdic.com/poltergeist.html, accessed June 2005.

medium.

The celebrated Afrikaans poet and author I D du Plessis captured the essence of the South African experience in this regard in a slim but fascinating volume published in the 1960s.[171] His scrupulous attention to detail and sources imbues the book with historic relevance aside, of course, from offering a superb source of first-person accounts. But first, an incident he translated from an old Afrikaans newspaper, the 21 July 1937 edition of *Die Burger*:

> The peaceful life of a family in Lansdowne has been cruelly disturbed since last Thursday by some mysterious agency. Creepy stories of a spook which appears in various forms, such as a shadow gliding through the house and disappearing as noiselessly as it comes, were told to a representative of *Die Burger* by several excited members of the family.
>
> After the disappearance of the shadow, they declared, the crockery and bedding, for which the spook seemed to have a decided preference, had to bear the brunt. Even while being watched the thing carried out its work of destruction. It seemed to prefer a particular bedroom, but in the kitchen and dining room the furniture also suffered. The cushions of the couch would fly through the air and land on the floor in the middle of the room. Crockery in the kitchen was shattered in the presence of members of the family.
>
> At first the children were suspected. When Mrs Smuts, who lives in the house with her daughter-in-law and grandchildren, came home last Thursday and found the bedclothes on the floor, the children were blamed and in spite of strong denials all received a good hiding.

[171] *Poltergeists of the South*, 1966.

But when these pranks were repeated that same evening while there was no one in the room concerned, the family became suspicious and the help of a neighbour, Mrs Olive Strong, was called in. She went to the 'spook-room' and put everything to rights, but had hardly shut the door when she heard a noise in the room. On returning she saw pillowslips being pulled off the pillows and the sheets and blankets being thrown in a heap in the corner of the room. Again she tidied up everything, made sure there was nobody in the room and took up her position outside the window. The curtains moved apart and she could see the blankets rise in the air, to be hurled through the room.

The family was thoroughly mystified and went into the dining room to discuss the affair. While they were doing this the cushions on the couch rose one by one and floated through the air. In a rage Mrs Strong threw them back again. Apparently the spook got angry too, for soon afterwards the falling of crockery in the kitchen was heard. They rushed into it just in time to see a teapot rise and fall to pieces on the floor.

The news soon spread, and on Saturday evening a large company gathered in the dining room, intent on catching the spook. While they sat there the room was turned upside down again. This time the sideboard was pushed into the middle of the room.

That same night the daughter of Mrs Smuts who was sitting near the kitchen door suddenly shrieked that she had seen a 'spook'. She declared she had seen a white woman moving about a foot above the ground and that her head was invisible. Other members of the family affirmed that they plainly 'felt' the presence in the room. It became cold in the room and a strong current of air was felt to blow through it, apparently from nowhere.

> The real Jonah of the household is EW, a Cape Flats farmer who has recently come to live with the family, being a good friend. Since his arrival everything has gone wrong. The actual 'spooking' takes place in his room, and all the crockery which has so far been broken belonged to him.
>
> With nervous gestures he gave a description of his first night in the house: In the middle of the night the room suddenly became very stuffy. At the window he saw a woman who had threatened him before. There was no one near him and he felt no hands upon him; but suddenly he was held fast and collapsed.
>
> Since that night he has neither been able to eat nor sleep. The woman he saw at the window is (according to him) the cause of it all.
>
> During the last few evenings the house has attracted more visitors than even the Lansdowne cinema. Mrs Smuts declares it is impossible to keep the house tidy with so many people coming and going ... The present tenants do not intend staying longer than the end of the month.[172]

There is something comical about a homeowner being worried about how neat the house is when her household is beset by apparently demonic forces. However, this case became even more celebrated as a result of the report and new disturbances. 'A large crowd gathered round the house and even entered it,' *Die Burger* reported the next day. 'At one time it was so crowded that there was no room in which to move ... A number of constables came along and emptied the house of these inquisitive people ...'

The telling clue that this is a poltergeist of a different

172 Du Plessis, 1966, pp17-20.

colour is the presence of the menacing woman, suggesting black magic rather than emotional or ghostly energy. This is a common thread in South African poltergeist reports which tends to be absent in Western reports.

Du Plessis gives an account of similar poltergeist activity occurring at the beginning of the twentieth century on a farm near Schweizer-Reneke, described first hand by the brother-in-law of the farm owner. The informant prefers to remain anonymous. After a few odd experiences that had drawn inquisitive onlookers, the farmer had asked him to come and stay with him on the farm.

Among the phenomena they witnessed were: bread-pans and flatirons on the side of the oven moving into the oven; an ash-bucket moving out of the kitchen of its own volition, floating round the house and emptying itself on to the ash-heap; a table with drawers being moved around an outside room; a jug of water being thrown over the two men; blankets being pulled off their beds while they lay in them; a heavy force pushing down on both of them as they shared a bed; on one occasion a blow that left a scar on the farmer's chin; and ... stones thrown at them from every angle, described with the telling comment, 'It was very strange to see how slowly the stones came.'

They gave the phenomenon a name: Old Griet, 'for it was held that an old Coloured woman had brewed all the trouble'. However, the 'ghost' itself was seen in the shape of a man: 'It walked bent forward, taking long strides, and had big feet. It wore a large broadrimmed hat and its clothes were in rags.'[173]

The falling stones are a particular form of poltergeist activity occasionally mentioned in Western reports, but almost always in the South African equivalents. According

---

[173] Du Plessis, 1966, pp39-43.

to *Hauntings*,

> Hurling stones is an archetypal poltergeist activity that has been reported around the globe from as early as the 9th century: in AD 858, the little German town of Bingen-on-the-Rhine was pelted with rocks; in 1592, stones weighing as much as 20 pounds apiece rained down on an Oxfordshire, England, farm; in 1903, a Dutchman living in Sumatra was awakened in the middle of the night by rocks falling on him from his bedroom ceiling.[174]

Du Plessis records this last case in great detail, along with its relevance to South Africa: 'the flying objects moved in the same way in Cape Town's Malay Quarter and in Sumatra. The Sumatran case gives an indication of the link between local and general poltergeist phenomena.'[175]

Du Plessis then quotes from a 1919 Italian work which examines no less than 46 cases of stone-throwing. One of these was the Sumatran case, reported by a Mr Grottendieck from Dordrecht on 27 January 1906, and carried in the journal of the Society for Psychical Research. Grottendieck was sleeping in a hut in Palembang after a journey of exploration through the jungle when he was awakened by stones falling from the ceiling. He woke his helping hands and they made a thorough search of the surrounding area. At one point he fired shots into the air, and the events unfolded in a classic sequence.

The first result of this was that the stones fell thicker than ever in the hut; but now it appeared that the servant who had been drowsy before this, became wide awake; and

---

[174] *Hauntings*, Time-Life Books, 1989, p59.
[175] Du Plessis, 1966, p60.

as soon as he saw the stones falling, he screamed that they came from the Evil One and fled into the jungle. As soon as he disappeared the stones ceased to fall.

Grottendieck was questioned by the chairman of the Society for Psychical Research, and told him, among other things:

> The stones fell remarkably slowly, so that even if one accepts deception, there yet remains something mysterious to explain. It seemed as if while making a parabolic descent, they slowed up and then crashed to the ground with great force.
>
> Even the noise they made was abnormal for it was too loud in relation to their slow descent.
>
> I have said that my servant seemed drowsy until the moment the gunshots had thoroughly awakened him. His drowsiness was noticeable in his abnormal, unusually slow movements. He got up, then went to the jungle and returned from it, all in an unusually slow manner. The weariness of his behaviour made the same impression on me as the slow manner in which the stones fell.[176]

Even before this, stone-throwing poltergeists had been active at the Cape. Eric Rosenthal referred to such phenomena as 'Malay tricks', and Du Plessis as 'Malay magic'. Rosenthal recalls one particularly striking example in the typically patronising style of the time:

> Mr Adolf Braun, printer and stationer, living at the top of Long Street and editing a local German paper called *Das Kapland*, was the victim of 'Malay tricks' at his home at 48 Orange Street, Cape Town, about 1886.

[176] Du Plessis, 1966, pp62-63.

Stones, pebbles and lumps of coal came hurtling on to the tiled roof, on to the veranda, across the outhouses, on to the water tank. When the clatter on the brickwork became an infuriating fusillade, when several windows were shattered into tinkling splinters, and when finally the Coloured servant girl reached the pantry with blue bruises on her swarthy skin, Herr Braun went to search for the hooligans responsible. He walked up the roadway, strolled to the college nearby, whose peaceful white buildings might possibly have been used as a shelter by the roughs, and found – nobody.

For several weeks the stones continued to fall with tantalising irregularity. They came from nowhere. The Editor waited at a corner from which the whole property could be overlooked. 'Bang!' down crashed a lump of prime Cyfergat coal and hit poor Kantas. 'Whiz!' – the German could note the course of a wooden block evidently shied from somewhere in space.

... (the police) had long known about the haunted building and were keen to help. Detectives and constables created a cordon round the villa and watched. The phantom stone-thrower aimed so well that several policemen received black eyes. In brilliant sunshine, the missiles kept dropping.

... At last Kantas gave notice. 'The ghost disliked me,' she said and packed her tin trunk. When the girl walked through the front door, the house was at peace again.[177]

Rosenthal offers no theory, but this case ties in perfectly with the time-honoured Western phenomena of a young girl as the 'channel' for poltergeist activity.

Du Plessis, on the other hand, comes to a firm conclusion

[177] Rosenthal, pp41-42.

after examining all the evidence and case studies such as these.

'In the light of the data given above, the cause of poltergeist disturbances seems to lie within ourselves,' he writes. 'The explanations offered represent the views of a number of investigators who feel convinced that, as ever, science stands on the brink of new discoveries; that "magic" does indeed take place, but that it is becoming possible to explain it in terms of natural forces.'

However, after briefly summarising the sceptical attitudes of most scientists and the argument of believers that, because the subconscious is involved, the ordinary methods of science cannot be applied, he acknowledges that 'science can hardly be expected to make this concession'.[178]

Elsewhere, Du Plessis makes his most telling comment of all, and one that sums up every argument in Chapter 10 of this book:

> Whatever the nature of magic may be, *belief* in it makes it an active and powerful force for good and evil; and interest in the subject is as real as when the unknown and the supernatural were regarded as one, and pioneers of science were burnt at the stake for their search after knowledge.[179]

However, we haven't made much progress in understanding poltergeists in the last century or so. In 1896 Frank Podmore, one of the authors of the *Census of Hallucinations* published by England's Society for Psychical Research (SPR), published an article claiming that poltergeists simply did not exist.

Having examined eleven poltergeist cases randomly

[178] Du Plessis, 1966, pp79-80.
[179] Du Plessis, 1966, p64.

selected from the records of the SPR, Podmore advanced a 'naughty little girl' theory, suggesting that trickery accounted for nearly all poltergeist manifestations, and that the girls and boys who so often seemed to be the victims of poltergeists were actually pulling the strings.[180]

It's certainly a thread that runs through many of the tales in this chapter. And as in the first story in this chapter, our final story even contains the unintended hint that this, indeed, is the key to many a stone-throwing poltergeist. In every other respect, it is similar to numerous reports that emanate from the townships and villages of South Africa. The story was reported in *People* in 1993:

Lydia Phelo cowered in terror, screaming, as stones mysteriously came to life and began to batter the inside walls of her home. This eerie attack by an invisible hand broke ornaments, crockery and a lantern.

The attack began at noon one day late last year. Lydia jumped up, startled, as her paraffin lamp exploded in a shower of glass.

'I screamed in terror,' said the 55-year-old widow of Boekenhouthoek village in KwaNdebele. 'I saw a stone move through the air on its own. There was no one who could have thrown it: there was nobody in the house except me and my nine-year-old granddaughter Bathabile.

'The stone came out of thin air. That's when I knew that something unnatural was taking place.'

George Masango, who lives next door, heard Lydia screaming for help.

'I ran round to her front door and a big stone came out of nowhere and hit me on the head. Nobody threw it – it just came from the air. I knew that supernatural forces were at

---

[180] *Hauntings*, Time-Life Books, 1989, p72.

work. Other stones hit me on the body, and I began to run. I ran out of the gate but I was half a kilometre down the road before the stoning stopped.'

During the next two days an atmosphere of panic spread through the village. Despite the neighbours' prayers and a visit by a priest, the stonings continued.

At 13h00 the following Saturday the Reverend Sam Malaza of the St John's Apostolic Mission Church visited the scene, and found a group of women praying outside the shack, too afraid to enter it.

The Reverend Malaza said a prayer before he attempted to join Lydia and Bathabile inside the simple, tin-walled home. But as he crossed the threshold, he was struck painfully by two stones, on the side of the face and the thigh.

The Reverend Malaza said a prayer, then left. Lydia Phelo decided to consult a witchdoctor in Hammanskraal, but her taxi never reached its destination. Stones began to fly inside the vehicle and the panic-stricken driver dumped his passengers at the Kwaggafontein Police Station, where Detective Sergeant Saul Komane was on duty.

'I managed to calm Mrs Phelo down and get the story out of her,' Sergeant Komane told *People*. 'Suddenly two golfball-sized stones flew to the floor between me and the girl. I looked up, startled. Bathabile was standing with her hands at her sides. As I watched, another two stones of the same size came flying toward me, one over each of her shoulders. I asked Lydia, "Do these stones come from your granddaughter?"

'Mrs Phelo began to get agitated, saying that Bathabile was not a witch. As she spoke, another stone flew over the child's shoulder!

'I decided to keep Bathabile at the police station for her own protection, while her grandmother went to stay with a friend nearby.

'The child told me an amazing story of witchcraft.

'The child alleges that a certain woman cast a spell on her because she hated Lydia.

'The woman made her dig a hole about one metre from the front door of the shack and put stones in it before filling it up again.

'Then she rubbed a greasy ointment on her arms and hung a bag full of stones behind Bathabile's back. Soon after that, stones began to fly.'

Major Aaron Mahlangu of the KwaNdebele Police decided to investigate the case personally.

'Although there are no laws against witchcraft,'[181] he told *People*, 'we keep a very close eye on such cases, because they can lead to violence.

'I went to their village with Bathabile and Mrs Phelo. When we reached the house, the child was calm and smiling but the grandmother was visibly shaking.

'Then a handful of small stones were projected from behind Bathabile. There were several police officers and a newspaper reporter present; all of us witnessed the same phenomenon.

'What I saw convinced me that this is a genuine supernatural occurrence.

'Now the girl is with her mother, a long way from here. My men are keeping a friendly eye on the people concerned, to make sure that none of them come to harm.'

The flying stones of KwaNdebele remain one of the most well-documented, yet one of the most baffling supernatural manifestations in recent history.[182]

---

[181] This is incorrect. The Suppression of Witchcraft Act of 1957 legislates against both witchcraft and accusing any individual of being a witch.

[182] *People*, 22 March 1993, p2, 'The mystery of the flying stones'.

Not so baffling, of course, after examining the preceding theories and case studies. But it would be foolish to say that all poltergeist activity can be reduced to the mischief of children or adults. It would require a massive global conspiracy of mischievous children, all playing their tricks in a coordinated manner that would fit into a suitable category of supernatural phenomena. The consistency between many of the reports, even given the peculiarities of the South African variations, does not support the 'naughty little girl' theory – despite blatant examples of 'naughty little girls' at play.

The South African poltergeist is at the same time unique and yet consistent with the poltergeists of the world. It is an expression both of South Africa's unique identity and its powerful cultural connections to the rest of the world. That, of course, is no more proof of the reality of the supernatural than the claims of the many children who have faked their own poltergeists over the centuries.

17

Who You Gonna Call?

If anything has made a mockery of the art of ghost-busting, it is the 1984 movie of almost the same name, *Ghost Busters*.

Thanks to that box office hit, no one may now legally call themselves ghostbusters as an official name, since the term has been trademarked by moviemakers Columbia Pictures. Unofficially, however, many teams and individuals style themselves in this way, although most are merely 'ghost hunters' who aim to make contact with ghosts rather than remove them. That would be anathema to the three movie professors of parapsychology played by Bill Murray, Dan Aykroyd and Harold Ramis. They employed a wide range of scientific and science fictional devices to detect, capture and eradicate ghosts.

Serious ghost hunters tended to be bemused or even offended, believing that the movie had made a mockery of their pursuits. In reality, however, self-styled ghostbusters are not very far removed from the absurdities of the movie version. First, however, we must make a distinction between ghost hunters and ghostbusters. The former see their pursuit as a scholarly one, aimed at verification of supernatural claims and reports, rather than involving action against the ghosts themselves. The latter play precisely the same role as the movie trio – merely using different techniques and different tools.

South Africa's most famous ghostbuster, by virtue of the ready access he offered the media, was Dr Ismail Ballim of Laudium near Pretoria, who claimed a doctoral degree in ghostology. When contacted by Eric Bolsmann for an interview for *Ghosts of Pretoria*, Ballim said: 'I am the world's greatest ghostologist and I look forward to meeting with you.'[183]

In an interview with *The Star* a few years earlier, he had claimed to be South Africa's only 'ghostologist'. The journalist who interviewed him, Mpine Qakisa, seemed to be on to something when she commented that 'Dr Ballim's activities read like a script straight from a horror movie'. He told *The Star* that he had studied the subject under the late Professor Mohamed Moegsien at the International Spiritual Institute in Johannesburg in 1948. In 1992, a the age of 86, he was himself teaching the subject at the Guidance Psychical Institute for Scientific Research in Edenvale, Germiston.

Ballim claimed his own personal typology of ghosts (see pp292-3 for more generally accepted categorisations), which included:

- Lantern Ghost: appears with a lantern, walks up to you, disappears and reappears further on.
- Beheaded Ghost: holds head under its arm to scare the living daylights out of you.
- Hand-type Ghost: attempts to slash you with what

[183] Bolsmann, p107.

appear to be sharpened fingernails.

- Twin-type Ghosts: bumps into you and chokes you; bangs doors and shifts crockery neatly from the table. Can be in two places at once.
- Blueprint Ghost (the nastiest of all): smacks you and leaves five-finger marks in a blueprint on faces and arms.[184]

As comical as this may sound, Dr Ballim crowned his interview with a bizarre claim: a few years ago he used his skills as a ghostologist to bring to an end the reign of terror of Vera, the vanishing hitch-hiker of Meadowlands, Soweto. Considering that Vera is a bona fide urban legend, the product of imagination and rumour, and is still claimed to be roaming Meadowlands, that is a rather extraordinary claim.

To his credit, Dr Ballim stressed that there are many medical conditions that lead people to think they are seeing ghosts, when in fact they are just hallucinating. However, in both the interview with *The Star* and his meeting with Eric Bolsmann, he claimed that he was able to capture ghosts in bottles, using a mysterious powder from Egypt and a yellow flower to lure the ghost into the bottle. This he achieves with a rather unusual technique. He will telepathically tell the ghost to get the flower out of the bottle. Once the ghost is in the bottle, it is corked. Then he will throw the bottle into the sea. 'Ghosts can't travel through water,' he says.[185]

In his meeting with Bolsmann, Dr Ballim made numerous claims and told numerous stories of haunting and poltergeist cases that he had resolved. However, the Vera claim is a strong indication of the veracity – or lack thereof – behind

---

184 *The Star*, 5 October 1992, p7, 'Ghosts can be very friendly, says Ismail'.
185 *The Star*, 5 October 1992, p7, 'Ghosts can be very friendly, says Ismail'.

many of these claims.

In the mid-1990s, I came across the story of a somewhat more modest ghostbuster: a man who had no public profile whatsoever in his lifetime, but had been sought out by people who tended to be referred to him by someone who knew someone who had heard of someone who had consulted this low-key figure. Such seekers of respite from ghostly troubles eventually found their way to Oom Joubert, who often went into action with his son, Martiens.

I often heard stories about Oom Joubert in Mpumalanga, and finally arranged to meet his son, Martiens 'Sop' Joubert in 1996. At this stage Martiens himself was already an old man with only memories of his father. On his impoverished farm in Mpumalanga, where the main business was a scrapyard, he was living testimony to the fact that ghostbusting is not a profession pursued for the sake of amassing fortunes. Martiens passed away a few years later, and little remains of his father's ghostbusting legacy, aside from a tape-recorded interview with Martiens.

In the interview, he talked mostly about poltergeist activity and the 'Islamic' sorcery known in Afrikaans as *goëlery*. He said his father had travelled to Dar es Salaam to study the art of getting rid of ghosts, but his main tool had been his own powers of persuasion: he would talk to ghosts and persuade them to depart from the earthly realm.

'He used to *gesels* (talk) with the ghosts where it was haunted and where spirits were wandering about,' said Joubert of his father. 'He didn't try to catch them – he just talked. When we were dealing with *toordery* (sorcery or black magic), those we caught. You couldn't see anything; it was *goëlery*. You would be sitting in a house and pots and things would fall down. Crockery broke and that kind of thing.'[186]

[186] Personal interview, Martiens Joubert, 11 February 1996.

One of the ghosts that he claims his father had got rid of had usually been seen as a light moving across the farm Paardeplaats close to Belfast. Joubert attributed it to a *dwaalgees* (wandering ghost) from the days of the Boer War that was also seen appearing and disappearing on the nearby railway tracks. He said his father had removed a few pound notes from under the railway tracks and had 'talked to that thing', and it disappeared for good. However, I had been told by the wife of the then owner of that farm, Jean Lack, that she had still seen the light in later years, after Oom Joubert's death. Her son Hilton, too, reported seeing the light.

Martiens Joubert knew it well: 'It was a small light that would suddenly become very big, and you would walk to it and the closer you got, the smaller it got again. And if you came very close, it disappeared. It used to move all along the railway line.'

He said he had also personally seen the ghost of a woman walking on the tracks at nearby Sunbury station, walking past the station and over a rise, and then suddenly appearing again where she had started off. The ghost appeared every day, in broad daylight. Oom Joubert went to speak to it, but she didn't want to talk, and 'just carried on walking'.

He claimed that he and his father had followed the ghost of a black man a number of times until it led them to the spot where his body was buried. The police were called to exhume the body, and it turned out that the man had been buried by his own family after he had died, but the family had moved away and his grave had been forgotten. Supposedly, the ghost could not rest until its body had been moved to a decent burial ground.

Just when one began to imagine that Oom Joubert and his son would have mistaken even their own reflections for ghosts, he told a story that made it clear he was open to natural explanations for supposed hauntings:

> We used to live down at Suikerboskop. In those days we used to go by foot – we didn't have vehicles. At Grootspruit near the rapids on the Stofberg road is a spot where two streams come together, and in that spot a man from Swartkoppies shot himself dead with a double-barrelled shotgun he had borrowed. They said this man now haunts the area, walking around at night. Many people talked about it and got excited about it. Many saw him. Many people ran their legs off from fear.
>
> One man visiting Belfast decided to go have a look on his bicycle. It was a bright Monday, and as he came down to the stream, he saw there is that white thing. A snow-white thing between the two streams. A big white thing. He was a little scared, but he put down his bicycle and walked closer. As he got to the spot, it disappeared. It turned out it was the moon, as it rose, shining on the water. It looked just like someone standing there. That was the ghost![187]

By now he had warmed up to the topic and his memories, that he at first had said were very vague, came flooding back. Bizarrely, a radio was playing in the background, filling the room with the strains of the hit song, 'If God was one of us'. Martiens now admitted he himself had also been a ghost hunter, and described the technique he had learned from his father for dealing with sorcery.

> My father also used *toordery* (sorcery), but never to do harm. He did it to catch villains and evildoers. He had his muti, steel pins and things. *Goëlery* you caught with a piece of wire and muti. If you used that and if there was a monkey or a cat messing about in the house and you then

[187] Personal interview, Martiens Joubert, 11 February 1996.

hit it with a sjambok you would hear somebody scream outside and the next day you would hear of someone who had been beaten up. They usually work their *goëlery* through someone they can control. It's a long process. I saw it, and I used to do it as well.[188]

At this he points to two old puncture marks on his arm.

That's where a black man, who used to *goël* in Lydenburg, bit me. There was a farmer there who had two pretty daughters. And every week one of his cattle died. He would arrive at the kraal and there was a dead animal lying there. It was *goëlery*. Then they started to hear something on the roof. Every night it would walk around on the roof and run an iron bar along the zinc sheets on the roof. They looked on the roof but found nothing, because it was hiding in the ceiling. So they asked my father to come down there. I went there with him. I was still young, 15 or 16.

We arrived and looked around, and my father set his traps. We went into their house and had a meal. I was with the two girls and with one of them I went to sit on a cane *bankie* (small bench) and we began to *vry* (make out).

There was a small room on the other side of the room and that's where they believed the ghost was, in the ceiling. And then I heard a zinc sheet on the roof move on the other side of the house. I took a Coleman lamp and I jumped up and ran to that room and leaped up the ladder. Just as I climbed up into the ceiling, she (the girl) came in with a light and I just saw a black shape moving in the ceiling and I dived on to this man and grabbed him round the neck. He clawed a deep hole in

[188] Personal interview, Martiens Joubert, 11 February 1996.

the wooden beam right next to my head. And he and I fell right through the ceiling and fell on to an army bed and flattened it. I was on top of him and then he was on top of me, fighting like crazy.

Then my late father and the owner of the house came in and we caught him, and tied him up. He had just four teeth, the canines, and they were as sharp as knives. When we first tried to tie him up, he caught the rope with his teeth and just cut through it. He had been living in the ceiling and using *goëlery* against the farmer. He used to lie on top of the wall in the ceiling, so that you couldn't see him. He made himself invisible.

The next morning my arm was pitch black where he had bitten me. I went to the hospital and got an injection. The police took the man away and I don't know what happened to him.[189]

By now it was raining hard. Martiens continued to describe numerous experiences with the supernatural and the bizarre over the years, from having conversations with a skull that his father had kept, to witnessing a 17-year-old boy with cuts all over his body, apparently inflicted by invisible creatures. While he had not witnessed the cutting, he saw the boy bleeding from his many wounds. Eventually, he said, the boy died of blood loss.

My late father and I travelled around a lot. We helped a lot of people. He studied black magic from Indians in Dar es Salaam and came back here, and I learned from him. I learned ordinary magic tricks as well. An Indian is a deadly *slamaaier* (an old Afrikaans term for the Cape Muslims known in English as Malays, the term being

[189] Personal interview, Martiens Joubert, 11 February 1996.

> a corruption of Islam and Malay). There were many Afrikaners doing this kind of thing, fortune telling, *goëlery*.
>
> Since I got so sick I lost contact with them and I gave it all up. They took my medicines and things and burnt them. I have died twice through not being able to be revived after operations.[190]

He described how, just five years before, he had been at death's door, the doctors had given up hope. A sangoma removed a snake from his body, and he recovered.

He told the story matter of factly, as if it were a perfectly normal occurrence. Most of the stories he told had that air of ordinariness, with no attempt to dramatise them – except, ironically, when he told of a natural event that had been mistaken for the supernatural.

He claimed that there were still many Afrikaners in Mpumalanga who practise sorcery, turning themselves into animals, causing frogs to come out of people's mouths, and other equally bizarre tricks.

Of course, for a ghostbuster, none of this is bizarre. It became clear both in the reported claims made by other ghostbusters and those I heard from Martiens Joubert that ghost busters have their own vocabulary. It is a vocabulary that takes the extraordinary and the unnatural and makes them seem ordinary and natural. It seems designed to cast the supernatural in the light of common knowledge and accepted practice rather than arcane secrets and taboo activity.

It is not even a case of attempting to paint the supernatural with a veneer of credibility or respectability. Rather, it is an attempt to reduce it to the mundane, where it sounds not

---

[190] Personal interview, Martiens Joubert, 11 February 1996.

only as if magical events of evil origin could really have happened, but also that taking on the manifestations of evil is part of the natural order of things.

In other words, it's a dirty job, but someone has to do it.

18

Reason to Believe

There are many perspectives for understanding a belief in the supernatural. There are even many perspectives for understanding these various perspectives. Two broad categories that crop up constantly are the scientific, or rational, and the spiritual, or supernatural. But even within each of these, there are huge grey areas between what can be regarded as scientific and what can be taken as supernatural.

Take, for example, the various explanations for poltergeists. Even those 'scientists' who insist on a 'rational' explanation, and then invoke the likes of subconscious sexual energy projected by girls reaching puberty, are in fact offering a paranormal explanation, as they assume a force that has not been demonstrated by conventional science.

Those who accept a supernatural explanation for paranormal events often attempt to dress it in the clothes of science.

The latter tend to dismiss any argument that undermines

the case for supernatural phenomena. Ironically, it is in the interests of such believers to set the most rigid conditions for accepting supernatural events as authentic. The less strict they are, the more likely their claims are to be subjected to ridicule.

The science of the supernatural

My favourite example of someone who attempts just this rigid kind of approach is Emily Peach, who starts her 'practical and down-to-earth' guide to investigating ghostly events with a chapter entitled 'Facts'. The opening lines read:

> The evidence for the existence of ghosts is vast and incontrovertible. Thousands upon thousands of recorded experiences, taken from sources all over the world and ranging over many centuries, all agree to their existence, their nature and their behaviour. To seriously question their empirical reality, one would have to postulate an enormous and ongoing conspiracy spanning countless centuries and involving such diverse individuals as Plato, Pliny, Cicero and Mrs S. from Croydon.[191]

The message is clear: you have no right to reject belief in ghosts. Peach herself points out, wildly inaccurately for a supposed scientist, that 'still nobody believes in ghosts'. The reality is that a high proportion of any given population shares a belief in ghosts, but that doesn't mean they are ready to believe specific ghost stories. It is for this very reason – to give ghosts an aura of credibility – that

[191] Peach, p11.

investigators of the paranormal have reached consensus on a classification of ghosts, and general agreement on what is contained and defined within each of these classifications. Says Peach:

> Apparitions may be divided into five basic categories or types which serve to define, quite precisely and according to possible causes and/or behavioural characteristics, exactly what kind of apparition is involved. These categories are:
>
> 1. Apparitions of the living
> 2. Experimental cases
> 3. Crisis apparitions
> 4. Apparitions of the dead, or post-mortem apparitions
> 5. Ghosts, or apparitions which habitually haunt certain places
>
> It is important to appreciate that these divisions are in no way artificial, and exist, in fact, solely because the collation and examination of some thousands of representative cases showed that apparitions fell of themselves into such categories.[192]

Note the definitiveness of it all, the rigid categorisation, and ... the insistence that it is based on scientific observation – although it does not invoke that exact term.

John and Anne Spencer, who begin their oft-quoted encyclopedia with a guide for ghost hunters, are a little more circumspect. They suggest that 'ghosts are not one single phenomenon but rather form a range of phenomena, each requiring differing approaches' and that 'knowledge of what you are expecting to see can actually influence the vigil; in the worst case it is possible for the ghost hunter to

[192] Peach, p17.

"hallucinate" precisely what he was expecting to see'. They offer their own classification of ghost phenomena according to 'type':

- 'Recordings' of past events
- 'Anniversary' ghosts
- Presences
- Poltergeists
- Interactive ghosts
- Time slips
- Ghosts of the living (including Doubles, Doppelgängers, Vardogers and Bi-locations)
- Ghosts of the dying (or crisis apparitions)
- Haunted objects
- Phantom hitch-hikers
- Frauds[193]

Less scientific than Emily Peach, perhaps, but certainly more practical, inclusive and open to scepticism. Incidentally, Peach offers an additional breakdown of how paranormal experiences must be evaluated, from the perspective of the observer:

- Spontaneous or experimental – was the observer caught off-guard, or was there an intention to spot the apparition?
- Veridical or delusive – based on the category of ghost, does the experience correspond with external facts, ie can it be verified according to the criteria of that category of haunting? Dreams and hallucinations are delusive;
- Subjective or telepathic, a result of one's own internal thought processes, or intrusion from outside.[194]

It may sound scientific, but it really only uses highly formal

[193] Spencer, J & A, pp3-15.
[194] Peach, p19.

language to describe normal differentiations in describing personal experience.

John and Anne Spencer's more 'popular' typology may not have the ring of science, but then it also does not claim the kind of certainty – within the bounds of the unknown – that undermines the credibility of many cheerleaders for the supernatural.

The sceptic's guide to the supernatural

Just as the supernatural has its typology, so does the debunking thereof. The 'open source' online encyclopedia Wikipedia, which is compiled and updated by its reader community at a surprisingly high level of quality, offers sceptics a clear system for questioning the supernatural.

Sceptics may seek to explain ghost sightings by applying the principle of Occam's razor, which argues that the simplest adequate explanation for any event or phenomenon is the most likely explanation.

This usually means that, first, the *sincerity and motive of the person reporting* will be called into question. For example, the lingering of ghosts is typically associated with seeking justice or revenge. Ascribing such motives and powers to dead people could be interpreted as a scare tactic directed at those who might consider murdering someone.

Second, the *possibility of a hoax or con* will be considered, with the reporting person assumed to be the victim. It seems possible that sometimes the telling of ghost stories might have been a way for secluded communities to scare off intruders. It is also conceivable that, when unsuccessful, this tactic could have been backed up by more or less elaborate set-ups with members of that community playing ghosts.

Third, *explanations grounded in knowledge about human physiology* will be proffered. For instance, the appearance of ghosts is often associated with a chilling sensation and pale, semi-transparent figures. But a natural animal response to fear is hair-raising, which can be mistaken for chill.

The *visual aspects of ghost reports could also be accounted for by human physiology*: the peripheral vision is very sensitive in detecting motion, but does not contain much colour or provide focused shapes; therefore, a moving curtain or other movement outside the focused view can create a strong illusion of an eerie figure.

The *natural occurrence of infrasound*, which are sounds below human auditory frequencies (below 20 hertz), could possibly explain the notions of feeling a 'presence' in the room, or unexplained feelings of anxiety or dread, as certain infrasonic frequencies are known to have these effects on the body.

Psychological factors are also often cited as natural explanations for ghost sightings: susceptible people might be prone to exaggerated interpretations of perceptions when visiting a site of unpleasant historical events. Certain images – such as paintings and movies – might 'programme' a person to automatically associate a certain structure or area as haunted because of what they have seen in the movies.[195]

The legendary nineteenth-century critic, journalist and man of letters Ambrose Bierce, author of many supernatural tales, came up with one of the most practical arguments of all against the existence of ghosts as we imagine we know them today:

There is one insuperable obstacle to a belief in ghosts. A

[195] http://en.wikipedia.org/wiki/Ghosts, Wikipedia, 'Ghost', accessed June 2005.

ghost never comes naked: he appears either in a winding-sheet or 'in his habit as he lived'. To believe in him, then, is to believe that not only have the dead the power to make themselves visible after there is nothing left of them, but that the same power inheres in textile fabrics. Supposing the products of the loom to have this ability, what object would they have in exercising it? And why does not the apparition of a suit of clothes sometimes walk abroad without a ghost in it? These be riddles of significance. They reach away down and get a convulsive grip on the very tap-root of this flourishing faith.[196]

For the ultimate combination of science and belief, there are few better examples than the incorrigible Albert Einstein, who combined a healthy irreverence with a simple expression of faith. He was once asked whether he believed in ghosts. He said he had never seen one, and added, 'When twelve other persons have witnessed the same phenomenon at the same time, then I might believe.'[197]

Who believes?

'The belief that people's spirits might manifest themselves after death was extremely ancient,' says history lecturer Johann Sommerville of the Department of History at the University of Wisconsin. 'Many much-respected classical authors (including Suetonius, Cicero, Livy and Plutarch) recorded the appearance of ghosts.'[198] In his history course on 'Society and Ideas in Shakespeare's England', he includes

[196] Bierce, A, *The Devil's Dictionary*, 1911, Republished by Project Gutenberg.
[197] Chaplin, C, *My Autobiography*, New York: Simon and Schuster, 1964, p321.
[198] http://history.wisc.edu/sommerville/367/367-102.htm, accessed July 2005.

lectures entitled 'Ghosts, Fairies and Omens and Magic and Medicine' – and makes it clear that early scientists often accepted supernatural causes for the otherwise unexplained.

Today, ghosts and science tend not to go together, but several scientific polls have tested the extent of beliefs in ghosts. Between 21 and 27 January 2003, Harris Interactive conducted an online poll within the United States among a nationwide cross section of 2 201 adults. It found that 51 per cent of the American public believe in ghosts (see Emily Peach's comment, p291), including 58 per cent of women, and 65 per cent of those aged 25 to 29 but only 27 per cent of those aged 65 and over. Age was one of two major factors in belief – or lack of belief – in ghosts. Aside from growing older, the other factor that will make an American's belief in ghosts fade is education. Of Americans with high school education or less, 56 per cent believed in ghosts. This fell to 52 per cent with some college education, 43 per cent for college graduates, and 36 per cent for postgraduates. In short, the older and better educated you are, the less likely you are to be haunted.

One of the most interesting findings of all was that there was an almost equal belief in ghosts among Christians and non-Christians – 50 per cent versus 48 per cent.[199] This indicates that a belief in a specific religion does not predispose to a belief in ghosts.

The South African magazine *De Kat* carried out a similar poll among Afrikaans-speaking South Africans some years ago. The sample was much smaller – 220 respondents – and the poll was limited to the Gauteng, Free State and

[199] http://www.harrisinteractive.com/harris_poll/index.asp?PID=359, 26 February 2003, The Harris Poll #11, 'The Religious and Other Beliefs of Americans 2003'.

Western Cape provinces. The magazine warned that, while all possible steps were taken to avoid errors and statistical imbalances, they did not pretend that the poll conformed to strict scientific requirements. Even so, some of the results were surprising.

Afrikaners turned out to be less superstitious about ghosts than is generally assumed, and certainly less so than Americans as a whole: only 37 per cent said they believed in ghosts. Surprisingly, belief in a god was at almost exactly the same level. On several religious and supernatural issues, it was possible to make a direct comparison with the subsequent US poll:

	Afrikaners	*Americans*
Belief in a god	88%	90%
Belief in heaven/hereafter	90%	82%
Belief in existence of hell	79%	69%
Belief in reincarnation	6%	27%
Belief in ghosts	37%	51%

Other questions asked by *De Kat* included belief in angels (88 per cent yes), belief in the existence of fairies, elves and gnomes (6 per cent yes), belief in existence of vampires and werewolves (11 per cent yes), and belief in witches (31 per cent yes).[200]

Another American polling organisation, Gallup, has been researching the topic for decades. Two years before the Harris poll, they released their ten-yearly study on Americans' beliefs in paranormal phenomena. Their findings on belief in haunting were startling:

[200] *De Kat*, May 1997, pp52-55, 'Wat glo Afrikaanse mense¿'

> What exactly do Americans believe in when it comes to the paranormal, the occult, and 'out-of-this-world' experiences? The Gallup Poll recently updated its audit of Americans' beliefs in a variety of these types of phenomena. The results suggest a significant increase in belief in a number of these experiences over the past decade, including in particular such Halloween-related issues as haunted houses, ghosts and witches. Only one of the experiences tested has seen a drop in belief since 1990: devil possession. Overall, half or more of Americans believe in two of the issues: psychic or spiritual healing, and extrasensory perception (ESP), and a third or more believe in such things as haunted houses, possession by the devil, ghosts, telepathy, extraterrestrial beings having visited earth, and clairvoyance.[201]

By 2005, the proportion of believers had gone up even further: the most recent Gallup survey showed that 'just about three in four Americans hold some paranormal belief – in at least one of the following: extrasensory perception (ESP), haunted houses, ghosts, mental telepathy, clairvoyance, astrology, communicating with the dead, witches, reincarnation, and channelling. There are no significant differences in belief by age, gender, education, or region of the country'.[202]

Sadly, no equivalent research has been conducted among other South African population and cultural groups. However, a great deal can be assumed from the religious standpoints of the major religions and denominations, since South Africa is regarded as a highly god-fearing nation.

---

[201] The Gallup Organisation, http://www.gallup.com/poll/content/login.aspx?ci=4483, 8 June 2001, 'Americans' Belief in Psychic and Paranormal Phenomena Is Up Over Last Decade'.

[202] The Gallup Organisation, http://www.gallup.com/poll/content/login.aspx?ci=16915, 16 June 2005, 'Three in Four Americans Believe in Paranormal'.

True believers

It is not surprising that most religions that believe in immortality of the soul also accept a belief in ghosts, since the former suggests the latter, and the latter to some extent depends on the former. Certainly, all the major religions have a view on ghosts, but some are unofficial and some are clouded in semantics.

The first analysis of the link between religion and ghosts was made by nineteenth-century philosopher Herbert Spencer, who proposed his 'Ghost-Theory' for the origin of religion. The theory was neatly summarised by none other than human rights icon Martin Luther King in a university course paper:

> The awe inspired by the dead, and the fear created by the dead who had passed beyond the control of the living, constitute the two factors which arouse a new sense in man; and as far back as we can go men are seen offering sacrifices to the spirits of their ancestors. This Herbert Spencer believed to be the most primitive form of religion. Animism is not original but derivative, being a generalized form of the belief in the spirits of dead ancestors reappearing as ghosts and choosing certain objects in Nature as their dwelling-place.[203]

King quickly dismissed this theory, arguing that 'the weakness of Spencer's theory is at the point of oversimplicity. The deification of ancestors is far too narrow a basis on which to rear the structure of religion.' Most commentators agree with this stance, and demand something more than fear of the dead as an explanation for either religion or ghosts.

---

[203] King, M L, *The Origin of Religion in the Race*, 9 February 1951.

Each religion and denomination, in fact, has a very different approach to the concept of ghosts, which in itself undermines Spencer's proposition.[204]

Judaism

The world's oldest spiritual guide, the Torah, comprising the first five books of the Bible, acknowledges the existence of ghosts by prohibiting attempts to consult them. But that is not, of course, where the story begins or ends.

'The Torah's reticence on the afterlife is understandable within its historical context,' argues Rabbi Elie Kaplan Spitz in a provocative book on the afterlife. 'The Torah rejected the class-based, afterlife-obsessed Egyptian culture in which the Israelites suffered.'[205]

Nevertheless, several examples of possession by spirits and attempts to call up spirits occur in the Torah and the books that were added to it to make up the Tanach, or Old Testament. The most famous of all, and the one used most commonly to prove biblical endorsement of a belief in ghosts, is the story carried in 1 Samuel 28:7-25, of King Saul going in secret to the Witch of En-Dor to ask her to summon up the spirit of the deceased prophet Samuel:

> 11 Then said the woman, Whom shall I bring up unto thee? And he said, Bring me up Samuel.
> 12 And when the woman saw Samuel, she cried with a loud voice: and the woman spake to Saul, saying, Why hast thou deceived me? for thou art Saul.

---

[204] Religious leaders of four of the major faiths and denominations in South Africa, namely Catholic, Anglican, Muslim, and Jewish leaders were asked to provide input for the following section. Where none was forthcoming, other sources were used.

[205] Spitz, p34.

13 And the king said unto her, Be not afraid: for what sawest thou? And the woman said unto Saul, I saw gods ascending out of the earth.
14 And he said unto her, What form is he of? And she said, An old man cometh up; and he is covered with a mantle. And Saul perceived that it was Samuel, and he stooped with his face to the ground, and bowed himself.
15 And Samuel said to Saul, Why hast thou disquieted me, to bring me up? And Saul answered, I am sore distressed; for the Philistines make war against me, and God is departed from me, and answereth me no more, neither by prophets, nor by dreams: therefore I have called thee, that thou mayest make known unto me what I shall do.
16 Then said Samuel, Wherefore then dost thou ask of me, seeing the LORD is departed from thee, and is become thine enemy?
17 And the LORD hath done to him, as he spake by me: for the LORD hath rent the kingdom out of thine hand, and given it to thy neighbour, even to David:
18 Because thou obeyedst not the voice of the LORD, nor executedst his fierce wrath upon Amalek, therefore hath the LORD done this thing unto thee this day.
19 Moreover the LORD will also deliver Israel with thee into the hand of the Philistines: and to morrow shalt thou and thy sons be with me: the LORD also shall deliver the host of Israel into the hand of the Philistines.[206]

As suspect as the King James version of the Bible may be, there is no mistaking what is being represented here. Some arguments have it that it was in fact not the ghost of Samuel that appeared, but rather a demon or angel pretending to be Samuel, and decreeing the punishment that Saul would

[206] The Bible, King James version.

receive for daring to violate a Divine injunction.

However, there is a strong body of thought that the prohibition did not relate to communicating with the dead per se. Says Rabbi Spitz: 'The biblical command is linked to idolatry, with a detailed description of the bones, incense and the knocking of arms that were used as tools to accompany incantations in consulting the dead.'[207]

He points out that the principal rabbinical leaders of Western Europe during the period between the seventh and twelfth centuries gave permission to consult the dead on the basis that the prohibition related only to consulting with the body of the dead, 'while calling on the spirit was permitted because the spirit was not "dead"'.[208]

In the sixteenth century, when Jewish law was codified into an accessible system for the common man in a work called the Shulchan Aruch, its author was explicit in this permission: 'To cause a sick person to swear that he will return after his death to tell him [his living friend] what he will ask him is permitted.' This ruling by Joseph Karo was not out of keeping with the tenor of the times, either. In his diary, Karo recorded matter of factly that 'for most of his adult life he had been visited by a *maggid*, a spiritual being, who helped guide him in many aspects of life, including the composition of the Jewish law code, the Shulchan Aruch.'[209] Spitz gives several other examples of important Jewish leaders who gave credence to the existence of ghosts and spirits of the dead.

The issue has been explored by Rabbi Gershon Winkler in two renowned books on paranormal events from a Jewish perspective, *Dybbuk* and *The Golem of Prague*. Today he runs the Walking Stick Foundation, set up to explore the links

---

[207] Spitz, p105.
[208] Spitz, p106.
[209] Spitz, p107.

between Judaism and the natural world, and attempts to blend the concept of shamanism with the role of a rabbi.

In an interview with Jeff Belanger, author of *The World's Most Haunted Places*, Winkler explained how stories of the dybbuk go back to ancient scriptures:

> In the Old Testament of the Bible, in the Book of Samuel (18:10), a bad spirit is briefly described as attaching itself to King Saul, the first king elected chieftain of the ancient tribes of Israel: 'And it came to pass on the morrow, that the evil spirit from God came upon Saul ...' Later in the Bible, in the Book of Kings, the prophet Elijah is possessed by the spirit of a dead man who is trying to get the prophet to trick the King into going to war when he wasn't supposed to.
>
> You have stories like that, that just nonchalantly mention spirits of people who have left us coming down to effect some change, some phenomenon in this world.
>
> Our scriptures and our mystical tradition are full of ghosts – ghosts meaning the disembodied soul still wandering around. We also have teachings about what in English they call 'demons,' but they're not all evil – they're called 'sheydim' in Hebrew. There are good demons and bad demons. According to our ancient tradition, demons are beings just like we are, just like animals are. They were created in the twilight of creation after the human being was created, right before the climax of creation, so that they're neither of this world, nor of the other world, but a little bit of both. There are teachings about how our ancestors like King Solomon dabbled in demonology, and he learned a lot of sorcery mysteries from the famous head of all the demons, Ashmedai.[210]

[210] http://www.ghostvillage.com/legends/2003/legends32_11292003.shtml, 29 November 2003. Belanger, J, *Dybbuk Spiritual Possession and Jewish Folklore*.

Winkler offers a fascinating example of a psychological approach to an imagined possession from the eighteenth century, around the time the first wind-up alarm clock was invented: 'A woman brought her daughter to her rabbi because she suspected a dybbuk. The rabbi diagnosed the young girl and didn't find any real signs of possession, so he sent her home with an alarm clock and told her to carry it throughout the day. The rabbi told the woman and her daughter that at 4:30 that afternoon, the dybbuk would leave the girl. At 4:30, the family believed the dybbuk was gone by the mere shock of hearing the bell go off at exactly 4:30.'

The lack of detail in the Tanach, or Old Testament, about the nature of the afterlife means that ghostly occurrences and their meanings are wide open to interpretation, but such discussions had fallen out of fashion by the twentieth century. The topic of ghosts is rarely raised as a serious issue for debate in Judaism today, although authors like the rabbis Spitz and Winkler have given some credibility to discussion of the topic, if not to belief in ghosts themselves.

Islam

There are many similarities between Judaism and Islam, but one area where they diverge dramatically is the topic in question: belief in ghosts.

At Islam Online, a web-based resource where anyone may ask for a fatwa – a legal ruling by an Islamic scholar or religious leader – Sheikh Hasanein Makhlouf was asked: 'Some people think that when someone is murdered, a ghost appears in the scene of the crime mimicking the gestures and the voice of the deceased. Does such a belief have any Islamic basis?'

He responded, in part:

What is being circulated among people that a ghost appears in a scene of crime or the like has no basis in Shari`ah. It is even impermissible to believe in such things.

Addressing this point in detail, late Sheikh Hasanein Makhlouf, former Mufti of Egypt, may Allah bless his soul, states the following: 'Such sayings have no basis in Shari`ah and are no more than superstitions. In the pre-Islamic period, Arabs used to believe that the souls of the dead and their decayed bones depart and turn into a bird that flies high in the sky. They used to give it the name "Hamah" or "Sada". The Arab poet Labid says: "After your passing away, no men are there sure. All people are 'Ham' (sing. 'Hamah') no more."' Among their fake beliefs was that the soul of a murdered stand by the grave saying: 'I am thirsty! I am thirsty!' They believed that it would not rest in peace until after the family of the murdered avenged his killing.

This was a natural outcome of the ignorance they felt in their hearts and the traditions and customs prevailing at that time. The advent of Islam put an end to such fake beliefs and baseless ideas ... Thus, the common idea of having a dead person appear in form of a ghost traces back to the false beliefs of the pre-Islamic era of ignorance. It is thus Islamically rejected to lend an ear to such things, let alone to believe in it.

... As we know that after death a person enters into a different world known as Alam Al-Barzakh, preparing to account for all his deeds. It's a place in transition before the coming of the Day of Reckoning. So it would be hard to believe that such a person would have time to roam about in the world of the living.[211]

[211] Islam Online, 24 September 2002, 'How Does Islam View Ghosts?' http://www.islamonline.net/fatwa/english/FatwaDisplay.asp?hFatwaID=82038

While many fatwas do not enjoy the support of all Muslims, and the Islam Online website is hardly objective or authoritative in its coverage of political issues, the viewpoint on ghosts appears to be widely held. It is thus all the more fascinating that the supernatural plays such a powerful role in the cultural history of Cape Muslims. The history covered in Chapter 2 implies that the form of Islam brought to the Cape in the seventeenth century was itself strongly influenced by the pre-Islamic traditions of Indonesia and Malaysia – countries rich in supernatural culture. This intrusion survives to this day in the belief in the many 'Islamic ghosts' of the Western Cape.

Catholicism

A firm belief in the existence of ghosts and demons among Catholics in medieval times, and continuing to the present day, is as much a result of decree as it is of religious conviction and superstition.

It goes back, largely, to the publication of a book called *Malleus Maleficarum*, meaning Witch Hammer, in 1486. It was, according to Wicasta Lovelace, writing on the *Malleus Maleficarum* website, 'arguably one of the most infamous books ever written, due primarily to its position and regard during the Middle Ages. It served as a guidebook for Inquisitors during the Inquisition, and was designed to aid them in the identification, prosecution, and dispatching of Witches. It set forth, as well, many of the modern misconceptions and fears concerning witches and the influence of witchcraft.'[212]

As Lovelace writes, 'It became heretical not to believe in demons or the devil ... And while the *Malleus* itself is

[212] http://www.malleusmaleficarum.org/, accessed July 2005.

largely unknown in modern times, its effects have proved long lasting.'

Protestantism

The history of the Protestant approach is a little more complex.

On behalf of the Archbishop of the Anglican Church in South Africa, the Reverend Canon Louis Bank responded to queries about the Church's approach to this issue in an e-mail on 7 August 2005. 'Generally the Anglican approach is to regard such phenomena as the product of psychological conditions,' he wrote, 'but to take the experience of those who claim to have them seriously and to minister to them compassionately.'

Johann Sommerville's lecture on *Ghosts, Fairies and Omens* offers a succinct overview of the response to Catholic belief by Protestants.

The Roman Catholic Church taught that at death the souls of those too good for hell and too bad for heaven were sent to Purgatory. Here they were purged of their sins by punishment, but might on occasion be allowed to return to earth to warn the living of the need for repentance.

Catholic beliefs in Purgatory and Limbo (an intermediate state between heaven and hell in which the Old Testament Patriarchs were confined until saved by Christ) were rejected by Protestant theologians.

Protestant divines insisted that the dead went immediately to hell or heaven – the former could not return to earth and the latter would not want to.

Protestants rejected Purgatory as a money-making device of Catholic priests eager to sell indulgences and to charge for saying masses for the souls of the dead.

However, popular belief in ghosts survived in Protestant

England. Moreover, various Scriptural references to the appearance of Samuel to Saul and of Moses and Elias to Christ (Mark 9:4) suggested that apparitions of the dead were not wholly impossible.

However they dealt with Scriptural instances, virtually all Protestant theologians held that any contemporary ghost was in all probability a demon trying to tempt us to sin. Just as miracles had ceased, so had angelic messengers from God.

Heterodox thinkers like Reginald Scot, Thomas Hobbes and Thomas White doubted the existence of all spirits – ghosts as well as souls. Their perceived atheism softened the attitudes of such Protestant theorists as Richard Baxter and Joseph Glanville to apparitions, and they saw these as possible proofs of the existence of the spiritual world.

Indeed, while Protestants formally dismissed the possibility of ghosts, key figures in the movement flirted with the existence of these entities. In an academic paper on the occult beliefs of the seventeenth century, George Macdonald Ross points out that many Protestant writers, such as Reginald Scot in *Discoverie of Witchcraft* and John Webster in *Displaying of supposed Witchcraft*, 'blamed Catholicism for perpetuating superstitious belief in ghosts, on the grounds that the doctrine of Purgatory, combined with a failure to realise that the age of miracles had ceased, encouraged the supposition that the souls of the newly dead could miraculously return to earth just as Christ himself had done'.

At the same time, says Ross, 'among the most credulous believers in ghosts were Protestants such as Joseph Glanville and Richard Burthogge; whereas the typical Catholic position was that of Marin Mersenne, who explicitly denied that souls could return either of their own volition or summoned by any necromancer'.

The normal explanation of ghosts was that they were evil demons which had made themselves visible by condensing the air into a human form ... Some Neoplatonists, such as John Webster (*Displaying of supposed Witchcraft*), maintained that ghosts were the fading traces of the 'astral body' (ie the 'animal spirits' as contrasted with the rational soul); but few followed Reginald Scot in explaining ghosts away as nothing but the product of melancholic imaginations on the grounds that spirits could not influence matter (*Treatise upon the nature and substances of spirits and devils*). This wide range of beliefs was reflected in the ambiguous portrayal of ghosts in contemporary literature, eg in *Hamlet* (1604) by William Shakespeare and *Doctor Faustus* (1589) by Christopher Marlowe. As for actual attempts to communicate with the spirit world, there was as much resort as at any time to seances, mediums, crystal balls etc, but because necromancy was taboo, the spirits contacted were invariably identified as angels, not as the spirits of the dead.[213]

Ultimately, belief in ghosts among Christians became a matter of church politics and doctrine rather than religion. Several scholars have noted the impact on supernatural belief made by the rise of atheism in the eighteenth century: rather than counter this form of rationalism by emphasising the church's own brand of rationalism, Protestant leaders relaxed their stance on belief in ghosts, as they saw such beliefs as a bulwark against atheism.

The result, says author Keith Thompson, is that from a situation where ghosts were treated as a product of Catholic fraud, it became 'more acceptable to believe in ghosts than to be a total sceptic. The possibility of ghosts was a reality

[213] MacDonald, G R, 'Occult Tendencies in the Seventeenth Century', in Friedrich Ueberwegs *Grundriss der Geschichte der Philosophie*, Reihe 5, 17 (Basel: Schwabe, 1998) pp196-224, accessed at http://www.philosophy.leeds.ac.uk/GMR/homepage/ueberweg.html, July 2005.

in the eighteenth century for many educated men, however much the rationalists laughed at them.'[214]

Since the eighteenth century, the rise of science and in particular the increasing sophistication of both scientific and statistical methodology has removed any certainty the Church was once able to provide on the nature of ghosts. As with the formal position of Islam, it is highly likely that Christian doctrine of the future will see belief in ghosts as belonging to a past era and not relevant to mainstream religious belief. This will, however, not change the fact that people will continue to believe in ghosts. The advance of computer technology, for example, did little to slow down the increase in such beliefs from the 1950s to the 1990s, as measured by the Gallup Organisation. The advent of the Internet since the 1990s has made it both quicker to debunk urban legends and easier to disseminate beliefs in the supernatural.

What to believe?

There is one conclusion that can be safely made about all the claims, counterclaims, religious doctrines and arguments discussed above: belief in ghosts evolves over time in response to social, cultural, political and religious forces. Ghosts can be defined and categorised according to the definer's religious affiliation. Ghosts can be experienced differently according to both religious and psychological disposition. Ghosts, in short, are every bit as much the product of internal processes of the mind as they may be of external phenomena.

Specifically religious experiences fall under the domain

[214] Thompson, pp705-706.

of faith, which by definition does not demand proof. The experience of ghosts, on the other hand, is clearly not subject to the formal tenets of faith, and the onus falls strongly on believers in the supernatural to prove that a particular event is a product of the external rather than the internal.

Does this author believe in ghosts? I certainly believe that countless people believe that they have encountered ghosts. I believe that science cannot prove or disprove the existence of ghosts. I also believe that science cannot yet explain all phenomena of the physical world or of psychological processes.

At the same time, I believe that most supernatural experiences and reports have a physical or psychological explanation, or are simply fabrications, sometimes unconsciously so. There may well be a tiny proportion of authentic, widely and authoritatively witnessed events that defy rational explanation, but these are far fewer in number than the vast chronicles of the supernatural would have us believe.

Most of what I have read, heard, seen and been told, I believe, is a product of the mind. Most of the rest, I believe, is a product of fakery and fraud. Of the little that remains, however, there is enough to convince me that ghosts *can* exist. Yet, there is too little to persuade me that they *do* exist.

Ultimately, it is not necessary to have a formal stance on the existence or absence of ghosts. If you wish to believe, no one can prove definitively that you are wrong, whether by science or by logic. And if you do allow science and logic to convince you that there is no such thing, no one can prove you are wrong either. If beauty is said to exist in the eyes of the beholder, meaning that the mind can make anything of what the eyes see, then ghosts can certainly be said to exist – in the mind of the believer.

Epilogue

Brave New Tokoloshe: The Supernatural Year of 1994

And so it came to pass that a new rain queen walked the streets of our cities, Aids-infested child rapists roamed Soweto, Satanists won the hearts and minds of Pretoria's young, and Winnie refused to pay for restaurant meals.

In the land of urban legends, a free, democratic South Africa became a very bizarre place in its first year, filled with dark miracles and sinister wonders.

Where fear and uncertainty had inspired a legion of myths and rumours before the 27 April 1994 elections, the safe arrival of a new nation brought in its wake a new kind of baggage: the baggage of suspicion. It was almost as if the miracle of a united, relatively peaceful South Africa was too good to be true. Everywhere people unpacked their personal demons and set them upon the psyche of the nation.

It was all summed up by Pinky-Pinky, an absurd amalgamation of legend and superstition that should have been ashamed to be seen in such a state: half man, half woman, half ghost, half tokoloshe, wearing trousers down one leg and a skirt up the other, upper face of a cat and mouth and chin of a snake; hiding in toilets and stealing pink panties. It had been around for a while – lurking in urban middle-class schools where superstition is not supposed to be part of the curriculum. It was such a convenient demon too: only children could see it since it never appeared to adults.

When Pinky-Pinky arrived at Moretele Primary School in Mamelodi north of Pretoria in October 1994, every child felt compelled to have experienced it – or be left out of the most dramatic event of their entire school lives. Call it psychic peer pressure: soon there wasn't a kid at the school who couldn't tell of a personal encounter with this brave new tokoloshe. The teachers weren't convinced, and called in the police.

What must Mamelodi police officer Lieutenant Elias Mawela have thought when he arrived to investigate a report of possible child molestation? He was told that the creature had slapped two girls and stolen one boy's socks. He was led to the toilets, where he conducted a fruitless investigation. So the pupils asked him to step outside because, they said, it would not appear to him. They gathered at the toilets to chant a new song:

My name is Pinky-Pinky
I live in the toilet
My father is a sangoma
and my mother is a witch.

Suddenly, the children came running out, screaming hysterically.

One of their parents went in with a monkey wrench, and

also came running out. He claimed something invisible had touched him.

Soon, all of Mamelodi was infested with the tale, and the next day scores of parents gathered at the school, demanding answers, demanding that the toilets be burned down, demanding, demanding.

But then they started listening to the children and discovered a strange fact: every description of Pinky-Pinky was different. Here was 'leg of cow and leg of fowl' or 'one leg looked like an elephant'; there was 'body like a rag doll' or 'body wrapped in pink cloth'. Some said it was a friendly ghost that would dance for you; others said it wanted to steal their legs to 'mend its child'.

A few days later, a Pretoria mother claimed Pinky-Pinky had made her child float through the air and caused his hand to be burned by making it stick to a hot geyser. After investigations, the mother was charged with child abuse.

Lieutenant Mawela closed his file on Pinky-Pinky. The anthropologists opened theirs. Professor Robert Thornton of Wits University's Department of Anthropology:

> As we look at social change in South Africa, we see the emergence of new boundaries and the development of new identities, along with the dissolution of old identities like the homelands. Ethnic identities are changing, and this involves the transcendence of old cultural boundaries and the invention of new ones. On top of that, it's a society in transition, and people are developing new ideas of what kind of identity is going to get them the goods. It's a case of which queue do you have to stand in to get to the front first? Having broader access to the social goods and economic goods depends on different kinds of identity, training, social networks. All of this has to be reassessed, and people have to reinvent their identities.

> These are the really crucial questions. When you see something like the Pinky-Pinky and the tokoloshe and LaMlambo (a river god that is believed to abduct passers-by), you have to see them as symbols of power, and you've got to understand them in terms of the new geometry of power, the new kinds of goods, and the new identities required to get into those goods. These issues do get experienced in all kinds of ritual, religious and quasi-psychological ways.[215]

At about the same time as the demon of confusion stalked the school toilets, a story emerged about a haunted minibus stuck forever on the side of a Free State road. It had been stolen from Lesotho, but had mysteriously broken down between Senekal and Ficksburg, and had for no less than two years stood under the shade of the trees by the roadside near Senekal. And it was inhabited by a powerful tokoloshe.

Even the owner of the adjacent farm was unable to come near it. Long-haul taxi drivers insisted they'd seen the minibus – but didn't dare go near it. As for the people of Senekal? They burst out laughing at the mere mention of the demonic vehicle – because it simply did not exist.

Meanwhile, white suburbia was rooting out its own demons – not to get rid of them, but to parade them as bogeymen for a nation gone astray. With the able assistance of the South African Police Services Occult Unit, the Satan-fearing public was able to hold on to its fear in a changed society.

The head of the Occult Unit, Colonel Kobus Jonker, claimed that no less than 22 murders in July and August 1994 could be attributed to Satanism. He even compiled a hit parade of Satanic activity: number one, Bloemfontein;

---

[215] Interview with Professor Robert Thornton, 1995.

number two, Vanderbijlpark; number three: Pretoria.

He had other statistics too: between 1989 and 1993, Satanist-linked charges included 21 murders, 5 attempted murders, 34 assaults, 14 sexual offences, 78 charges of damage to property and 36 of cruelty to animals. A total of 285 cases of desecrated graves had been recorded, and in one case, 15 people had been arrested in Port Elizabeth following the discovery of a human head.

The good colonel did not explain why no murder in South Africa had ever been proven to be a direct and deliberate result of Satanic ritual. Murders and other grim crimes have frequently been committed by people who were also involved in Satanism in one way or another, but then far more have been committed by Christians, just for instance.

Satanists, however, make wonderful bogeymen: they are superb grist to the mill of crusaders, and they enable us to turn our attention away from the social ills that inspire kids to get involved in dark rituals in the first place. But most of all, they are a scapegoat for our suspicions and fears about a world we cannot control or understand.

After all, for every one piece of obscure evidence that Satanists have been playing games and leaving signs and symbols, there are probably two or three real, horrifying cases of child mutilation in the pursuit of supernatural power. It's called muti murder, and it is little different from the intent and motivation ascribed to Satanist ritual killings. There is one big difference: it is real, and the victims all have names. Satanic murder in South Africa has been almost entirely fictional, existing largely in the realms of urban legend.

Muti murders, on the other hand, have left real, deadly evidence of the intent behind the killing. The big difference is that muti killers pose no threat to the pillars of Christian Nationalism, the official theology of the old South Africa.

April 27 1994 should have brought an end to the imbalance between the hunt for murdering Satanist and muti killers, in reality an imbalance between old South African and African belief. But, at least in the Occult Unit, the police clung to the theology of the old. If police officers can get lost in the land of urban legends, where does that leave mere uninformed mortals? Where do they find a road map through the misinformation of propaganda?

A lesson from Mozambique would serve us well: exactly six months after Nelson Mandela's inauguration, Joaquim Chissano's Frelimo emerged victorious in Mozambique's first democratic elections. It should have been a walkover. After all, the main opposition were the baby-eating, genital-mutilating, ear-carving monsters of Renamo. Yet about 40 per cent of Mozambican voters wanted Renamo as their government. In effect, the people voted their disbelief in urban legends. Renamo may have been nasty, but Frelimo were hardly choirboys. The mass consciousness was not to be fooled.

In South Africa, old habits clung to our consciousness.

Then deputy president Thabo Mbeki was so used to the lies of the police that he automatically assumed they were lying about the crime wave to get a bigger share of the budget. He instantly gave birth to a new urban legend: that the high crime rate was a fiction of media and police hype.

Winnie Mandela was so used to the abuse of power, or so we believed, that she took her entourage to an expensive French restaurant and refused to pay. When the manager called the police, one of the investigating officers wrote out a cheque for the full amount. A few days later, the manager was beaten up. Everyone knew the name of the restaurant. But of course nothing of the sort had happened. Winnie had eaten there, and had left early. Her bill was settled by one of her fellow diners. But someone saw her leave without paying, and another urban legend was born.

White conservatives were so used to horror stories about socialists, they readily believed that the new 'leftist' government was about to grant political asylum to Fidel Castro. By the time it was denied, it was already an urban legend.

The country's biggest daily newspaper was so used to the superstitions of its readers that, when it came across an urban legend that had criss-crossed the Third World, it shut off its collective sense of perspective, and filled its front page with the story of HIV-positive men who were raping township children in the mistaken belief that it could cure Aids. Ironically, they dismissed the belief itself as an urban legend, but failed to recognise the bigger myth.

Often the secret is to know when to start believing.

Unfortunately, not everyone provides the kind of cue Queen Elizabeth II gave South Africa. Already famed in Zimbabwe as the rain queen, for having arrived in dry-as-moth-wings Bulawayo on the day its drought had been broken a few years earlier, she now came upon a parched South Africa, its 11-month-old democracy thirsty for rain. It was a newly confident country that was far more in awe of its own leader than of any visiting monarch, and no one was about to strew petals where her feet passed. But by the time she left, the rains had come, the crowds had turned out after all, and a legend had become official. Thabo Mbeki had declared her Motlalepula – the Rain Queen.

For once, a nation was content to unite behind a myth.

Appendix

The tales children tell

Many ghost stories start life as broken telephone versions of stories children have heard and told and retold to their friends. I had the opportunity of experiencing the phenomenon first-hand when I was invited to give a talk on ghost stories to a group of Grade 6 and 7 learners at King David Primary School in Victory Park, Johannesburg.

I had been speaking for only a few minutes when the first hand went up. A child was eager to share her own ghost story. And then another hand. And another. A flood of ghost stories, beliefs and even experiences came streaming from this group of only a few dozen children. So popular was the very process of sharing ghost stories, I suggested the children each write down a ghost story that had been told to them as a true happening. The host of the event, the school's media centre manager Jackie Klevansky, then made it a class project for the Grade 7s. A few months later, she handed over the best of the stories. Some were truly excellent pieces of fiction, with fanciful tales told in the first person. Some were recountings of famous urban legends from around the country.

The stories I selected to reproduce here are those that the learners believed really happened, either to themselves or to friends or family, or stories that show how children express their belief in the way ghosts function.

A fascinating aspect of some of the stories is that, whether they are clearly identified as urban legends or told as first-person experiences, the tales all tend to carry archetypal elements of urban legends.

Almost delicious detail – such as child victims of a serial killer happening to have been bullies at school, or the sky thickening with mist the day a family arrives at a temporary home – reveals not only imagination at work, but the need for context, for a framework that gives justification for or warning of the events that unfold.

Such stories tend to reveal children as a natural filter for beliefs and fears, organising fearsome stories in such a way as to give structure to the unexplained. And, of course, organising them in such a way that they will give their friends as many sleepless nights as possible.

This House Appears to be Haunted
by Gabi Abrahams

This is a true story. A house that hadn't been lived in for years. My mom (in her youth) had the misfortune of being the first and hopefully last to live there. Well let's start from the beginning. My mom's house was being renovated. The racket was unbearable! So Bubbles (my granny) made a decision to find a place to stay until the house was done. They packed and off they went. They moved into the house down the road. My mom, uncle and granny all had ideas of what the house would be like. The sky thickened with mist. They saw the huge driveway and walked through the huge wooden doors. The house moaned and creaked with every footstep they took. That night was one my mom wouldn't forget. My mom dreamt of a woman stabbing her. Then she woke up to footsteps and no one was there to make the ghostly sounds. My uncle became desperately ill. All his animals tried to escape his eerie room. Knocks on the door and phones lifting added to the fear. They left after 3 months. She was interested in the history of the house and found a woman killed her husband and 3 sons. Maybe their spirits still haunt that house.

Aunty Rose

by Kelli-Paige Preston

One Saturday evening late in April my best friend Susan arrived to sleep at me. This was an exciting sleepover because my parents were going out. We were going to be alone. My parents left just after eight. Susan and I stayed up in my room talking. All of a sudden we heard the strangest noise coming from downstairs. We didn't think much of it but then the thumping started coming up the stairs. We became scared and locked the bedroom door. The thumping stopped in an instant. We had to investigate what the noise had been so quietly we crept downstairs.

Walking into the kitchen the smell of rose oil hit the air. I picked up the phone to call 911 but the phone went dead. The lights flickered and the curtains moved. We ran upstairs as fast as we could, hearing a bang, bang, bang sound behind us. When we reached the top stair the bang noise stopped instantly. We looked behind us but there was nothing there,

NOTHING! That night we fell asleep with difficulty even though we locked the bedroom door.

In the morning there were rose petals scattered across my dressing table. My mom couldn't have put them there because we had locked the bedroom door the previous evening.

A few days later I told my mom about what had happened. She said that I had had an aunty named Rose who had died tragically many years before on a late Saturday evening in April.

The Kaplans Ghost

by Jeffrey Mendelson

In the residence of the Kaplans is a black, old, haunted chair. In that chair (apparently) sits an old, dull woman ghost. This old woman sits in that chair all day long. If you sit on that chair she gets upset and gives you terrible nightmares.

One day I was at their house and we all heard a noise. A bowl was lying on the wooden floor in the same room the old woman sits in. It had to have been the ghost because nobody was around to throw it onto the floor because we were either in the kitchen or upstairs in the bedroom. It had to have been picked up and moved because of the other things around it. If it had just fallen it would have hit the other ornaments. We were all a bit nervous after that.

Another time I slept at Josh's house and I sat on that chair. Then one of the Kaplans said I must get off and say sorry to her immediately otherwise she would get cross. I didn't believe him, so I didn't move.

That night I had a very bad dream. The next morning I told Josh. He said it was my fault because I didn't believe him. After that I say hello to her whenever I 'see' her. I don't actually mean it. I didn't believe in ghosts before and I don't now. It was all coincidence. Or was it?

The Ghost in a Safari Suit

by Kim Snoyman

Everyone knows that the business school of Wits University is haunted. Ghosts haunt it every night of every year. This is a particularly scary story of a ghost in a safari suit. You may not (have) heard of this, it is not an urban legend. This is the story of a poltergeist that haunted a guard named Walter.

Walter was a guard who worked at Wits for about 20 years. Until then, he had not believed in ghosts. He knew the Business School was haunted, that a woman in a white wedding dress lurked in the darkness. She searched for her husband every night.

Furniture moved. Doors creaked. It WASN'T the contraction of wooden beams.

One night in the thick darkness of winter, Walter's shift began. He walked around Block E's bottom floor. He saw ghosts, but they dissolved into the wall.

Walter was an old African man with greying hair and a wrinkling face. He was certain tonight no intruders would dare to enter the top floor, it was already haunted and very eerie. But being a guard it was his job to check the top floor on campus. He walked through the creaking doors. Something wasn't right. No ghosts? No screaming? It was much too quiet to be normal. Though nothing was ever normal at Wits.

Walter, worried at the building being too quiet, shouted, 'Is anyone there? Is anyone there?' No one answered. He checked rooms 3 to 12 with no problem. Suddenly a ghost in a safari suit appeared. Walter had not seen him before (and he had seen all the ghosts). He assumed it was an intruder and loaded his gun. He smashed open the door with the butt of his gun. He saw the ghost in the safari suit and told him to get out or else he would shoot. The ghost wouldn't listen and so Walter popped the trigger and the bullet sailed through the ghost's torso. The ghost, in his defence, threw a dustbin at his head and disappeared. The next morning he had a large bump on his head from the dustbin. Since then, Walter has never seen the ghost in the safari suit again.

Rondebosch Ghost House
by David Fine

It happened about 100 years ago, in a house on Milner Road, Rondebosch, in Cape Town.

100 years ago in that house a family of 5 people lived. That family had many, many enemies, because the father, Max, was a judge, and before that, a lawyer. He was very successful and had sent many people to prison. The mother, Jane, was a very successful policewoman. Finally, the three children, Mark, Frank and Jerry, were bullies in their grades at school.

On one stormy night, it was announced that a dangerous mass murderer, Tom Killer, had just escaped from Pollsmoor. Max and Jane both knew Killer. Jane had been the one that caught him and Max had sentenced him to life imprisonment. Quickly they gathered the children together and told them that they thought that Killer might come after them. Frank said that they must seal all the entrances.

'Right, I'll go do that,' Max said.

He left the room to go to the front door and lock it. The family waited. And waited. Suddenly they heard a horrifying scream. Jane said, 'Oh no, something's happened,

I'm going to look for him.'

The children stayed in the room, waiting for their mom, petrified.

About an hour later, they heard another terrifying scream! Now the children were absolutely terrified! What had happened to their parents? Finally, after many silent minutes, Mark said, 'We have to go and find them.'

Terrified, the others followed him. They got to the entrance hall. What they saw made them scream. Both their parents were lying there. Dead! The look on their faces was of pure, undiluted, terror. The children started trembling. At that moment, out of the shadows, stepped a man, Tom Killer. In one hand he held a knife, in the other, a gun. He killed all three of them, and then turned the gun on himself.

Ever since, even a hundred years later, people never enter that house. Children play games, daring each other to get into the house, but they never get further than the front gate, because you can hear the wails of that family, and the serial killer. You hear the terrified screams of the children. The maniacal laugh of Tom Killer. And finally, worst of all, the parents' wails, from looking into the eyes of Tom Killer.

Scary enough? Not scary enough? In the minds of children, ghost stories serve many functions, and only one of those functions is to scare others. As suggested above, another is to give structure to supernatural beliefs as well as to bring understanding to their own experiences. In this sense, children absorb and repeat ghost stories in much the same way as adults do. The fundamental difference is that children have neither become jaded by such stories nor overexposed to countless elaborations. This means their understanding of the stories remains fresh, even if the source is not.

Untainted by cynicism or over-explanation, these are ghost stories in the raw, and provide the foundation for the emergence of many a ghost legend in the corridors and dormitories of schools and hostels. When the origin of one of these legends seems just too obscure or too unlikely, it should be sought not in the pages of history, but in the ways of the mind of a child.

References

Bolsmann, Eric (1997). *Ghosts of Pretoria*. Be My Guest Publishers.

Da Costa, Yusuf & Davids, Achmat (1994). *Pages from Cape Muslim History*. Pietermaritzburg: Shuter & Shooter.

Du Plessis, I D (1945). *Tales from the Malay Quarter*. Cape Town: Maskew Miller Longman.

Du Plessis, I D (1966). *Poltergeists of the South*. Cape Town: Howard Timmins.

Goldstuck, A (1990). *The Rabbit in the Thorn Tree*. Johannesburg: Penguin Books.

Goldstuck, A (1993). *The Leopard in the Luggage*. Johannesburg: Penguin Books.

Goldstuck, A (1999). *The Aardvark and the Caravan*. Johannesburg: Penguin Books.

Guide to the Kramats of the Western Cape (2001). Cape Town: Cape Mazaar Society.

Laubscher, B J F (1963). *Where Mystery Dwells*. Cape Town: Howard Timmins.

Markowitz, Arthur (1956). *With Uplifted Tongue: Stories, Myths and Fables of the South African Bushmen told in their manner*. CNA.

Morrison, E W B (1901). *With The Guns in South Africa*. Hamilton, Canada: Spectator Printing Co.

Mutwa, Vusamazulu Credo (1965). *Indaba, My Children*. Johannesburg: Blue Crane Books.

Niehaus, Isak (2001). *Witchcraft, Power and Politics*. London: Pluto Press.

Peach, E (1991). Things That Go Bump in the Night. The Aquarian Press.

Pearse, G E (1956). *The Cape of Good Hope: 1652-1833*. Pretoria: Van Schaik.

Roll, W & Storey, V (2004). *Unleashed: Of Poltergeists and Murder. The Curious Story of Tina Resch*. Paraview Pocket Books.

Rosenthal, Eric (1949). *They Walk By Night*. Cape Town: Howard B Timmins.

Spencer, John & Anne (2001). *The Encyclopedia of Ghosts and Spirits*. London: Headline.

Spitz, E K (2000). *Does the Soul Survive?* Woodstock, Vermont: Jewish Lights Publishing.

Taylor, Troy (1997). The Ghost Hunter's Guidebook. Whitechapel Press.

Thompson, K (1978). *Religion and the Decline of Magic*. London: Penguin.

Watson, Stephen (1991). *Return of the Moon: Versions from the /Xam*. Cape Town: The Carrefour Press.

Williamson, Margaret (1993). *Haunted Corners: South Africa's Own Ghost Stories*. Johannesburg: Jonathan Ball Publishers.

Zukov, Gary (1979). *The Dancing Wu-Li Masters: An Overview of the New Physics*. New York: William Morrow and Company.